Christi J. Whitney is a former actress with a love for the arts. She lives just outside Atlanta with her husband and two sons. When not spending time with them or taking a ridiculous number of trips to Disney World, she can be found directing plays, making costumes for sci-fi and fantasy conventions, obsessing over Doctor Who, watching superhero movies, or pretending she's just a tad bit British. You can visit her online at www.christijwhitney.com or connect on Twitter @ChristiWhitney

Grey

CHRISTI J. WHITNEY

Book One of the Romany Outcasts Series

HARPER
Voyager

HarperVoyager
An imprint of HarperCollinsPublishers Ltd
1 London Bridge Street
London SE1 9GF

www.harpervoyagerbooks.co.uk

This Paperback Original 2015

First published in Great Britain in ebook format by HarperVoyager 2015

A catalogue record for this book
is available from the British Library

ISBN: 978-0-00-812045-0

Set in Sabon by Born Group using Atomik ePublisher from Easypress

Printed and bound in Great Britain

To the E.H.S.T.S.
You know who you are

1. Dreams and Waking

'Sebastian!'

I hear my name, but I can't answer. I'm trapped by the image in my head.

It flashes again.

Rainbow-scorched leaves. Gypsy music.

Caravans of faded paint.

'Sebastian Grey!'

Dark and nothing.

I struggled for words. 'Yes, sir?'

'Are you joining this group or not? I need to get a list . . . '

Another flash.

Bonfires. Starless night.

A girl dancing. Ribbons in her hair.

'For the last time, Mr Grey, *wake up*!'

My mind ripped free. I jolted, launching papers into orbit.

For a split second, I wasn't convinced of my surroundings. Then, as fluorescent lights bored through my skull, it hit me.

I was in the middle of class.

And twenty-five pairs of eyes were staring straight at me.

All my school supplies littered the floor – textbooks, papers, colored index cards. Everything except the pencil that I'd somehow snapped between my fingers. I coughed and hunkered in my seat. Across the aisle, Avery leaned sideways in his desk, giving me the look I'd seen way too many times: the one that questioned my sanity.

'Crap,' I whispered.

I'd done it again.

Mr Weir moved closer. He glowered at me from under spidery eyebrows. I prepared myself for the tirade. But just as he took a wheezing breath, the bell rang. I shrugged and gave him my best smile as the room reverberated with slamming books and screeching chairs.

Mr Weir grunted and waddled back to his desk, my outburst promptly dismissed as more important matters – like the end of the school day – took precedence. I dropped to one knee and recovered my textbook.

'Hey, Sebastian, you okay?' Avery towered over me. 'What just happened there?'

I blinked away the lingering haze. 'It appears I must have dozed off.'

'Seriously, man,' said Avery, his brows shooting up. 'Who talks like that?' He knelt and picked up one of my library books, examining it with a shake of his head. 'I swear, sometimes I think you read way too many old books. They're messing with your head.'

I snatched it out of his hands. 'I don't read old books.'

'You read Shakespeare.'

2

'That's different.'

Avery laughed, shoving papers at me. 'Sure it is.'

I stuffed them in my bag, taking care to hide my tattered copy of *Hamlet* from Avery's prying eyes. We squeezed into the crowded hall, avoiding locker doors banging open and shut around us.

'You never answered my question, you know,' Avery continued.

'I realize that.'

We strolled in companionable silence down the hallway. Okay, maybe I was the one who was silent. Avery Johnson – senior superlative and social giant – had something to say to everybody we passed. At the end of the corridor, he stopped.

'Okay, what was it this time?'

'Nothing,' I replied. 'I fell asleep.'

'Yeah, right,' Avery said in an amused huff. 'That wasn't a nap. That was a complete zone out. Same as this morning in gym, when you stood there like a zombie until Alex Graham smacked you in the face with the ball.'

'I'm athletically challenged.'

'Try strange,' he replied.

'Can you maybe find another expression to stare at me with? It's not helping.'

Avery went dramatically serious. 'Sorry.'

'Oh, that's better,' I replied. 'I feel much more comfortable now.' Avery's features didn't change. There'd be no avoiding it this time. I worked out my confession. 'Okay, so you know when you stare at a camera flash and then you keep seeing the glow, even after it's gone?'

'Yeah . . . '

I gripped the strap of my backpack. 'Well, I keep seeing this same thing in my head, like a camera flash. Only not a light. An image. It used to just happen at night, but now I'm starting to see it during the day.'

'What exactly do you keep seeing?'

'A girl.'

Avery whistled slyly. 'Must be some dream, eh?'

'No, it's not like that.' My head throbbed. I pinched the bridge of my nose between my fingers. 'It's not a dream.'

'A vision, then,' said Avery, lighting up like Christmas. 'You can see the future! Or maybe the past. You know, like that guy on TV. The one that helps the cops solve cases and junk.'

I grinned sideways. 'If only. 'Cause that would be kind of cool.'

'And profitable,' added Avery. 'We could totally . . . '

'Hate to disappoint,' I said, holding up my hands before he could spout off some money-making scheme that I would – mostly likely – lose cash on. 'But I don't have dreams, visions, premonitions, or anything worth printing up business cards for. It's just an image. I probably saw it in a book somewhere.'

'Well, whatever it is, when you come out of it, you do this jerking spaz thing.' He demonstrated for my benefit. 'Like a bad episode of *Sebastian Can't Dance*. Maybe you should ease up on the caffeine.'

'Oh, you're hilarious,' I said, shoving him towards the exit doors. I wasn't about to tell Avery I'd seen the image every night for two months, and I couldn't remember the last time I'd had any decent sleep. I'd reached the limits of sharing. 'Glad to know I covered all the basics of self-embarrassment. Maybe next time I'll work up a drool.'

Avery pushed open the set of metal doors, flashing a Cheshire grin as he passed through. 'Hey, don't worry too much about it, Sebastian. It's not like it's the first time you've done something weird.'

*

My brother Hugo owned a tattoo shop on the edge of town, near the railroad tracks. It was a hole-in-the-wall, crammed between a flea market and a convenience store; just the kind of place where you'd expect to find people injecting ink into each other's arms. A neon sign hung over the door flickering the words *Gypsy Ink Tattoo Parlor*. A woman's face, showing her with flowing hair and hoop earrings, adorned the front window.

I eased my sputtering old van into a parking space with a sigh of relief. Memories of Sixes High School faded away as I opened the shop's painted black door and stepped out of the blinding sun.

The eclectic style of the *Gypsy Ink* fascinated me, with its bright red walls and linoleum floor – black-and-white checked – like an old diner. A coffee table scattered with tattoo magazines faced the front counter, flanked by two dilapidated purple leather sofas. The art was a portfolio of skulls, roses, and half-naked women.

I dumped my backpack in a rickety armchair and reached for the stash of candy Hugo kept in a plastic monkey head next to the register. My gaze went automatically to the enormous framed picture hanging behind the counter: a colorful caravan of Gypsies gathered around a campfire.

I popped a fistful of gummy bears in my mouth and frowned at the painting. I wondered if I'd looked at the picture so much it had imprinted itself onto my psyche. And if it had, then how was I supposed to get rid of it? I squinted at each figure on the canvas. The image my brain kept conjuring definitely resembled the Gypsies in the painting, but not an exact match. My reverie was broken by a rough, friendly voice from the back of the shop.

'Hey Sebastian, is that you?'

'Yeah, it's me.'

It was uncanny how Hugo could do that. My brother always seemed to know who was in the shop. It was both creepy and comforting.

'Grab us a couple of sodas, will you? I'll be out in a minute.'

I heard the buzz of Hugo's ink needle. I snagged two sodas from the shop's refrigerator then grabbed a container of beef jerky and a jumbo bag of salt-and-vinegar potato chips off the shelf. I deposited my stash on the coffee table and flopped on the closest sofa. Popping the lid off the container, I started in on the jerky and leafed through a magazine while I waited for Hugo to finish.

Five minutes later, a lanky kid appeared, sporting a bandage of plastic wrap on his bicep. Hugo entered just behind, slapping him on the back and giving a speech on tattoo aftercare. The kid, looking pale and relieved, shook my brother's hand and left, jangling the string of bells above the door.

Hugo laughed and plopped beside me. My foster brother *looked* like a tattoo artist. He was wearing a pair of jeans that were so splattered and tattered they should have been burned. His black T-shirt was rolled up to his shoulders, showing off arms covered in a myriad of designs that extended to the fingers of both hands. A swirling tattoo sprouted out of the collar of his shirt, winding its way up to his right ear. His dark hair and goatee would have made a Viking proud.

He reached for his soda. 'So, how was school today?'

Because he was thirty and ran his own business, Hugo felt the need to act parental with me, even if I was technically an adult and not legally under his care. I shrugged and ripped open the bag of potato chips.

'It was okay, I guess.'

6

Hugo leaned back, taking a swig from his can. 'That good, huh?'

I scarfed down the chips and let my gaze drift over the waiting room. It was usually quiet this time of day around the *Gypsy Ink*. The shop didn't officially open until noon, and most of the regulars came during evening hours. 'So, where are the guys?' I asked, steering the conversation away from school.

'Kris took the day off, and Vincent and James are next door at the store. We're down to a just a few sodas and a bag of . . . ' He trailed off, noticing the empty beef jerky container and the damage I was doing to the family-sized bag of chips. 'Make that a few sodas. Man, Sebastian, you eat more than anyone I know. Where do you put it all?'

I turned the bag up to my mouth. A few crumbs bounced off my shirt, sprinkling the floor. 'I can't help it if I'm always hungry.' I crushed the bag in my hand and tossed it across the room. It dropped easily into the trash can at the door. 'I'm a growing boy, Hugo.'

He shot me a look, but I couldn't interpret it very well. Another ability of Hugo's that unnerved me was the way he could just close off his emotions, like shutting blinds on a window. One minute, I knew exactly what he was thinking, and the next, it was as if I didn't know him at all. 'Well,' he said, 'you're going to eat us out of the shop. You know that, don't you?'

My lips curled into a grin. 'I'll pay you back one day. If you'll teach me to ink, I'll work for you.'

'Yeah, yeah, that's what you say.' Hugo leaned forward, ruffling my hair affectionately. 'But for now, just do your homework and then sweep the floor. I've got to clean up my work area.'

He'd never been receptive to my tattoo artist idea. It was always talk about high school and graduation with him. He left the room while I rifled through my backpack for my calculus book and binder. The sound of my brother rummaging through things in the back made me stop and smile.

Though we weren't related by blood, Hugo Corsi was the only family I had. I didn't like thinking of myself as a foster kid, but I'd grown up in a state-run group home. I probably would have stayed there until I aged out of the system, but Hugo's parents had changed all that.

Not long after they asked me to live with them, the Corsis went to Europe to take care of some major family business, but they said they wanted me to stay in Sixes and finish school. Hugo owned a small apartment attached to his tattoo parlor, and he volunteered to take me in.

Of course, I was grateful to Hugo. Because of him, I had a home and some semblance of a family. The *Gypsy Ink* was all I knew, but I was comfortable here.

I struggled through the math problems and managed to have them done by the time Hugo reappeared in the waiting room.

'How's pizza sound?' he asked. 'Kris has a customer coming in tonight, so he's going to pick up some food on the way over.'

My stomach rumbled. 'Pizza would be great. Make sure he gets enough.'

Hugo shot me that look again. 'Don't worry, he *knows* how you eat.'

It was getting dark outside, and the shop's fluorescent lights threatened me with a headache. Hugo saw me rubbing my temples, and he switched on the lamp, dousing the overhead bulbs. The throbbing in my skull dissipated, but the annoying pain spread to my back. I rolled my shoulders, pressing my fingers into the tense muscles.

'So, how's the back?' Hugo asked, sitting down beside me. He busied himself with straightening the magazines, but I could hear an edge to his voice.

I sighed and gave a one-shouldered shrug. 'Not bad.'

'Is it getting worse?' Hugo studied my hand as I rubbed my neck.

'It's a little stiff. Maybe I'm sleeping on it wrong or something. It hasn't bothered me until just now; probably from leaning over my notebook too long.'

Hugo's examination made me a little uncomfortable. Sure, my back had been giving me trouble off and on the last few weeks, but Hugo was staring at me like I'd gotten into all his ink and had a graffiti-fest on the wall.

Suddenly the front door swung open, and Vincent and James burst in, bearing plastic bags of groceries. James saw me first and chucked his bags into the armchair before grabbing me in a headlock and hoisting me off the couch.

'Hey, Sebastian! How was school today, man?'

He set me down, and I scrambled out of his grasp. The man was huge, with muscles flexing under his tattoos and a shock of brown hair pulled haphazardly into a ponytail at the nape of his neck.

I rubbed my protesting shoulders and backed away before James decided to pick me up and toss me across the room in another friendly display of affection. 'It was fine, James.'

Vincent – who was tall, red-headed, and sported the most tattoos of anyone in the shop – tossed a package of paper towels and toilet paper in my direction. 'You know better than to ask him, James. We never get details.'

'We should work on that,' said James.

I rolled my eyes. 'Well, I'm hungry and I've just had paper goods thrown at me. Sorry if I'm not in the mood for story time.' Vincent flashed me a lip-pierced grin. I tucked the packages under my arms. 'I'll be right back.'

The bathroom of the *Gypsy Ink* was not the cleanest place in the shop. After all, the responsibility of maintaining it fell to four guys who were having a good day when they remembered to brush their teeth and change their underwear. Since coming to stay with Hugo, the job of keeping it decent for customers had become mine. I complained, but I couldn't really do anything about it. I had to earn my keep, so to speak which, apparently, included bathroom detail.

I flicked on the light and surveyed the damage. It wasn't too bad, so I decided to put off cleaning until the next day. I tossed the packages under the sink and hurried out, passing the rooms where the guys did their tattooing. Each one matched their personalities, from my brother's bright orange walls to Vincent's pirate theme.

I started to round the corner into the waiting room when something pulled me up short. Everything was strangely quiet. I paused and listened. And then, I heard my name. The guys were talking, but their voices were low, barely above whispers. Instinctively, I pressed my back against the wall and slid forward so I could hear.

'If this is true, it changes everything.'

'We don't know that.'

'We can't jump to conclusions without proof.'

'But we can't wait either.'

'Hugo, what have you seen?'

There was a pause in the conversation, followed by my brother's slow intake of breath. 'I can't be sure yet,' he said. 'And until I am, nothing will be done, understand?

Now, shut up, all of you. He'll be back any second. Get out the pizza.'

The others abruptly switched the conversation to trivial things. I continued to lean against the wall, ignoring the ache in my shoulders. This was more important. I'd just eavesdropped on some big secret, and it was pretty obvious why I'd been left out. Whatever they'd been whispering about, it had to do with me.

My stomach grumbled and I pressed my hand against my torso. Maybe they'd been discussing whether I was ready to learn how to tattoo, something I'd been begging Hugo about for months. If so, then I definitely wanted to know.

I put on an easy smile and launched into the room. 'So, what were you guys talking about?'

Hugo glanced up from the cash register. 'Nothing important.'

'Are you sure?' I pressed. 'Because it sounded like . . . '

'Just shop talk,' he said, cutting me off.

I met my brother's eyes and read the look. I wasn't going to get anywhere with the direct approach. I switched gears while I debated my next attempt. 'Hey, Kris,' I said, eyeing the pizza boxes in his hands. 'It's about time. My stomach's threatening to eat itself.'

'Yeah, I got your food right here,' Kris replied. 'Just try to save some for the rest of us, eh?'

There were four pizzas: two were cheese and two were loaded with meat. I normally opted for the cheese, but tonight, the meat had my number, and I piled six slices onto my plate and ripped through them like there was no tomorrow. James shook his head incredulously at me, and I grinned back.

The guys talked about the shop and their customers and about the repairs Hugo was making on his bike. Vincent said his girlfriend was going to stop by, and James thought

11

that his wife might also show up. I listened in silence as I worked through the pizza, but fragments of their whispered conversation filtered through my head.

'Sebastian.' Hugo frowned at me. 'You look tired. Why don't you go back to the apartment? Maybe watch some TV? Kris has a customer coming in, and we're going to stick around and help close up after.'

The hint was far from subtle.

There'd be no secrets spilled tonight, unless I forced it. My brother was worse than a maximum-security prison when he wanted to be. But I was patient. Or maybe just tired. Sitting around had made my back worse and, combined with my lingering headache, had pretty much beaten the curiosity out of me. I'd catch my brother tomorrow. Whatever he was keeping from me, I had a better chance of prying it out of him when he was alone.

'Sure, Hugo. Whatever you say.' I looked at my empty plate and considered grabbing another slice of pizza, but opted against it. I took another soda instead and hoisted my bag over my shoulder. 'Well, I guess I'll see you guys tomorrow.'

'Nighty night,' said Vincent.

'Don't let the bedbugs bite,' added Kris.

James grinned. 'And don't forget to brush your teeth.'

I hurled an empty pizza box at his head and rushed out before he could catch me. The last door on the hall led to home: Hugo's nondescript apartment contained a simple kitchen, two bedrooms, one bath, and a living room.

I dumped my bag and stepped over a small glass table to reach the love seat. I curled up in the cushions, planning to watch television for a while, but I'd barely made it to the Discovery Channel before my eyelids started to droop. Within minutes, I was asleep.

*

I wasn't sure at what point Hugo came in, but when I woke, it was 3 o'clock in the morning, and a blanket had been draped over me. I shifted, letting out a groan. My shoulders were killing me. I tried massaging the stiff muscles as I stumbled to my bedroom. Once there, I flopped down, face first, onto the hard mattress.

Sleep never returned. The image of the Gypsy girl flickered through my mind, but staring at the clock every fifteen minutes kept her appearance to a minimum. When the numbers registered 6:00, I got up and scrabbled for the nearest pile of clean clothes, retrieving a pair of jeans and a faded T-shirt. I ducked into the bathroom, got ready, and took a critical glance in the mirror.

I shoved my fingers through the dark mass of hair plastered to my face. The summer had done nothing for my skin – not that it had much chance – since I spent most of my time indoors or with my hood pulled low to block the searing Southern sun. My friends went to the beach; I worked in Hugo's shop or read in the apartment. I felt more comfortable there.

My eyes were rimmed with dark circles, betraying my lack of sleep over the past few weeks. I scowled and reached for the hood of my jacket. As I did, I noticed something strange, just below my right temple. I tilted my head towards the mirror. It was a chunk of gray hair, as wide and nearly as long as my thumb.

'You have got to be kidding me,' I said to the mirror.

It didn't talk back, but my phone alarm did. I messed with my hair until I managed to cover up the silvery streak. I didn't know if I was starting to go gray at the ripe old age of eighteen, but I'd have to figure out the hair thing later. If I didn't leave now, I'd be late for school. I flicked off the light and left Hugo's apartment.

The shop was dark, but I didn't need help finding the vending machine. I confiscated two bags of chips, a package of Oreos, and a Pop Tart, hoping they would appease my crazy appetite until lunch. I smirked at my handful of snacks. Hugo was right. I *was* going to eat him out of house and shop. I let myself out and locked the door behind me.

2. *Hope and Fear*

My stomach didn't make it past fourth period. It rumbled loud protests – which I ignored – as I hurried down the aisle of the Sixes High School auditorium. Most of the class had already assembled. I slid into the third row and dumped my backpack in Avery's lap. His face contorted.

'Ow, man! Whatcha got in there? A bowling ball?'

'Why do you ask?' I plopped down smugly beside him. 'Oh, I guess because that's something a really weird person would do.'

'Okay, okay,' he said, shoving my bag at me. 'I'm sorry about what I said yesterday. I was just making an observation, that's all.'

Everybody has their quirks. For the most part, I accepted mine. But I didn't need my recent blank-outs adding to my already sizable list. I slid my book bag underneath the seat and grinned. 'Apology accepted.'

'Hey, Sebastian,' said a voice behind me, 'are you going to audition for the play?'

I tilted my head to meet Katie Lewis's bright blue eyes. She was practically bouncing on the seat behind me. Katie may have given some substance to that cliché about dumb blondes but, in reality, her grade point average put her at the top of our class.

15

'Ah, no, I don't think I'll be auditioning. I'm better back-stage, you know, in the shadows, where I can't be *seen*.' I didn't consider myself a theater person – even though I did like Shakespeare – but after helping with one of the drama department's shows, Katie had twisted my arm until I joined the club.

'Oh whatever, Sebastian. It's our senior year. You should at least *try*.' She tapped her pencil against my arm. 'You never know, right?'

'Leave the acting stuff to Avery and Mitchell,' I replied, jerking the pencil playfully out of her hands. 'Just give me a paintbrush, stick me behind a wall, and I'm perfectly happy.'

'Yeah,' said Avery. 'As long as you're not on a ladder.'

'Hey, I tried to warn the stage crew. Putting an acro-phobic artist on anything higher than a chair is just asking for trouble.'

'I'd never seen somebody's face *actually* turn green before.'

'Well, it's a gift.' I made a mental note to request another crew assignment for this year's production.

The bell rang, and Ms Lucian sauntered through the doors, toting a stack of colored papers. She seated herself on the edge of the stage. No one knew exactly how old Ms Lucian was, with her youthful face and red-tipped black hair, but she'd been teaching drama at Sixes for a long time.

'Good morning, my darlings,' she said in a pleasant voice. 'How are we today?' There was an eruption of less than favorable responses from the masses. Ms Lucian's brow arched 'Okay, forget I asked.'

She began to call the roll. I hugged my legs to my chest and rested my chin on my knees. The drone of student names seemed to go on forever.

A girl's face, veiled in shadows . . .

Her hands stretching. Reaching. Pleading . . .

A sharp jab to my stomach knocked me back into reality.

'You're doing it again,' Avery whispered harshly.

Ms Lucian glanced over her clipboard, her eyes fixing on me. For a moment, I thought I caught something in her gaze, but then it was gone. 'Did we not get enough sleep last night, Sebastian?' she asked.

'My apologies.' Avery kicked my chair. 'I mean, I'm sorry. No, I didn't, really. Get enough sleep, I mean.'

Behind me, Katie smothered a laugh.

'Well, let's try to work on that, all right?' Ms Lucian looked disapprovingly at my posture. 'And do take your feet down off the seat, please.'

'Yes, ma'am.'

What was going on with me? After all the sleepless nights, I supposed dozing off in class was pretty much a given. But zoning out like this was unnerving. I rolled my shoulders and tried to concentrate.

Ms Lucian continued. 'Class, your assignment today is a project, but before you all kill each other choosing groups, listen up.' She presented the papers. 'I received these fliers in my mailbox this morning. The Circe de Romany is coming back to town, and they will be here for an extended run. According to this advertisement, they've got a lot of stuff going on at the Fairgrounds over the next few months, so you might want to check it out. Who knows, there might be some extra credit involved if you attend some of their performances.'

Ms Lucian distributed the fliers, and everyone pored over them excitedly. I wasn't sure why, but my stomach suddenly bottomed out.

'Check this out,' Mitchell said loudly in my ear. He held the paper in front of his freckled face and then shoved it at me. 'Finally, something to do on the weekends besides movies and bowling.'

I took the paper, looking it over skeptically. 'So this is a carnival, as in, cheap rides and overpriced cotton candy?'

'Nah,' said Avery. 'It's way better than that. They were here two years ago, don't you remember?'

'I wasn't here two years ago, Avery.' I glanced up with a wry smile. 'Thanks for noticing.'

'Oh, right.'

Katie rolled her eyes at him. 'You're an idiot.'

'Well, I noticed you, buddy,' said Mitchell. He raised his arm dramatically. 'It was halfway through our sophomore year. You walked into class, looking all lost and confused. I said to Katie, "Hey, it's the new kid! Let's tell him they hold PE classes on the football field and see if he falls for it!"'

'Ah yes, fond memories,' I replied. 'And so was the detention I got afterwards.'

'That was freaking amazing,' said Mitchell, puffing out his chest.

'Remind me again,' I said, crossing my arms. 'Why are we friends? Oh yes. Because I have a soft spot for charity cases.'

Mitchell punched me in the shoulder. 'Nice.'

'So anyway,' said Katie, pulling our attention back, 'to answer your question, Sebastian, the Circe de Romany come through Sixes every couple of years. They have rides and games, all that carnival junk. And they put up this huge tent and have all kinds of special performances. It's actually pretty awesome.'

I studied the list of shows on the flier. It was true that Sixes came up lacking in the field of recreational activities. It was easy to see how something like this could cause a stir.

18

Mitchell leaned over to Katie. 'So the Romanys will be back in school?'

My stomach did that same weird elevator drop again, and the muscles in my neck went crazy tight. I watched Katie, suddenly interested in her answer, even though I didn't have a clue who Mitchell was talking about.

'Oh gosh, yeah, she's totally coming back,' Katie said, beaming happily. 'We've been talking a lot lately online. She says the Circe has leased the Fairgrounds until next spring, so she gets to attend school here for her senior year.'

Avery folded the flier, stuffing it into his pocket. 'Just her?'

'No, her brother's coming too,' Katie replied. 'He's not big on the home-schooling thing. He's bored.'

'He'd better be going out for the football team,' said Mitchell. 'He was a starter, back during freshman year, before they left town.'

The conversation continued, but I gradually lost interest. Whoever the Romanys were, I'd arrived in Sixes long after they'd left. Still, I couldn't ignore the feeling in the pit of my stomach like a case of nerves. But since I didn't have anything to be nervous about, I chalked the sensation up to my hunger. When the bell rang for lunch, I was seriously relieved.

The school's campus resembled a small college, with separate buildings devoted to particular areas of study. As we made our way up the hill to the Common Building, the potent smell of school cafeteria food hit me full in the face. The odor grew worse as we crammed our way through the doors.

The cafeteria was packed, and I was glad our group opted for the picnic tables in the courtyard. Avoidance of crowds ranked high on my quirks list. We fought through the food line and escaped into the great outdoors. Avery made a beeline for a couple sitting at one of the far tables, and I held the door open for Katie as we followed behind.

'Bet he's going to rag Brandon and Emma,' she said as Avery sprinted away. She gave me one of her knowing looks and smiled. 'You know they're like an official couple, as of yesterday.'

'That's nice,' I said politely.

Her smile turned sly. 'So, now it's your turn.'

'Oh no,' I said, using my lunch tray as a barricade. 'I'm immune to your schemes. No more trying to set me up. You *do* remember the Becky Drummond fiasco, don't you?'

'What?' Katie shrugged. 'She was perfect for you.'

'She said I smelled like moss. Who *says* that on a first date?'

'Okay, maybe not *perfect*.'

'I know you feel it's your God-given duty to bring me up to acceptable social standards,' I said, trying my best to look solemn, 'but I assure you, I'm a pathetically lost cause. Use your oozy matchmaker charms on some other poor soul.'

'Oh, come on, Sebastian.' Katie nudged my shoulder. 'You're funny, you're sweet . . . '

'And you sound like a commercial for a dating agency.'

Katie sighed. 'Well, points for trying, I guess.'

'Yeah,' I grinned. 'Always points for trying.'

Her laugh told me I'd won the battle. For now.

The afternoon sun was bright, even for autumn, and I yanked up my hood. I felt Katie's disapproving stare. I'd be getting a lecture from her on the benefits of sun exposure before the day was through. She'd given me a few, usually when I'd back out of one of her trips to the lake. When it was sunny, Katie practically lived on her father's boat, soaking in the rays. But the sun and I had never been friends. I resented the pounding migraines it inflicted, so I tended to hold a grudge.

We pushed through mingling students until we reached our table. Avery was sprawled across it, punching Brandon on the arm and congratulating him for snagging Emma, a cute girl with curly, sand-colored hair.

'Hey, guys,' said Brandon, scooting over to make room for us, 'did everybody hear about the Circe coming to town?'

Anxiety jolted through me at the mention of the carnival. I pressed a hand to my stomach, not feeling as hungry as I had before.

'Yeah, we were talking about it last period,' Mitchell replied, holding up his slice of square-shaped pizza and examining it critically before taking a bite.

Katie pulled a bright green phone from her purse. 'Yeah, and that reminds me, I've totally got to find out when they're coming to school. I can't believe it's been two years!'

'Let me know what she says,' said Brandon as he polished off a strange concoction that I assumed was meant to be a burrito. 'It'll be cool to see them again. Maybe they'll get us backstage passes or something to one of the shows.'

Emma laughed. 'Yeah, like they'd let you back there, Brandon. You'd break something!'

He put a hand to his heart in mock hurt. 'Hey, I'd be careful. I just like to look at stuff, you know?'

Avery pelted him with a hamburger bun, and everyone began talking about the Circe again. The louder their conversation got, the ickier I felt. I tugged my hood lower and studied the pile of soggy fries on my tray. The image of the Gypsy girl threatened the edges of my vision, but I stubbornly blinked her away. Freak class was *not* in session right now. I refused to provide Avery any more ammo to use on me today.

'Check it out, guys!'

Mitchell pointed over the courtyard, and we followed his gesture passed the front of the school where the town's main road ran parallel to the campus. A bright caravan of large tractor-trailers was passing by. Red paint spelled out the phrase *Circe de Romany*. The lettering was set against a background of orange and gold, with a design of swirling green vines and yellow flowers as the border.

Behind the trucks rolled several expensive-looking tour buses, branded with the same logo, and a cluster of smaller vehicles brought up the rear of the procession. The entire courtyard paused, watching the caravan amble down the road like a bright, twisting serpent.

The soft jingle of Katie's phone caught my ears. 'It's her!' she said. 'They're coming in tomorrow to register for classes!'

Avery leaned forward, rubbing his chin. 'Well, I'll make a point of being available to show her around.'

'Yeah, I'm sure you will, Avery.' Brandon huffed.

Lunch resumed, but I'd lost my appetite. I never skipped out on meals, but suddenly the three mustard-drenched corn dogs staring up at me were completely unappealing. Was I coming down with something? I pushed the tray aside and unscrewed the lid of my bottled water instead, wishing I had some aspirin. Beside me, Katie happily sipped a juice box. I cleared my throat, trying to appear casual, but feeling strangely unsettled.

'So, who is the *she* you keep talking about?' I asked.

'Josephine Romany,' she replied.

Hot chills ripped through my insides, like I'd plunged into a pool of lava and liquid nitrogen at the exact same instant. The shock was so strong that it sucked the air from my lungs. I pitched forward, clutching the edge of the table. Was it food poisoning? I stared at my plate. I hadn't even eaten anything yet!

Katie grabbed my arm. 'Sebastian?'

My airway opened again, and I could breathe. Was this an allergic reaction to something? I squinted up at the sky. Gradually the feeling passed.

'Just a bad headache,' I replied, pushing thoughts of various ailments from my brain.In a flash, Katie's hand was in and out of her bag, this time, holding a bottle of Tylenol.I took it gratefully. 'Thanks, mom.'

She poked me hard in the ribs.

The bell echoed through the courtyard, announcing that our brief stint of freedom was over. A collective sigh swept through the masses as students converged on trash cans and doors, disposing leftovers and shuffling to their next destinations. I parted ways with Katie, still feeling uneasy. Not to mention I'd barely touched my lunch.

The courtyard sloped downhill, ending at a covered breezeway. The shade felt good after being in the harsh sun, and I shoved my hood back, pushing hair out of my face. My stomach had settled, but my mind continued to swirl. The image of the dancing girl flashed in my head like the neon sign over the door of the tattoo parlor. But now, each time the image appeared, a name accompanied it:

Josephine Romany.

'Sebastian, are you still there?'

I transferred my phone to my other hand as I buckled the seatbelt. 'Yeah, I'm here.'

'Weren't you listening to me?' Katie asked.

I paused, trying to remember what we'd been talking about. The two hours since lunch had been a blur, and my brain was mush. 'Um . . . '

Katie sighed on the other end. 'The project Ms Lucian talked about in class today,' she continued impatiently. 'When are we going to work on it?'

'I'm sorry,' I replied, starting the engine. 'The pounding in my head's making it difficult to think.'

'Another headache?'

'You know me and sunny days,' I said dismissively. I stepped on the gas and coaxed my old van onto the road. 'But about the project. I don't know if I can do it this week. Can I get back to you?'

'Yeah, just don't wait too long. I know we've got almost a month to work on it, so Ms Lucian's not going to cut us any slack, and the rest of our group is totally avoiding me about the whole thing.'

Katie hated procrastinating on anything related to school-work. This was probably killing her. 'Look, don't worry about it. I'll talk to the guys, and we'll come up with a day to work on it. I promise, we won't let you down.'

'Thanks, Sebastian,' she replied, sounding relieved. 'You're not nearly as much of an idiot as the rest of your species.'

I chuckled. 'I think you mean gender.'

She giggled. 'No, I don't.'

'Talk to you later, Katie.'

'Bye.'

I tossed the phone on the passenger seat and rubbed my temples. By the time I made it through town and steered my van into the parking lot of the *Gypsy Ink*, my headache had traveled, setting up residence between my shoulder blades. The last thing I felt like doing was homework.

I shuffled through the waiting room, giving a brief wave to Kris, who was busy behind the counter. I'd grab a quick snack and then lay out flat on the floor of the apartment for a while. Just until the aching eased. I paused in the hallway just outside the door of Hugo's workspace. I didn't have to

24

say anything. My brother knew I was there.

'Hey, Sebastian.' He glanced up from his sketchbook. 'What's up?'

'Do you have any sports cream?' I leaned against the wall and squinted as a sharp pain lanced through my shoulders. 'My back's killing me.'

Hugo's brows settled low over his dark eyes. 'In the drawer beside my bed.'

'Okay, thanks.'

I continued down the hallway, followed by the weight of my brother's stare. He probably thought I was trying to get out of work, which wasn't a bad idea. I chucked my bag on the bed and rummaged through Hugo's nightstand until I located the tube of medicine. I worked the cream into my back, but it felt as if someone was digging long fingers between my shoulder blades, attempting to separate muscle from bone.

I gave up with the cream and stumbled to the bathroom on a quest for aspirin. Just as I reached for the medicine cabinet, another shock of pain doubled me over. I gripped the edge of the counter and straightened. My gaze flicked to the mirror. For a moment, I almost didn't recognize the face staring back. I was crazy pale, even for me, and my skin made the hazel color of my eyes look dull. But then I noticed something else. Another chunk of gray was poking through my disheveled hair.

What kind of sickness produced symptoms like these? There had to be some reasonable explanation. I was just stressed. My body was worn down. I needed a weekend of sleeping in and watching mindless movies. Then I'd be back to normal. I jabbed my fingers through my hair until the discolored strands disappeared beneath the surface of the black.

But it didn't matter. I knew it was still there.

And I was beginning to get just a little concerned.

25

3. Lost and Found

Katie was waiting for me in the school's main lobby the next morning, holding a chicken biscuit in her hand. The sight of warm food made my mouth water. My breakfast had consisted of a bag of potato chips and three protein bars. I eyed the foil package innocently.

'Is that for me?'

'Of course. You're always in a better mood after I've fed you.'

I grabbed the biscuit and hugged Katie at the same time. 'My hero.'

'Hey, I'm doing this for my benefit, not yours. I've seen how you get when you're hungry.'

Katie tapped endlessly on her phone as we strolled to our lockers. She opened the door with one hand and pulled out a book. I managed to sneak a quick peak in her locker mirror. The two gray streaks in my hair were pretty well hidden. That was a relief. So was the fact that my back pain had disappeared, along with the image of the dancing girl. I'd actually slept most of the night. But something new was bothering me.

I took a bite of chicken biscuit, and I was surprised at how unsettled it felt in my stomach. I chewed in silence, letting my mind wander back to the day before, and the talk about the Circe de Romany.

Katie pocketed her phone. 'You're really quiet today.'

I raised an eyebrow.

She smirked. 'Okay, quieter than *usual*.'

'Maybe.' I paused a moment. 'Um, Katie?'

Apparently something in my expression was amusing. She twisted a strand of hair around her finger like a gold ring and winked at me. 'Um, Sebastian?'

'I was just wondering if you heard any more about the Romanys?'

Her brows lifted. Yes, she was definitely amused. 'I have. Why?'

I played with the biscuit wrapper, choosing to stare at it rather than meet Katie's gaze. But we'd been friends for a while, and it didn't take long for Katie to read my thoughts.

'Uh huh,' she said. 'By Romanys, you mean Josephine.'

Warm-and-cold sensations spiked through my body again. I pressed against the lockers to cover my reaction, but blurted, 'What makes you think that? I don't even know her!' I abruptly stuffed a huge bite of chicken into my mouth to shut myself up.

Katie reached up and flicked a piece of biscuit off my shirt. 'Cute, Sebastian.' Her look made the blood rush to my cheeks. 'But I'm sure all the guys have been talking about her,' she continued. 'So naturally, you're interested, right?'

'No. Just curious. That's different from interested. Everyone else seems to know these people, and you're obviously pretty close to her.' I attempted a smile. 'I just wanted a heads-up, that's all.'

The heated chill passed, leaving only the warmth of embarrassment. This was almost worse than my zone outs.

'Well, Josephine's awesome. I totally get what they all see in her. Just remember one thing', she jabbed her finger into my sternum for emphasis; 'I consider myself her best friend, and I'm looking out for her. So don't get any ideas.'

A startled laugh escaped my throat. 'No worries there. Lost cause, remember?'

'I'm signing you up to the audition, Sebastian,' announced Mitchell, leaning smugly over his seat in the auditorium.

'Don't even think about it,' I replied sternly. I continued to scribble in my theater notebook. 'I'm not kidding.'

He only laughed.

I ignored him and studied my artwork. The massive circular patterns looked like batches of gray smoke engulfing the paper. Or maybe it was a representation of my churning insides. I hadn't felt right all day. No, make that the last two days. Or whenever it was that I'd first heard about . . .

Katie's phone vibrated beside me. She glanced down excitedly at the text. 'Guess what, guys! Josephine's in the office signing in.'

She was here.

It was as if the air had been squeezed from my lungs. My notebook dropped from my hands. Cold rushed over my skin, and I leaned forward, feeling myself in danger of falling out of my seat.

'Sebastian?'

Ms Lucian stood over me. I swallowed hard and pried my fingers loose from the armrests. 'I'm fine,' I said, automatically, before she could ask. But I wasn't. It felt like I was suffocating. 'I'm going to check out some props for our project.'

I bolted out of the chair and up the stairs to the stage. I could feel everyone watching me the entire way. As soon as I had parted the curtains and was safely out of sight, I fell against the wall and slid to my knees. I stared into the rafters, then looked away before I imagined plunging to my death over the edge of one of the pieces of scaffolding.

Maybe I wasn't diseased or suffering from cafeteria food poisoning. Maybe I was having a nervous breakdown. I was sick and shaky, and my body felt like I was taking a shower in alternating cold and hot water.

But why?

There was no telling what Avery and the others were probably saying about me. This was rapidly moving out of the realm of quirky. This was teetering on insanity. I put my head between my knees and prayed for the bell.

My pride sank to the bottom of my Converse as I stood in front of the call-board, staring at the audition sheet for the drama department's production of *A Midsummer Night's Dream*. My name was in the middle of the page. Mitchell had signed me up for auditions, the next afternoon.

The fact that he'd done it while I was hiding out backstage was just plain irritating. If I backed out now, they'd never let me live it down. But I wasn't an actor and had no intention of embarrassing myself – or Shakespeare – for that matter. As much as it stung my ego, I was going to have to bail out.

As I continued my inner debate, the door to the auditorium opened. Class was over and everyone had filed out to lunch, so I assumed Mitchell had returned to gloat. But no one appeared. Then, someone knocked on Ms Lucian's door. Since her office was around the corner, I didn't see who had entered. But I could certainly hear the voice.

'Excuse me, Ms Lucian. Could I speak with you?'

It was the most beautiful sound I'd ever heard.

Ms Lucian gave a polite reply and enquired as to how she could help. The voice spoke again.

'I'd like to audition for the play, if that's still possible.'

The teacher gave an enthusiastic affirmative, followed by instructions for finding the call-board.

'Thank you,' said the voice.

There was silence. Then I panicked. The voice would soon be at the call-board. I shivered harshly. Something in my gut told me to get out of there before it was too late.

But just as I reached up to scratch off my name, I caught a whiff of perfume. No, not perfume. It wasn't like the overpowering department store stuff that Emma wore, or even the fresh, fruity concoctions Katie slathered on every morning at her locker. Not that those weren't nice. But this was more like a scent; exotic, like flowers and spices from some strange place I could never afford to visit. My fingers froze over the '4:00' time slot. Then, another hand hovered over mine, gracefully wielding a pink pen. It wrote a name with a gentle flourish.

Josephine Romany

I couldn't remember how to breathe.

The voice drifted across my ear. 'Are you auditioning?'

'No,' I managed. 'No, I'm not.'

There was a delicate intake of breath behind me. My cheeks burned, and my feet felt bolted to the floor. I couldn't move, much less turn around.

'*A Midsummer Night's Dream* is a great play,' said the voice: Josephine Romany's voice. 'I'm sure they'll need plenty of guys.'

'Well, I don't know about that. I mean, yeah, it's a great play . . . I just meant . . . I mean, I'm not sure yet . . . about auditioning. I haven't thought much about it.'

What was I *saying*?

'Well, you really should.' Her voice was liquid sunshine. 'Everyone should give live performance a chance.'

'Okay,' I said, trying desperately to remember why I'd been so intent on scratching my name off in the first place. 'I'll do it.'

'Good.' There was the click of a pen and the pull of a backpack zipper. 'Well, I've got to stop by the registrar's office. I'll see you later . . . '

She trailed off purposely. My name, I realized with a start. She wanted my name! It took me a second to figure out what it was. 'Sebastian.'

I smelled that sweet, exotic scent again. It made me dizzy – but a good kind of dizzy – a swirling bliss that I didn't want to end. I put a hand on the call-board to keep from pitching forward.

'I'll see you later . . . Sebastian.'

The way my name sounded in her voice sent a current of electricity pulsing down my neck. It surged along my skin, unlike anything I'd ever felt before. I turned just in time to catch a glimpse of green shirt passing through the doors. I wiped my hand across my eyes, trying to sort out the craziness in my head.

I felt sick, almost queasy, but also elated, as though I was floating miles above that cloud nine place people talk about. How could such bizarre emotions exist at the same time? And why did they revolve around Josephine Romany; a girl I hadn't even had the nerve to turn around and meet properly? My gaze drifted to the sign-up sheet. Fate, it seemed, had decided to give me another chance. There, right above my name, was hers.

We were auditioning in the same time slot.

*

'You're auditioning for the play?' James looked at me incredulously.

'It's against my will, believe me.'

I'd barely walked through the door of the shop before he'd started yelling for some fresh paper towels. No one else was around, so I plucked a roll from under the counter. A young woman was his latest victim. She leaned over the back of his leather office chair as the burly man finished up an elaborate rose and butterfly combination on her back. She was quite the bleeder, and James kept dabbing his cloth, mopping up the red droplets seeping through the design.

'Nice work,' I commented.

'Thanks,' James muttered, concentrating on the last bit of shading. The needle stopped and he grunted in satisfaction. 'Check it out and see what you think.'

The customer scrutinized her fresh ink using the long wall mirror. 'It's great, James,' she cooed. 'Thanks a lot.'

The woman left and James followed me into the waiting room. He deposited money into the register. 'So, why the school play, Sebastian?' he asked. 'I didn't think you were the acting type.' Before I could answer, he snapped his fingers. 'Oh, I got it! It's a girl, isn't it?' He rocked back on his heels triumphantly, daring me to disagree.

'Mitchell signed me up.' I wasn't about to mention my encounter at the call-board. The guys gave me a hard enough time about my dating life as it was. 'As a dare.'

'School play?' my brother asked causally as he emerged from his room.

How did Hugo *do* that? Even fifteen feet down the hall, behind a closed door, and with a tattoo pen buzzing, he'd still managed to hear my news.

'Yeah,' I admitted. 'Auditions are tomorrow.'

'O-kay.' He drew the word out sarcastically. I shuffled towards the couch. 'Hey, don't sit down yet,' he said. 'I need you to pick up some Chinese takeout. We've got a busy evening.'

I sighed and held out my hands, waiting for Hugo to fork over the money. 'I don't get paid enough for this.'

He grinned back at me. 'Yeah, you do.'

I ran the errand, and within minutes, we were all sitting around the coffee table, piling up plates of Mongolian Beef. I didn't have the healthiest of diets, I realized, as I topped mine off with a helping of crab Rangoon.

'So what do you have to do for this big audition tomorrow, Sebastian?' Vincent asked around a mouthful of noodles.

'Read from the script, I guess.' I wiped my hands against my jeans before snatching up the last box of rice. 'I'm scheduled for 4 o'clock.'

Vincent chuckled. 'You look freaked out.'

'More like petrified,' agreed Kris.

I pressed my fork into the carton, smashing the rice until it resembled mashed potatoes. 'Well, it's just . . . there's this new girl in school . . . '

'I knew it!' James declared. 'You've got a thing for her!'

Ugh. It was like having a pack of annoying big brothers.

'No, I *don't*, James.' I raised my fork and stared at the chunk of disfigured rice clinging to it. 'I figured I'd be up on stage with Katie, or even Mitchell. But this girl's the only one in my time slot. I'm just a little nervous, I guess.'

Kris whistled. 'Must be one intimidating chick.'

'That's just it. I don't even know her.' I took a bite and chewed thoughtfully before continuing. 'But, you know, the strange thing is, when I heard her name yesterday, I got this really weird feeling that I *should*. I can't explain it.'

Hugo shoved his plate aside. 'Why do you say that?'

'Well, because it's not possible. She's new at school – as in – she literally just registered for class. Katie says she's part of that carnival that came into town yesterday. It's called the Circe de . . . '

'We know the one,' Hugo said curtly.

Everyone paused.

Then Kris cleared his throat. 'Well, I think you'll ace it, Sebastian.'

Vincent jumped in. 'Still can't figure out why you'd want to audition for something like that, girl or no girl.'

'I'm just doing it to save face, Vincent. It's not like Ms Lucian will cast me.'

My brother returned to his food, as did the others, and we passed the rest of the meal in silence. But the room felt tense, and I began to wonder if Hugo had issues with the carnival, or maybe somebody who worked there. Hugo *was* pretty opinionated. Whatever the case, I could tell he wasn't going to talk about it that night, and I'd learned, if I pushed my brother for details when he was in shut-down mode, I found myself with an additional list of chores.

I had way too many chores already.

After dinner, I bagged everything up and hauled it out to the dumpster behind the strip mall. The air was cool, and a gentle breeze rustled through the treetops. The stars were barely visible through the haze of city lights. I loved the night. Everything was quiet, peaceful. Comfortable. I sighed contentedly, despite the fact that I was carrying smelly trash to an even smellier dumpster.

When I returned, the crew had cleared out, but Hugo was waiting for me. He motioned me to follow him down the hall. Something about the way he squared his shoulders as he stepped inside his workroom made me uneasy.

'Sit down, kid.' He patted the second-hand dentist's chair he used for costumers. 'I think it's time you had a little initiation.'

My eyes widened. 'Are you serious?'

Hugo had always been against my getting a tattoo, which was a little hypocritical of him, in my opinion. I was the legal age, and I was planning on going into the business after graduation. I couldn't see his hang-up. But every time I mentioned it, he'd tell me there was no need to rush. A tattoo artist telling someone *not* to rush into a tattoo? Something had to be wrong with that picture.

I eased into the room with about as much confidence as a rat approaching a chunk of cheese in a trap. 'So what's changed?'

Hugo positioned his rolling chair, and a strange look flashed across his face, followed quickly by a cool smile. 'I thought you might need a little good luck for the audition tomorrow.'

I settled into the orange fabric of the dentist's chair and regarded my brother suspiciously. This wasn't the Hugo I was used to; the one who treated me like a kid. Auditioning for a high school play didn't seem important enough to change his strict opinion. But here he was, setting up his workstation for my tattoo.

My tattoo.

'Wait.' I sat up rigidly. 'Just what exactly did you have in mind?'

Sure, I wanted to be inked, but I hadn't actually decided *what* I wanted yet. Hugo didn't answer. He meticulously poured ink into small containers and then mixed the colors. He used black and white, as well as a shimmering silver ink I didn't remember seeing in his supplies.

'What's that?' I questioned, pointing to the ink.

'It's a new color I've been wanting to try,' he said, flatly, absorbed in his preparations. Okay, so maybe I wasn't a rat.

35

I was a guinea pig. But all the guys in the shop had been the test subject for one tattoo project or the other over the years. Looked like it was my turn now.

When Hugo was ready, he grabbed the pen, his demeanor business-like. His foot hovered over the pedal. 'Ready?'

'No stencil sketch? No Sharpie drawing?'

In all the times I'd watched Hugo at work, I had never seen him simply take the needle to skin. He put a hand on my shoulder. The smile that tightened his lips was genuine enough, but it didn't quite reach his eyes.

'Trust me,' he said. Hugo's eyes glazed as if he was concentrating on something only he could see. He shoved up the left sleeve of my jacket and flipped my arm over, exposing the pale skin along the inside of my wrist. 'Now, hold still.'

I swallowed hard. 'Don't do something stupid, please.'

Hugo didn't respond. He was already focused on his task. His foot pressed the pedal, and the familiar hum of the pen filled the air. I looked away, setting my jaw in preparation. The initial touch stung, the needle moving in and out of my skin so fast that my arm tingled. The tingle grew into pain which intensified as Hugo began to carve a design into the tender flesh of my wrist.

Adrenaline kicked in, engulfing my body in an exciting buzz. But my arm ached, sort of like the time I'd hit my elbow weird on the edge of the counter while dodging one of James's wrestling moves. It made my eyes water, and I couldn't decide whether I wanted to laugh or let out a string of unpleasant words. Though I was tempted to watch the process, I focused on the wall. At last, the mechanical drone of the pen ceased. The wheels of Hugo's rolling chair squeaked as he pulled away from me.

'You're done.' He sounded oddly relieved. 'Go ahead, check it out.'

The tattoo was black and gray – Hugo's specialty – but I was startled by the design. Permanently inked into my wrist was a dandelion flower. Each gray petal was painstakingly detailed and eerily lifelike. The stem and two jagged leaves wrapped around the outside of my wrist. Of all the things I thought Hugo might be putting on my skin, this image didn't even appear on the radar. I could feel my brother waiting for my reaction.

'What is this?' I asked, stunned.

Hugo tossed a wad of paper towels into the trash. 'I think my artwork's pretty decent. Can't you tell?'

'I know what it is, Hugo. I mean, why this? I was expecting tribal artwork or, at the very least, something black and tacky. But . . . a *flower*?' The shock was wearing off. Had my foster brother seriously just inked me with a dandelion?

'It's what you're supposed to have.' The tone of Hugo's voice squelched my rising irritation. 'Don't doubt your brother, Sebastian.'

James's bearded face appeared in the doorway. 'Look who's finally been initiated, Vince!' he boomed over his shoulder. 'Sebastian's gotten his first ink!'

Vincent entered the room and grabbed my arm. His gaze flicked briefly to Hugo, who was leaning against the wall, watching silently. I felt that vibe again, as if there was some-thing they were keeping from me. My shoulders tightened.

'So what's really going on, guys? Is this some kind of joke?'

'Not at all,' Hugo replied. 'We've been talking about your apprenticeship for a while. And I've finally decided that you're ready.'

I blinked, still leery. 'That's it?'

'I was going to surprise you next week, but in light of your audition tomorrow, I thought you could use a little good news. So, what do you say, Sebastian? Are you ready to join us?'

'So that's what all the weirdness has been about? All the talking behind my back was because you were keeping this a secret?'

James snapped his fingers. 'Yep, you got us.'

I stared at my new tattoo. The elegant detail Hugo crafted into it made the dandelion look ancient, not just minutes old; as though I'd always had it there, perched gracefully along my wrist. 'So what does this dandelion have to do with being an apprentice?'

The others looked at Hugo, but he kept his gaze on me, regarding me carefully. 'Not much, actually. It's more a matter of clan tradition.'

'Clan?' I glanced around the room, but the others continued staring at my brother. 'Am I missing something here?'

'We're Gypsies, Sebastian,' said Hugo.

'Well, that explains a lot.'

'I'm serious.'

'Gypsies?' I repeated, sitting up straighter. I thought about the shop, its name, and all the paraphernalia. Even the folk music they'd occasionally play in the lobby. I'd always assumed it was just a theme; a gimmick for the tattoo parlor. 'You mean like, *real* Gypsies?'

'Yeah,' he replied. 'Like *real* Gypsies.'

'So, what, do you like tell fortunes on the side?' I quipped, still convinced this was part of the joke. 'Got a crystal ball hidden under the counter I don't know about?'

'Don't believe all the crap you see in movies, Sebastian.' Hugo began cleaning up the workspace. 'My parents come from a long line of Roma.'

It had only been over two years since Zindelo and Nadya Corsi had left for Europe, but I had a hard time remembering their faces. 'Roma?'

'Some people consider the term "Gypsy" disrespectful,' Hugo continued. 'It's a name given to us by the *gadje*, the non-Roma. The truth is we've been called lots of things: Travelers, Black Dutch, Tinkers, you name it. But Gypsy suits us just fine.' He crossed his arms, looking proud. 'You could say we move in different circles.'

James cuffed me on the shoulder. 'That just means we do our own thing around here.'

I glanced at my brother, feeling the sting of betrayal. 'Why haven't you ever told me?'

'You never asked,' Hugo replied lightly, but his smile faded as he caught my look. 'I picked my own time to tell you, Sebastian. Who we are . . . our lineage . . . it isn't something to be taken lightly. It's important that this remain a secret from anyone outside of the Roma.' The corner of his mouth tightened. 'We keep a low profile.'

'Who is *we*?'

Hugo flicked his head at the others. 'Clans are made up of different Gypsy families, with one head family usually in charge. We all belong to the same clan: the Corsi.'

I stared at the men; the ones I'd come to regard as family. I'd never seen them so serious before. Suddenly, they didn't look like the same ragtag gang of tattoo artists who hung around my brother's apartment and doted on me like a kid brother.

'And the flower?' I asked again, holding up my arm.

'The *dandelion*', Hugo corrected, 'is symbolic. It's been used by all the Outcast clans for centuries. It represents persistence and survival.'

'So it's a good thing, right?'

Hugo laughed; an oddly choked sound. 'Of course it is, Sebastian. Why else would I have given it to you?'

'I don't know. Payback, maybe? For all the times I bugged you about getting a tattoo?'

'It's an important part of our heritage,' he explained. 'I wanted to wait until the right time, that's all.'

I studied my foster brother, trying to take it all in. Thinking of Hugo as a Gypsy was just, well, *weird*.

He knelt next to my chair. 'But keep that heritage bit to yourself, Sebastian. There's a lot more of us than you might think, and not all clans get along.'

'What, like rival gangs or something?'

Vincent snorted from across the room. 'Hardly.'

'We just like to stay out of each other's way,' said James.

'I'm starting to get that,' I replied, looking at him dubiously.

'But it's nothing you need to worry about,' Hugo interjected. 'Just don't go telling all your friends that you live with a bunch of Gypsies, okay?' His smile returned. 'Low profile, remember.'

'A funny request, coming from a guy who named his shop the *Gypsy Ink*.'

He looked smug. 'Ever heard of hiding in plain sight?'

'Okay, okay,' I relented. 'I'll keep your little secret. But I do have one question.'

'Shoot.'

'If you're Gypsies, what does that make me?'

A singular look came into Hugo's eyes. 'Does it really matter?'

I frowned. 'No, I guess not.'

'Good.' Hugo held out his hand. 'Then welcome to the clan.'

4. Rise and Fall

I was pouring a glass of orange juice the next morning when Hugo shuffled into the kitchen. He was rarely ever up before nine, and it was only a little after seven. 'Hey,' I murmured, cautiously. Hugo was about as much of a morning person as I was.

He almost smiled, which I took as a good sign, so I proceeded to make myself a heaping bowl of cereal as he fumbled with the coffee maker. I curled up at the kitchen table, and after Hugo poured his coffee, he joined me.

'So how's the tat?' he asked over the rim of his mug. I set down my spoon and pulled up the sleeve of my shirt. Hugo gave it a casual glance, and then a double take. He lowered his mug. 'Whoa,' he breathed, suddenly awake.

'Okay, not the response I was expecting,' I said, checking out my arm to see the cause. The top layer of skin had peeled away during the night, leaving the design intact, glaringly detailed against my pale skin. I shifted my glance to Hugo, bewildered. 'What is it?'

Hugo took my wrist, held it closer, and examined the tattoo with an expert's eye. 'I've never seen a tat heal this fast,' he commented. 'There's no redness, no swelling.' He ran a finger over the dandelion. 'Is it tender?'

'Nope.'

Hugo dropped my arm – almost too quickly – it seemed. 'Guess you're a fast healer, kid.'

'Or maybe I just heal faster than Gypsies do,' I ventured. 'We should run a study or something.' My brother returned to his coffee, ignoring my attempt at humor. I gritted my teeth, still not completely over my feelings from the night before. Hugo had always been pretty guarded, but I didn't think he'd keep me in the dark about something he considered this important. 'Sorry,' I said after a few minutes of silence, choosing to push away the left-out feeling. 'It's just that I'm having a hard time believing you guys are Gypsies.'

'Why? Everyone has a heritage, Sebastian. We all come from somewhere.'

I jammed my spoon into my cereal. 'Yeah, I guess you're pretty lucky to know yours.'

I could feel Hugo's eyes on me, but I didn't press the issue; either about my foster brother's Gypsy roots or the lack of my own. I was dangerously late for school already. I polished off a third bowl of cereal without saying another word. Hugo still hadn't finished his coffee by the time I dumped my leftover milk and grabbed my backpack.

'Well, I've gotta get to school.'

'Yeah,' Hugo replied, staring hard into his mug.

I paused in the doorway and tilted my head, trying to figure out if I was being paranoid or if Hugo was acting a little strange. With it being so early in the morning, it was difficult to tell. 'Okay, well, I'll see you this afternoon, I guess.'

Hugo snapped out of his preoccupied silence. 'I expect a full report later on about this whole audition thing,' he said with a wide grin.

I groaned. I'd almost forgotten about my impending torture. 'Well, don't get your hopes up. There won't be much to report.'

As soon as school ended, I raided the vending machines. My nerves had returned, and with them, my appetite. Lunch had been the equivalent of eating rubber. I polished off three packs of crackers on my way to the auditorium, and was opening my fourth when a sharp pain cut through my wrist. I dropped the package, and wrapped my fingers around my tattoo. Maybe I wasn't as quick a healer as Hugo thought.

I spread my fingers and examined the dandelion. It looked exactly the same as it had at the breakfast table, but my skin throbbed like bad sunburn. I shook out my arm, collected my spilled snack, and opened the front doors.

No one was in the lobby when I arrived, and I was glad for the chance to collect my thoughts. But just as I leaned against the wall, the door flew open and the stage manager – sporting a clipboard and an attitude – burst into the lobby.

'Aren't you in the 4 o'clock slot?' he demanded.

'Yeah,' I replied.

'Well, you're late.'

'What?' The clock above the door read 3:50. 'I thought . . . '

'Never mind,' he huffed, cutting me off. 'The rest of your group's already inside.'

I followed him in, and the door clanged shut behind me. The stage lights were on, but the rest of the auditorium was dark. The stage manager scurried down the aisle as I found a seat in the back row. On stage, Katie and Avery were in the middle of reading a scene. Avery's booming voice echoed through the house. He was good.

Really good.

This was going to be embarrassing.

When they finished, Ms Lucian – who was seated in the second row – thanked them for their efforts. Katie spotted me as they exited, and she waved encouragingly. Avery punched me across the shoulder. I didn't see Mitchell, but that was okay.

I would kill him later.

While Ms Lucian wrote in her notebook, a strained quiet enveloped the room. The anticipation felt like a vice cranking against my lungs, each moment increasing the pressure. It squeezed drops of sweat from my forehead, dampening my hair inside my hood. It was just a stupid audition. It wasn't as if I was delivering a speech to the United Nations. Why were my hands shaking so much? Finally, Ms Lucian lifted her head and addressed the auditorium.

'Josephine Romany.'

I craned my neck to see, though I really didn't know who I was looking for. All I knew was her voice; the sweet, exotic smell of her perfume. And the awful, wonderful, twisting of my stomach as it made sailor knots beneath my T-shirt.

And then, I knew. My anxiety had nothing to do with the audition. I was nervous about *her*. Near the front, a girl rose and made her way down the aisle; movements fluid and smooth, like a professional artist. I braced myself against the seat as Josephine seemed to float up the stairs, out of the darkness and into the light.

Beautiful just didn't cut it. The Bard himself would've stabbed me with his quill for my lack of words, but nothing seemed to fit her. She wasn't fashion magazine beautiful, like the cheerleaders who sat in front of me in science with their dress-code-breaking skirts that made it hard to concentrate. Josephine Romany was something else, something outside of Sixes; from some other place and time.

Her full lips didn't need lipstick, and the way she smiled made her whole face glow. She looked out over the audience, tucking a strand of hair the color of hazelnut coffee behind her ear. Thick brows lifted over the most amazing eyes I'd ever seen: large and luminously green. The glow of stage lights clung to her tanned skin.

As she stood waiting for instructions, the air around me hummed. It was the same electricity I'd experienced at the call-board, and it reminded me of the way I'd felt when Hugo had given me my tattoo – weirdly uncomfortable and alarmingly pleasant – all at the same time. I stared at her, fascinated, unable to look away.

'Sebastian Grey.'

Ms Lucian peered into the audience, and I was horrified to realize she was searching for me. This was it. I had to go stand up there with this new girl who was doing all kinds of unexplained things to my insides. I stumbled out of my seat, head numb and legs wobbling as though I'd never used them before. I struggled to maintain some semblance of composure as I walked with heavy steps to my own funeral.

'Break a leg, man,' Brandon whispered as I passed.

A script was slapped into my hands and, suddenly, I found myself next to Josephine Romany. I felt euphorically sick.

'Hello again, Sebastian,' she said.

I wanted to make eye contact; to actually look into her face for the first time instead of just seeing her from afar, but I also wanted to remain upright and coherent, so I merely nodded in her direction. 'Hey.'

Ms Lucian rapped her pencil against her notebook, demanding our attention. 'All right, I want you both to turn to page sixteen.' She waited while we found our places.

'Josephine, if you would read for Hermia, and Sebastian, please read for Lysander.'

I'd read *A Midsummer Night's Dream* more than once, and I knew that Lysander was one of the romantic leads. This was going to be terrible. The words swirled on the page. *Just don't pass out*, I pleaded to myself.

'Sebastian, are you all right?' Ms Lucian studied my face carefully. 'You don't look as though you're feeling well.'

I planted my feet, determined to see this through. 'I'm good.'

'All right then, let's begin.'

Josephine had the first line. 'Be it so, Lysander,' she read in a low, clear voice. 'Find you out a bed; for I upon this bank will rest my head.'

'One turf shall serve as pillow for us both,' I said through clenched teeth. 'One heart, one bed; two bosoms, and one troth.'

Somewhere, Shakespeare *had* to be laughing.

I was no Avery, but I survived the audition by keeping my head firmly buried in the script and my thoughts glued to the words on the page. I had never been happier than when Ms Lucian interrupted and thanked us. Josephine left the stage first, and I followed, my legs still feeling like liquefied jelly.

Josephine glided ahead of me in the aisle, tossing her hair over her shoulders as she walked, carefree and obviously unaffected by what had been fifteen of the most gut-wrenching minutes of my life. I felt more confused than ever. My palms were sweaty, my brain was gooey, and I had all the coordination of a two-year-old. What was going on with me? Auditions were over, and I'd seen the elusive Josephine Romany.

The mystery was over.

So why did I still feel so weird?

Everyone had gathered in the lobby. Katie whirled and clutched Josephine's arm as soon as we appeared. I hovered near the door, still feeling like an idiot, but unable to take my eyes off the new girl. I rubbed at my wrist, which was throbbing to the beat of my pulse.

'Oh my gosh!' Katie cooed. 'You were so good! You're totally going to get Titania!'

'You were great too,' Josephine replied cheerfully.

'That was a lot harder than I thought it would be,' Katie went on, barely drawing a breath. 'I can't believe I didn't wet myself right there.'

Brandon jumped in. 'Aw, you were great, Katie. You too, Josephine.' He spotted me. 'And you were pretty decent, I guess.'

They all looked at me then, and I smiled, fully aware that Josephine was watching as well, even though I couldn't bring myself to meet her gaze. 'Thanks for the encouragement, Brandon.'

'Ah, it was good for you, Sebastian,' he said. 'Who knows? Maybe Ms Lucian will take pity and actually give you a part.'

'Stranger things have happened,' I replied.

Josephine was still looking at me, and I knew I should've said something to her, but what would've made sense? I couldn't reverse time, and I was pretty sure I'd destroyed my first impression. I wanted to melt into the lobby's concrete wall.

Katie saved me from any further embarrassment by pulling her away from the group. 'Well, we'll see you guys later. We're heading to the mall.'

I watched them go, feeling as if I was in a trance. I had total tunnel vision on Josephine as she opened the door and slid inside Katie's car. But as soon as they pulled out of the parking lot my head cleared, and the world refocused. I stuffed my hands into my pockets, hoping I hadn't looked as stupid as I'd felt.

'I gotta give you credit, Sebastian,' said Mitchell, approaching me. 'I didn't think you'd actually go through with the audition.'

I shrugged. 'Hey, I'm always up for a challenge.'

Avery attempted a serious expression. 'Did you have fun?'

'Oh, tons. It ranked right up there with chickenpox and root canals.'

'You've gotta stop taking yourself so seriously, man,' Avery declared. 'What's life without a little risk? And you lucked out today. You got to read with Josephine.' He dropped his arm around my shoulder. 'What about that?'

I shrugged him off. 'So?'

'Oh, come on. She's pretty hot.'

'Definitely,' agreed Mitchell.

'And with that whole carnival girl vibe she's got going on . . . '

'That's enough,' I snapped.

Avery looked stunned. 'Excuse me?'

I felt a rush of heat as a frightening surge of anger blazed through me; the kind that made me want to hit something. I paused, shocked at my own emotion. I didn't get like this. Indignant, sure. Even ticked off, on occasion. But nothing like this.

This was raw, barely controllable, anger.

I took a deep breath. It had to be leftover nerves from the audition, that's all. I took a few more breaths and pressed my fist against my leg. Something inside me finally released, and the harsh emotion disappeared as quickly as it had come.

'Sorry,' I said, putting on an easy smile and playing down my reaction. 'Listen, I've got to go home and, you know, recover from this audition thing. Maybe get a little therapy. I'll see you guys tomorrow, okay?' I ignored their stares as I pushed open the lobby doors and rushed out.

What was wrong with me?

5. *Sink or Swim*

I considered skipping school the next day, but there was no point. I'd already seen Josephine Romany – and thoroughly embarrassed myself in the process – so that was over. Things could go back to normal now.

But I found myself constantly thinking about her, and the more I tried not to think about her, the more it happened. I wanted to see her, to somehow make up for my awkward reaction – which made even less sense to me than it did the day before – but then I'd feel mortified at the thought of seeing her – and I realized it was because I didn't want to see her, which made absolutely no sense.

Feelings like this couldn't be normal.

I transferred my lunch tray to one hand so I could massage my aching shoulders. Much to my dismay, and despite aspirin and a tube of muscle cream, they hadn't loosened at all. If anything, the cramping tightness had gotten worse. Avery shifted closer as we walked through the courtyard.

'Did somebody go to the gym last night?' he asked hopefully.

'Sorry, Avery,' I replied, covering my irritation with a smirk. 'I'm not going to join your fitness club, even if they *do* have really good smoothies.' He tried to look wounded, but I wasn't buying it. 'I'm just a little stiff today,' I added. 'The weather, I guess.'

Avery glanced at the sky and cocked an eyebrow. 'The weather?' It was a perfect autumn day – one that begged for football and bonfires – not aching joints and muscles. 'Look, Sebastian, I know you've got a full year on me, but that's old people talk, man.'

'I said it's the weather, okay?' I grinned under my hood. 'Now shut up or I'll beat you with my cane.'

'Yes, *sir*.'

The gang was assembled in the courtyard, but with one addition: Josephine sat atop the table, chatting with the others. I instantly put on the brakes, my blood pounding in my ears. All attempts at normalcy crumbled. Avery pushed ahead, oblivious to my reaction.

'I was so excited when my parents said we were staying in Sixes,' she said to Katie. Her face lit up as she talked. 'I really like it here.'

'Well, it's cool to have the Circe back in town,' Mitchell squirted a packet of ketchup on his hot dog. 'It's been pretty boring around here.'

'I'm glad you got switched into drama, Josie,' said Katie. 'I barely see you all day.'

I grimaced as Katie called her Josie. It seemed too plain for someone like her.

She was sunlight reflected on a pond.

'Speaking of hiding out,' said Avery from across the table, 'where's Francis? Did he register for drama, too?'

Josephine laughed. 'My brother wouldn't be caught dead in a drama class. You know what a big jock he is.'

Avery straightened, bowing out his broad chest. 'And what's that supposed to mean? You can't be a jock and participate in the theatrical arts?' He flexed his broad arms for emphasis. 'Is that what you're saying?'

'Of course you can,' Josephine replied, clearly entertained. 'But trust me, you don't want Francis anywhere near the stage. He claims he's too much of a tech-head for the artsy stuff.'

'Yeah?' Brandon set down his soda and leaned forward. 'So what does that make us?'

Katie smiled. 'Well-rounded.'

Josephine propped her chin in her hand. 'So, my birthday's on Monday.' She was met with a chorus of well wishes and she laughed. The sound gave me a pleasant rush. 'Thanks, guys,' she continued, 'but my parents are insisting on throwing me a party . . . turning eighteen and all that. I have to humor them, but spending a whole evening with my troupe is not exactly what I'd call a party. I mean, honestly, I see them every day.' Everyone was listening and, like a seasoned performer, Josephine milked every moment of their attentive silence. 'I asked my parents if I could bring some friends from school, that is, if anyone is interested.' She tilted her chin, looking around the table innocently. 'I'd love it if you all could come. It's at the Circe, of course. Monday night at seven. What do you say?'

It wasn't really much of a decision. An invitation to a party at the Circe de Romany on a weeknight easily topped the most exciting weekend plans in Sixes. Everyone talked, and Josephine seemed pleased, and I found myself smiling at her. Then I realized I was still standing there, frozen, stupidly holding my tray. Josephine saw me.

'What about you, Sebastian?' she asked. 'Can you come?'

The dancing girl whirls. Green eyes meet mine.

Blinding pain. A shriek in the dark . . .

*

Everything snapped into focus. I barely kept my tray from crashing to the ground. I took a step back, clutching the plastic handles, trying to breathe again. All this time, all those zone outs. The image of the Gypsy girl. It wasn't from the painting in the tattoo shop. It was *her*.

It was Josephine.

My mouth dropped open before I had the good sense to clamp it shut. All eyes were on me now, and Katie's were so large that I thought they might pop out of her head. Josephine blinked at me, waiting for my answer. I concentrated all my energies on declining her invitation. There was no way I could attend her party. Not when just looking at her made me freak out.

'Sure.'

The word escaped my lips completely against my will, and the sensation felt like plunging down a long flight of stairs. Josephine's expression turned strangely solemn as she stared at me.

'Good.'

After another dinner of Chinese takeout, I collected the *Gypsy Ink* trash and prepared to make my nightly pilgrimage to the garbage bin.

'Don't be long,' said Vincent, tossing me another bag from his workroom. 'There's another load waiting for you by the counter.'

'Some Friday night,' I replied, transferring garbage around until I could get it all in one trip. 'Most people go to the movies. I've got a date with a Hefty bag.'

Vincent followed me to the back. 'And whose fault is that? I figured you'd be hanging out with Katie.'

'Nope,' I said, kicking the door open and shoving myself through. 'She's doing something with Josephine.' My scalp tingled when I said her name.

Vincent raised his brows. 'The girl from the audition?'

'Yep.'

My scalp tingled again, growing rapidly into an annoying itch. I pressed the side of my head into my shoulder, trying to scratch without dropping the garbage bags. Vincent watched me with amused curiosity.

'Problems?' he asked through quirked lips.

I tried using the other shoulder. The itch just seemed to spread. 'Hugo's got to stop buying that cheap crap shampoo.'

Vincent thrust another bag into my chest. 'What, discount brand not good enough for you, pretty boy? Next you'll be asking for body wash and those loofah things my girlfriend uses.'

'At least I take showers,' I said with a broad grin. 'You should try it sometime. Really helps with the smell.'

I tucked the bag under my arm and hurried down the steps before Vincent retaliated with more trash. The door clanged shut behind me. So maybe I was sans plans for the weekend, but I didn't mind. I wasn't feeling particularly social. With all the weirdness I'd been experiencing lately, along with my teetering emotions, the thought of a couple of days away from everybody at school was pretty appealing.

My feet crunched over the gravel, and the sound echoed off the concrete walls. The lane was wide enough for a car, but the building on one side and the hedge of thick pine trees on the other made it feel enclosed, even stifling. The only illumination came from a sickly orange streetlight teetering precariously from a post.

The glow reminded me of the bonfire in my recurring image. And at that moment, I realized something: I hadn't seen a single flash of it since lunch. Since I'd realized Josephine was *the girl*. Another mystery solved, I decided, as I closed the distance between the shop and the garbage area. I'd obviously seen Josephine's picture somewhere – probably at Katie's – since they were apparently good friends.

In other words, I was cured of the whatever-it-was – which should've been a relief – but I wasn't totally back to normal. My insides hadn't felt right since the afternoon before, not to mention my throbbing back, the unexplained slivers of gray hair I'd kept carefully hidden, and the fact that I couldn't stop thinking about Josephine Romany, no matter how hard I tried.

Or how many chores I hid behind on a perfectly decent Friday evening.

I heaved the garbage bags over the side of the dumpster, determined to ask Hugo for a raise. Maybe his little Gypsy clan wasn't rich, but I figured enduring the dumpster smell was worth some extra cash. With my hands free, I could finally dig them into my hair for a decent scratch, but my head wasn't tingling anymore. Or maybe I just wasn't thinking about it because of the repugnant smell of the alley. I sniffed, wondering when the stench had gotten so bad. It was enough to clear my sinuses. I brushed my sleeve disgustedly across my nose and turned around to head back to the shop.

Then I heard it: a shuffling sound from the other end of the alley. It wasn't unusual for someone to be behind the building, dumping trash or breaking down boxes. But it wasn't the sound that bothered me. My skin began to crawl, and the base of my skull throbbed to the rhythm of my steadily quickening pulse. The atmosphere around me felt suddenly dark.

Very, very dark.

I pressed my back against the cold metal and peered around the dumpster. The building was black and ominous. Under the feeble light the rows of doors gaped at me like hollow, fathomless eyes. The alley was deserted.

'Hello?' I called out into the darkness.

The only reply was the creaking of an old pine tree as a breeze chilled the October air.

My breath spewed out in white puffs. I set my jaw to stop my chattering teeth, and pushed myself away from the trash bin, eyeing the back door of the shop.

A shadow passed across the alley. No, it was more than a shadow. It was like smoke; blackened and thickly curled. It crept along the ground, clinging to the gravel and trash, enveloping the road. It could've been fog, but it moved too quickly. As if it had some kind of purpose.

Fair is foul, and foul is fair. The line from *Macbeth* ran through my head as I watched the mist slither closer, leaving a translucent trail. *Hover through the fog and filthy air.*

The air seemed to whisper jumbled sounds; like many voices speaking to me at once . . . none distinguishable or pleasant. My blood dropped to subzero levels. I could feel my heart crashing against my ribcage. I remained perfectly still, hardly daring to breathe. The mist continued to roll towards me, gaining in breadth until it stretched the width of the alley.

The door to the shop seemed a hundred miles away.

The smoke rose and hovered above me like a storm cloud. I could feel energy swirling inside it; a presence; alive and vibrant, propelling it downward. It drifted against my skin, cold and warm. I crouched, digging my shoes into the mucky ground, ready to make a run for the door. Then a strange female voice whispered in my ear.

We've found you . . .

I shot forward, propelling myself across the alley. But I didn't get far. A gust of wind slammed into me like a freight train. The impact ripped the air from my lungs. I ricocheted off the dumpster and skidded, face first, across the dirt. Gravel sliced my palms, tore at my knees. My head rattled. Darkness invaded my vision. I felt my body trying to stand, to right itself, but I was losing consciousness. Something registered through the fog: a door banging open. I choked, gasping for oxygen as I crumpled to the ground.

I wasn't sure how long I lay in the slosh and grime of the alley. I heard the scratching of an animal in the dumpster and the buzzing of the streetlight. But time itself passed out of reach and beyond my comprehension.

Then, arms were around me, lifting me from the ground. Vincent's hard, lean face was close to mine, his dark eyes worried. I could smell his sweat and the hint of teriyaki on his breath.

'Are you hurt?' He sounded scared. 'What happened to you?'

'S-something . . . ', my throat felt coated with sand, '. . . attacked me.'

'*Attacked you?*' Vincent released me and jogged a few paces down the alley. His head twisted back and forth as he examined the road. Or, at least, that's how it seemed. His form was blurry. I wiped my eyes with the edge of my sleeve. He returned and knelt beside me. 'Are you sure, Sebastian? There's no one out here.'

'It was . . . ' The words didn't make it past my teeth. *The wind?* I glanced at the scraggly pine branches swaying in the breeze. Then I noted the slimy tracks I'd left across the ground. Had I slipped, lost my balance in the mud? I looked at Vincent through narrowed eyes. 'What are you doing out here?'

'Looking for you,' he replied. He didn't meet my gaze; he was staring somewhat awkwardly at my hair. I brushed it out of my face as he continued. 'You've been gone almost half an hour.'

'Seriously?'

'Come on,' he said quickly, 'let's get you inside.'

He helped me to my feet. My palms itched and my right temple throbbed, but the rest of me seemed to be in working order. My lungs felt clear, and there was no trace of the mist anywhere in the alley. I glanced dubiously over my shoulder. Had I imagined it? Already, the details of what just happened felt fuzzy in my head. We entered the shop, and Kris glanced up from the counter. His eyes widened as he looked at me.

'Um, your hair's gray.'

I stared at him. 'What?'

Vincent grabbed a mirror from the counter. I flipped it over and met my reflection. And I couldn't believe what I saw. Kris was right. My hair *was* gray, but not the whitish gray of the elderly. It was a vibrant shade of pewter.

Only a few strands of my normally black hair remained. I tentatively brushed my fingers through it. My hair felt the same. But the shade was something out of the paint department at the hardware store. I'd heard of people's hair changing color due to fright or trauma, but nothing like this.

'Okay, what's going on?' I peeled my gaze from the mirror. 'Is this another weird Gypsy tradition? First tattoos, then hair dye? Did my brother put you up to this?'

Vincent didn't blink. 'You'll have to ask him.'

As if on cue, the front door banged open. Hugo stomped through, ushering a gust of wind. 'Did you guys see the fog?' he said, shedding his jacket. 'It looks like we're going to . . . '

He caught sight of me, instantly registering my new hair color.

But he didn't seem surprised. His face hardened for a moment, then relaxed into an expression I couldn't totally place.

Almost like satisfaction.

'Your hair's gray,' he said.

'Yeah, we just covered that,' I replied.

'Looks good on you.' Hugo brushed passed me and chucked his jacket on the counter. 'Hey, Vincent, can you grab that book for me? I've got some research to do on a Gothic tat for a customer.' Vincent hauled a large leather-bound book from the shelf behind the counter and handed it to my brother.

'Hold up,' I said, tossing the mirror aside, 'is this gray hair part of some kind of initiation thing? I thought you already said I was in the club.'

'It's not a club,' Hugo replied. 'We're a clan. And no, having gray hair doesn't make you Roma.'

'Then it has to do with my being your apprentice, doesn't it? Your form of tattoo artist hazing.' I paused, thinking. My scalp had only started itching after my shower earlier that evening. My gaze cut to Vincent and back to my brother. 'You put something in my shampoo, didn't you?' Hugo had never really been the prankster type, but the other guys were always pulling something on each other. 'Trying to get me to change my mind?'

Hugo cracked open the book and flipped through the pages. 'Hmm . . . '

I smirked darkly and crossed my arms. My brother was stubborn.

But so was I.

'Well, it's going to take a lot more than flowery tattoos and hair dye or tossing me around the alley to get me to back down.'

Hugo glanced up with a sharp look. 'Tossing you around?'

'Yeah,' I replied. 'One of you guys was out by the dumpster, trying to freak me out.' Everyone just looked at me. I let my gaze circle the group, studying their blank faces. 'Okay, then,' I continued, allowing my smirk to lengthen into a casual smile, 'if that's the way you want to play, bring it on. You're going to apprentice me this time, Hugo. Nothing's going to stop me from doing what I want with my life.'

For a split second, Hugo seemed to freeze. As he studied me, another expression flickered across his face. Conflicted, maybe even uncertain. But then, the blinds were closed again, and it was gone. Hugo tucked the book under his arm. 'Well, I've got to get these sketches done. I'll see you guys later.' He smiled at me. 'As for you, *Mr Apprentice*, you'd better get yourself cleaned up and grab a mop. You've tracked mud all through the shop.'

6. *Sighted or Blind*

'Mr Grey, please remove your hood.'

I glanced up from my math problems. 'Sir?'

Mr Weir stood over me, obviously irritated. 'Your hood, Mr Grey,' he said, pointing to a laminated list of rules on the wall. 'No hats or coverings in the classroom.'

I looked around self-consciously. Everyone was in a typical Monday morning stupor, working drearily at their desks. Only Avery stole a glance at me over the edge of his textbook. I sighed and reached up, pushing back my jacket hood. Avery made a weird choking sound.

Alex Graham turned around in his seat directly in front of me. He looked me over in his typical 'everyone on the planet is beneath me' way and sneered through his nasty mountain-man beard. 'Nice.'

My chest grew warm underneath my jacket at his insult. I didn't need any more negative attention from Alex. He singled me out for ridicule enough on a daily basis as it was. I hunched in my seat and narrowed my eyes back at him, feeling the heat churning into irritated anger. I clenched my teeth, determined to keep my stupid, newfound emotions under control. *No freak outs, Sebastian.*

Mr Weir cleared his throat disparagingly, and continued moving down the row, checking students' work. Alex snickered and turned back to his graffiti effort on the desk with his pen. As soon as the coast was clear, Avery leaned across the aisle and poked me with his pencil. He aimed his eraser at my hair, silently indicating the obvious question.

'Just trying something new,' I whispered.

No one needed to know that I'd tried to dye my hair back to its original shade all weekend, but with no success. I'd rinse out the solution, only to find the same slate gray color mocking me in the mirror. I didn't know what Hugo and the guys had used on me or how long it would last. But for now, it appeared my new hair was permanent.

In the parking lot after school, we made our plans for the evening. Or rather, everyone else made the plans while I stood in the back of the group, adjusting the hood of my jacket and tugging it as low as possible. I'd been slammed with comments about my hair all day. Katie had given me several disapproving looks, and Emma had even threatened to stop by later and 'repair the damage'.

'Hey, I saw Erica on my way out,' Mitchell said as he leaned against his car. 'She said Ms Lucian's going to post the cast list for *A Midsummer Night's Dream* at six tonight.'

'Finally,' said Katie. 'I've been freaking out all weekend.'

'I'm sure you'll get a part,' said Emma, from under Brandon's arm. He had her pinned against his car door and was proceeding to suck on her ear. 'I can't wait to see who got cast.'

'Okay,' said Mitchell, ignoring them. 'I vote we meet here, check out the list, and then head to Josephine's party at the Fairgrounds. Is that cool with everybody?'

Josephine's party.

I'd forgotten all about it.

'Works for me.' Katie retrieved her keys from her purse. 'Somebody text me as soon as you see the cast and let me know. I made the mistake of volunteering to help with the party, and now Josie's made me her slave for the next few hours.'

Avery winked. 'Remember, you promised you'd get Josephine to introduce me to some of those hot Circe performers.'

Katie wrinkled her nose. 'Don't get your hopes up.'

She got in her car and drove off. The rest of our group exchanged goodbyes and quickly dispersed. Avery pointed at me over the hood of his Jeep.

'You're still coming, right?' he asked, opening the door.

I hesitated. I wasn't the party type, but I'd told Josephine I'd be there. And I couldn't pass up the chance to prove that I wasn't a complete bumbling freak. The gray hair wouldn't earn me any points, but at least maybe I could talk to her this time and not come off as a total idiot. 'Yeah, I'm coming.'

I pulled out of the parking lot right behind Avery, and I was halfway home before an unsettling thought struck me. I didn't have a birthday present for Josephine.

'I can't show up without something,' I groaned aloud.

My rumbling van seemed to agree, so I turned around and headed back into town. Sixes was filled with dozens of shops, and I decided to try my luck in the historic district. Maybe I could find something unique there. Josephine just didn't seem like the card and candy type. I chose a promising street and eased the van into a parking slot near a line of antique stores.

The first shop was called *Antiquities and Such*. I opened the bright pink door and ventured inside. Strands of Christmas lights framed the shelves and piano music drifted from a pair of frayed speakers. The smell of old things tickled my nose.

An elderly lady looked up from her magazine and smiled somewhat warily at me.

'Can I help you, young man?'

I smiled back. 'I'm just looking, thank you.'

She nodded and returned to her magazine, and I ducked into the first aisle. Row after row of delicate collectibles taunted me. The sight was discouraging. What would Josephine like? I'd barely talked to her; if one could count a few awkward sentences as actual conversation. I should have asked Katie's advice, but it was too late now.

I checked my phone. It was already 5:30 p.m.. I was running out of time, and I wasn't going to find anything here. I spun around, fumbling for my keys, and dropped my phone in the process. It clanked against the glass shelving. As I knelt to pick it up, I noticed the bottom shelf was empty, save for one object: a porcelain figure.

She was dressed in a patterned skirt and peasant top, painted bright orange and yellow. The artist had captured her in the middle of a dance, with her arms extended, her back arched, and her hair billowing. Lifelike green eyes stared back at me, holding my gaze so intently that I could have sworn she was real. I leaned in closer; captivated.

A Gypsy figurine that resembled Josephine Romany. *Romany*. I could almost hear the wheels clicking together in my head. Could it be that the traveling circus was made up of Gypsies, too? Is that why Hugo had abruptly cut me off when I mentioned their arrival? Was there still more my brother wasn't telling me?

'Young man, can I get that for you?'

I toppled backwards off my heels, narrowly missing the breakables on the shelf behind me. I blinked up at the wrinkled face. 'It's her,' I murmured.

The woman looked at me as if I'd escaped from a mental institution. 'Well, I'm glad you like it. I'll package it up for you.'

She took the figurine and hobbled to the counter. She rolled the porcelain girl in crinkled paper and bundled it into a bag.

'That will be fifteen dollars.'

I scrounged up enough bills to pay for the gift. Back inside my van, I placed the bag on the passenger seat and stared at it, feeling a little hazy. Was I cursed with seeing Josephine in every dancing image for the rest of my life? I forced my gaze away from the gift and glanced in the rearview mirror instead.

I shoved back my hood and raked my fingers through my hair as if I could somehow brush out the pewter sheen. But nothing changed. I had to hand it to the guys. They were taking this initiation pretty seriously. I gave my head a fierce shake, yanked on my hood, and drove back to Sixes High School.

I'd given little thought to the cast list until I arrived. I just wanted to look at the sheet, congratulate those who had gotten roles, and commence with the most difficult part of my day: Josephine's party.

'Okay, Sebastian,' I said, 'let's get this over with.'

A crowd had gathered to see the audition results, and I eased closer to the posted sheet, trying not to draw attention. The first thing I noticed was all the leads. Josephine was Titania, Queen of the Fairies. She would be perfect. Brandon had snagged Lysander, and Emma was Hermia. I doubted their love scenes would take much effort. Avery won the part of Oberon, and I was proud that Katie had been assigned the role of Hippolyta. Of course, I would have to give her some good ribbing over that name.

And then I saw the unexpected: my own name. I looked away and back. Sure enough, there it was, right next to the character of Nick Bottom, the weaver. I cringed, knowing exactly what was in store for me.

As if on cue, Mitchell's mischievous face came into view. 'Hey Sebastian, isn't Nick Bottom the guy who gets turned into an ass?'

Avery shoved Mitchell while the rest of the group laughed. *The ass.* I sighed deeply. *Perfect.*

7. Fire and Ice

My van protested as I hit every pothole on Fairground Drive. But none of my passengers seemed to care. They were too busy discussing the cast list. I'd volunteered to drive – not because my van held the most people – but because it provided some distraction. And not from the incessant joking about my role in the play, either; I was used to Mitchell and his junior high level pranks. They didn't faze me.

But attending Josephine's party was a different story.

'Look, guys,' Emma squealed, nearly jabbing me in the eye as she pointed over my shoulder from the back seat. 'We're here!'

'Way to state the obvious,' said Brandon, pulling her back into his lap with a laugh.

She poked out her bottom lip. 'Not funny.'

He leaned in for a kiss, and I shifted the rearview mirror so that I didn't have to witness any more of the public displays of affection that pretty much summed up their relationship. But Avery craned his neck around from the passenger seat and made gagging noises.

The Fairgrounds was a twenty-acre expanse designed for recreational activities, just outside town. As I pulled through the gates, evidence of the Circe de Romany was everywhere.

An enormous tent loomed overhead, covered with lush red and gold stripes. Bright pavilions and booths, in similar colors and trimmed with green, lined the perimeter of the grounds. Katie met us in the parking lot, flushed and beaming like a blast of sunshine.

'Pretty cool, huh?' Katie was at my elbow as we piled out of the van.

'It's all right,' I said, 'I mean, if you're into this sort of thing.'

She grabbed the edge of my jacket and yanked me down to her level. 'Listen to me, you social invert, you're going to have fun tonight.' Her blue eyes narrowed playfully. 'Understood?'

My lip twitched into a grin. 'Does fun include hovering dangerously close to the exit door, looking for the most opportune moment for escape?'

'You're impossible.'

She tried to hit me, but I dodged out of the way with a laugh.

Avery jogged up. 'This is awesome!'

'I know,' Katie replied. 'And Josie said the Circe's added some new acts and expanded the carnival since their last visit.'

Avery looked as if he was in heaven. 'More games and rides?'

Katie bounced on her toes. 'Yep. And I hear the new shows are going to be really cool.'

I locked up the van, noting the numerous cars in the lot. Josephine had apparently wasted no time making friends. Just as I stuffed my keys into my pocket, a stocky young man strolled through the fence. A broad smile flashed across his tanned features.

'That's Francis, Josephine's twin brother,' Katie said, following my gaze.

'I didn't know she was a twin.' Granted, I didn't really know much about Josephine at all, but I could see the sibling resemblance. 'So, is this his party, too?'

'Well, technically. But he's not big into parties.' She crossed her arms. 'Sounds like someone else I know.'

'I have no idea what you're talking about,' I replied in my most innocent voice.

'Hey, guys,' said Francis as he approached. He was friendly, and I got the feeling that, despite Katie's words, he'd be perfectly at ease with any party thrown his way. 'Thanks for coming. Glad it's not gonna be just us carnies tonight.'

'We won't let you down,' said Brandon.

Francis led us through the opening, speaking over his shoulder as we walked. 'Josephine wanted to have the party in the Big Tent.' He gestured to the massive structure. 'But we're behind on setup, and it's a mess inside. So we're in the Holding Tent around back.'

'What's that?' Emma asked, flitting out of Brandon's grasp as he tried to lick her neck.

'It's the smaller tent where we dress and warm up for shows,' Francis replied. He rolled his eyes as he saw Emma and Brandon exchange a slobbery kiss. I smiled to myself, liking him already.

Avery jabbed my ribs every time he saw something inter-esting. I was in danger of being permanently bruised by my Neanderthal friend before we reached the party. Just as I started to give him a good shove into the nearby fence, a sharp pain in my wrist brought me up short. I pulled up my sleeve and rubbed at the tattoo. Why was it hurting again? Avery caught sight of the inked design, and his mouth dropped open.

'Man, you've been holding back on me!' He twisted my arm to see. 'When did'ya get the new body art?'

'A couple of days ago. My brother finally gave in.' I yanked my arm back when I saw the look on his face. 'Yeah, I know, it's a flower. But it wasn't my choice. Hugo did it.'

'Wouldn't have been my choice either,' Avery said, sounding almost sympathetic. 'But actually, it's not that bad. I mean, that's some serious detail work!'

'It's no big deal.' I shoved my sleeve back down.

'So it's like a theme then, huh?' Avery's eyes darted to my hood. 'The new hair, the tattoo. Gotta look the part, right?'

'The part?'

'Yeah, the whole tattoo artist apprentice thing. Didn't you say your brother's gonna start training you?'

I half laughed. 'Oh yeah. I'm not letting him out of it this time.'

No matter what he throws at me, I thought.

My wrist flared with pain again, and I pressed my fingers against it. Avery shot me a curious look, but didn't say anything else. We hurried to catch up with the others. Francis took us around the Big Tent to another just behind it, half the size of the first.

'Here we are,' he announced, peeling back the canvas flap. 'Come on in.'

It was nearly dark outside, but the Holding Tent was illuminated with lights. They were everywhere: hanging from the tent supports, running along the walls, and lining the tables. Inside, it looked like a quarter of the senior class had turned up for the party.

I scanned the crowd warily, suddenly feeling a bizarre need to memorize every person in the room. I zoned in on a couple of football players scratching their names into the canvas wall of the tent with a knife, their bodies hunched to hide their actions. I narrowed my eyes, feeling a strange burst of anger underneath my sternum.

I breathed in through my nose and let it out through my mouth. The anger was still there. I closed my eyes, jostled by the fierce heat of emotion. Where was it coming from? The sensation was beginning to scare me, and I bit down on my lip, commanding my body to relax. Gradually, my muscles eased, and the emotion dissipated.

'Sebastian,' said Avery, punching my arm. 'You coming or not?'

I shook myself off and nodded, stepping through the opening.

'Ah-ouch,' I gasped suddenly.

Avery stared at me. 'What?'

The tattoo was burning, worse than before, like slices of hot metal in my skin. I clenched my fist and shook out my arm. 'Artwork's still a little tender, I guess.'

Avery studied me for a moment, then hoisted his present under his arm. 'Well, time to schmooze with the birthday girl.' He pointed and winked.

Josephine Romany sat in the middle of a group of people on a red, circular couch. Avery rushed forward, diving comically into the cushions and causing general bedlam. I forgot about my wrist as I looked at Josephine. She'd changed for the party, wearing an emerald dress that matched her eyes. Her hair was clipped back with a silver butterfly, and jewelry sparkled at her neck, ears, and wrists.

Avery flirted with the female attendees, his long legs sprawled out in some girl's lap. I felt a twinge of envy: Avery never had awkward moments. 'Get over here,' he called to me. 'You're missing all the fun.'

I waved, but there was no way I was joining them. Talk about awkward. I retreated to a large table cluttered with expensively packaged gifts. I unzipped my jacket and retrieved the brown bag, trying to camouflage it in the pile, but it stood out against the colorful array. I reached out to swipe it back.

'This is so freaking awesome,' said Brandon, leaning over my shoulder to check out the gifts.

I backed away, leaving mine. 'There's a lot of people here.'

Brandon smirked. 'Well, it *is* a party.'

'So people keep telling me.'

I scanned the crowd again, watching the movements and body language of everyone around me like I was working security. It felt weird, but I couldn't seem to refocus my attention.

Emma stopped playing with Brandon's hair and frowned at me. 'Whoa, you don't look so good, Sebastian.'

Sweat trickled down my neck. 'It's just hot in here,' I replied, pushing my fingers against my stinging wrist. My skin was on fire.

A man and a woman wafted through the entrance, flanked by a large group of people: the Circe de Romany troupe. Their eccentric clothing, hair, and make-up suddenly made the rest of the party seem dull. I leaned against the table and tried to focus on the new arrivals rather than the uncomfortably rising temperature.

'Welcome, everyone,' said the man. 'I'm Nicolas Romany, and this is my wife Sabina. We want to thank you for coming to Josephine and Francis's birthday party. Sixes has become one of our favorite touring locations, and we're glad to be back.'

Spontaneous applause erupted through the tent. Sabina Romany stepped forward. She looked like an older version of her daughter. 'We'd like to invite you to enjoy some early carnival fun. We've set up a few rides and booths, just for tonight. Francis, why don't you show our guests the way?'

In a rush, kids were flooding out of the tent flap, with Francis in the lead and Avery on his heels.

'Let's go check out the games,' said Brandon, slapping me on the back.

'I'll be there in a minute.'

He shrugged and looped his arm over Emma's shoulders, following the crowd outside. My eyes fixed on Josephine. She was sitting alone on the couch. At the sight of her, the jellified feeling returned. I was burning up, but I didn't know if it was from the heat or my nerves.

Okay, Sebastian. You can do this. Just walk over there and talk to her.

I wiped my face, stepped forward, then instantly backpedaled. A man had broken away from the lingering Circe group and was approaching the couch. He was lean and tall, and probably in his early twenties, though it was difficult to tell; his deep set eyes and angular face made him seem older. His hair was like black ink, perfectly styled, and his clothes were the well-tailored kind. All in all, he looked like he'd just stepped off a red carpet. He leaned down and planted a kiss on Josephine's glossy lips.

I felt like I'd swallowed a bucket of ice water.

'Josie, I have something for you,' he said in a voice out of a jewelry commercial.

Her eyes lit up. 'What is it?'

Of course, she had a boyfriend. A girl like that couldn't be single. The scorch of disappointment burned hotter than my feverish temperature. I knew I needed to turn away, but my body refused to move. I watched as the man – wearing a model-worthy smile – produced a small, rectangular box. My head swirled. Josephine opened it and took out something that resembled a necklace.

I didn't see anything else.

The ice in my stomach exploded into nausea. I clutched my torso, stumbling for the door. I burst through the opening and hugged the support rope, trying to keep upright, though I couldn't see straight. It was the worst I'd felt in days. I took frantic gulps of autumn air, trying not to puke or pass out, or whatever my body was desperate to do for relief. The cold burn of oxygen was like medicine. Gradually the queasiness subsided. I pressed my hands to my face until my vision cleared. My skin was hot, almost clammy.

'Great timing,' I said to no one in particular.

Now I could add stomach bugs to my record of ill-timed incidents, like having your hair dyed gray right before getting a part in the school play. Or attempting to talk to a girl at the exact moment her boyfriend arrives.

I took a deep breath, and then a scent I recognized with startling clarity flooded my nostrils. I spun so quickly that I nearly lost my balance. Josephine Romany stood at the entrance of the Holding Tent. Any attempt to act casual seemed impossible.

Josephine approached. 'Sebastian?'

I blinked at her, numb for words. My chance at the second first-impression was diving faster than a stalled-out plane. My tongue finally dislodged itself from the roof of my mouth. 'Hi, Josephine.'

I was surprised at how good it felt to say her name, as if it was meant to roll off my lips the way it did.

'Are you okay?' she asked, searching my face. 'I saw you run out.'

I wasn't sure what startled me more: the fact that she'd noticed me or the fact that she cared enough to enquire. 'Oh, sure, totally fine. I just needed some air. It was really . . . hot . . . in there.'

Josephine didn't seem convinced. Her head tilted as she studied me. I tried to smile but ended up squinting at my shoes instead. There was a long pause.

Mayday. Plane down.

'Hey, would you like a tour of the Ferris wheel?' she asked suddenly.

My head snapped up. 'A tour?'

Her smile melted my insides. 'Well, sure. We haven't gotten much chance to talk since I arrived, and now it looks like we're going to be in the school play together . . . ' She trailed off, looking at me with a sort of friendly pity.

We have a survivor.

I felt a little confidence return. I hadn't totally self-destructed. At least, not yet.

'That sounds great,' I replied.

'That is, if you're sure you're feeling all right,' she added quickly.

'No, I'm good. Everything's good now.'

'Awesome,' she said, sounding happy. 'No one around here ever wants to ride it with me.'

Ride it?

The thought hadn't occurred to me.

'Oh.'

'Oh?' she repeated in a light tone.

'I have a problem with heights,' I confessed.

'Well, we don't have to, then.'

'No,' I said, hastily. 'I'd love to ride with you.'

What was I doing? I hated being in the air. And with my stomach already doing somersaults, the chances of embarrassing myself beyond repair were pretty good. But I couldn't refuse. Josephine could have asked me to ride a unicycle down a telephone wire, and I would have done it. I didn't know whether to be happy or horrified. As she looked up at me, I decided on the first.

Josephine led us away from the crowded game booths to a less populated section of the Fairgrounds. We turned a sharp corner and then the Ferris wheel loomed into view. Its large form consumed the night sky. It was an impressive size for a carnival ride, and I counted twenty green and yellow cars on the circular frame.

'Well, there she is,' Josephine said. 'We call her Bessie.'

'Bessie?'

'Yeah,' she replied, darting through a short, roped-off line. 'Francis and the other riggers hate her because she's such a beast to put up.'

A gray-headed man leaned out of the small booth at the gate as we approached. He gave Josephine a short wave. 'Two for the wheel?'

'Yes, Karl. I found a willing victim at last.'

My body threatened a cardiac rebellion, but I had to admit, the thought of being Josephine's victim was thrilling.

'Well, climb in and I'll send you up,' Karl chuckled, ducking back into the booth. 'You're the first customers I've had all night.'

'Poor Bessie,' said Josephine, winking at me.

Our car was bright yellow. Josephine climbed in first. There was a single safety bar, which did nothing to help my acrophobia. Being this close to Josephine was nerve-shattering enough, but now, I was about to be hoisted dozens of feet off the ground. The engine chugged to life. Metal squeaked and groaned, and our car began its circular journey.

'Sebastian, are you sure this is okay with you?'

Josephine was settled comfortably on her side of the car. The breeze had wrestled a few strands of her hair free from the clip, and they fluttered like angel wings around her face.

'It's not that bad.'

Behind her, the roofs of the pavilions sank from view. It *was* that bad. But I wasn't about to let her know. I gripped the bar fiercely. My entire life I'd hardly given a girl more than a second glance. Now, suddenly, I couldn't take my eyes off one.

And I was going to be sick all over her.

Josephine smiled. 'You know, for an actor, you're not that great a liar.'

'Really? I thought I was masking my feelings of abject terror pretty well, under the circumstances. I haven't curled up into fetal position. Yet.'

'Ah, something to look forward to, then.'

'Maybe. But I should warn you, my acting skills are about as subpar as my lying. I don't know how convincing a fetus I'll make.' *Brilliant, Sebastian.* I groaned. 'Pretend I didn't just say that.'

Josephine laughed. 'Delete button pressed.'

I returned the laugh, feeling relieved. 'Thanks.'

Josephine turned her face into the breeze. 'So, if you don't think you're a good actor, why did you audition for the play?'

'It was a dare from Mitchell. But believe me I came really close to backing out.'

'Why didn't you?' she asked, her brows furrowed with curiosity.

I studied the safety bar and tried to keep my mind off the arcing circle we were making in midair. 'Just changed my mind, I guess.' I remembered the way I'd felt when Josephine had appeared behind me at the call-board, how easily her small persuasion had altered my plans. 'I don't really like to act.'

'Well, you should rethink,' she replied. 'You had a really good audition.'

I glanced at her. 'You have to be thinking of somebody else. I was the guy stumbling over his lines and sweating profusely. Not my finest hour.'

Her musical laugh filled the Ferris wheel car. The more I heard it, the crazier I was about it. 'No, I was referring to you, Sebastian. You have a nice voice; soft and quiet, but strong. You don't give yourself enough credit.'

She was looking at me with that same curious expression, and I felt my cheeks flush. I needed to change the subject, and fast. My gaze drifted from her eyes – which wasn't an easy task – and I caught sight of something glinting against her neck.

'So, is that a birthday gift?'

Josephine touched her throat. 'Yeah. He wanted me to open it before everything got too busy with the party.'

'The guy you were talking to in the tent?'

'Quentin Marks,' she explained. 'He works with me.'

My shoulders cramped at the name, but I didn't know why. No more than I'd understood why hearing Josephine's name that first time had sent me reeling. I stretched my back, wondering why she didn't say he was her boyfriend. I made a wish that they were related, cousins, maybe. Weren't circus families supposed to be really close?

Our yellow car was slowing down as it neared the top, and I concentrated harder on Josephine; watching as she wrapped her fingers around the length of black silk. Attached to the ribbon was a sparkling object, cylindrical in shape and liquid black.

'So what is it?' I asked, switching topics.

'It's a pendant. Actually, it's a family heirloom.'

Maybe the relation thing wasn't as far-fetched as I thought. Josephine turned the face of the pendant into the light so I could see it better. Inside the casing was a shimmering, multi-layered patterned. I leaned forward, my nerves forgotten as I grew mesmerized by the bright shape within. It was a yellow dandelion, surrounded by swirling leaves.

A dandelion?

I jolted in surprise. My tattoo burned underneath the sleeve of my jacket. I opened my mouth, but before I could say anything, Josephine slid closer. I couldn't remember what I was going to ask.

'It's made from cut glass,' she said, untying the ribbon and holding the pendant out to me. 'Feel how smooth it is.'

I was startled to feel my hand move of its own accord. My fingers closed the distance, and then I was touching the unblemished surface of the pendant.

'It's very bea . . . '

Suddenly, everything was spinning, and a blinding pain shot through my wrist and up my arm. I clutched the safety bar, crying out as my body convulsed. The movement jostled the car, and Josephine gasped as the pendant slipped from her hand. She dove for the falling necklace.

The next moments happened so fast. I saw Josephine's body teetering over the edge of the safety bar. Her momentum had carried her too far, and she was going over. I lunged frantically, grabbing Josephine's arm. I flung her back into the safety of the car, but my own momentum became my doom.

Everything was in sharp focus as I fell.

The car's yellow paint was blinding against the night sky. Every individual light on the spokes of the wheel burned brightly. Josephine's face was as enrapturing as an angel's; her mouth opened in a scream. The breeze was cool against my face.

And then, I hit.

My lungs burned like I'd been underwater. I tried to move, but my body was numb. I had the odd sensation of floating down a sluggish stream. Everything was warm and quiet. Then, sounds drifted through my brain.

At first, they were indecipherable, muffled. But gradually, the sounds became voices wafting around me; a meaningless jumble. I knew I needed to come back from wherever I was. The ground was hard beneath me. My head ached. My back stung.

I squeezed my eyes tightly, then opened them. Immediately I regretted it. I groaned as my brain beat against my skull. Blurring colors refocused around me, and I realized that I was lying on my back on the cold concrete.

'Ouch.'

It wasn't the most eloquent thing to say, but it was the best I could manage. My throat was as scratchy as sandpaper, and I could almost see the little dancing birds circling my head like they did in cartoons. I tried to sit up but felt a pair of hands pushing me back.

'Don't try to move, son.'

I squinted through the pain. Someone was kneeling over; his head was bent close as he examined me. It was the same man who'd been running the Ferris wheel; the one Josephine had called Karl.

Josephine.

I pushed myself up, shoving his hands away. 'Josephine,' I said through clenched teeth. 'Is she all right?'

Karl stared at me. 'How in hellfire . . . '

I shoved my hair out of my eyes and looked past him, searching for Josephine, but the only thing in my vision was the Ferris wheel; a monstrous skeleton against a graveyard of starry sky. My heart pounded as I remembered just how closely she'd come to toppling over the safety bar and plunging to the ground.

Instead, it had been me.

Suddenly, I went cold all over.

What had just happened?

Karl's hands were on my back, pressing and prodding. 'No broken bones,' the old man muttered softly. 'I don't understand it, Quentin.'

The man from the party leaned over me. Dark hair framed his perfect face, and his lips were pressed into a firm line. 'How did you survive that?' he demanded.

'I . . . I don't really remember much,' I said, rubbing my shoulder.

He knelt down, pressing his face closer. 'I saw you fall from the car. You landed flat on your back.'

My stomach clenched. 'I don't . . . '

'What were you doing up there?'

'Quentin, give the boy some air,' ordered Karl.

He narrowed his eyes at me for a moment, then rose. I placed my fingers gingerly against the back of my head. I groaned, and Karl was examining me again.

'You're getting an impressive knot back there, but you seem to be fine, otherwise,' he said. I could hear the disbelief in his voice. 'You're one lucky kid.'

I tried moving around a bit. Karl was right. I seemed to be in one piece. Quentin kept staring at me, his piercing gaze traveling from my face to my gray hair and back again. I reached self-consciously for my hood and shrugged it on.

'Where's Josephine?' I asked again. 'Is she okay?'

It was Quentin who answered. 'She's fine. I sent her inside.'

'But she's all right?'

Karl patted my arm. 'Perfectly okay. She wanted to stay out here until you came back around, but I told her you'd be all right. She was pretty shaken up after we got her off the wheel, and I thought it best she go on inside to her parents.'

'That's good,' I replied, testing the lump on my skull. 'What about her necklace?'

Karl shook his head, chuckling. 'Also safe and sound, thanks to you. Now, I recommend you go home and take it easy. And see a doctor if you begin feeling dizzy or nauseous.' I must have looked at him funny. He frowned. 'I'm the troupe's personal trainer, son, and I've got medical training. I know what I'm talking about.' I rolled my shoulders and the pain eased, but my head was still swimming. Karl scratched his beard. I could tell he was a little unhinged, but he was covering it up with a cool demeanor. 'Have you eaten at all today?' he asked.

I tilted my head at the strange question. 'A few times.'

'Well, you should probably find a ride home. You're in no condition to drive.'

'I can't. I drove a bunch of people here.'

'I'm sure they can find other ways home,' Quentin interjected.

I stared at him dully. Something about the guy felt wrong, but I couldn't put my finger on it.

'Sebastian!' Katie came barreling out of nowhere. 'I just saw Josie. She said you hit your head. Are you okay?'

I pushed myself up, and Karl helped me the rest of the way to my feet. I looked at Katie, bewildered. Why had Josephine only told her I'd hit my head? Everything was a little hazy, but I was pretty sure I'd done a lot more than that.

Quentin touched Katie's arm. 'Your friend's fine,' he said in his smooth, movie narrator tone. 'But I'm going to take him home.'

I jerked in surprise. 'There's no . . . '

'Oh, but he drove us here,' Katie said, interrupting me.

Quentin smiled. 'I'm sure one of you could drive his car.'

Her head bobbed. 'Oh, sure, of course! Sebastian, we'll get your van back to your house, don't worry.'

I stumbled forward. 'That's really not necessary . . . '

Katie darted around Quentin and caught my arm, steadying me. 'Please let Quentin take you home. You look terrible.'

'Thanks.'

'No, I'm serious, Sebastian. You look . . . ashen. Like death or something.'

'Wow,' I said, smirking groggily. 'That's even more encouraging.'

'I didn't mean it like that,' Katie replied, 'but you definitely need to go.'

'She's right,' agreed Karl. 'Let Quentin drive you.'

Though I didn't like the idea of movie guy taking me home, it didn't look as if I had much choice. Plus, a few curious partygoers had arrived on the scene, and I felt anxious to get away before I brought more unwanted attention on myself.

'Okay,' I said, reluctantly.

Katie held out her hand, and I fished my keys from my pocket. 'Do you want me to come with you?' she asked.

'Go back to the party, Katie,' Quentin replied, speaking for me. 'Josephine would hate it if you left.' He flashed a smile that showed off perfect teeth, white against his dark skin. 'I'll make sure your friend gets home, don't worry.'

Katie stared at Quentin, a giddy expression on her face. She was always a goner for any guy who was remotely handsome. But when she looked back at me, she was all serious again. 'You're sure you're okay, Sebastian?'

I forced a smile. 'Yeah, Katie, I'm totally fine. Go have fun. It's a party, remember?'

'Okay,' she said, relieved. 'I'll come by and see you in a little while.'

'Don't worry about it. I'll probably just take some aspirin and pass out. My head's killing me. But I'll see you at school, okay?'

She squeezed my hand. 'If you're sure.'

'I'm sure.'

'See you tomorrow, then.' She hugged me gently and sprinted away.

'I'll pull my car around,' said Quentin. 'Stay here with Karl.' He swiftly disappeared around one of the pavilions.

'Put some ice on that head of yours, son,' said Karl, 'it'll help with the swelling.' He stroked his beard again. 'That was some fall,' he muttered, almost to himself.

I nodded absently. I wasn't thinking about my fall anymore. I was thinking about what had happened just before it. The dandelion pendant; the weird sensation; the shock of touching it. Had Josephine felt the same thing, or was I going crazy?

A black SUV pulled up. Quentin let down the window and motioned for me to get in. Karl reached for the door.

'Take care of yourself, son,' he said.

I climbed into the seat and turned to say goodbye to the gray-headed trainer. As I did, I could have sworn I caught a glimpse of emerald eyes peering around the corner of one of the pavilions.

Quentin eased the SUV out of the lot and down a small side road I hadn't noticed before. It dumped out onto the main drive heading into town. I curled up against the window, resting my head in the crook of my arm. I imagined Josephine in the middle of her party, opening presents and enrapturing her audience with bright smiles and musical laughter. I could see her dandelion pendant dangling from her neck. My wrist was still throbbing, though only faintly now. I held it gingerly between my thumb and forefinger.

Quentin asked for directions. I gave him, in as few words as possible, the quickest route to the *Gypsy Ink*. I thought I saw him stiffen at the mention of the shop, but my head felt so thick that I could have imagined the whole thing. All I wanted to do was crawl into bed. When we arrived, I fully expected Quentin just to let me out at the door. Instead, he parked the SUV and got out.

'So, you live here,' he said as I joined him outside.

'Yeah, my brother has an apartment around back.'

He studied the building. 'Interesting.'

I got a sickening jab in my gut as I brushed past him. Something definitely wasn't right about the guy. The shop's neon lights were too bright, and I shielded my eyes from the glare as I pushed open the front door. Inside the *Gypsy Ink*, the guys were lounging on the sofas, listening to music. Vincent was the first to speak.

'Hey, man, what are you doing home so early?'

Hugo's brows lowered suddenly. 'Are you okay?'

'He's fine.'

All eyes went to Quentin, who had followed me into the shop. I felt something shift and tense in the atmosphere. Hugo rose slowly. The others followed suit. Everything went deathly still. I swayed a little on my feet, wondering when the music had stopped.

'What happened?' My brother asked evenly.

I was getting more strange vibes, and I put a hand to my forehead.

'He had a little accident at the Circe tonight,' Quentin replied in an equally even tone. 'We thought he needed to come home, so I drove him. One of his friends is taking care of his car.'

The two eyed each other for several seconds.

'Thanks for bringing him back.' Hugo replied, finally.

'No problem.' Quentin wore a strange thin-lipped smile. 'Though you should keep a better leash on your stray.' I glanced up sharply. His dark eyes shifted to me. 'Have a good night, Sebastian,' he said smoothly. 'Sorry you had to miss the party.'

I heard the bells jingle as Quentin left, but the room was spinning too much. I reached for the couch, but I was falling. James caught me in his massive arms before my face smacked the floor. I blinked, but he refused to come into focus.

'Don't feel well.' My voice sounded slurred.

Hugo was leaning over me. 'Sebastian, what happened?' he demanded.

I felt heavy with sleep. 'Fell,' I murmured. 'From the Ferris wheel.'

I didn't see Hugo's reaction. Everything dimmed, and I was out like a light.

8. Fight or Flight

A knock at the door sent me sprawling. I hit the floor, crouched on all fours. Fuzzy red dots blinked above me. When they shifted into focus, I realized I was staring at my alarm clock. I staggered to my feet and flung open the door. Hugo was leaning against the wall.

'Late for school,' I grumbled.

'I let you sleep in,' he replied.

He *let* me sleep in? I was usually out the door before Hugo ever woke up. My brother looked tired, as though he hadn't slept at all.

'Made you some breakfast,' he added.

Was I dreaming? In what world did Hugo Corsi ever get up before me *and* have breakfast on the table?

'Shower first,' I said with a yawn, running a hand through my matted hair.

Hugo grunted. 'Probably a good idea.'

I stumbled to the bathroom, stripping down as I went. The scalding water coaxed the stiffness from my shoulders, but it didn't eradicate the churning in my gut. What exactly happened to me last night? I left puddles on the tiled floor as I dried off, and I scrubbed my slate colored hair. I touched the base of my skull hesitantly, expecting to find a huge knot, but there was nothing.

'Huh?' I said out loud.

'Come on, Sebastian,' yelled my brother from the kitchen. 'Food's getting cold!'

I threw on some clothes and hurried through the apartment. Kris, Vincent, and James were there, along with James's wife, Genella. I'd always liked Genella. She was smart and funny, and had bleached blonde hair with black tips that flipped out in every direction. When she saw me, she rushed over, jewelry clanking.

'Oh, God, Sebastian!' she said, taking my face between her hands. She studied me with wide eyes but thankfully didn't mention my hair. 'Are you okay? James told me about your accident last night.'

'I'm fine,' I replied, smiling sheepishly and blushing at her attentions. 'Just took a little fall.'

'Yeah,' said Kris. 'From the freaking Ferris wheel.'

The image of Josephine careening over the side of the car flashed before me. 'Well, everything's still a little fuzzy,' I said, slipping out of Genella's grasp and plopping down at the table. Maybe the ride hadn't started yet. Maybe I'd just imagined falling all that way. 'Some guy named Karl checked me out. I think he was a doctor or something. He said I'd be okay.'

'And are you?' asked Hugo.

The room was heavy and eerily quiet. 'Well, yeah,' I said, pondering how many times I'd been asked that question over the last few days. 'Actually, I feel great. Must not have been as bad as I thought.'

Everyone looked at Hugo again. He handed me a plate of sausage and biscuits. 'You *could* skip school today, if you're not up to it. It's not like you'll miss that much, right?'

'Yeah, just my government test and a vocabulary quiz. No big deal.' I quickly stuffed a piece of sausage in my mouth as Hugo looked at me sharply. 'But seriously, Hugo, I'm good. We've got our first rehearsal for the play today, and I kind of need to be there.'

James dropped the frying pan into the sink. 'Whoa, you got a part?'

'Could you maybe try and not look so shocked?'

He chuckled into his beard and turned on the faucet. 'Sorry.'

'Congratulations,' said Kris, raising his fork in a salute.

Vincent clapped me on the back. 'Told you so.'

'Yeah, I guess you did,' I admitted. 'And, actually, I think being in the play might be fun.'

Hugo gave me the look-over. 'You sure you're feeling okay?'

I grinned. 'I'm sure.'

'All right, then,' he replied. 'Guess you'd better eat your breakfast.'

Both subjects were dropped as we helped ourselves to the heaping mound of eggs James had arranged on a plate. Hugo sipped on his coffee and read an issue of *Rolling Stone*. As I ate, I caught a glimpse of my tattoo poking out from under my sleeve. The skin was still a little red, but it didn't hurt at all. It was as if everything that had happened was just some weird dream. Then a thought occurred to me.

'Hugo?'

He flipped a page in his magazine. 'Yeah?'

'How do you know Quentin Marks?' My brother glanced up. 'Last night, when you guys were talking, I don't know, it was like you knew him.'

'We've known him a long time.'

The emphasis on 'we' wasn't lost on me. After giving me the tattoo, Hugo had insisted that I was part of the clan. But I wasn't, really. After all, I wasn't blood. I was just a . . .

Stray.

Quentin's voice echoed in my head. It was an odd choice of words. 'This is crazy,' I said, choosing to ignore the Quentin connection for the moment. 'I mean, it's like you've got this whole secret world going on.'

'Well, it just never came up, Sebastian.' My brother leaned back in his chair. 'We keep to ourselves. Most Outcast clans do.'

'So what does that *mean*, exactly?' I asked. 'The Outcast thing. Did your family get kicked out of the elite Gypsy clique or something?'

Hugo seemed to ponder his answer. 'The Corsis were part of a particular old tribe of Roma in Europe. We call them the Old Clans. Anyway, a few centuries ago, some . . . disagreements broke out. Our family was one of several clans that *chose* to break away from the tribe. We wanted to make new lives for ourselves, develop new traditions. Some Outcasts settled in small towns like this. Others decided to be more nomadic.'

'You mean like the Romanys.'

'They're a pretty big clan,' he replied, his tone casual. 'And one of the oldest.'

I pushed my plate away, digesting this. Josephine was definitely a Gypsy. I supposed I'd already figured it out the moment I'd made the connection between her and my image. Josephine's dandelion necklace still glimmered in my mind. It hadn't felt like a coincidence when she showed it to me, and Hugo had said lots of clans used the flower as a symbol. 'So, the Romanys are the same type of Gypsies as the Corsis? Outcasts?'

'Yeah. All the clans that broke away were given that label.'

'But you don't get along with them.'

Hugo's lips drew into a tight line. 'The Romanys and the Corsis haven't always seen eye-to-eye over traditions and junk like that, but I wouldn't say I have a problem with them, necessarily.'

I traced my tattoo with my finger, a little overwhelmed. In the space of a few days, I'd learned that, not only was I living with a clan of Gypsies, but the girl I'd just met was one, too. 'How many clans actually live here?'

'Just ours. But others, like the Romanys, pass through. This town's considered a Haven, a place where Outcast Gypsies can meet or do business. We're the only ones who've made it a permanent home.'

'Wow,' I said, 'talk about feeling out of the loop.'

My foster brother stood and dumped his coffee in the sink. 'It doesn't matter now. You're one of us, Sebastian. I wouldn't have given you that tat if you weren't.' He glanced at the clock. 'Well, I've got to get to the shop. Got an early client coming in.'

Before I could say goodbye, my brother's large tattooed body was out the door.

By the time I reached my locker, the bell was ringing for third period. I shoved a few books in and slammed the door. My mind was still whirling from my conversation with Hugo. Suddenly, arms circled my waist. Panic rushed through me. I spun, breaking the hold and threw myself against the locker.

Katie's mouth gaped open in shock.

Where had that reaction come from?

'Oh, hey,' I said.

'Man, you're jumpy today,' she said, recovering. 'Can we try that again?'

'Sorry about that.' I returned her hug, chastised. 'It's been a weird morning.'

She tilted her head to the side, lips pursed thoughtfully. 'How so?'

I started to tell her about Hugo and the guys, and then I remembered my promise to keep quiet. If the Romanys were as secretive as the Corsis, I doubted Katie had a clue about her Circe friend's roots either. So I worked up a quick lie. 'My brother's just been stressed with stuff around the shop.'

Katie's brows furrowed. 'Well, I'm glad to see you're okay. You looked awful last night.'

I hoisted my bag and made a face. 'Please don't talk about last night, Katie. I'm trying to erase all evidence of it from my memory as we speak.'

'Must have been pretty embarrassing, huh?' Her tone was sympathetic. 'Josie said you hit your head pretty hard on the safety rail getting out of the car.'

I barely controlled my surprise. 'She said that?'

Josephine probably didn't want to scare her, I reasoned. Unless I imagined the whole thing. Suddenly, I wasn't too sure of anything from the night before. Maybe I'd been suffering from feverish delusions. Or the flu.

Or I was just going nuts.

'Don't worry about it, Sebastian.' Katie chirped, steering me into class. 'It could've happened to anybody. Anyway, it was sweet of Quentin to take you home. He's a really nice guy.'

'Yeah,' I replied. 'Real nice.'

She peered up at me, studying my features under my hood. 'You're sure you don't need to make a doctor's appointment? You still look kind of . . . sick.'

Yup, definitely the flu.

'I always look this way before class,' I replied. 'I'm allergic to math.'

The rest of the day was a blur until rehearsal. I shifted uncomfortably in the auditorium chair. There was no way I should've been in the play. Not Shakespeare. And definitely not a romantic comedy. But Josephine's encouragement had stuck with me. Maybe I'd imagined that conversation on the Ferris wheel along with everything else, but I'd made up my mind to give this thing a try. Mitchell could laugh all he wanted.

I was going to act.

The auditorium door opened, and Josephine walked in, talking with another girl.

'It's so pretty,' the girl was saying.

'Thanks,' Josephine replied, her fingers playing along her throat. 'It was a really thoughtful gift, you know?'

My eyes flicked to the object in her hand. It was the pendant. The yellow dandelion shimmered brightly inside the glass. The symbol of the Outcast Gypsies. I remembered the way it glimmered when she'd shown it to me. The horrified look on her face. The whoosh of air from my lungs as I hit . . .

The room tilted, and I clung to the seat in front of me. I felt sick all over; hot and cold at the same time. I breathed heavily, willing myself not to pass out.

'Whoa, easy man,' Avery said, leaning away from me. 'Please don't tell me you're going to barf.'

I shook my head, squeezing my eyes shut. Slowly, the feeling subsided to a dull, churning sensation in the pit of my stomach. 'Danger contained,' I said, offering a disarming smile. I mopped my brow with the back of my sleeve. 'Note to self: Stay away from the corn dogs at lunch.'

Avery laughed so hard he launched his chewing gum.

By the time the room righted itself, Josephine was already in her seat. I wiped my face again. My body was picking the worst possible times to act up. But – sick or not – I had to go talk to her. I had to find out what really happened last night.

But I wasn't going to get the chance. Not yet. Ms Lucian appeared in the aisle, toting a large notebook. She stopped at our row. Avery hid the wad of gum with his shoe.

'I wasn't expecting to see you today, Sebastian,' she said. 'I heard about last night. I won't hold it against you if you miss this one rehearsal.'

She'd *heard*? As far as I knew, only three people had seen my accident. Everyone else just thought I'd been a klutz. Maybe that's what she thought, too.

'It's nothing, really. Didn't even leave a mark. But I'd like to stay, if you don't mind, Ms Lucian. I don't want to miss anything.'

'Very well,' she consented.

I smiled as she continued up the aisle, but I felt terrible. My insides were gnawing at me, and I was convinced someone switched on the heat in the auditorium. My wrist burned under the sleeve of my jacket. I rubbed it tenderly, wondering if I was allergic to the ink. Avery leaned against the armrest and nudged me from my thoughts.

'Man, I can't believe some of the people Lucian let in this play.'

'Look,' I said, 'I never wanted to audition in the first place, so just give me a br . . . '

'Not you,' said Avery, cutting me off, amused. He pointed. 'I meant him.'

Alex Graham lounged on the front row, his head in the lap of a girl who was wearing way too much make-up.

'Oh,' I said, bringing myself back to reality. 'It's funny, but I thought you had to, you know, actually *attend* school to participate in extra-curricular activities.' Alex spent more time in suspension than anyone in the senior class. I sighed. 'What's he doing here?'

Avery snorted. 'What do you *think*?'

I turned away, disgusted with the ensuing make-out scene between Alex and the girl. 'Maybe Ms Lucian's making him do the play as punishment.'

'Some punishment,' said Avery, his tone laced with sarcasm. He crossed his arms and slouched in the chair, clearly moping.

'You're actually jealous, aren't you?'

'Dude, he's swapping spit with Candace Steinberg. Who wouldn't be? In fact, I'd go congratulate him, if I didn't hate his guts so much.'

'Wow,' I replied. 'Classy.'

Ms Lucian held up her hand, bringing us to attention. 'Congratulations are in order,' she announced. 'You beat out the competition. Now we've got a lot to do. This may be an abridged version of *A Midsummer Night's Dream*, but we only have a couple of weeks, so there's no time to waste. I want everyone on stage with a partner, one you don't know very well.'

Avery leapt out of his chair with an excited whoop. Couples formed quickly, but I noticed Josephine lingering near the curtains, surprisingly partner-less. I hesitated, rubbing my aching shoulders. She hadn't acknowledged me since arriving. What if she didn't want to talk to me after last night? What if I'd freaked her out with my unintentional stunt?

Our eyes met suddenly. A strange expression flittered over her face, and her hand strayed to the pendant. It was only then that I became aware of the increasing pain in my wrist, as though I was holding it over an open flame. Josephine moved towards me. A vibe of electric current hummed through my body, steadily building as she came closer.

A shadow passed across my face, blocking Josephine from view. Alex Graham towered over me, his lips turned up in a foul smirk. I rolled my eyes. Seriously, what had I ever done to this guy to put me on his radar? I tried to step aside, but he pushed his hairy face into mine. His breath choked me. I wondered how Candace Steinberg could even stand being near him.

'Didn't you hear me, man?' he sneered. 'I said you're too late.'

I blinked, confused. 'Too late for what?'

Alex dug his fingers into my bicep. 'Go find another partner. Josephine's with me.' He shoved me backwards with a laugh and turned to face her. 'We don't know each other very well,' he said, leering obscenely. 'So I'd say that makes us a perfect match.'

Josephine's green eyes went wide.

His words rammed into my brain. *Josephine's with me.*

Something inside me snapped. I whirled on Alex.

'No, she's not,' I hissed.

Alex's face registered surprise, then irritation.

'Back off,' he spat.

I scanned him quickly, noting his body mass, his posture. My brain locked it all into place, without me even trying. Before I could figure out what was happening to me, Alex took a swing.

I dodged the clumsily thrown punch. My upper lip curled as fury scorched through me like a forest fire. Heat burst through my shoulder blades. I sprang forward, a fistful of his shirt in my hand before I even knew I was moving. Then Alex was on his back, staring up at me in shock.

'Sebastian!'

The voice was Josephine's. A cold chill doused the current like water on a flame. It was then I realized I was crouched over Alex, my other hand poised to strike. I swallowed hard as I met Josephine's gaze. She looked confused, and perhaps a bit horrified.

'What are you doing?' she whispered.

It was smothering quiet. The eyes of the entire cast, including Ms Lucian, were riveted on me. No one moved. No one spoke. My hand shook as I released Alex's shirt. He scrambled up, his face crimson.

'That's enough!' said Ms Lucian firmly. 'Alex, to the principal's office. Now.'

Alex glared at her. 'Yeah, whatever. I'm done with this crap anyway.' He jumped to the floor and shoved open the doors. They banged loudly behind him as he stormed out.

Ms Lucian dumped a pile of scripts on the stage. 'Everyone, I want you to read the first scene of the play on your own.' She turned to me. 'And Sebastian, I want to see you in my office.'

Ms Lucian settled behind her desk. I stood in front of her, hands clenched to keep them from shaking. My head was pounding like the subs at a rock concert.

'So,' she said finally. Her expression remained pleasant, even amused. 'Want to tell me what just happened?'

A wave of erratic emotions crashed over me. I felt the lingering burn of anger in my veins, the overwhelming desire to beat Alex Graham senseless. But it was nothing compared to the embarrassed shame that flooded my face and turned my palms sweaty. 'I'm really sorry, Ms Lucian. I don't know what got into me.'

'Well, I'm sure Alex started it,' she replied with an irritated sigh. 'I didn't want him in my cast, but I was told it would give him an incentive to attend school. After this, he can consider himself cut from the show.' Ms Lucian propped her elbows on the desk. 'But we're not going to talk about Alex. We're going to talk about you.'

I looked down. 'Okay.'

'I must say, I was surprised by your actions,' she went on. 'I've always thought of you as the quiet, easy-going type. Such aggression doesn't seem like you at all.'

No, it definitely doesn't.

'I've just been feeling a little . . . off, lately.'

'Is there something going on, Sebastian? Anything you're having difficulty dealing with?' Her gaze passed over my forehead – noting the gray scruffs of hair poking out of my hood – and then continued across my face. 'Is there something that's troubling you at home, or making you angry?'

Her questions caught me off guard. 'I . . . I'm not sure.'

A slight hardness appeared in the corners of her eyes. 'You don't have to tell me, Sebastian. But you should talk to someone. Does Hugo know you're not feeling well?'

My head jerked up. 'You know my brother?'

She smiled at me; a weird smile. 'We're old friends.' Ms Lucian studied my face carefully, as if she was reading a book. 'And no, I'm not a Gypsy, if that's what you're wondering. I just happen to know a few.'

I stepped back, shocked. Even my drama teacher was in on the whole secret Gypsy society thing? It was like some bizarre movie plot. 'How did you . . . I mean . . . ' I broke off, unsure of what to say.

'I've lived in Sixes a while,' she said. 'But before that, I knew some Corsis, down in Savannah.'

'But I thought Gypsies didn't really reveal themselves to . . . ' My mind fumbled for the still unfamiliar word. ' . . . *gadje*.'

'That's true. But once you've befriended a Gypsy, those rules can sometimes change.' Ms Lucian pushed herself away from the desk and crossed the room. 'But back to the matter at hand. I'm not going to turn you in for this incident, Sebastian. But you're going to have to promise me one thing.'

'What's that?'

'You need to tell Hugo what happened today.'

I groaned. 'Can't I just take a detention instead?'

She smiled slightly. 'Sorry. Not an option.'

I hesitated. Telling Hugo I'd almost gotten into a fight was the last thing I wanted to do. But if Ms Lucian really was a friend of my brother's, chances were, she'd tell him anyway. 'Okay. I'll talk to him.'

'Good,' Ms Lucian replied, opening the office door. 'Now, let's get on with rehearsal, shall we? But I'd like you to sit out for a few minutes, just until you've collected yourself.'

'Thank you.'

I followed her out, feeling more dazed than anything. I collapsed into a chair in the back row while Ms Lucian divided the cast up into scenes and began rehearsal. It didn't take long for the rest of my group to find me.

'Hey, guys,' I said, trying to be casual.

They didn't buy it.

Mitchell stared at me as if I'd just yanked off all my clothes and streaked across the stage. 'Dude, what *was* that?'

Avery beamed like a proud parent. 'You almost had Alex soiling his pants, man!'

I remembered Alex's face. I remembered the electrifying current. And I remembered the intense need to . . .

'Josephine!' I snapped, nearly jumping out of my seat. I frantically searched the auditorium until I saw her on the far side of the large room, reading over lines with a group of girls, mercifully oblivious to my latest outburst. 'Is she all right?'

Katie seemed irritated. 'You mean other than being freaked out by you?' She shook her head at me. 'What's gotten into you? One minute you're doing your little socially awkward thing, and the next, you look like you're going to rearrange Alex's face!'

I flinched. 'I'm not sure what happened.'

'Jeez, Sebastian,' Katie reprimanded, 'I don't get you lately.'

Avery clapped me on the back. 'Oh, don't listen to her. It was awesome, man! I'd never seen that guy look so scared! I thought you were going to go all Animal Kingdom on him!'

'I guess I should have skipped rehearsal today,' I said, rubbing my forehead.

'Maybe so, Sebastian,' said Katie, her irritation fading. 'You're not acting like yourself.'

I couldn't have agreed more.

9. *Darkness and Light*

I'd avoided Hugo most of the afternoon, trying to figure out what to say to him. He wasn't going to be happy about my near incident with Alex. But I had to tell him – not just because I'd promised Ms Lucian, but because something was definitely going on with me – something a flu shot couldn't fix.

I leaned against the counter, watching Vincent count up the money from the register, but my gaze kept shifting to my reflection in the small vanity mirror. My pewter hair accentuated the sallow tone of my skin and highlighted the hollowed places above my cheeks. Even my eyes seemed different, more grayish than their usual hazel. Katie was right. I did look sick. I turned the mirror away from me.

'So how much longer am I stuck with this hair color?'

Vincent opened his mouth, but before he could speak, Hugo stormed into the waiting room from the hall. His eyes fixed on me.

'I need you to go back to the apartment, Sebastian.'

I looked up in surprise. 'Excuse me?'

'Go to the apartment,' he repeated, his tone serious, even tense.

'Why?'

'We're expecting visitors.'

Visitors? Since when did the *Gypsy Ink* ever have visitors? Friends, yes. Customers, definitely. But visitors? That strange, unbidden anger fluttered inside my stomach. 'Are you having some dinner party you neglected to tell me about?'

'No time,' said Vincent, pointing to the window.

There was nothing out there; not a single car in the parking lot. Nothing but fog.

Fog.

'Hugo,' I began, feeling my neck prickle. 'The other night, out by the dumpster . . . '

He shoved me towards the counter. 'Hide,' he commanded. 'Now.'

The door of the shop swung open, and I ducked behind the counter. I clutched my abdomen as an icy sensation spread through my guts. It was the same thing I'd felt when I met Quentin Marks; the same coldness as when I'd seen the smoky mist behind the shop. Was it some kind of warning?

I knelt on the tiled floor and stared up at the Gypsy painting. I could see the reflection of the waiting room in the glass. Three figures hovered side by side, just inside the door. They were bundled as though they'd just stepped off a ski lift. Hats and scarves obscured their faces. Long jackets clung to their shoulders. The dark fabric swirled together in a mixture of hues that seemed to shimmer in the light.

Hugo positioned himself in front of the counter. 'Can we help you?'

'We're here for our appointment,' said the shortest figure. It was a female voice, smooth and deep. Somehow familiar.

'Right this way,' Vincent said steadily.

The tattoo artists retreated to their rooms, and the three figures followed as though they knew exactly where to go.

102

Their movements were slow and heavy, yet graceful. As they passed the counter, the coldness twisted inside my belly. The air turned foul. I gagged and hastily covered my mouth, holding my breath until the figures disappeared down the hall. Every inch of my body was on edge and frozen.

Who were these people?

Hugo appeared at the counter, and I jumped. He motioned for silence as he reached past me and pulled a large book from the shelf. 'Go back to the apartment,' he whispered harshly.

'What's going on?' I whispered back.

Hugo knelt, fingers gripping my shirt, eyes boring into mine. 'Just do as I say. We'll talk after they're gone, but for right now, I need you to go back to the apartment and stay there.'

My brother squared his shoulders and left, giving me no chance to argue.

I'd seen Hugo deal with some pretty rough people: guys that would come into the shop drunk and violent, demanding refunds for tattoos they no longer wanted, or trying to cause trouble. None of them had ever fazed Hugo, though. I'd witnessed him – on more than one occasion – manhandle an unruly client right out the front door.

I could grit my teeth and say whatever I wanted under my breath about Hugo Corsi. But I wouldn't cross him. I couldn't. I wrinkled my nose against the nasty smell permeating the shop, then I hurried to the apartment and shut the door behind me.

A half hour passed before Hugo and the guys joined me.

I'd been pacing the living room like a restless animal. With each pass, I'd catch a glimpse of myself in the wall mirror and a fresh wave of uneasiness would pass through me. Hugo entered first and collapsed on the sofa.

'Hugo, what's going on?' I demanded. 'Are you selling on the black market or something?'

'Nope.'

'Owe the mafia money?'

'Uh uh.'

'Then *what*?'

He looked out the window, watching rain pelt against the glass. 'It's nothing, Sebastian. Everything's fine. I'm just having to play some cards right at the moment. I can't say more than that.'

Anger simmered inside me. 'Why are you trying to keep me out of this, Hugo? Is it because I'm not a Gypsy, like the rest of you? You said I was part of the clan, and now you're treating me like an outsider.'

'You are part of the clan, Sebastian. There are just some people who've been a little misinformed about a few things, and I'm trying to straighten the whole thing out. Like I said, it's nothing.'

I pressed my hand against my torso. I didn't feel cold anymore. Was everything actually fine, as Hugo claimed?

'Okay, so if you won't talk to me about your covert operations, then let's talk about stuff that *is* going on.'

His head snapped back. 'Like what?'

'Like the fight I nearly got into at school.'

The room went uncannily silent.

Hugo stiffened. 'What fight?'

I sighed and dropped into a chair, putting my head in my hands. All my revved up emotions had left me drained. 'I don't know what happened, Hugo. I just got really angry with this kid, and I couldn't control it.' I closed my eyes, shivering at the memory. 'I just snapped. I had him on the ground, and I wanted to . . . '

104

'What?'

Everyone was looking at me. I stared at my shoes. 'I wanted to tear him apart, Hugo,' I said hesitantly. 'It really freaked me out. I've never felt like that before.' I ventured a glance at my brother. 'Ms Lucian should've sent me to the office, but she said she'd let it go, if I told you what happened.'

'Well, you're lucky Esmeralda was looking out for you, then,' he replied.

Esmeralda. It took me a moment to realize he was referring to Ms Lucian. My class schedule only listed her first initial. 'She said you guys were friends.'

Hugo sat back. 'She's right.'

'Another thing you failed to mention.'

'Well, forgive me if I neglect to run every part of my life by my kid brother,' Hugo snapped. He pushed himself to his feet. 'Has it ever occurred to you that some things just aren't your business, Sebastian?'

Ouch.

'Look,' Hugo said, softening his voice, 'I didn't mean to go off on you like that. It's been a rough day. I know you've been dealing with a lot lately, and then we dumped all this Gypsy stuff on you. I'm sure what happened at school today was no big deal. If Esmeralda's willing to drop it, then so am I.'

Okay, so that had gone easier than I'd expected, but his answer didn't make me feel any better. 'So what about everything else?'

Hugo stepped into the kitchen, and I heard the fridge open, followed by the squeak of a cabinet and the whoosh of gas on the stove. I frowned. Since when did the walls in this apartment get so thin?

105

James settled into the place Hugo had vacated. His thick brows were pinched together in a way that looked strange on his normally jovial face.

'What do you mean, "everything else"?'

I worked the words around my mouth. 'I . . . I think I might be sick.'

'Sick how?' questioned Vincent.

'Like from your fall at the Fairgrounds?' James interjected. 'You mean like, as in you might need to go see a doctor kind of sick?'

I shook my head. 'No, it's not that.'

Was it my imagination, or did James look relieved?

'Then sick how?' repeated Vincent.

'I just don't feel . . . right,' I replied. 'I can't really explain it.'

James and Vincent exchanged looks, and I felt James subtly increase the distance between us. There was something in the air that reminded me of the night I'd overheard the whispered conversation about my apprenticeship. Or, at least, that's what I'd been led to believe the guys had been discussing. I was getting all kinds of contradicting vibes. I clenched my hands, determined not to have another angry outburst.

'Why are you guys looking at me like that?'

'You know, Sebastian,' said Kris from the other side of the room. 'You could just be stressed. Have you ever considered that this whole audition and play business might have you worked up?'

And Josephine, I thought, but I wasn't going to admit that to the guys.

'Yeah, maybe.' I stood and rolled my shoulders, trying to loosen the muscles. A flash of lightning illuminated the room, and my reflection in the wall mirror looked almost ghostly in the dim glow. 'Listen, can we maybe call a truce on this initiation thing?' I pointed to my hair. 'I know the tattoo's a done deal, but all this other stuff's getting old. Call me crazy, but I'm kinda fond of the way my hair used to look, you know, before you guys dumped paint on my head, or whatever you did.'

I glanced back at the guys. They were staring at me; that same strange look that was becoming a little too frequent for my comfort. Just then, Hugo appeared from the kitchen, a glass in his hand.

'Here.'

I took the cup and studied its contents. 'Warm milk?'

'It'll help you sleep.'

I couldn't resist smiling, despite the circumstances. 'What are you, my grandmother, now?'

He watched as I downed the drink in one gulp. Hugo nodded in satisfaction and took the empty container out of my hands. 'Okay, Sebastian. You're right. There are some things – some Gypsy things – that have been going on the last few weeks. So I'll make a deal with you. You head off to bed, and I promise we'll sit down and talk everything out tomorrow.'

'Why not tonight?'

'Well, for starters, you look pretty beat.'

The others voiced their agreement. I started to argue, but I *was* feeling pretty tired. Actually, I was suddenly exhausted. My knees wobbled a little. It felt as though I'd been plugged into some power source that had abruptly run out of juice. I rubbed my temples wearily.

'You sure you don't want to stay home tomorrow?' asked James.

'Can't.' I yawned loudly. 'Rehearsal.'

Vincent's pierced lip shifted into a frown. 'But I thought you were sick.'

'Just need some . . . sleep.'

I couldn't see straight anymore I was so tired. And all kinds of bizarre, fatigue-induced notions were dancing through my brain, like the idea that Hugo had somehow drugged the milk. I yawned again and forced my eyelids open as I maneuvered around the sofa. *Tomorrow*. Tomorrow I'd find out what Hugo and the guys had been up to behind my back. I didn't care about anything but my pillow and a dark room. I shuffled, heavy-footed, down the hall.

'Goodnight, Sebastian,' I heard Hugo call.

I barely made it to my bed before sleep took me.

10. Sanity and Madness

The school day passed with the speed of a three-legged turtle. As soon as play rehearsal ended, I shrugged on my jacket and bolted for the door. I couldn't get out of there fast enough. And it didn't have anything to do with the jabs about my hair or my health, or the hushed conversations about the incident between Alex and me.

I needed to get home before anything else happened.

The feverish sensation was back, this time, with a vengeance. Though I'd slept like the dead the night before, I felt hung-over and scattered. I used the theater chairs for support as I hurried up the aisle of the auditorium, afraid I was either going to puke or pass out, neither of which would be a favorable end to my day.

Then I smelled a familiar fragrance drifting from behind me.

'Sebastian?'

As if on autopilot, my body pulled up short, just as I reached the last row. I tried to retreat into my hood, to mumble some excuse and keep walking, but my motor functions wouldn't obey. Instead, I found myself turning around to meet her green-eyed gaze.

'Yes, Josephine?'

Saying her name felt incredible. It sent a blissful rush through my insides, easing the sickness, but making me dizzy at the same time. I leaned hard against the seat to keep my balance. Josephine adjusted her messenger bag across her shoulder. She was wearing a flowing green shirt that looked amazing against her skin. Green had to be her favorite color. It had definitely become mine.

'I've been wanting to talk to you all day,' she said. 'But you're hard to track down, even in rehearsal.' She tilted her head to the side, studying me. Then she smiled a smile that warmed me all the way to my toes. 'You haven't been avoiding me, have you?'

Yes, I have, because you probably think I'm a complete psycho at this . . .

'Of course not,' I said quickly. I started to laugh, but clutched my wrist instead. It stung like crazy. I considered taking the opportunity to ask her about the Ferris wheel thing, but I was so enthralled watching her, that it didn't seem important anymore. I cleared my throat. 'Ah, what did you want to talk about?'

'I'm a little worried about our scenes,' she said simply.

Her answer caught me off guard. 'Our scenes?'

'Well, two weeks isn't a lot of time to put on a play, and I don't know how many chances you and I will have to work on our parts together in rehearsal.' Her lips puckered gently. 'So I was wondering, would you mind coming by today to go over lines with me?'

Don't sound stupid, my mind shouted at me. I hurried ahead to open the auditorium door for her. 'You mean, at the . . . Fairgrounds?'

Way to go, Sebastian.

'Yes, at the Fairgrounds,' she said, brushing against me as she passed through the door. 'I have to get some practice in for my circus routine, but I've got about an hour free. Can you come?'

'Absolutely.' I didn't understand what to make of these yo-yo feelings I had around her, but I wasn't going to worry about it right then, not when she was looking at me, turning my legs into melted butter.

'So, what do you think of the play so far?' she asked as we maneuvered through the crowded parking lot.

'I think it's going to be good. You're doing an amazing job as Titania. I love watching you.' I clamped down hard on my lip. That last bit was probably too much. But she didn't seem to notice.

'Thanks. I have to admit, I've always wanted to play her. I adore Shakespeare.'

'Me too,' I said quickly. I was sounding way too desperate, but I couldn't make myself stop. I was worse than a gushing fire hydrant.

'Really? Well, what's your favorite play?'

'That's a pretty loaded question,' I replied, glad for a chance to recover. 'I guess it depends on whether you're talking tragedies or comedies. Or histories, even. I'm not as big into his sonnets and all that, but there are some that are pretty cool.'

Josephine stopped walking and looked up at me. 'You really *do* like Shakespeare,' she said, sounding impressed.

I kicked at a stray pebble, heat spiking up to the roots of my hair. Most guys didn't voluntarily read things like *Hamlet* or *Much Ado about Nothing*. Shakespeare could be considered a form of cruel and unusual punishment. 'Well,' I began, trying to play it off as best I could, 'I think . . . '

'Hey, Josephine,' said a smooth voice.

111

The remains of my answer died on my lips. Quentin Marks strolled towards us. Muscles tightened along my back, and I went cold all over.

Josephine practically glowed.'Quentin!'

He wrapped her in a hug, lifting her in his embrace as he planted a kiss on her lips. I looked away and curled my fingers into my palms. My theory about their relationship disintegrated like paper on fire. I searched for a quick and subtle escape, like a giant rabbit hole. Out of the corner of my eye, I saw Quentin return her to the ground. She cuffed him lightly on the arm.

'I've missed you,' she said.

'Well, I'm here now.' He took her bag and flung it casually over one broad shoulder. 'Ready to go?'

I edged off the sidewalk, but Josephine immediately turned, catching me in mid-step. Her expression was strangely intense. Something about the way she looked at me made my heart bounce under my sternum.

'So, I'll see you in a little while?' she asked.

'Sure,' I replied, hoping I didn't sound too eager. 'I'll be there.'

'Remember . . . the Fairgrounds.' She winked.

'What's going on?' Quentin looked as though he'd just realized I was standing there.

Josephine curled her arm around his. 'Sebastian and I are going to work on our scenes for the school play.'

'I see,' he replied, studying me. 'Hey, Sebastian. How's the head?'

'Good as new,' I replied.

His gaze returned to Josephine. 'Today? Do you think that's a good idea? You know we've scheduled a long practice, and you've got a lot to cover.' He cast a sideways glance my way. 'Maybe some other time?'

Though he'd directed the question to Josephine, it was obvious that he was expecting me to answer; to bail out. The tone of his voice had changed – a slight variation – but I picked up on it, loud and clear. Something crackled through my stomach like icy fire. I pressed my fingernails into my palms, working to keep my face unexpressive.

'Just an hour.' Josephine rubbed his arm. 'It won't interfere.'

I focused on Quentin, scrutinizing every move and reaction, storing the information in the back of my mind, though I didn't know why. I'd never really been one for details, but things had changed drastically over the last few days. I found myself doing it a lot more, so much that it was beginning to feel instinctive.

His mouth curved easily, but his body language conveyed that of someone trying a little too hard to appear relaxed. 'Okay, Josie. It's your call.'

'Just an hour,' she repeated, giving Quentin a peck on the cheek. Then she waved at me. 'I'll see you soon, Sebastian.'

Quentin put his arm around her shoulders, spinning her towards his SUV. I watched the vehicle roar out of the parking lot, my blood pounding in my ears. Something wasn't right. A burst of heat shot through me, and a sound I didn't know I could make rose from my throat. Something registered in my peripheral vision. I whipped around, snarling.

'Hey, easy, Sebastian!' Mitchell cried, throwing his hands up.

'I have to follow her. She's not safe.'

Mitchell looked at me as though I'd lost my mind. 'I'm going to take a chance here and say she's probably fine, buddy.'

'No, she's not,' I hissed. My shoulders pinched together. 'She's not.'

My head was screaming at me. I pressed my fingers into my temples. Mitchell glanced away uncomfortably. I had to get a grip on my emotions. I breathed in hard through my nose and squeezed my eyes shut until the anger released me from its grip. Common sense told me that Josephine was fine, but the compulsion to jump into my van and take off after her was nearly overwhelming. I planted my feet until, finally, the urge passed.

What the crap was going on?

'Well . . . ' said Mitchell, looking as awkward as I felt.

Before I could either apologize or explain away my latest out-burst, Avery arrived on the scene, inadvertently coming to my rescue. He slapped me good-naturedly on the back, totally oblivious to everything.

'What's up, guys?'

I rubbed my shoulder, feeling more like myself again. 'You know, Avery, some people might take offense at your greeting tactics.'

He laughed. 'Let me know if you meet one.'

Katie bounded up beside me, her face flushed. 'Rehearsal totally rocked today! I can't believe how soon the show's going to be here!'

I grinned at her, relieved for yet another distraction. 'So, how are you doing as the Hippo, by the way?'

'*Hippolyta* is coming along quite nicely, thank you. That is, if her Theseus would learn his lines. Wesley totally sucks!'

'Why don't you tell us how you really feel,' said Mitchell.

Katie shrugged. 'You know I only speak the truth.' She started to say something else, then her gaze shifted to my hood. She leaned forward. 'Wow, Sebastian, I just realized that your eyes are the same shade as your hair,' she mused. 'I mean, like totally exact. Did you do that on purpose?'

'Contacts,' I lied, simply.

She propped her chin in her hand, forming her own opinions, probably. 'It's almost creepy.'

114

'Um, thanks?'

'Part of this tattoo artist phase he's going through,' said Avery, cutting in on our conversation. 'And, not that standing here talking about Sebastian's lack of normal fashion sense isn't riveting and all . . . but I'm starving. Are we going or not?'

'Going where?' I asked, casually jerking Avery's bag from his shoulders as payback for his comment, and smiling as his books dumped on the ground.

'Not cool!' He knelt to pick them up.

'To the diner across the street,' Katie replied, ignoring our antics. 'You coming with us?'

'I can't,' I replied. 'I told Josephine I'd come to the Fairgrounds to work on our scenes for the play.' I managed to keep my face carefully arranged as I spoke, but my pulse quickened the moment I said her name out loud.

Katie's brows shot up. 'Oh really?'

'It's no big deal.' I hugged her quickly. 'Gotta go.' I sprinted across the parking lot, ignoring Katie's demands for details. 'See you guys tomorrow,' I shouted over my shoulder. I climbed into my van and pulled out before I had the good sense to change my mind.

I steered onto Fairground Drive, tapping my fingers against the steering wheel, barely able to sit still. My nerves were strung tighter than the telephone wires above the road. I knew Hugo was probably waiting for me at home. After all, he'd promised we'd talk. But his secrets seemed way less exciting, compared with what lay before me.

Just ahead, the Sutallee River wound through the rich autumn forest, splicing the landscape like a watery whip. The Sutallee Bridge stretched across it, looking like something out of an old Norman Rockwell painting. I crossed the bridge and continued down the road until I reached the gated entry of the Circe de Romany. Then I parked the van and got out.

The red and gold tent loomed against the overcast sky. More pavilions had been assembled, and bright pennants fluttered in the breeze. Carnival rides of every size and shape dominated the Fairgrounds. Flashy publicity posters lined the fence, announcing the Circe's opening, just weeks away. Behind the tent, motionless, was the Ferris wheel. I shuddered and looked away.

The gate was closed and locked. I peered through the iron bars, looking for signs of life. My stomach sank. What if she'd forgotten about our practice? How important could an amateur high school play be to a member of a circus troupe?

The minutes crept by, and I grew restless. I gauged the height of the fence, wondering if I could scale it. As I pondered the possibility, my head went painfully cold, like a brain freeze from too much ice cream too fast. When I looked up, I realized why. Quentin Marks was strolling towards the gate. He studied me through the fence, and there was something in his expression I didn't care for.

As if he enjoyed seeing me behind bars.

11. Drought and Rain

'Hey,' I said with a nod, determined to be polite. 'Is Josephine here?'

Quentin's smile was carefully placed. 'Of course.'

'We're supposed to rehearse,' I continued, getting the feeling he was taunting me. 'Could you let me in?'

He produced a set of keys from his pocket. The gate creaked loudly on its hinges. Once I was inside, he closed the gate with a bang.

'Follow me.'

It felt as though I was intruding on his territory, and he was going to turn on me any minute, like it was some big joke, and kick me out. But he walked with an easy stride, seemingly oblivious of my presence. The back of the property was lined with brightly painted trailers and buses, all arranged in a circular pattern. Quentin stopped in front of the largest vehicle and knocked on the door. He stepped inside and motioned me to follow.

I entered a small living room, crammed with furniture: a dark blue couch, a patterned chaise, and several other mismatched pieces. The decor reflected the tastes of a family who'd traveled extensively. Artwork hung from every available space on the walls, and ornate curtains framed the narrow windows.

Quentin smiled again, more serpentine than friendly. 'Have a good rehearsal.'

Before I could reply, Quentin was out the door. The ice thawed in my stomach, but my lip curled away from my teeth, and I got a weird urge to growl at his retreating form. I really didn't like that guy.

'Hey, man.'

The voice came from the kitchenette. A boy my age lumbered out, waving at me with a fistful of sandwich. I knew him from the circus party. It was Josephine's twin brother, Francis. He leaned against the wall.

'Hey,' I replied. 'Is Josephine here?'

Francis grinned around a mouthful of food then raised his voice. 'Jo, your acting buddy's here!'

Josephine appeared from a short hallway at the other end of the room. 'Thanks for coming Sebastian,' she said, nudging her brother out of the way. 'Would you like something to eat or drink?' She opened the refrigerator.

'Ah, sure.' I tugged at my sleeve, feeling out of place as I stood in the middle of the Romanys' cramped living quarters. 'That would be great.'

Francis flopped on the couch, sprawling his thick legs along the cushions and flipping the buttons on the remote control. I crossed to the chaise and perched on the edge, rubbing absently at my tattoo as I waited for Josephine to reappear.

'So, how's the play going?' Francis asked. 'Jo says you guys are crunched for time.'

There was something easygoing about Francis – a definite contrast to Quentin – who was so aloof and reserved.

'We are,' I replied. 'I mean, we've gotten a lot done, but there are still scenes we've barely covered.'

'Yeah, like this scene you're doing with her, right? The one where she falls in love with you.'

I became suddenly interested in the program on the television. 'Yeah, like that one.'

. . . *Where she falls in love with you.*

As with my character in the play, I didn't have a chance with someone like her – not that I was trying – I reminded myself. She was taken and obviously happy. And even if she wasn't, Josephine and I were barely even friends. No matter what kind of straitjacket-worthy emotions I felt around Josephine, this was just a rehearsal, nothing more.

'Here you go, Sebastian.' Josephine handed me a can of soda and a plate of Oreos.

'Thanks.'

She sat on the end of the couch. She smelled so good I had to resist a sudden, powerful desire to sniff the air. *Normal. Just act normal.* The plate of cookies rattled in my hand. I set them aside and concentrated on opening the soda instead. Josephine slapped Francis on the leg.

'Do you mind?' she said in a chastising voice. 'We need to rehearse.'

He grunted and rolled off the couch, tossing the remote on the cushions. As he passed by he patted my shoulder.

'Good luck, man,' he chuckled. 'Jo's a diva.'

He ducked as a cream-colored pillow soared through the air, aimed at his head. Then Josephine and I were alone in the room. I cleared my throat, fumbling at my jacket zipper. The temperature had kicked up several degrees since I'd entered the trailer, which was insane. I liked Josephine. A whole lot. Probably more than was healthy, especially

119

considering her annoying, intimidating boyfriend. But even that didn't explain what kept happening to me when I was around her.

Every time I was around her.

'So, are you ready to begin?' I asked, yanking myself from my thoughts. 'I know time is fleeting.' I cringed on the inside, knowing if Avery had been around, he would've accused me of another of my 'old books' talk. 'I mean, you've got a rehearsal coming up, right?'

But Josephine only smiled. 'There's time,' she replied, picking up my plate and holding it out to me. 'You need to eat first.'

'You don't have to tell me twice,' I said, snagging an Oreo. 'I never turn down food.' While I ate, grateful for a distraction from my fever, I fought the urge to scratch at my tattoo, which felt as if it was crawling along the top of my skin.

Josephine took a pillow into her lap and played with the fringe.

'Thanks for doing this, Sebastian,' she said. 'I know it's out of your way and all.'

'It's no trouble. I didn't have anything major at the shop today.'

'Your brother's shop?'

I glanced up, surprised. 'Yeah.'

'Quentin told me that's where you live.' Her expression grew thoughtful. 'I didn't know Hugo Corsi had a brother. But we don't spend a lot of time with other clans, and we pretty much keep to ourselves when we're in Sixes.'

Of course, she'd know about Hugo's Gypsy clan. She was part of her own. But it still felt bizarre to be talking about it as if it was just completely normal stuff. Then suddenly I realized that, to her, it probably was.

'Well, that's because he's not really my brother,' I confessed. 'His parents got me out of foster care almost three years ago. When they went to Europe on business, Hugo took me in so I could finish school here in Sixes.'

Josephine gasped then clamped her mouth shut like she'd just revealed a top secret battle plan. She gripped the pillow so tightly that I could see her fingers turn white. 'I just thought . . . I mean, because you're with the Corsis, I thought you were one of us.'

'Oh, I am,' I said rapidly, to alleviate her distress. 'I mean, not technically. But I know about your family. And Hugo's.'

'But you're not a Gypsy.' Josephine paled underneath her tanned skin as if my revelation had drained the life out of her. 'We don't reveal ourselves to *gadje*. That's like, rule number one with my people. It's serious business. If you do, you could be shunned, turned out of the clan.'

I slid my thumb underneath my sleeve, feeling the heat from the tattoo I'd kept carefully hidden since the night of the party. It seemed now that my tattoo had less to do with good luck or apprenticeship, and more to do with assurances; as though making me an honorary Corsi would guarantee I'd keep the Gypsy thing a secret.

'It's okay, Josephine. Hugo let me in, or whatever you want to call it. He said you guys like to stay under the radar, so it's definitely not something I'd go spreading around. I haven't even said anything to Katie, and that's saying a lot. She can pretty much pry anything out of me.'

Josephine relaxed at my comment, and her slight smile returned. 'Trust me, I know. That girl's got people skills, and she's not afraid to use them.' The smile faded. 'I've always liked those kinds of people, you know? The ones that are like open books, all the time. I guess maybe because

I'm kind of the opposite. Keeping our identity hidden is hard sometimes, but it's what we have to do. It's a matter of survival.'

'Wow,' I said, leaning into the plush cushions and trying to absorb what she said. Suddenly, Hugo didn't seem so far-fetched anymore. 'That's crazy. I didn't think people still lived like that, at least, in this country. No offense, but it all feels like folk tales and history to me.'

'Traditions and customs are what keep our heritage alive, Sebastian.' Her shoulders drew back and her chin lifted. I felt as if I'd wandered into forbidden territory. Josephine lowered her brows, and it seemed as though she were trying to determine if my Gypsy ignorance was for real. 'Roma are strict and set in our ways, even the Outcasts. Our laws determine how we live, where our place is in the clan, what our future will be . . . '

A crease formed between her eyes as she drifted off. Her voice had changed – I couldn't place it, exactly, and she sounded kind of like Hugo – but her tone was different to his, and the words felt rehearsed somehow, almost as if she was trying to convince herself.

'Huh,' I said. 'And here I was thinking Hugo was putting on some kind of show with me; all drama and mystery and secrets.' I pulled on the cuff of my sleeve and shook my head. 'Like it was all some lead-up to my working as an apprentice in the shop. But I guess at least some of what he's been telling me is true.'

Josephine's forehead softened, and she studied me with a curious expression. She leaned forward, tilting her head, attempting to get a better look at my face underneath my hood. 'I'm getting the feeling you haven't always known about your brother's heritage.'

I frowned. 'Actually, not until a few days ago. Hugo acted like it was no big deal, said it just never came up. But, it feels strange that he's never shared this with me before now. I don't know, maybe it has to do with the Circe coming to town.'

'Well, I'm sure he had his reasons, Sebastian. I don't know your brother or the Corsis really well, but I do know what it's like growing up in a Roma family. We keep a lot of secrets, even from each other.'

'Doesn't that bother you?'

She paused. Her gaze flicked to the door of the trailer, and she studied the curtained window. 'All the time,' she said, her voice noticeably quieter. Hushed. 'But you find ways of dealing with it.'

She looked at me again; the same intently solemn expression as the day she'd invited me to her party. An unexpected flash of knowledge passed between us, and in one slow blink of her eyes, I realized there was more to Josephine than she allowed anyone at school to see, more than maybe even the people closest to her knew. And suddenly, I wanted to know everything about her.

More than anything in the world.

Josephine brushed her hair away from her cheek and laughed, breaking the moment, but a trace of it remained, lingering in the air with a mysterious life of its own. Her silence wasn't a closed door to whatever I'd just witnessed, but it wasn't an invitation, either. Not yet. I had the sense to recognize that, at least.

'Well,' I said, changing gears before I said anything I'd regret later. 'Hugo promised we'd talk tonight about all this clan stuff, so maybe I won't sound like so much of a Gypsy newbie the next time we talk.'

To my relief, Josephine nodded. 'You know, it's nice talking to someone outside the Circe without having to worry if I'm going to slip up and say something to the *gadje*. My father doesn't like me attending public school, but he gave in, after Francis and I begged him for a month.' Josephine set her pillow aside and straightened the books on the coffee table. 'I like school, but I'm not exactly comfortable there, either.'

'Yeah, I know the feeling.'

Her fingers paused over the cover of a photography book. 'Something we have in common, then.'

This time, I felt as though Josephine was the one peering into the cracked door of my life. She hovered there a few breaths, and then continued. 'So, anyway, it's nice to know that you're a *diddikoi*.'

'Is that a compliment or a curse?'

Josephine flashed a smile that reminded me of sun on water. 'Roma use the term for different things, but for Outcasts, the word means someone who is a friend to the Gypsies. Believe me, it's a huge compliment.'

'Well, that's a relief,' I said, mirroring her grin. 'So, how many more Gypsies do you know? Besides my brother's clan?'

'The Circe's made up of many families, but outside of us, there are several Outcast clans spread all over the Southeast. Since we travel, we pass through other Havens a lot.'

'So it really is like Hugo said. There's more of you than people think.'

'Uh huh,' she said with a knowing spark in her eyes. 'Some of us hide under the obvious covers, like a traveling circus. Others choose more subtle ways to blend in.'

'Yeah, I'm sort of figuring that out,' I said, watching as Josephine played with the ribbon at her neck. I couldn't see her pendant, but I knew it was hidden beneath her shirt. I wiped a trickle of sweat from my temple, feeling uncomfortably warm. 'But then, Hugo told me about the dandelion symbol the Outcast clans use, and then you showed me your necklace on the Ferris wheel . . . '

My words died off as our eyes met.

'Yes,' she said softly.

I continued with caution. 'But I don't really remember the rest.'

Josephine clasped her hands in her lap. 'I dropped my pendant, just as we were getting out of the car. You tried to catch it, and then you hit your head on the safety rail.'

'And . . . that was it?'

She broke our gaze and stared at the television. 'Karl was looking you over, so I ran to get Quentin, and then Katie came . . . and I tried to check on you, but there were all the party guests, and then, by the time I came back, Quentin was driving you home.' She sighed heavily. 'I wanted to say something to you the next day but, I don't know, it was like you were avoiding me.'

'Maybe a little,' I confessed. I couldn't tell her my real reasons, not when I'd just discovered she didn't actually think I was a mental case. 'I felt pretty idiotic after the whole thing. I'm apparently sadly uncoordinated. Everything from that night is still kind of fuzzy. Thanks for clearing it up.'

Josephine seemed visibly relieved. I guess I should've been, too. At least I knew now that I'd imagined the details of the accident. I probably had a concussion. Maybe going to the doctor wasn't such a bad idea, after all.

She reached for the soda can, which was dangling precariously from my hand. 'Are you finished?' she asked politely.

Josephine was looking at me with those eyes of hers, and I could hardly think anymore. The Ferris wheel was suddenly the farthest thing from my mind. 'Ah, sure.'

She tapped her chin with one finger. 'Then I guess we can start where Titania wakes up and sees Bottom for the first time.'

The reality of what I was about to do hit me like a tsunami in the face. Neither the Ferris wheel nor and Hugo and his Gypsy roots concerned me anymore. Performing with Josephine was far more nerve-wracking. 'I'm ready.'

'Why don't you take your hood off, Sebastian?'

As much as I didn't want to comply, it was as if I couldn't refuse. Some unseen force had switched on the autopilot again. My hand moved, and the next thing I knew, I'd slipped my hood from my head. I glanced up anxiously. Josephine's eyes widened. She took in my gray hair – the dye job wasn't much of a secret anymore – but I could tell my sallow complexion bothered her.

'I've been sick,' I said, instantly self-conscious.

'I've noticed,' she said, looking concerned as she locked on my eyes. 'Ever since my birthday party. And it seems like it's getting worse. Have you been to the doctor?'

She'd noticed me that much?

I shook my head. I knew the way I looked had nothing to do with my head injury. It was something else. 'It's just stress and lack of sleep.'

'Are you sure? Katie said you haven't been . . . '

Josephine trailed off, and I could tell she was trying not to say too much.

'Haven't been what?'

'Acting like yourself,' she replied hesitantly.

I grimaced. I'd really done a bang-up job putting myself in the best possible light for a girl I hardly knew. Josephine didn't mention my incident with Alex, but I knew she had to be thinking it. 'Well, Katie's right. And I'm sorry. I'm not usually so . . . high strung.'

126

To my surprise, Josephine smiled. 'So what are you, then? Usually.'

I paused, trying to remember the last time I'd felt like myself. Or maybe I'd always been this way. It was getting harder to tell. 'I'll be fine by the time the play rolls around. At least, I'd better be. I don't think I want to be on Ms Lucian's bad side.'

Her smile widened. 'I don't think I want to either.' She stared at me for a moment longer, as if trying to decide whether she wanted to ask me something else. But she didn't. 'Okay, well, let's pick up the scene with Bottom's entrance. Does that work?' She curled up on the couch. 'You have the first line, I think.'

I retreated behind the chaise, thinking over the blocking notes from rehearsal. Josephine rested her head on her hands, shutting her eyes in pretend sleep, waiting on me to begin. My heart was beating so loud I was sure she could hear it. I was supposed to sing my lines, but I opted to say them instead, and I picked up halfway through my speech to save Josephine from any unnecessary torture.

'The throstle with his note so true. The wren with little quill.' I strolled in front of the couch, past the sleeping Titania. Josephine yawned dramatically.

'What angel wakes me from my flowery bed?' she cooed.

I continued my lines, trying to appear oblivious as Josephine rose from the cushions. I felt a strong sense of peace as she approached, but I also felt her every move like a shock through my nerves. I fumbled through my next line. 'The finch, the sparrow, and the lark, the plainsong cuckoo gray, whose note full many a man doth mark, and dares not answer "Nay".'

Josephine slid her hand down my arm as she faced me. My fragmented emotions were wiping me out, and I couldn't process either one. I swallowed hard as she took my hand, trying to concentrate on her lines and not on her lips as she spoke. 'I pray thee, gentle mortal, sing again. Mine ear is much enamored of thy note; so is mine eye enthralled to thy shape.' She grasped my other hand, and I was conscious of how clammy they felt against her soft skin. My face flushed when she raised my hand to place it against her cheek. 'And thy fair virtue's force perforce doth move me on the first view to say, to swear, I love thee,' she continued, leaning her head into my palm.

Josephine's lashes fluttered against my fingers. I'd never had the opportunity to observe her this closely, and I didn't want the moment to end. I was feeling so many things for her at once.

'Methinks, mistress, you should have little reason for that. And yet, to say the truth, reason and love keep little company together nowadays.'

Josephine smiled up at me with Titania's smile. 'Thou art as wise as thou art beautiful,' she replied.

According to the blocking of the scene, she was supposed to kiss my hands. I wasn't sure what she was going to do, and I wasn't sure what *I* would do if she did. Josephine paused, and I stared back at her, feeling the electricity in my body rising.

The trailer door swung open. She dropped my hands at the same time that I jumped back, catching my leg against the table. The tiny piece of furniture toppled, launching cookies and orange soda. I lunged forward, snagging the can out of the air before it could wreak havoc on the plush carpet, but the cookies were a lost cause. I knelt to pick them up.

Quentin stepped into the room with a commanding air and a mocking smirk. 'Sorry to interrupt, Josie. But we've got to cut your little practice short. Andre's moved the schedule around, and you're up next.'

Josephine turned to me, an apologetic look on her face. 'Well, I guess I have to go.'

She reached for the plate. Our fingers touched briefly. 'It's fine, Josephine,' I said quietly. 'I understand.'

She took the food into the kitchen. When she returned, Quentin slipped his arm around her waist. 'They're waiting on you, Josie,' he said, guiding her to the door. 'I'll walk Sebastian out.'

She paused in the doorway. 'Thanks for coming today, Sebastian. I feel better about our scene already.'

Josephine glided out of the trailer and was gone. Quentin gestured to the door, and I moved quickly, eager to get out into the open. I was feeling suddenly trapped. As I passed the kitchen, something caught my eye, stopping me dead in my tracks. There on the counter, alongside a pot of flowers, was my porcelain figurine. The Gypsy girl was still in her frozen dance, her delicate arms raised and her long hair spread in stationary perfection. A lump formed in my throat.

We reached the front gate, but instead of opening it, Quentin leaned against the bars, regarding me coolly. 'I like you, Sebastian,' he said, 'so I'm going to give you a piece of advice.'

'Advice,' I repeated, instantly suspicious.

His smile tightened. 'You should stay away from Josephine.'

'I don't think that's possible, Quentin,' I replied, feeling my shoulders stiffen. 'We *are* in the play together.'

'I'm sure you'll find a way.'

I took a deep breath, choosing my words carefully. 'I'm not after your girlfriend, if that's what you're implying. I get that you're together. I just want the play to go well, that's all. You don't have to worry about me.'

Quentin seemed surprised by my answer. That, in turn, surprised me. It wasn't as if I was any competition, even if I *was* pursuing Josephine – which I wasn't – I reminded myself firmly. Quentin pulled himself from the iron bars and produced his keys. Something in his eyes reminded me of one of Hugo's looks; odd and completely unreadable.

'You're right, of course,' he said in a lighter tone. 'Sometimes I can be a little possessive. But I care about Josephine, and right now, she needs to stay focused on her job here. I didn't mean to imply anything.'

'So first you threaten me, and now you're apologizing for it?'

'Of course not,' he said, unlocking the gate. 'I'm just saying I may have been a little out of line. Now, I'm sorry I can't hang around and chat, but I've got to get back to work.' He opened the gate, and I stepped through. It clanged shut behind me. I looked at Quentin through the iron bars, finding myself on the outside once more. His smile arched. 'See you around, Sebastian.'

He turned and walked back the way we'd come, tossing a casual wave over his shoulder at me; one I couldn't help feel was mildly triumphal.

12. *Betrayal or Trust*

'I need to talk to my brother.'

Vincent glanced up from the arm of his customer. 'Right now?'

'Yes,' I said, exasperated. I was still reeling from my visit to the Fairgrounds. 'Where is he?'

Vincent shifted the needle to his other hand and scratched his ginger-colored goatee. 'He's not here. He went up to Tennessee this morning.'

'Why?'

Vincent returned to his work, grabbing a cloth to wipe away a bit of blood before continuing. 'Had some guy in Chattanooga who wanted a full sleeve done.'

'When will he be back?'

Vincent's needle traveled gracefully up his victim's arm, drawing a perfect arch to the outer edge of a Celtic cross. 'Pretty soon.'

'Well, I'm going to grab something for dinner,' I said, backing out of the room.

Vincent shot up, his foot slipping off the pedal. The customer looked up in alarm, but the red-haired tattoo artist never noticed. 'Hugo doesn't want you going anywhere.'

'Excuse me?'

'He called about an hour ago and told me to relay the message to you when you got home. He wants you to stay here until he gets back.'

'Okay,' I said. 'But I'm getting some food first.'

'Didn't you hear me?'

I laughed. 'Yeah, I heard you Vincent. But I'm eighteen. It's not like Hugo can ground me or anything.' I waved my hand. 'Don't worry, I'll bring you back something.'

'I'm serious, Sebastian. Stay here.'

'Not going to happen, Vincent.' I headed for the door. I hadn't noticed Kris in the waiting room until he and James moved in front of me, blocking my exit. I stared in disbelief. 'You're kidding me, right?'

Kris shrugged. 'Just following orders, Sebastian.'

'*Orders?* What is this, the military?'

'Nope,' James replied. 'If it was, we'd be demanding a little more respect from the private.'

I was used to the guys giving me a hard time, little-brother style. But their lame initiation joke was wearing on my nerves. I stepped forward, intending to push past them, but James countered, his massive form towering over me. I stared at his large form, and suddenly, a fiery rage boiled inside me. The onslaught caught me off-guard, nearly knocking me off my feet. My body hunched defensively, and I felt my lip pulling back from my teeth.

'Let me by.'

My words came out more like a growl. James straightened with an overly casual flair, but his eyes were uneasy. 'Please, Sebastian. Just cooperate for tonight, okay? When Hugo gets back, he'll explain everything.'

Kris leaned against the door. 'Trust us.'

I'd seen enough movies to know that when someone said to trust them, that was exactly what you *weren't* supposed to do. But these guys were like family. I studied their faces. Or were they? I was just a kid with no parents and no home; a charity case Hugo had, for whatever reason, decided to take in. And I definitely wasn't Roma.

The guys continued to stare me down, their smiles more grim than joking. If James and Kris were serious about stopping me, I doubted I'd be able to make it to the door. They made imposing obstacles. I gritted my teeth and choked down the anger. It wasn't easy. The emotions were powerful, every bit as powerful as the ones I felt around Josephine. But these were way different.

Around her, I was a mixture of serenity and anxiety. What I felt as I stared at James and Kris, what I'd felt when I'd almost attacked Alex in rehearsal; these emotions had a life of their own. They were wild animals, trapped inside me, clawing at my lungs and threatening to scale their way up my throat. I kept trying to shut them out, to pretend they weren't there.

To pretend I wasn't terrified of what they were doing to me.

'Come on, Sebastian,' Kris said steadily. 'Just hang out here, and I'll grab us some food, okay?'

The guys weren't going to budge, and unless I intended to fight my way out, I wasn't going anywhere tonight. I took a deep breath. The ugly fury retreated once more, disappearing with the same unnerving speed as it had manifested. I breathed out, this time in relief. 'Fine. I'll play it your way. But I'm expecting some major compensation for this.'

It was Kris who spoke. 'Pizza?'

'No pepperoni.'

'Sure,' he replied.

I flung myself into the couch, still feeling the bite of my emotional battle. This growing struggle was really messing with my head. Kris grabbed some money from the register and left. I leapt up, pacing restlessly, flexing my fingers. They were sore and stiff, like my back. I tried to think of a reasonable explanation for Hugo's weird behavior, but kept coming up blank. When had life stopped making sense around here? I was hungry, I was irritated, and I needed something to distract me before I lost my mind.

I headed for the apartment, deciding to watch television while I waited. But as I reached for the light, I paused. Something about the room didn't feel right. I brushed my hand across my eyes. The blinds were closed, lights were off, but I could still *see*.

I ground the heels of my hands into my eyes. Then I looked again. Everything in the room was crystal clear, from the collection of candy wrappers on the table to the titles of the books on the shelf. Objects stood out in stark detail, but in grayscale, like an old photograph, totally visible in the dark.

'What's going on?' I whispered into the stillness.

My stomach clenched. I bolted through the apartment and into the bathroom. The mirror glared at me. My breath wrestled inside my lungs as I slowly touched my face with my fingertips. Against the strange pewter color of my hair, my skin looked ashen. My irises were gray. Even my lips and the dark circles beneath my eyes seemed discolored. Whatever was going on with me, it was getting worse. And I couldn't keep pretending I was okay with it. My gaze drifted to my wrist. The dandelion tattoo glimmered with a silvery sheen in the gray light of my revved-up vision, as though the ink had a life of its own.

My tattoo.

134

The events of the last week banged through my memory like gunfire. I'd been treating all my bizarre symptoms as though they were unrelated incidents: the worsening sickness, the careening emotions, even the fear that I was teetering into insanity. But what if they were all connected somehow?

I switched on the light, squinting for several moments until my eyes adjusted from the grayscale vision into normal sight. Then I studied my reflection again, this time more carefully, taking in every detail. My eyes didn't just look brighter above the hollows of my sockets. They *were* brighter. More intense. I swallowed hard, raking my hands through my hair as I realized something else. Nothing remained of my original shade, not even a streak of black. My hair had changed over the last couple of days. Just like my complexion.

This wasn't an initiation. The guys hadn't been playing pranks on me. This was real. As I traced the inked design on my wrist, it suddenly dawned on me why Hugo didn't want me leaving the apartment. Why he'd been acting so weird and secretive. I wasn't crazy after all. Something was wrong with me.

And Hugo Corsi knew exactly what it was.

It was nearly eleven when Hugo returned. James had just flipped the 'closed' sign over in the shop window, and the others were cleaning up. I managed to keep my seat on the couch, giving my brother enough time to get in the door, but I was growing more anxious by the second. I was ready for answers.

Hugo chucked his bag onto the counter. 'Is there any coffee around here?' Kris poured him a cup, and my brother eased into the purple couch opposite me. He looked exhausted.

'Nice trip?' I asked.

'Pretty good,' he replied.

'Okay, Hugo.' I squared my shoulders. 'Let's hear it.'

'Sebastian . . .'

'No, Hugo,' I growled. 'No more shutting me out. You promised we'd talk, so let's talk.' My brother set his coffee aside as casually as if we were about to discuss the stock report. The action fueled my rising anger, but my next question took it out of me again. 'All this covert Gypsy business you've been dealing with lately . . . it has to do with me, doesn't it?'

Hugo barely moved. 'Yes.'

I leapt from the sofa, my heart pounding in my chest, my calm demeanor slipping away. 'I'm not stressed, and I don't have the flu. Something else is wrong with me, and you know what it is.' I yanked up my sleeve and thrust my wrist into the light. 'God, if I didn't know better, I'd think you poisoned the ink.'

Hugo flinched, or as close as I'd ever seen him come to such a reaction. His eyes met mine. They were cold and sharp, but their piercing focus wasn't directed at me. It was as if he was staring deep within himself. 'You're not poisoned. But you're right about one thing.' Hugo's voice matched his stare. 'There is no initiation. There never was.'

I froze in the middle of the room.

'Then what's happening to me?'

The room went silent. I shifted my gaze to the guys, but they avoided my stare. All attention was focused on my brother. My senses kicked up a notch. I heard a crinkling sound and noticed Hugo fiddling with something in his coat pocket. Crumpled paper. His fingers clamped and unclamped around it. The muscles in his hand were as tight as the ones in his tattooed neck. Finally, after a pause too long to mean anything good, Vincent approached Hugo and put a hand on his shoulder.

'You've got to tell him, Hugo. There's no reason to keep waiting. It's happening. We've all seen the changes in his behavior. And just, *look* at him. How much more evidence do you need?'

They all stared at me then, and their expressions sent a tremor down my spine.

'Test him,' said Kris.

Vincent nodded. 'Then we can know for sure.'

Hugo looked sharply from one man to the next, and I felt the tension of the standoff. The hair rose on the back of my neck. Hugo drew the paper from his pocket. An envelope. A letter? He rose and set it on the counter. Something changed in my brother's face, and I knew that whatever it was they were suggesting he do, Hugo was going to give in. I waited in silent anticipation, ready for anything.

Hugo stepped directly in front of me.

'Hit me,' he said.

I *thought* I was ready for anything.

'Excuse me?'

He grabbed my shirt and yanked me to him. My surprise vanished. Heated coals ignited in my stomach. 'You heard me, Sebastian,' he snapped, so close I could feel his breath. 'Hit me.'

My brother was *telling* me to punch him? I had to admit, I'd dreamed of doing such a thing more than a few times, but this was stupid. 'I'm not going to hit you, Hugo.'

He laughed harshly. The sound grated my nerves with a force I hadn't expected. I was aware of the others pressing around me, hemming me in. My breath caught in my throat. They were doing it on purpose. They were trying to rile me up. And it was working. As though someone had flipped a switch inside me, my body began to shake. The dark emotions were returning, this time with a lot more power.

'Sebastian, the tattoo on your wrist isn't there by accident,' Hugo said, releasing me. 'If it does its job, then we'll know. Now quit wasting time and hit me!'

'Then what happens?' I asked, struggling to smile though the elevating anger. My voice sounded raspy, like I was talking through a snarl. 'I get one shot in, then you pound me to a pulp in typical big brother fashion?'

'I'm not your brother. You're just an orphan I took in.'

My humor died as hurt sliced through me, exposing the fear I'd held underneath for so long. Shocked tears pricked the corners of my eyes. 'Hugo . . . '

'You heard me,' he continued. 'Now, do something about it.'

The guys moved closer, boxing me in, leaving no escape. The muscles in my back were so tight I couldn't hold my body upright. I hunched over, panting raggedly, glaring at Hugo as my hurt melted into anger. Fierce, gut-wrenching anger. The room, the guys, everything was coated in red. I wanted to be scared of what was happening, but the dark emotions rising inside me wouldn't allow it. They ripped up my throat, forcing a growl.

'Come on,' he yelled.

This was wrong.

Hugo shoved me hard. I stumbled into the couch.

Red fury. Rage like lava.

No control.

No control.

'Hit me, you gray-haired freak!'

I leapt at him with a wild cry. My hand shot up, fingers spread, and I swung. There was a cracking sound, followed

138

by sharp pain in my fingers, and my body slung forward with the force of the blow. Hugo's head snapped around, his large body flailing.

He sank to the floor.

I gasped for breath, hunched and tense, waiting for Hugo to attack. But he didn't. Instead, he rolled over, holding his face as blood trickled through his fingers. James shifted back with a wary look. Vincent knelt beside my brother. The sight of Hugo on the floor quenched the fire in my veins and cleared my head. The emotions dropped in a sickening weight in my gut. I stared, open-mouthed and petrified.

'Oh God . . . I'm sorry, Hugo.'

His hand slipped from his face. Four red gashes striped his cheek. I jerked upright, shocked at the wound. What had I done? Kris stared at me then reached down and snatched my arm, holding it out.

'Well, Hugo,' he said. 'I'd say you have your proof.'

I stared, disbelieving, at my hand. Glinting in the light, in place of where my fingernails should have been, were a set of ugly gray claws.

13. Day or Night

I huddled on the couch, staring dully ahead.

Hugo emerged from the hall with a strip of gauze taped to his cheek. I looked down guiltily. I'd just attacked my brother. With my bare hands. The lack of control I'd felt was appalling. It wasn't me. I curled my fingers tighter inside the sleeves of my jacket, feeling the rough edges of my nails – or what used to be my nails – against the skin of my palms. Like my hair, they didn't seem to belong to me anymore.

An hour ago, I'd just wanted to talk. Now, all I wanted to do was run, straight for the door, leave this all behind and pretend none of it happened. But that wasn't an option.

'Sebastian,' said Hugo, his voice low and even, as if reading my thoughts. 'I'm sorry for coming at you like that, for saying what I did. But we had to know if everything really was set in motion. Your response had to be purely emotional and instinctive. It was the only way to be sure. Now that we are, the best thing for you is to stay here, in the shop. It's for your own safety.'

For *my* safety? I'd just left marks on his face with my *claws*. Goose bumps broke out along my arms. It was like sitting in a doctor's office, waiting to receive news you already

140

knew was going to be bad. 'Just tell me the truth, Hugo. Whatever it is.'

My brother's jaw worked as he deliberated. I braced myself for the worst. His eyes flicked to my wrist. 'Your tattoo isn't just a tattoo, Sebastian. It's a brand.'

The word hit me like a slap. '*Brand*?' A few days ago, I'd thought Hugo inked me with a flower as some sadistic, brotherly payback. It had been a fleeting notion, a joke. But the word my brother used scraped my insides raw. 'I don't understand what you mean.'

'Branding is an ancient art, nearly dead to the Corsi clan. But my parents knew how, and they passed it on to me.'

'So it's some Gypsy symbolism thing,' I huffed. My nerves were starting to prick at my anger again. 'Sounds more like something you do to a herd of cattle.'

'You're right.' Hugo propped himself against the front counter. There was that look again, the near-flinch. 'And why do ranchers brand their animals?'

'I don't know, Hugo. To mark their property, I guess, so people know who they belong to.' My reply echoed heavily in the room. The other guys were deathly quiet and completely still. I was growing increasingly uneasy. 'Okay,' I continued cautiously. 'The dandelion proves I'm part of the Corsi clan.'

'In a manner of speaking.' The expression on my brother's face was grimly composed, as if he was sitting in a business meeting he didn't want to attend. 'But the dandelion isn't the brand. I chose the design for all the reasons I told you about when I inked it. The power of the brand comes from the ink itself.'

I pulled up my sleeve and rotated my wrist. The edges of the design shimmered in the light. 'What did you use?' I asked warily.

'It's made from a special powder called *prah*,' he answered, his tone almost clinical. 'We sometimes call it gypsy dust. It's mixed with regular ink and injected into the skin using a special needle.'

I remembered seeing the strange silver ink during my tattoo session, but I hadn't actually watched Hugo carve the design into my wrist. 'But why did you do this?' I held out my hands. The claws looked hideous, sprouting from my nail beds like gray teeth. 'And what does it have to do with these? Or what just happened?'

'I branded you because you were showing signs of emerging, Sebastian. The difficulty sleeping, the complaints about your back. And then the way you've been acting lately, with all your erratic emotions. My parents told me what to watch for, before they left you in my care.'

My head swam. 'They knew about this?'

'It's why they took you in.'

'You aren't making sense,' I growled, wishing I could remember more about my own past. Or my foster parents. 'Emerging from what?' I stood and moved to the counter, running my hands through my hair. As I did, I caught myself in the mirror: my thick claws, pewter hair, and pallid complexion. My breath lodged painfully in my lungs. 'Hugo, what . . . what *am* I?'

He stared at me for a long moment.

'You're a guardian, Sebastian.' Hugo retrieved a large leather-bound book with gilt-edged pages from behind the counter. I recognized it as the one he'd been looking at the night my hair had turned gray. 'You're the product of a blood feud,' he continued. 'One that started a long time ago. Being a guardian is your duty.'

It felt as though a heavy weight had fallen on me. 'And who am I supposed to guard?'

Hugo dropped the book on the counter. It landed with a resounding thud. 'Us.'

'The Corsi clan?'

He nodded.

'From who?'

'The Outcasts have always had enemies. When I said clans don't always get along, I meant it. Some view us as renegades, living outside Gypsy law. And believe me, stuff like that isn't taken lightly among the Roma. But it's not just Gypsies that we have to worry about. There are other things out there, too.'

'You mean the visitors from the other night.'

'It's why we keep a low profile.'

My mind went to Josephine and the Romanys. 'Do all the Outcasts have . . . protectors?'

'Most of them, yes. But guardians like you are rare these days. You could say you're a unique case.'

I didn't like the sound of that. 'There are other people like me?'

'You're not a person, Sebastian. You're a guardian.' He moved to the large Gypsy painting and ran his hand purposefully over the canvas, pausing near the top. Though I'd studied the scene a hundred times before, I suddenly noticed something new. Hidden in a grove of trees, so faint that I almost missed it, was a gray creature. Eyes glinted from a formless face, its gaze fixed on the Gypsy bonfire.

I backed away, catching my leg on the edge of the couch. 'What is that thing?'

'We've been keeping an eye on you, waiting to see if you were really what my parents claimed. That's why I haven't said anything before now. Even with your hair and everything, I wasn't convinced, but now, we know. I'm sorry, Sebastian, but it's only a matter of time before your body catches up to your calling.'

'Well, can't you stop it?' I said, hearing panic in my voice. 'Remove the tattoo, or ink over it or something? I don't want to be this guardian thing!'

'It's not the tattoo that's changing you,' said Vincent. 'It's who you are.'

'When the Outcasts fled Europe, back in the day,' continued Hugo, 'a lot of knowledge about guardians was lost or reduced to stories. And what resources we do have aren't very reliable. For instance, you shouldn't have been able to hurt me once I branded you.' Hugo touched his bandaged cheek. 'But obviously, you did. So there's something missing in the process. Something I haven't figured out yet.'

'But . . . '

'I'm trying to get some answers,' said Hugo, cutting me off. 'I want to help you, but you're going to have to trust me.'

There was that word again. 'Hugo, I'm trying to believe that. But all these secrets . . . '

'Are for your own protection.' Hugo's voice went cold. 'You don't know what you're capable of.'

I glanced at the gauze on Hugo's face. I remembered the way my body had reacted to his threats. The dark emotions that built up inside me until they exploded. The surge of instincts I couldn't control. I hadn't felt scared then, but I did now, so much so, that I couldn't stand anymore. I sank down onto the sofa. 'What *am* I capable of?'

Vincent stood. 'You need to show him, Hugo. You can't protect him anymore.'

The two friends faced each other. My brother's glare was dark, commanding. But Vincent stood his ground. I could sense the unspoken agreement of the others. Hugo's hand strayed to the book, his finger tracing the edge.

'What's with the art book?' I asked.

'It's not art,' he replied, his voice was a heavy, resigned sigh. 'It's history.' He opened it, flipping through several pages. I watched in hushed expectation. He stopped somewhere in the middle and turned the book around. 'Here, Sebastian,' he said, holding it out to me. 'This is who you are.'

I hesitated a moment, then moved forward. I took the book in my clawed hands and retreated to the far wall. The decorated pages were old, many of them torn. The section Hugo had indicated was filled with ornate pictures and flowing script. Some of the writing was in French, but the other languages were unfamiliar. At the top of the left page was a header.

Gargouilles et Chimera

Directly below were several drawings, all depicting ancient cathedrals and cemeteries. The largest picture – old and painstakingly done – was of the famous Cathedral of Notre Dame in Paris.

'I don't understand,' I said, looking up.

'Turn the page.'

I grasped the paper gently and flipped it over. Pictures of the cathedral's legendary gargoyles filled the page, a collection of strange animals and grotesque faces.

I turned the page again.

While the previous images had been somewhat familiar, the next set of drawings was not. These statues weren't animals, but human. Some sported large wings. Others had brutal horns, sharp claws, and thrashing tails. All wore the same fierce expression as they stared down from their pedestals and ledges like frozen guardians.

Guardians.
Gargoyles.

'What is this?' I whispered, my throat constricting.

Hugo's gaze was steady. 'Your brethren.'

I slammed the book closed. 'A gargoyle?' I stared in disbelief. 'You think I'm a *gargoyle?*' The others stared levelly back at me. I shoved the book into Hugo's hands and pressed against the wall. 'You guys have been sniffing ink way too long.'

'So says the guy with gray hair,' muttered Kris.

My knees gave way and I slid to the floor. 'No,' I said hoarsely. I shook my head back and forth, trying to rid myself of the images I'd just seen. I was sick. I wasn't some stone-faced beast. 'That's impossible.'

Hugo knelt in front of me. 'No, it's not. Guardians have been around for centuries. They're an important part of our history. They've always protected us.'

'I'm not a gargoyle, Hugo.'

My brother kept talking. 'There's a reason my parents brought you to us. A reason we need protecting. I don't know what it is yet, but I'm going to find out.' His voice sounded distant, as though he was underwater. 'Do you hear me, Sebastian?'

I leaned against the wall. The paint felt cool against my skin, but the rest of me was on fire. This was worse than going insane. This was a nightmare. I clenched my hands, then jerked in surprise. I raised them to my face. The claws had disappeared. I stared, refusing to believe it at first, and I flexed my fingers tentatively, afraid they would suddenly return. But they didn't. I had normal fingernails again. I breathed a ragged sigh of relief. 'They're gone . . . '

'I told you,' Hugo said. 'The process has just started.'

Anger flared inside me.

146

'And I told you,' I replied, pushing myself to my feet. 'I'm not a gargoyle, and I don't want anything to do with your superstitious Gypsy lore. Whatever you did to me with that ink, I want you to fix it.'

'I can't,' he said lowly. 'Not until I find out exactly what's going on. I went up to Chattanooga today, looking for answers. It was a dead end, but I'm not done. We're going to help you through this.'

I bit my lip, staring at the floor. The tone of Hugo's voice held finality. My simmering anger fizzled as quickly as it had come. 'All right, so when you do, when you find out what's going on with me, will I be . . . okay . . . again?'

Hugo didn't blink. 'You'll be fine.'

His assurance rang hollow in my ears. I squeezed my eyes shut with such force that my sockets ached. But when I opened them, the nightmare remained. The guys looked at me with expressionless faces. How could things possibly be fine after this? Was I supposed to learn how to tattoo while dealing with disappearing and reappearing claws? Find a way to explain my stupid anger management issues to a client if I suddenly lost control?

The book seemed to glare mockingly at me from Hugo's hands. My head ached. I just wanted to look normal, to feel normal again. But could I trust my brother after the way he'd been acting?

Did I really have a choice?

'What am I supposed to do?' I asked wearily.

'Go to bed,' he replied. He tucked the book under his arm and moved to the doorway. 'The best thing for you now is to remain with us. Stay here until I've had a chance to get some answers. Don't worry, Sebastian,' he said as he crossed the room, 'you belong to us now.'

His words echoed ominously in the room.

14. To Be or Not To Be

'Lights up! Lights up!'

The stage manager flew by, barking into his headset. I recoiled into the shadows to avoid any unprovoked verbal abuse. I couldn't believe we were well into our performance of *A Midsummer Night's Dream*. But the demanding pressure of the show had been one of the best things to happen to me over the last two weeks. It kept me busy at school.

And away from the shop.

Hugo insisted I stay at home and, for the most part, I did. I knew he felt better when he could keep his eye on me. But there'd been no more incidents since that night. The claws hadn't reappeared, and as long as I wore my hood and mumbled excuses about lingering health issues, I could pretend none of it had happened, which is exactly what I'd been doing. Because there was no way I was going to let this condition, or whatever it was, keep me from the school play.

Or the chance to see Josephine.

Being near her was the only thing that felt right. Not that I'd talked to her. I didn't really talk to anybody. Not anymore. I couldn't explain what was going on with me, so it was easier to function as a shadow: going to school, attending rehearsals, and hiding at home. It was amazing how quickly people were willing to leave me alone. But it was awful. I didn't *want* to be this person I was turning into: the freaky recluse. I felt lost.

'You don't look so good.'

I whirled around, almost hitting Brandon who was dressed to the hilt as Lysander. He swept back his cloak, proudly displaying his costume, which included a very cool theatrical sword. He was the poster boy for confidence, something I was seriously lacking these days.

I pushed down a twinge of jealousy. 'What?'

'You look like you're about to puke your guts out, man.'

'Oh.' A bead of sweat trickled down my neck. I was just a few scenes away from being onstage with *her*. My face twisted, and Brandon shot me a look that bordered on alarm. 'Just stage fright,' I insisted.

'Okay,' he said, as if he wasn't totally convinced. 'Well, break a leg. I hear my cue.'

He slipped through the curtains, and I sighed in relief. But as I peered through the opening, air hitched in my throat. Josephine was gliding across the stage.

Her hair was curled and woven with green ribbons that spilled down her back. The dress she was wearing – her Titania costume – rolled off her shoulders like a Greek toga, falling in gentle folds, clinging to every curve.

I was scared to move, afraid I would miss something she did or said. I wanted to be near her, wanted to feel that chaotic tranquility again. The more I thought about being around her, the more I felt my emotional control slipping, like when Hugo had threatened me. My breathing grew shallow, the edges of my vision blurred with a strange tunneled effect. I gripped the curtain for support.

'Hey, you! Stay out of the wings!'

I leapt back at the voice. The curtain ripped, fabric coming away in my fingernails.

In my claws.

I panicked, ducking my hands behind my back as the stage manager's eyes bugged out of his head. He stared at the massively thick curtain. It looked as if someone had taken lawn shears and shredded it. While he gaped, I took the opportunity to make a hasty retreat to the empty dressing room. Once there, I frantically rubbed my hands together.

'No, please. Not now. Not now.'

I flexed my fingers, and closed my eyes, willing the disgusting claws to disappear. I *had* to get through this night. I had to prove to myself I could be normal and then I could prove to Hugo that he was wrong, and that it was all going to get better. After a few minutes – and several prayers – I looked at my hands. I had fingernails again. I sputtered in relief. It was my jittery nerves. I'd gotten too worked up, like the night in the shop. But the claws were gone now. I was okay.

The door opened abruptly, and I was taken captive by the make-up crew, who were assigned the task of getting me into the donkey make-up I'd need for my next scene. Ten minutes later, I was waiting in the wings with my huge donkey ears and painted face.

The time had come to make a literal ass of myself onstage. I shook my stiff limbs and flexed my muscles, determined to be the best Nick Bottom in all of amateur theater history. But as I opened my mouth to practice my opening line, a fragrance filled my nostrils, and sent me reeling in tortured pleasure.

'I just wanted to say break a leg,' said Josephine brightly. 'You're going to do great.'

I grinned sheepishly, at a total loss for words. It was the first time we'd spoken, apart from running lines, since our rehearsal in her trailer. 'You too. I mean, with the breaking of the leg.'

Ms Lucian appeared out of the darkness, dressed in black. Her red-streaked hair was tucked behind a headset. 'Are you two ready?' she asked. I nodded, donkey ears flopping. Josephine laughed. I blushed. Ms Lucian pointed with her pencil. 'I'm afraid you're going to have to take that off,' she said. 'No jewelry onstage.'

Josephine touched the ribbon at her neck, and the dandelion pendant sparkled under the blue work lights. I blinked hard against a rush of dizziness. Her fingers closed around the glass. 'But I've had it on the whole time,' she protested.

'It was only just brought to my attention by the stage manager,' said Ms Lucian. 'But don't worry. I'll hold onto it for you.'

The feverish sensation was back, smothering me with heat, making me woozy. My wrist throbbed to the beating of the blood in my veins. It seemed as though the closer I was to Josephine, the most lopsided I became. The drama teacher held her hand out expectantly for the necklace, but Josephine hesitated.

'I can't,' she said.

'And why is that?' asked Ms Lucian.

Josephine shrugged apologetically. 'I know this sounds silly, but I promised someone that I wouldn't.'

Ms Lucian shifted her gaze to me. 'Something wrong, Sebastian?'

'No,' I replied quickly.

'Please, Ms Lucian,' Josephine continued, 'I'll make sure it's hidden under my costume.'

To prove her point, she tucked the pendant inside the fabric of her gown. I felt instantly better, as if someone had mercifully turned the thermostat down a few degrees.

'All right,' Ms Lucian relented. 'But keep it out of the stage lights. It casts a horrible reflection.'

She gave us a parting nod and disappeared into the backstage abyss. My head swirled with another rush of heat, and I glanced over to see Josephine playing with the necklace once more, her graceful fingers running along the glass casing. The dandelion seemed to come alive under her touch.

'You like to look at this, don't you?' Josephine asked suddenly. My eyes snapped wide as I met her gaze. 'I've noticed you doing it a lot, whenever you're looking at me.'

The blood drained out of my face. 'I'm sorry.'

'Don't apologize, Sebastian. I'm flattered, really.'

I grasped for something that wouldn't make me sound crazily obsessed. 'It's the Gypsy thing. I've got one, too. I mean, not a necklace, of course. The dandelion.' Geez, I was rambling like an idiot. Impulsively, I pulled up my tunic sleeve and showed her. Other than Avery, no one had seen my artwork outside of the shop.

Josephine reached out, as though she was going to touch the design, then pulled back. 'It's beautiful,' she said, leaning in to examine the tattoo. My wrist ached, and my head went all fuzzy again. 'The Romanys use dandelions in our family crest. We have them in the Circe logo, too.'

'And then, there's your pendant,' I added. 'You said it was a family heirloom, right?'

She tucked the necklace inside her toga with one hand and tugged at a ringlet of hair with the other. 'Quentin said it belonged to his grandmother, and he wanted me to have it.' A stain of pink graced her cheeks and she looked away. 'We're sort of promised to each other. I know that sounds weird to *gadje*, and most outsiders don't understand our ways.'

I worked hard to produce a smile. 'Well, I'm not *gadje*, remember?'

Josephine smoothed a few wrinkles in her costume and played with the braided cord at her waist. 'It's not a law or anything, but it's a tradition, and it's expected . . . especially in my case.' A strange look flickered over her face, and she continued at a rapid pace. 'I mean, with my family. Anyway, Quentin and I practically grew up together. He's a great guy, and I love him.'

It was like falling face first into a snowdrift. I pressed harder against the wall to steady myself. The intensity of my reaction threw me. The only girl I'd ever felt something for was completely out of reach – that was bad enough – but my erratic emotions were getting out of control. What did this have to do with the stuff Hugo claimed I was going through? I shook myself off. Josephine was looking at me oddly, and I knew I had to say something.

'Well . . . ah. . . break a leg.'

Josephine's brows shot up, and she laughed. 'Thanks, Sebastian. You're sweet. You're the strangest person I think I've ever met, but you're sweet.'

At that moment, the stage manager materialized, tapping his foot impatiently. 'It's your cue, Titania.'

'See you on stage,' she said to me. Then she turned on her heel and followed the stage manager around the curtain.

I stood there, shaking from head to toe. Fifteen minutes before, I'd been ready for our scene. Now, I wasn't sure I would survive it. The music faded, and the lights dimmed on our Athenian woodlands. On the other side of the stage, Josephine emerged, taking her place on Titania's fairy bed. She closed her eyes in pretend sleep, and the stage manager signaled my cue. I adjusted my donkey ears, mustering my courage.

And stepped out into the light.

'O monstrous! O strange!' shouted Quince, pointing at me. 'We are haunted!'

The other actors yelled, running away in feigned terror. The audience laughed.

'I see their knavery,' I recited, faithfully. 'This is to make an ass out of me, if they could, but I will not stir from this place, do what they can. I will walk up and down here, and I will sing that they will hear I am not afraid.'

There was a rustle in the air as Josephine moved behind me. Her touch was soft against my shoulder. I'd never felt so drawn to anyone or anything in my entire life. It was more than attraction or longing.

It was like being home.

'Out of this wood do not desire to go,' she purred into my donkey ear. 'Thou shalt remain here, whether thou wilt or no.'

Josephine led me to Titania's fairy bed, but I may as well have been on a trip to my own coffin. I was twisted up inside; a packaged deal of stage fright and embarrassment, with the added torture of being so near Josephine that I could see the pulse beating in her neck. I sprawled out among the flowers as a dozen glittering fairies surrounded me. Josephine hovered closer.

Her fingers played along my arm while fairy girls danced around me. I was going complete cartoon-character goofy, and I knew that if I didn't pull myself together, I was going to ruin the scene. I stared over the audience, focusing on the wall and trying to keep my composure, as Josephine swooned. Then, without warning, movement in the back of the house caught my attention.

154

Three cloaked figures glided through the doors. They moved with a heavy – though graceful – gait, taking up positions against the wall. The strange visitors from Hugo's shop. Tendrils of mist floated above them like cigarette smoke, barely visible in the darkened auditorium. Then I felt it – that uncomfortable coldness in my gut – like a warning beacon. Everything around me faded, including Josephine. All I could see were the figures.

'Sebastian, it's your line!'

I met the gaze of a panicked fairy. *My line? I had a line?* My mind was blank, and I could only stare dumbly back at her.

'Sebastian?'

My eyes darted to Josephine. That weird place inside me ignited, snapping something to life: an uncontrollable instinct. A desire to protect. It was so strong that I bolted to my feet. The figures hovered near the aisle. My lip curled, and I stepped in front of Josephine. Red haze filtered through my vision as a growl rumbled deep in my chest. I forgot about my lines, the play, and everyone else. All that mattered was protecting Josephine.

'Sebastian, please . . . '

Her soft voice cut the haze. Her eyes were wide and pleading. Slowly I became aware of the awkward tension, both on the stage and in the audience.

And I was the cause.

The stage manager's face jutted through the curtain. 'Finish the scene!' he whispered frantically.

Finish the scene.
Finish the scene.
Finish the scene.

Everything shattered into clarity as my senses rushed back. Every eye was on me, everyone waiting for me to continue.

Josephine touched my arm. I took a deep breath and looked to the back of the house.

The figures were gone.

I quarantined myself in the dressing room, scrubbing off the remains of my make-up. The play had recovered from my freak-out and continued without a hitch, and the audience rewarded our efforts with a standing ovation.

After patting my face with a towel, I studied myself in the mirror, dismayed. My skin was ashen, my eyes strangely bright above the darkened circles. I could ignore Hugo's words about guardians and brands all I wanted, but it didn't matter.

I *was* changing.

The rest of the cast had cleared out by the time I left the dressing room, but I huddled deeper into my hooded jacket anyway. I didn't want to see anyone after the evening's fiasco. Unfortunately, I wasn't going to get that lucky. As I rounded the corner, there was Josephine, her back to me, talking on her cell. She'd changed into her street clothes, but her hair was still in its Grecian ringlets, the green ribbons fluttering as she moved.

'No, Quentin,' she was saying. 'I already made plans. I know you're looking out for me, but I'll be fine.' She listened for a moment then sighed loudly. 'All right.' There was disappointment in her voice. 'I'll see you tonight.'

She ended the call and rammed her phone into her bag. I'd never seen her flustered or irritated before. Butterflies skittered in my stomach, and I knew I needed to just turn and walk away. But I couldn't master the strong compulsion to stay near her.

'Hey, Josephine,' I said with some hesitation. She gasped in surprise and whirled around, dropping her bag. I flushed and knelt down to pick it up.

156

'Hey, Sebastian,' she said, taking the bag from my limp fingers. 'Thanks.'

'I'm really sorry about tonight,' I said.

Her smile was polite but unengaged. 'Don't worry about it. Stage fright happens to everybody.'

I studied her face from the safety of my hood. Her thoughts were clearly somewhere else. 'Are you okay?' I ventured, hoping she wouldn't think I'd been eavesdropping on her phone call.

She looked at me a moment without speaking. Silence fell between us; not uncomfortable, but electrically charged. I took an uncertain breath, waiting.

'Sebastian, could you drive me home?' she asked suddenly. 'That is, unless you're planning on going to the cast party. I didn't think you would, you know, since you've been so distant the last couple of weeks . . . ' She trailed off, and the same faint blush returned to her cheeks. 'I'm sorry. I didn't mean it like that.'

She was right, of course. I had been distant and I wasn't going to the party. The remainder of my Friday evening plans consisted of picking up fast food and locking myself in my bedroom. That was, until now.

'I'd love to,' I said.

Josephine seemed relieved. 'I'll get my things and meet you out front, okay?'

I nodded, dazed at my stroke of good luck. 'Okay.'

Josephine took off down the hall. My heart went into palpitations, slamming crazily against my ribcage.

'Hey, Sebastian!'

Katie was jogging towards me, and I met her halfway. I hoisted her up, swinging her in a wide circle. She shrieked and wriggled in my grasp until I released her.

'You were great tonight, Katie.'

She stared at me as if I was crazy. 'Wow, what happened to you?'

I grinned guiltily. 'Sorry.'

'Totally not complaining,' Katie laughed. 'It's good to see you acting almost normal again. What's the cause of this good mood of yours?'

'I'm driving Josephine home tonight.'

Katie raised an eyebrow. 'How'd you swing that one?'

I shrugged.

'You realize she's with Quentin, right? They're like, practically engaged.'

Leave it to Katie to state the obvious.

'I know that.' What I didn't know was what to make of my feelings. I *did* know I was supposed to be close to Josephine, but there was no way I could explain that to Katie. 'Since I'm not going to the cast party, I suppose that made me the obvious choice.'

'Oh.' Katie frowned. 'I thought you meant *after* the party. I can't believe Josie's not going. Guess she's too busy, what with the Circe opening soon. But I really wish you would go, Sebastian.' Her blue eyes darkened with concern. 'You need to get out more.'

'We'll hang soon,' I replied, reaching for her hand. I'd missed Katie's friendship the last few weeks more than I could tell her. But I had too much to sort out, too many questions without answers. 'I promise.'

Her face relaxed and she gave my hand a squeeze. 'I'm holding you to that, you social invert. Now, I've got to get going. I told Mitchell I'd ride with him.'

Katie sprinted off, and I hurried down the stage steps. A few people still loitered in the aisles. I studied the back doors.

Had the mysterious figures been real or just a hallucination? Reality was getting difficult to decipher these days.

Josephine met me in the lobby. We climbed into my van and made our way through town. We rode in silence for a while, which suited me fine. Just being with her felt right and nothing else really seemed to matter.

The quiet was broken with a single word.

'So.'

Josephine leaned against the door, her body turned in my direction. The glittery remains of her fairy make-up made her eyes sparkle like emeralds.

'So,' I replied.

She tucked a green ribbon behind her ear. 'We haven't really gotten a chance to talk much lately.'

'I know,' I said guiltily. I'd wanted nothing more than to talk to Josephine, but I didn't trust my social skills anymore. 'And it's totally my fault. Hugo's kept me really busy at the shop.'

'Have you worked in the tattoo shop a long time?'

I nodded, thankful for the question. It was always easy to talk about the *Gypsy Ink*. 'Yes. Well, since Hugo took me in. I'm hoping he'll let me work there, after graduation. He finally agreed to apprentice me and teach me the trade.'

'Sounds like a career that suits you,' she replied. 'Katie showed me some pictures of the set work you did on last year's play. You've got some serious art skills.'

I tried to control the surprise riding across my face. Josephine and Katie had obviously talked about me on more than one occasion. But instead of boosting my confidence, the knowledge only fueled my nerves. 'Thanks. I've always liked drawing and painting. Who knows, maybe I'll go to art school one day.'

'Katie said you moved to Sixes a couple of years ago,' Josephine continued. 'Where'd you live before here?'

The shift in conversation caught me off guard. 'Different places.'

'Like where?' she asked, sounding genuinely curious.

I sighed, feeling embarrassed, like I usually did when someone asked about my past. Normally I'd just play it off, but for some reason, I couldn't do that with her. 'Before living with the Corsis, I was in a group home,' I said, keeping my eyes on the road. 'At least, that's what they tell me.'

'What do you mean?'

I gnawed on my lower lip, a habit I seemed to be developing around her. 'There was a car accident, according to my case file. I suffered some head trauma, but I lived. My parents didn't. So I ended up in the care of the state.'

Josephine gasped. 'Oh, God, I'm sorry! That must have been horrible.'

'I guess it would've been,' I replied with a shrug. 'But I don't remember any of it; not my parents, not the accident. To tell the truth, I barely even remember the Corsis. My time with them just sort of runs together in my head. In fact, nothing really fell into place for me until I came to live with Hugo.'

'And it doesn't bother you?' Josephine's forehead creased. 'Not knowing, I mean.'

'Well, I'm just used to not knowing,' I replied. 'Actually, I haven't ever told anybody this before, but the truth is, I don't think I really *want* to know. The past is the past, kind of like a door that's bolted and locked from the other side. I can't do anything about it, so I guess I've just accepted it.'

'You don't strike me as the accepting-your-fate kind of guy.'

'Well, I'm very multi-layered.'

I felt her smile, but she pressed on. 'If I had that much empty space in my life, it would be hard for me to accept it. Everything has a place and a purpose, and it would eat me up inside, not knowing what that was.'

I tugged at my collar. It was getting hot inside the van. 'I never thought of it like that.'

'How old were you?' she asked softly.

'Fifteen.'

We both fell silent. I could almost read Josephine's thoughts as she pondered my answer. After a few moments, I heard her gentle intake of breath.

'But that's practically your entire life.' Her voice had the quality of someone at a funeral; trying to be as delicate as possible with a difficult subject. 'I can't imagine not remembering my whole childhood.'

'It's okay, Josephine, really. Like I said, I know how it sounds, but it's true. It doesn't bother me that much. I have a life here now, and I've got my whole future ahead of me.'

'And you've got a lot more restraint than most,' she replied. She twisted her hair ribbons around her finger, pulling them taut and letting them go again. 'Personally, I don't like the unknown. When I have questions about something, I have to find out the answers. I guess you could say I'm a little neurotic that way.'

I caught the point. My mysterious lack-of-life was on her radar now. Her curiosity was giving me an excited, terrified buzz. But as much as I wanted to know about her, I didn't want to know any more about myself. I put on an easy smile, ready to change the subject. 'So what about you? Where've you lived?'

She hesitated, then returned my smile. Her brow smoothed. 'Well, we don't really *live* anywhere for long. We have certain towns, like Sixes, where we'll stay for a while, but mainly we just travel around. I've been all over the South and even up the East Coast and into Canada. With all our traveling, it's hard to keep up with schoolwork. I love coming here, because I actually get to attend school like a regular person. I know I said I don't always feel comfortable around *gadje* because of the distance I have to keep, but sometimes, it feels good being considered just a normal, run-of-the-mill teenager.'

'Yeah, I miss that,' I said under my breath, before I could stop myself.

She sat up in the seat. 'Ah, so you're saying you used to be normal?'

I chuckled and tried to ignore the blood rushing to my head. 'Oh, definitely not. I've always been a little off, no question about that.'

'And lately?'

'Lately,' I said in my best, easy-going voice. 'I've been insane. Nothing a strait-jacket couldn't cure, though.' I forced a laugh and immediately steered the conversation back to Josephine. 'So, do you like it? The Circe, I mean.'

She took the conversation offering, though not without a curious lift of her brows. 'Well, I don't know any different. It's been my life since I was born. It's difficult sometimes,' she continued, her tone growing serious. 'The traveling, never settling down, always working. And we've really been under a lot of pressure. Quen . . . my parents have been hard on me. I don't have much free time.'

'That sounds rough.'

'It's okay. But it's been nice doing the play. It's something outside of the Circe, you know? Quentin didn't approve, but my parents convinced him I needed a little break.'

'Why didn't he approve?' I asked, cautiously.

162

'Long story,' she sighed.

Another lull fell between us. It seemed we both had things we wished to keep to ourselves. I turned onto Fairground Drive, not realizing how dark it had become until we emerged from the thick canopy of trees. I squinted, finding it difficult to see.

So much for my weird night vision ability.

I pushed the thought from my mind. I didn't want to think about what was going on with me. The whole seeing in the dark thing had only happened that one time, anyway.

'Everyone loved your performance tonight,' I said, eager for more conversational distraction.

'Well, just for the record, you did a great job as Nick Bottom,' she replied. 'Not everyone can pull off the donkey ears, you know.'

'Thanks. Too bad they don't have an awards category for that.'

'You should audition for more shows, Sebastian.'

'I like theater and all, but the spotlight's not for me. I don't do well with the attention. I never have.' I shrugged and gave a short laugh. 'Maybe that's why I've got friends like Katie and Avery. It makes things easier.'

'Makes what easier?' she asked.

I shifted in my seat. I wasn't used to all this soul bearing. 'I don't know. Blending into the background, maybe? I've always felt that's where I fit. But that probably doesn't make too much sense.'

'You know, not everyone chooses to hide in the background,' Josephine said in a soft voice. 'Some of us can do it right in the middle of the limelight.'

I glanced sideways at her. 'Why would someone like you need to hide?'

When Josephine didn't reply, I turned my head to get a better look. Her lips were pressed close together, and I saw the delicate movement of her neck as she swallowed. Here it was again: a glimpse into the mysterious levels of her life, but this time, I wasn't going to let the door close so quickly.

'Josephine?'

She jerked, coming back from her thoughts. Her lips softened. 'Sorry, I just mean I think everyone needs to get away from the pressure of life.' Her shoulders rose, then dropped. 'My family is kind of . . . important to the Outcast clans. My father is in charge of a lot of stuff, and well, we just have a different status than the others. Makes it kind of hard to hide, sometimes. But I've gotten pretty good at it, when I want to.'

So, Josephine was more than just the daughter of the circus boss. I wondered what pressures she dealt with; what was so overwhelming that she'd want to hide. I'd made some progress, but I wasn't going to train-wreck it. One level at a time.

'Well, you were a great Titania,' I said, turning my attention back to the road and tugging on my hood. I could feel the weight of Josephine's stare, even though my eyes were fixed ahead. 'I just hate that I almost screwed up our scene, especially after all the work we put into it.'

There was a long pause.

'What did you see out there tonight?' she asked.

My hands tightened on the steering wheel.

'Nothing.'

'Sebastian, I *know* you saw something,' she pressed, her voice eager. 'This look came into your eyes; scary intense, just like that time in rehearsal when Alex threatened you, and then once, when I was with Quentin. Your face changes and your eyes get . . . strange.'

'Strange?'

'They take on this sheen like . . . ' Josephine puckered her lips in thought. ' . . . like silver.' She frowned. 'I don't know you very well, Sebastian. And you've always seemed a bit out there, not that it bothers me or anything. But lately, you just been . . . well . . . different.'

'Maybe a little,' I replied. It felt like a confession.

'Does it have to do with me?'

My stomach bottomed out. 'What do you mean?'

'I don't know. It's just that, whenever you're around me, you act really weird.'

'I'm sorry.'

'No, don't be.' She smiled. 'You apologize too much.'

'I'm sor . . . '

I cut myself off before I could finish, and she laughed. I couldn't help laughing back. The Sutallee Bridge rose before us, looking less like Norman Rockwell and more like something out of *The Legend of Sleepy Hollow*. A dense fog had begun to roll in, settling heavily across the road.

My van crept across the bridge, the old planks creaking under the wheels. Trees moaned eerily under the weight of a sudden breeze, and they flung their leaves across the gravel. I pressed on the gas, eager to reach the Circe. The mist was at the level of my windows, reducing visibility. It curled against the glass, staring at me without eyes. A cold tingle spread from the base of my skull.

This was no ordinary fog.

'In all seriousness, Sebastian,' Josephine continued, 'you look different these days, too. I thought it was just your hair, but it's more than that.' She leaned closer. 'There's something else going on, isn't there? Something besides being sick, like you told me before.'

I sank deeper into my hood, staring at the road. Her question hung unanswered between us. The fog continued to thicken, and my stomach turned as I felt a deep chill sinking into my bones. Josephine touched my shoulder.

'Is there anything I can do to help?' she began in her sweet voice. 'I just . . . '

Josephine's sentence died in her throat. A dark figure loomed in the middle of the road, directly in the path of my van.

I jerked the wheel. Josephine screamed. Brakes screeched and rocks spewed as we careered across the road. I whipped the van in the opposite direction but the gravel gave way, and we fishtailed off the road. The van ploughed into a tree. The sound of crumpling metal pierced my ears.

Then everything went silent.

15. *Free or Bound*

I was trapped in a timeless void. Only silence and stillness. When I forced my eyes open, I was staring at cracks in the windshield. Mist coated the glass. I smelled metal and dirt. The passenger side was caved in. The seat was crumpled where Josephine had been.

Josephine.

I jerked in panic. Then I felt arms. They clung to my neck. A head was pressed against my chest. Heavy breaths pierced my shirt, warming my skin. I noticed my arm around her waist, and I gulped.

'Josephine, are you all right?'

Her body jolted at my words, as though coming out of shock. Her arms slipped from my neck, and I was cold again. 'Yeah . . . I think so,' she murmured. 'What happened?'

Though I'd only caught a brief glance of the figure in the road, I knew I'd seen it before . . . I knew I'd seen *her* before. Goosebumps sprouted from my skin. I couldn't see anything outside but billows of fog. As much as I wanted to keep my arm around Josephine's waist, a stronger drive compelled me.

I had to protect her.

'Stay here.'

Josephine nodded, wide-eyed. I wrenched open the door, shoved down the lock, and shut the door firmly behind me. The mist was so thick that I could only guess at the placement of my feet. A breeze stirred, oddly warm, almost sickening. Or was it the stench in the air? I hunched forward, my skin crawling. The mist swirled and parted.

The figure was nowhere to be seen.

Something thumped above and behind me. I spun, skidding in the gravel. Another figure crouched atop the van. It was larger than the first and decidedly male. Mist clung to its body like a second skin. I couldn't see the face, but I could feel the mocking stare. The figure gripped the metal roof and leaned over the window. Josephine's face paled as she saw it, her terrified eyes luminous through the glass.

Her fear ignited something inside me. A fierce sound burst from my throat, and I lunged for the van. My foot connected with the front bumper, and I launched myself onto the hood. I landed on all fours, white-hot fire racing through my veins. I dove forward but tackled only air as the figure sidestepped and flung its arms wide. It lifted off the van and into the night. The mist engulfed it, and then, the figure was gone.

I stared at the spot where the figure had been moments before. Inside the van, Josephine was gaping at me, her hands pressed to the windshield. I sniffed the air. The stench was gone, too. I jumped to the ground, landing lightly in the gravel. I made a quick circuit around the vehicle.

The trunk of an oak tree was firmly embedded in the van's passenger side, and the front tire was mangled. There was no way we'd be driving the rest of the way to the Circe. I continued on around. Something white glinted against the back door handle. It was a scrap of paper, no bigger than a business card. There was writing on the paper, in a thick, heavy hand. Even in the darkness, it was easy to read.

This is a test.

I flipped the card in my hand. There was nothing on the other side. Kris's voice suddenly came back to me as he'd spoken to my brother.

'*Test him.*'

Hugo's test had ended with a slashed face. Now someone else was taking a turn? I shoved the paper into my pocket and surveyed the road. It was one thing to come after me. But Josephine could've been hurt. The thought sent fiery indignation through me. I could see the entrance to the Circe, just ahead. Good. I'd get Josephine to safety. Then, I'd come back and hunt these people down. And when I found them . . .

'Sebastian?'

I jerked so hard I nearly hit Josephine as she rounded the back of the van. She gasped and ducked out of the way. Her presence melted the haze in my head, and my heart instantly flew up my throat.

'I'm . . . sorry.'

Josephine didn't meet my eyes. She was staring at my hand, which was gripping the door handle. In the dim light, gray claws glinted inhumanly from my fingertips. I flinched and stuffed my hands into my pockets. Josephine looked dangerously close to horrified. 'Sebastian, how did you *do* that?'

My pulse raced, but I gritted my teeth, determined to stay calm. 'I was just trying to scare him off.'

'But you *leapt* on the roof!' She looked like she was trying to convince herself of what she'd seen. 'Like serious, Olympic kind of *leapt*!'

169

'Adrenaline kicked in, I guess.'

'And your hand . . . '

Don't panic, Sebastian.

'What? Oh, I just banged it on the van door.' I conjured up every peaceful thought I could come up with, willing calm into my body. I took a breath, and slid my hand from my pocket. 'See?'

Josephine studied my hand, which was, thankfully, just a normal hand, except for a slight discoloring along the edges of my nails. The strange residue actually looked kind of like bruising and helped my lie.

'Are you sure you're okay?' she asked.

The tone of her voice was laced with suspicion, and as she frowned up at me, I got the feeling she wasn't referring to my injury. We'd been dancing around secrets all night, and we both knew it. Another awkward moment slipped between us.

'Yeah, I'm fine,' I replied, finally. 'I'm just glad you're all right. If I'd reacted sooner, turned the other direction, maybe.'

'But you did react. I didn't even see it until . . . ' Josephine hugged her arms. 'Sebastian, what were those things?'

'They weren't things,' I said, sounding more sure than I felt. There was something inhuman about the way the figures had vanished. 'Just some drunks who wandered from the main road and got lost. They're gone now.'

'That one just stood there in the road, like it was asking to be hit.' Shock radiated from her voice as she stared ahead. 'If you hadn't swerved . . . ' Her hand flew to her mouth. 'Oh God, how's your van?'

'Not drivable, I'm afraid.'

She pulled out her cell phone and flipped it open. 'There's no service.'

170

'Not out here,' I answered, glancing at the heavy branches above the road. 'But we're pretty close to the Fairgrounds, if you don't mind walking.'

Josephine nodded. 'Yeah, let's get out of here. I'm really creeped out.'

And she definitely looked like it. I hovered close to her as we walked, constantly scanning the woods, the road, even the sky. I wanted her to feel safe with me, but inside, I was as freaked out as she was. Josephine's gaze strayed in my direction, and I wondered if I added to her fear by my actions, not to mention my pole-vaulting imitation.

Minus the pole.

We made our way along the road, and I listened to the padding of Josephine's feet on the gravel, the whisper in her throat as she breathed; the swish of ribbons against her long neck. It was unnerving how in tune I was to everything about her. I could also tell she wanted to say something, but we continued on in silence. Pale light from the lampposts illuminated the gate, and beyond the iron bars, lay shady outlines of tents and pavilions.

'You know,' said Josephine, gently breaking the quiet between us. 'I want you to consider me a friend.'

I stole a quick glance in her direction. 'Of course I do, Josephine.'

'So can we talk? I mean, about what's going on with you?'

I sucked in a breath then looked down to hide my alarm. What could I possibly say that wouldn't sound like I was crazy? 'It's nothing, really.'

'Sebastian.' The way she said my name gave me butterflies. She stopped walking and placed her hand on my arm. 'Please, tell me.'

My stomach knotted as I fought the urge to spill my guts right then and there. Josephine waited patiently, her eyes full and deep, like pools, sucking me in. I shoved my hands deeper into the pockets of my jeans.

'Well,' I began. 'A few weeks ago . . . '

The sound of boots crunching on gravel made me stop. The same instincts I'd fought with earlier kicked in. Before I could stop myself, I was in a crouch, upper lip curled back, fingers digging into the gravel. A strange noise welled up from my throat. Josephine cringed in surprise.

'Get behind me,' I hissed.

A man stepped from the darkness, lantern in hand, moving towards us like a ghost from another time. He wore a heavy cloak around his shoulders. He peered at us through the bars.

'Who are you? What are you doing here?'

I narrowed my eyes, sizing the man up and weighing my odds. He was roughly my build, maybe a little taller. I could take him. But another man appeared with a dark creature at his side. I smelled wet fur, heard the rattle of a chain, and a dog's low growl.

'I asked you a question, boy,' said first man. 'Now, answer me.'

'Phillipe?' said Josephine.

The man lifted the lantern higher. 'Josephine?'

'Yeah, it's me,' she replied, smiling in relief.

I rose from my crouch, coaxing my muscles to straighten. Arctic air blasted my insides as Quentin Marks materialized behind the others and moved into the lantern's glow. The light flickered over his face, shadowing his features.

'Josephine, where've you been?' he demanded. 'I thought you were getting a ride home.'

Quentin had already made it clear he didn't want me near his girlfriend. Once he heard what had just happened, I doubted he'd let Josephine out of his sight again. I squared my shoulders, ready for the worst.

'We had some car trouble, back at the bridge,' she replied. 'So we had to walk the rest of the way.'

I did my best to conceal my surprise. Josephine had every reason to bolt after everything she'd been through, and especially after what she'd seen *me* do. But as our eyes met, I didn't feel as if we were keeping secrets from each other. This time, we were sharing one. Was it possible that she felt some kind of connection to me, too?

Quentin unlocked the gate. 'Well, I want you inside. There's been a break-in at the Circe tonight.'

Josephine gasped. 'Is everyone okay?'

'Everyone's fine,' he replied. 'And we've just finished searching the grounds. The thieves are long gone. But your family's pretty shaken up. Let's get you inside, Josie. I know they'll want to see you.'

'But what about Sebastian?'

Quentin's steady gaze shifted to me. 'He can use my cell to call home.'

Despite his congenial expression, I got the feeling Quentin would've preferred bashing my head in with his phone rather than letting me use it. The muscles in my back went taut, but I managed to smile back at him with dead-calm politeness.

'Thanks.'

'We could give you a ride,' said Josephine.

Quentin's stare weighed about a thousand tons. My fingertips ached almost as much as my shoulders. I didn't want to risk another appearance of my claws or a slip of control. Tonight had been bad enough.

'The guys are at the shop,' I replied. 'They can be here in a few minutes.'

Josephine hesitated, and for a split second, I thought I saw something like regret in her face. But, then it was gone.

God only knew what she was thinking about me. 'Okay.' She slipped through the gate and turned to me. 'Thanks for everything, Sebastian. I guess I'll see you at school on Monday?'

'Sure thing,' I said, keeping my voice as casual as I could. Josephine vanished around a striped pavilion.

'I'm sure you want to let your brother know where to come pick you up,' said Quentin, holding out the cell phone.

He'd used that same tone with Josephine: deadly smooth, almost demanding. Someone accustomed to giving orders and having them followed. My insides bristled, and I clenched my hands into fists inside my jacket. 'No, thanks. I think I'll just walk home.'

'Have it your way.' Quentin stepped back and closed the gate. He regarded me coolly through the bars. 'But I'd be careful out there, if I were you.' He faded from view as the night closed in around him. 'You never know what's lurking around in the dark.'

16. Calm and Panic

No lights were on in the *Gypsy Ink* when I returned. Had Hugo gone again? The sign wasn't in the window, and the door was unlocked. An icy shiver crept up my arms. Something didn't feel right.

I pushed open the door, and as I did, a white object fluttered to the tile floor. It was another scrap of paper, and on one side – in the same heavy handwriting – was another message.

1163 Chimeras Street
Do not keep us waiting.

I shoved the paper in my pocket and eased the door shut. The air inside was stifling, like a humid summer night. The shop smelled of rotting fish. I lingered near the window, trying to see into the waiting room, but there wasn't enough light. I concentrated harder, and then, suddenly, my surroundings flashed into vivid detail, as though someone had switched on a lamp. My freaky ability was back. Slowly, I let myself adjust to my enhanced vision.

One purple couch was overturned, and magazines littered the floor. Wisps of mist clung to the walls. My shoulders contracted, and I forced them back. I inched closer. My movements were unnaturally silent. I gripped the edge of the counter and peered around it. There was a body on the floor, turned upward and lifeless.

It was Hugo.

My gut screamed a warning, and then something struck me from behind. Pain lanced my shoulders as I hit the counter. I tried to catch my balance, but the attacker engulfed me. We tumbled to the ground. Its weight crushed my lungs, and I struggled to break free. I shoved my feet into the dark mass, snarled, and kicked as hard as I could.

My attacker fell back and rolled into a crouch. A snarl of equal fury resonated from beneath the heavy clothing it wore. Instinct took over. I launched into the figure, hurtling us both into the wall. The picture over the counter jolted free and shattered. Glass sprayed across the floor.

His arm caught me across the mouth. I slid across the glass-strewn floor, shards embedding in my skin. The figure suddenly changed tactics and lunged for Hugo's lifeless body. I blocked his path, slashing at the air with my claws. The figure screeched and retreated. I leapt over my brother protectively, letting out a threatening hiss.

I braced for a counter-attack. But it never came. My attacker regarded me from under a deep hood. Despite my night vision, the face was lost in shadows. As I watched, mist formed out of nothing, growing so thick I couldn't see. In the space of a breath, it was gone. And it had taken the figure with it.

I glared at the empty shop, body shaking with adrenaline, daring the thing to return. Slowly the instinctive haze lifted and released me from its hold. I knelt over my brother's body. His face was deathly pale. I clasped his shoulders.

'Hugo!'

He was cold.

'Oh God . . . Hugo!'

I shook him, desperate. This wasn't happening. Why him? Hot tears pricked my eyes. I slumped forward, head bowed. Then a strangled cry interrupted my grief. Hugo's face twisted in pain.

'Let. Me. Go.'

I was still clutching his shoulders with an iron grip. Blood oozed between my fingers where my claws had pierced through shirt and skin. I jolted back in horror. Hugo pushed himself up, grunting in pain. Color seeped into his face, and his eyes cleared.

'Hugo, I thought you were dead.'

My brother didn't answer at first. He did a quick survey of his head, probing his temple. I noticed a small gash, like he'd hit his head. Then he examined his shoulder. Blood trickled down his arm from my clawed grip, and he brushed it away. His expression hardened like baked clay. 'What did you *do*, Sebastian?'

'I came in and saw you, and then someone . . . or something . . . attacked me. I tried to fight it off, but then the thing just vanished. I'm sorry. I didn't mean to hurt you.'

A wave of guilt careened into me. Hugo had been hurt, no, by the looks of it, nearly killed. If I'd been in the shop, if I'd stayed home like he'd wanted me to, then maybe I could have prevented this.

'That's not what I meant.' Hugo wobbled to his feet. He grimaced with the strain, but there was fire in his eyes. 'Who did you protect tonight, Sebastian?'

'What do you mean?'

His eyes narrowed. 'Who did you *protect*?'

'You, I guess,' I replied, confused. 'I mean, that . . . '

'No,' Hugo snapped. 'Not me. If it were me, you would've been here. Your instincts would've kicked in, and you would have *known* I was in trouble.' He stared me down, sending a chill up my spine. 'So I'm asking, for the last time. Who did you protect tonight?'

I clutched my head, feeling as if it was about to explode. Images of the dark figures at the Fairgrounds flashed through my mind. I could still feel the intense protective urges I'd been experiencing since . . .

'Josephine Romany,' I said suddenly.

A muscle in Hugo's neck bulged. The air between us hung heavy. My arm stung from the broken glass, but I didn't move, didn't breathe. He lumbered past me and collapsed into the armchair. His gaze drifted to the window.

'I should have realized it sooner,' he muttered. 'Or maybe I refused to see the obvious. You shouldn't have been able to hit me the other night, not if you were protecting me.' His brows knitted together. 'There's been a mistake.'

'A mistake with what?'

Hugo looked at me. 'Your charge.'

'My what?'

'The person you're meant to protect.'

My breath caught in my throat. 'You mean Josephine.'

Hugo's eyes narrowed dangerously. 'You're meant to protect us, not them. Something's interfering.'

'The Romanys,' I said quickly. 'There was a break-in at the Fairgrounds tonight. Maybe they were in some kind of danger?'

'Is that where you were?' Hugo scowled. 'I told you to come straight home after the play.'

'Josephine asked me for a ride.' My thoughts immediately went to her. I'd been trying to convince myself she was safe since I'd left her. 'Maybe I should go back to the Fairgrounds, just to make sure everything's okay.'

'No, Sebastian. That's the last thing you need to do.'

'But you just said I was supposed to protect her.'

'No, I didn't,' he replied curtly. 'I said there was a mistake. I don't want you getting involved with the Romanys.'

'What are you talking about, Hugo?' I gritted my teeth against another harsh emotional rush. 'I don't even know them. How can I be involved?'

He ignored my questions. 'Stay away from them.'

'I can't promise you that, Hugo,' I forced myself to take slow breaths. 'Especially when you're not giving me any reason why I should.'

My brother drew his shoulders back and glared at me. 'The Romanys have made some powerful enemies, Sebastian. Ones that you, of all people, don't need to come up against right now. You should've come home tonight, and you don't need to hang out with a member of their clan.' Hugo rubbed his arm, and his fingers came away stained with blood. 'You've done enough damage tonight. Let me handle this.'

I didn't budge. 'What was that thing? What did it want with you?'

'It doesn't matter.' His eyes took on an ominous glint. 'Let it go.'

My anger ignited again. 'Hugo, I found you lying on the floor. Attacked by some creature and unconscious! That's not something you just let go.'

My temperature was rising, and sweat beaded along my forehead. I pushed away from the counter and stomped through the waiting room's cluttered debris. Hugo shot to his feet and met me at the front door.

'What are you doing?' he demanded.

'Not letting it go,' I said. I zipped up my jacket. 'Don't worry, I won't be long.'

Hugo's silence followed me all the way to the parking lot.

In the past, the thought of my van abandoned on the side of the road would have bothered me. The old clunker was the only thing I'd ever called my own. But now, such things seemed unimportant. Let it get towed to a junkyard, for all I cared. I could manage.

The October night was crisp and clear. The stars sparkled above like flecks of glitter on a velvet canvas. I jogged across the road to the railroad tracks, which led straight into town. I leapt onto the rail, on a whim, but instead of teetering as I expected, my feet were steady on the narrow beam. Unnaturally steady. I dropped my arms to my sides and took several steps, testing my newfound balance. I took a cleansing breath of autumn air.

Then I started to run.

I sprang lightly on the balls of my feet, gliding along the rail. Each footfall was as sure as if I was running on the ground. I'd never had balance this good before, and the feeling was exhilarating, almost like flying. For a moment, I forgot about all the freaky stuff happening, and I felt myself grinning as I picked up speed. Main Street veered off to the left, but I stayed on the tracks, following them into Sixes' historical district.

I knew exactly where I was going: a section near the outskirts of town scheduled for renovation years ago but never completed. I leapt from the tracks, skidding down the gravel bank to the road I'd been searching for: Chimeras Street. The pavement was badly cracked and needed repair. Weeds poked through jagged fissures in the sidewalks, and rows of abandoned buildings stood forlornly on either side of the street.

It was like entering a ghost town.

The hair on my arms rose as I searched every broken window and board-covered door. I couldn't shake the feeling that I was being watched. I fished the second paper from my pocket, flipping it between my fingers. My claws had disappeared again, but my nails remained dark gray. I crumpled the paper in my fist. The faded numbers above store fronts and factory entrances took me closer to my destination.

1157 . . . 1159 . . . 1161 . . .

My feet stopped in front of a rusted gate that opened into a courtyard of dead grass and overgrown weeds. Looming before me was an ancient-looking cathedral, fashioned entirely out of gray stone. The lofty spires were a familiar sight; I'd observed their pointed tops many times from the window of the *Gypsy Ink*, all the way across town. But I'd never been this close to the building before. An old historical marker leaned against the front steps, its faded gold lettering barely legible.

Cathédrale de Gargouilles
Established 1832
Jacques Gringoire

Mossy vines grew rampant along the cracked walls. Portions of stained glass windows glistened through boarded slats. Along the rooftop, stone figures – some human-like, some animalistic – were silhouetted against the dusty sky. Their Gothic faces stared out over Chimeras Street with expressions of noble ferocity; mirror images of the drawings in Hugo's book. I shuddered and hurried up the marble steps.

Massive wooden doors groaned open on aureate hinges, ushering me inside a cavernous room. Dim light filtered through the space, illuminating the deteriorated remains of what had once been a beautiful sanctuary.

I hesitated, starting to regret my decision to come. I had no idea what I was dealing with. The air inside the cathedral was eerily warm, but my body felt frigid. Nervous sweat trickled down my back.

'Hello?'

My voice echoed back to me. I scanned the room and the rafters above, but I could see nothing. And then, a faint breeze began to stir. It moved through my hair and chilled my skin. Drifting on the gentle current was a voice.

'Welcome, Sebastian Grey.'

The blood crackled in my frozen veins. The voice didn't speak again, but I could feel something in the room with me. Seconds passed. Then minutes. I dropped into a crouch out of some instinctive urge.

Mist drifted between a row of immense columns, and from within the mist, four figures materialized. The first three were the mysterious creatures I'd already encountered. Each wore an array of gray-colored clothes, simple and non-descript. The two male figures flanked the female. Standing near the trio was a man with a tall, sturdy frame.

'Thank you for meeting with us,' he said.

'I didn't have much choice,' I snapped. 'You totaled my van and attacked my brother.'

Mist wafted around the female's face, and I felt her laughter. 'We're not your enemies, Sebastian.' Her voice was smooth and resonant.

The three figures circled me slowly. I couldn't keep my eyes on all of them at once, and I shifted around in my crouch, feeling trapped. 'You said you wanted to talk. So talk.'

The female figure was at my side – quicker than I'd have thought possible – and she crouched down, mimicking my posture. It was still difficult to see her through the shroud of mist and heavy clothing, but her foul smell burned my nose. 'So your little clan hasn't told you anything,' she mused.

My lip curled again; that same involuntary reaction I couldn't seem to manage. 'They're trying to protect me.'

'Are you sure about that?' she answered. 'Or are they trying to control you?'

'What do you mean?'

The tall man flicked his hand, and she cowered back. 'You'll have to forgive Anya,' he said. 'She's a bit impatient. He nodded at the others. 'Matthias, Thaddeus . . . give our guest some space.' The figures retreated to the columns as the man moved closer. 'You know, Sebastian Grey,' he continued, 'you were a difficult one to track down. The Corsi clan has hidden you well.'

I rose slowly. 'Who are you?'

He was obviously human, and mist didn't cling to him as it did the others. Dark wide-spaced eyes in a tanned face, which was framed with long black hair. A pinkish scar ran from his temple to the corner of his thin mouth. 'My name is Augustine,' he said, pulling his lips into a smile. 'It's a pleasure to finally meet you.'

'Not exactly the word I'd have chosen.'

The man – Augustine – strolled to the center of the room, seating himself on a discarded pew. 'You're right, Sebastian. Perhaps we did not go about this the best way. But, you see, we don't have a lot of time.'

My anger was slowly growing, replacing the nervous fear. 'Okay, so I'll make this brief,' I said. 'Starting with my brother. Why did you try to kill him?'

Anya drifted around the column. 'We never intended to kill him,' she answered. 'Otherwise, he'd be dead. We were merely seeking confirmation.'

'Of what?'

Augustine rubbed a finger along his scar, looking thoughtfully at me. 'Your existence, Sebastian. We had our suspicions, but couldn't be certain. You hadn't shown any physical signs of emerging.'

Damp hair clung to my forehead, and I shoved it away. 'So you've been looking for me.'

'Of course I have.' Augustine brushed invisible flecks of dust from his shirt and smoothed the fabric with a casual grace, as if we were having the most normal conversation in the world. 'Shadow creatures are quite rare these days, but gargoyles are even more so. Too many of your brethren have been destroyed over the centuries. To find an unsealed guardian like yourself is remarkable.'

'Hugo never said anything about a seal,' I said warily.

'Interesting.' He leaned forward, lacing his long fingers together. 'It would seem the Corsis are trying to manipulate this situation for their own purposes. You have, after all, been given a brand.'

I grabbed my wrist. 'How did you . . . '

'They sensed it,' Augustine said, gesturing to the three figures. 'The brand is the first step in an irreversible process to seal a guardian to his Gypsy charge.'

The others made eerie, hissing sounds.

Augustine held up his hand, and they fell silent. 'But I can offer you a way out.'

'A way out of what?'

He pressed his laced fingers to his lips, watching me carefully. 'Once a guardian is sealed, he becomes trapped in servitude

184

to the Gypsies. It is, of course, the reason the Corsis gave you that tattoo. What I couldn't figure out, however, is why Hugo Corsi hadn't sealed you to his clan. It made no sense.'

'A mistake,' I murmured, almost to myself. 'He said it was a mistake.'

Augustine's face went strangely blank. But then, his casual smile returned. 'That may very well be. Sadly, many of the intricate details surrounding gargoyle branding have been lost over the years. It is quite possible that he made an error. Or, there could be another explanation.'

I shifted impatiently. The man was irritatingly slow, as though he enjoyed drawing everything out. I wanted him to get to the point, but I forced myself to hold my tongue.

Augustine's brows drew together over his dark eyes. 'At first, I believed the Romany girl was simply a foolish romantic notion of yours, a pure coincidence. But Anya was suspicious. In fact, she observed the two of you together for some time before she ran your van off the road.'

I staggered under the force of his words. 'So that was the test?' I ripped the paper out of my pocket and flung it to the ground.

Augustine leaned back. 'We wanted to see what you would do, should the life of the girl be put in danger.'

Anya flitted closer. 'Plus, it was fun.'

A hot flash burned through me. 'You keep away from her.'

The three figures struck defensive postures. But Augustine merely crossed his arms nonchalantly over his chest. 'An impressive display of anger from one so young of your kind,' he remarked. 'Of course, that very trait – those primal, unrestrained emotions – is one of the reasons you're so easy to control. But the girl isn't our concern right now. You're our priority.'

'But why?' I demanded. 'I'm nothing special.'

'Are you so sure about that?'

Augustine gave a quick nod. The figures leapt forward. I ducked as an arm swung at my face. I rolled, coming up in a crouch, a hiss playing across my lips. I felt supercharged, ready for anything. Another movement caught my eye, and I lunged, knocking one of the males off his feet. The other rushed at me, and I whipped around, catching him by the throat. My fingers tightened. And then, I saw my horribly clawed hands. I recoiled from my attackers and backed against a column. The hard stone dug through my shirt.

Augustine looked pleased. 'Do you still think so, Sebastian Grey? Can you still pretend you're just like everyone else?'

I panted. 'What do you want from me?'

'We don't want anything from you,' he replied, sounding surprised. 'We came here to save you from *them*. We came to show you that you have a choice.'

'A choice in what?'

'In whom you're going to serve, Sebastian.'

An ominous silence permeated the sanctuary. Augustine and the gray figures looked at me expectantly. Then Anya approached. The mist peeled from her body, and I saw her clearly for the first time. Underneath the hood her skin was chiseled gray, like a marbleized statue come to life. Long hair shimmered like polished pewter, split on either side by demonically canted ears, framing a face highlighted in dark shadows. Silver eyes glittered in her shadowed face, and as she smiled, dark lips pulled back to reveal rows of sharp, jagged teeth. 'You see, little gargoyle fledgling,' said Anya, her voice haunting, 'you're one of us.'

'Not quite yet,' said Augustine, almost chiding. He kept his eyes on me. 'Right now, he's nothing but a Gypsy pet.

186

But you could be so much more, Sebastian. You have special talents; talents that the Gypsies want. They seek to control you, and if you do not change your current course, they soon will.' He ascended the broken altar at the front of the room. Moonbeams filtered through the stained glass, bathing his face in pallid light. 'The process is already much farther along than I would like.'

I had a sinking feeling in my chest. 'The process?'

'Of course. The bond is already strong, isn't it?' Augustine's eyes pierced into mine. 'You feel it, don't you; the insatiable pull towards the one assigned as your charge. The desire to protect at all costs.'

I clutched my wrist tightly between my fingers. In my mind, I saw the image of the pendant hanging so delicately against her chest, the dandelion glimmering inside the glass.

'Josephine,' I said in a low voice.

'Yes, the Romany girl. I don't doubt you've even dreamt of her, imagined yourself defending her from danger. Am I correct?' He smiled when I didn't answer. 'Somehow, despite the efforts of your ignorant brother, the Romany girl appears to be the one you're intended for. You must break this growing bond with her before you are permanently sealed and under Gypsy control.'

I let go of my wrist. What they were demanding was impossible. To stay away from Josephine was impossible. She was the only thing that made sense. 'I can't.'

'Yes, you can,' Anya replied coldly. 'Don't let them trap you.'

'No one's trapping me.'

Augustine looked at me with something like sympathy in his gaze. 'Sebastian, you are about to find yourself in the middle of feuding Gypsies with grievances older than you are. Get out while you can. Let us help you.'

Sweat glazed my temples, but I didn't bother to wipe it away. The tension in the room was unbearably thick. 'What do I have to do?'

'If this bond is broken before you are sealed, you will be free. You will no longer be plagued with that enslaving desire to protect her; that desire that consumes all your thoughts and actions. You know exactly what I mean.'

Yes, I did. I felt it every moment of every day. I was concerned about her safety. No, I had become obsessed with her safety. It was all I thought about. *She* was all I thought about.

'I know.'

'Let the Gypsies worry about themselves, Sebastian. Your brother's motives are not in your best interests. He has only taken care of you because he wants to use you. It's time to step out from under him and live your own life. You can move on and forget about all this.'

'But Josephine . . . '

Augustine's face smoothed, and his voice took on the quality of a parent trying to comfort a small child. 'She'll be fine,' he crooned. 'She has her own protectors.'

'Like Quentin Marks.'

I wasn't surprised that he knew exactly who I was talking about. 'Among others, yes.'

Anya paced with irritation, her fists clenching. 'Then it's settled. Break your ties and be done with it.'

My anger bristled. 'I don't understand why I matter this much to you,' I snarled. 'Why do you care?'

'Why?' she echoed. 'Because we've been there before . . . myself, Matthias, and Thaddeus. We've been enslaved by those wretched Gypsies. And we want revenge for all the suffering that . . . '

Augustine descended suddenly on Anya, catching her hard across the mouth with his fist. 'Silence!'

She hissed and fell back, slinking to join her companions. She didn't appear hurt, but her eyes were molten silver as she glared at him.

'Go, all of you,' Augustine ordered. 'You have duties to attend to.'

Anya nodded curtly. Mist gathered around them, followed by a heavy flapping sound. I caught a glimpse of what looked like leathery wings, but then, the trio was gone. Augustine's attention returned to me.

'Anya was out of line,' he said apologetically. 'She doesn't think too highly of the Outcast clans. But, then again, neither do I.' He went on. 'You see, those gargoyles were once under the control of clans much like your brother's. But I rescued them, showed them what they were truly capable of.'

'And what's that, exactly?'

His lip twitched mysteriously. 'You will learn for yourself, soon enough.'

I leaned my head against the column. I didn't know what to do or what to believe anymore. Augustine lifted his hand, stopping just short of touching my shoulder. It was intended to be a comforting gesture, but it made my blood run cold.

'All the insanity will end, Sebastian,' he said softly. 'If you break your ties. You'll be yourself again, not ruled by thoughts and emotions you cannot control. Don't you want that?'

I studied my clawed hands, feeling my chest tighten. I thought of my dream of being a tattoo artist, like Hugo. Or even attempting art school in the future; a future that I was in charge of, not someone else.

I raised my eyes to meet Augustine's. 'If I break the ties, will I be normal again?'

'Trust me, Sebastian,' Augustine replied. 'Everything Hugo has tried to manipulate will end. Confront the Corsi clan with what I have told you. Your eyes will be opened to their true motives. Hugo seeks to use you. I seek to empower you.' Augustine moved away. 'But you must decide soon.'

'Why?'

'Because each moment you spend near Josephine Romany will only make this more difficult for you. You've been weakened by the bond too much already. Once you've reached your decision, come and see me. I will be here, in the bell tower.'

I'd been furious moments before. Now, I felt numb. 'All right.'

Augustine produced something from his pocket. 'And please, accept my apology on Anya's behalf for her over-enthusiasm with your test.' He tossed me a set of keys. 'You'll find your van parked around back, good as new.' Augustine smiled, his pink scar twisting upward. 'Now go. The Corsi clan will be wondering what happened to their pet.'

He regarded me for a moment, then turned and walked out of the room. The hollow clang of the door echoed in my ears.

17. Turbulence and Tranquility

My van was parked behind the church – just like Augustine said – and he hadn't been kidding on the 'good as new' bit. No one would've guessed it'd had an up-close encounter with a tree. I turned the key in the ignition, and it rumbled to life.

As I drove through town, passing the high school, everything felt surreal. It was like watching my life being played out by a stranger. I adjusted the rearview mirror and scrutinized my reflection. There was no denying the similarity in my hair and skin tone with Augustine's companions. I swallowed hard. Would I end up looking just like them?

I needed to go home, to confront Hugo. But instead, I found myself crossing the Sutallee Bridge into the Fairgrounds. Ever since I'd left Josephine, I'd been unsettled. Augustine called it a growing bond. All I knew was that the separation was driving me insane. Until I had proof she was safe, I couldn't go back to the shop.

It was well past midnight. She'd probably be asleep. I'd just drive around the fence, check the grounds. Nothing intrusive. Make sure Josephine's all right and the feeling would go away. I was sure of it.

The Fairgrounds' iron fence rose against the blackened sky. Security lights cast a sparse glow over the grounds, steeping everything in shadows. I parked the van well off the road. The last thing I needed was to be mistaken for a burglar.

I scurried along the perimeter of the fence. When I reached the caravan of buses and trailers, I was surprised to find them all dark, even at such a late hour. I doubled back for the front gate, growing increasingly restless. I knew I was experiencing that freaky pull Augustine had talked about, but I couldn't help myself. It was as though my body wouldn't listen to reason. I had an overpowering desire to get inside the Circe before I did something crazy.

Crazy.

That was it. If I *was* crazy, then why not act on it? I spotted an old magnolia tree a few yards away. It was taller than the fence. A smile slid over my face.

Perfect.

I took off running and leapt, grabbing hold of the nearest branch. I swung myself onto it with surprising grace. Like my balance, my dexterity had definitely improved. I crouched on the branch, taking inventory of myself. My senses were heightened and alert. My heart beat stronger in my chest. I felt recklessly alive.

Were gargoyles supposed to feel this way?

Taking a deep breath, I began to climb the tree. The higher I went, the better I felt. My fears melted away. Soon I was well above the fence. I settled into another crouch, feeling oddly secure on the narrow branch, as if I'd been doing stuff like this my whole life. Dark asphalt spread like a vast pit below me. My rational mind told me that a jump from this height wasn't safe. And it would hurt.

But instinct told me otherwise. In fact, the new compulsion was so strong that it blocked out a lifetime of logic and experience. And suddenly I knew that, if I jumped, I would be fine.

So I did.

My feet pushed against the branch – propelling me outward – and I sprang into the air. The sensation was more like flying than jumping. I sailed effortlessly over the iron bars and made my descent on the other side. My body braced for the hard impact, but it never came. Instead, I touched down lightly on the balls of my feet, my hands assisting in balance as I dropped to all fours.

I'd barely made a sound.

My head snapped up, and I glanced back at the fence. *I'd actually jumped over it!* I pulled myself together and took a look around. The only interior light seeped from the opening of the main tent. I moved quietly, keeping to the darkest shadows. Once I reached the structure, I pressed against the thick canvas and peered through the entrance.

Inside was a scene from another world. A large, circular stage dominated the middle of the tent, surrounded by rows of audience seating. Curtains of wispy fabric and ornate set pieces decked the performance space. Filtered stage lighting wrapped everything in a cozy, candlelit glow.

On the stage, an assembly was gathered.

Some were dressed in costumes, others in work clothes. Nicolas and Sabina Romany graced the center of the group, with Francis hovering nearby. But there were no happy expressions, as there had been at Josephine's party. I spotted Josephine at the edge of the stage. Quentin was next to her, his muscular arm draped over her shoulder.

My upper lip curled of its own accord, and I had to repress the strong urge to hiss. *Calm down, Sebastian.* I'd wanted to make sure Josephine was safe. She was. I needed to leave before someone caught me. I didn't need to be a part of this. My head buzzed, and I recognized the sensation for what it was: my instincts overruling my common sense.

I wasn't going anywhere.

I slipped inside and ducked behind the audience stands, creeping close enough to hear. Nicolas Romany stepped forward, and the circus folk quieted.

'Thank you for gathering on such short notice,' he began. 'And I apologize for interrupting your rehearsals. I know you've been working late hours getting ready for the show. But there have been rumors circulating about tonight's events, and I thought it best that we meet before they got out of hand.'

The crowd murmured among themselves.

Nicolas raised his hand. 'It was just a simple case of robbery, nothing more. The men got away with some petty cash. They escaped before the Marksmen could track them down, but we've called off the search. Nothing else was taken, and no one was hurt. Since it's not our custom to involve the *gadje* in our affairs, I decided not to call the police.'

Though I didn't understand why, my chest tightened, and I had to bite back a rising snarl. The circus folk glanced nervously at each other. Then, suddenly, Quentin's voice rang out.

'You may be convinced that's all it was, Nicolas. But I'm not.'

The crowd shifted uneasily.

Nicolas regarded Quentin. 'Why do you say that?'

'Because whoever it was, they got past our defenses tonight. I've expressed my concerns for weeks now that someone was following us.' Quentin glared from under his dark brows. 'I think we should cancel the show until we've thoroughly investigated this. I don't want anyone from this clan in danger.'

Sharp cries rose from all sides of the stage, especially from those in costume. I caught Josephine's horrified look.

'But we're scheduled to open on Sunday,' she protested.

Quentin wasn't deterred. 'So we postpone until a later date.'

'We can't do that,' said Sabina Romany. Her gently commanding presence seemed to calm the crowd. 'We've worked too hard, Quentin. And we desperately need the profit.'

Francis, who'd been silently observing the exchange, spoke up. 'And what's the big deal anyway, if somebody's following us? We're a big clan. We've got protection. I don't understand why we freak out every time there's an incident.'

'Because it's my job to keep the Circe safe,' Quentin shot back. 'That is, unless you want to debate the law, Francis.'

His voice dripped with contempt, as though he was trying to invoke some kind of response from Josephine's twin brother, but Francis only shrugged.

'I'm just saying we tend to overreact, no matter what town we're in. This is supposed to be a Haven, right? And the Corsis live here. Why don't we get their help with this? Find out if they know anything.'

'We're not associating with that clan!' Quentin's body went rigid. 'They don't have any regard for our laws!'

'Calm down, Quentin,' Sabina said quietly.

'We may not agree on everything,' he went on, turning his attention to Nicolas. 'But as the head of the Marksmen, I'm in charge of security. I think there's a threat out there, and until I know what it is, I don't feel comfortable letting the Circe open as usual.'

'It's not your decision,' said Nicolas coolly.

Quentin's usually calm demeanor appeared dangerously close to breaking. 'But Josephine was attacked tonight!'

My eyes darted to her as she pushed herself up from the stage. 'I'm fine,' Josephine insisted. 'No one actually attacked me. It was just a couple of drunks, and Sebastian fended them off.'

Quentin spun, his face clouded with the wrath of a storm. 'You stay away from him, Josephine. He's nothing but trouble.'

I pressed my back harder against the canvas wall. It didn't sound like Josephine had told him the full truth about the figures on the road, but did Quentin somehow know about me? I ground my teeth so hard my jaw ached.

'What are you talking about?' Josephine demanded.

He knelt, putting a hand on her shoulder. The crowd had grown quiet again, all attention fixed on him. 'It's for your own safety,' he said, reverting to his hypnotic voice. 'Yours and your family's.'

He sounded just like Hugo.

Josephine opened her mouth, but Nicolas pushed forward before his daughter could reply. 'We aren't sure of anything yet, Quentin,' he said in a cautionary tone. 'Don't jump to conclusions.'

'Oh, I'm perfectly sure,' Quentin challenged back.

For several moments, no one spoke or moved. I crouched lower, trying to force my quivering body to still. My headache returned, and I reached up to pinch the bridge of my nose between my thumb and finger.

While Quentin defiantly held Nicolas' gaze, Sabina moved towards her daughter. Josephine seemed confused, and most of the circus folk shared her expression.

'Do you trust this boy?' Sabina asked.

A tornado swirled in my stomach as I realized she was talking about me.

'I hardly know him,' stammered Josephine.

Her mother leaned forward. 'But do you trust him?'

'Yes, I do,' she replied. 'It's just . . . '

'Just what?'

Josephine's face changed, and her head turned. My breath hitched as her gaze swept over the space where I was hiding. For a second, I thought she saw me. 'I don't really know what to make of him,' she said finally.

Feelings for Josephine that had nothing to do with protection welled up inside me, and I clenched my fists, trying to ignore them.

Quentin glared at Sabina. 'You see?'

'At first, he unnerved me,' Josephine continued, avoiding Quentin. 'He was always watching me, always giving off this really weird vibe.' She paused, her eyes shifting suddenly to the entrance of the tent. I froze, until she looked back. 'But I don't feel the same way now. Especially after tonight. I don't know, it's like he's looking out for me. If Sebastian hadn't been there, I don't know what would've happened.'

Nicolas and Sabina exchanged glances. Francis frowned. But Quentin; I'd never seen Quentin look so angry with Josephine. Something rumbled deep in my chest, and I inched closer to the stage, looking for the best way to get a clear shot at his throat.

'If he hadn't been there tonight, you wouldn't have been in danger in the first place,' Quentin fumed. He grabbed her hand. 'Josephine, I don't want you going near him . . . '

'Stop.'

Nicolas's firm voice sliced through the air. Quentin raised his chin insolently, but he obeyed. He released Josephine and moved away.

197

'I have a lot to think about,' Nicolas said. 'But we're not going to solve anything tonight.'

Francis stepped forward. 'But, Father . . . '

Nicolas shook his head. 'Tomorrow, we'll meet again and discuss our next course of action. Until then, everyone, don't leave the Circe without my knowledge and permission. You're dismissed.'

I was shocked at how quickly the circus troupe obeyed. It reminded me of the way the guys listened to Hugo. I slid from the entrance as the crowd broke into smaller groups and left the tent. Soon, the stage was empty, save for Josephine and Quentin. I crouched in the darkness, watching.

'Quentin, tell me what's going on right now.' I could hear the strain in her voice. 'What does Sebastian have to do with anything?'

'You've always known your family had enemies, Josephine. It's why we move around so much.'

'And you think Sebastian . . '

'Is one of them,' he finished.

'But he's one of the Corsis. They're not our enemies.'

Quentin huffed. 'They're not our friends, either.'

'I don't believe that,' she murmured.

'Did anything else happen tonight, Josie?' Quentin's face was difficult to read. 'Anything you're not telling me?'

A sinking feeling crept into my soul. My anger fled, and I was left with pure and simple dread.

Josephine moved to the edge of the stage, looking out over the empty audience. 'I told you, there were some idiots out by the bridge and Sebastian ran them off. That's it.'

Quentin's lips drew into a tight line, but then, his face relaxed. 'Well, I'm just glad you're okay. You had me really worried, Josie. Now, come on, I'll walk you to your trailer. It's been a long day.' Quentin stood a few feet from her, his hand outstretched, but Josephine didn't move. 'Aren't you coming?'

She scanned the tent again, hesitating as her gaze neared my hiding place. 'Not yet. I want to finish the last section of my routine.'

'The show's going to be canceled,' he replied. 'You don't need to rehearse anymore tonight, Josie.'

'Father never said we were canceling, Quentin.'

'No, he didn't,' he admitted. 'But Nicolas listens to me, and he'll see reason by the time I'm done. Now, please, come back to the trailers.'

'Just a few minutes.'

'Fine. I'll stay with you.'

'Please, Quentin. I just need a moment alone to clear my head.'

His face clouded. 'I can't let you do that, Josephine.'

'I'm not going to be long,' she snapped. Then she softened and approached him, lifting up on her toes, and kissed him. I wished I hadn't seen it. 'Twenty minutes, and I'll be back in my trailer. I promise.'

He looked as though he was going to refuse, then his arms came around her. 'All right,' he relented. 'But no more than that. I'll be waiting on you.'

He leapt off the stage and went out, though I couldn't be sure if he was gone or waiting outside, keeping a close eye on his girlfriend. I scowled at the floor. Somehow I'd become the enemy of a group of people I didn't even know.

Josephine looked over the rows of bleachers, but I knew she couldn't actually see me. If I was quiet, I could sneak out without her knowledge. She never needed to know I'd been . . .

'Sebastian?'

I jumped at the sound of my name, knocking noisily against the metal seats. Josephine didn't seem surprised. I sighed and stepped into the aisle.

'Hey, Josephine.'

Her hand slid to her throat, her fingers wrapping around the pendant at her neck. 'I knew you were there.'

I took a deep breath. 'How?'

'I'm not sure, exactly.' She looked embarrassed. 'I . . . I felt you.'

My head went all woozy, but I planted my feet, determined not to go into freak mode. 'You did?'

Josephine didn't answer. Instead, she seated herself on the edge of the stage and dangled her legs over the side. After a long silence, a frown touched her lips. 'How long have you been here?'

'Long enough.'

Josephine wrapped her arms around her knees. 'Then you know you should probably go.'

'I'm sorry for intruding,' I replied quickly. 'I just wanted to make sure that you were all right.'

'Why all this concern?' she demanded, though her voice was gentle, confused. 'I barely know you, Sebastian.'

I nodded, studying the floor. 'I know.'

'So why do I feel like I *should*?'

I lifted my eyes to meet hers, and the sight of her face jarred the breath in my lungs. 'I'm sorry,' I said again, backing up. 'I'll let you get back to your rehearsal.'

'Wait.' Her voice rang in my ears, and instantly, there was electricity in the air. She tilted her head. 'You know I'm supposed to stay away from you.'

'Yeah, I heard.'

'I don't know, Sebastian,' she replied, her brow creased. 'At first, I just thought it was simple jealousy.'

I couldn't hide my astonishment. 'Jealousy?'

Josephine's lip curved slightly. 'Quentin's always been a little overbearing; boyfriend's prerogative, I guess. But he's been keeping a special eye on you.' She grew serious. 'I didn't think much about it at first, until he started talking about you. He was pretty upset that you took me home from the play.'

'I'm not trying to cause trouble.'

'It's not that, Sebastian,' she replied. 'Quentin and I have been together a long time. Fights happen. But this is different. It's like he's scared of you.'

'Why would that be?' I asked carefully.

'I'm not sure,' she said, shaking her head. 'You're with the Corsis, and he's always suspicious of other clans, no matter where we travel. But that doesn't really explain it.'

'So he hasn't said anything to you directly?'

My voice sounded tense in my ears, but Josephine didn't appear to catch it. She sighed and drummed her fingers on her knees. 'No. That's how it is around here. The people in charge only tell us stuff when they feel it's necessary.' She paused and glanced over her shoulder toward the tent flap. 'I'm not buying the robbery story my father told the troupe. I think there's something else going on. I haven't seen Quentin this on edge in months, but I swear, he's like a brick wall with me lately. I know he thinks keeping me out of things is for my own good, but it's so . . . '

'Frustrating?' I offered.

'Yeah.'

Josephine's shoulders slumped. I wanted so much to pull her close. I concentrated on the back wall instead. 'It's hard not knowing what's going on,' I said. 'Especially when you feel like everyone else around you does.'

Her fingers played in her hair, and I couldn't help watching. Every movement she made burned itself into my memory.

'So we're both in the same boat,' she replied.

'Yeah,' I said. 'I suppose we are.'

Our mutual confession felt like a bridge, suspended between this fragile and strange relationship – whatever it was – waiting for one of us to step first, to test its strength.

Her lips puckered in thought. 'We should probably do something about that.'

'What do you suggest?' I asked, my skin tingling with wary anticipation.

She tilted her head, looking me over. Her gaze made me uncomfortable and excited all at once. 'Well, for starters, maybe we should level with each other.'

The floor seemed to tilt underneath me. I sank down onto the first bleacher and propped my elbows on my knees, head forward, trying to breathe evenly. She was right. We'd both been skirting around things, especially the last few days. 'Okay.'

'Sebastian?'

'Yes?'

'What are you?'

My muscles contracted until I felt my bones would crack with the pressure. She peered down at me, trying to see my face within the depths of my hood. The question hung heavy in the air; Josephine's first step across the expanse.

'I know I said you hit your head when we got off the Ferris wheel,' she continued, speaking quickly, as if she was trying to finish before she changed her mind, 'but you didn't. You fell out of the car . . . from the top. From the top, Sebastian! That had to be almost a thirty-foot drop. But you were back in school the next day, perfectly fine.'

'Fine is a relative term,' I said, trying to smile, but failing miserably. 'I don't feel like I've been fine for a really long time.' I paused, taking several breaths in the silence, letting the reality of my words sink in. I studied my fingernails before pressing on. 'So why didn't you say anything before?'

'I said I knew something was going on with you.'

'I mean, about my fall.'

Josephine closed her eyes. 'Because I convinced myself I'd made it all up.'

'Yeah,' I replied, rubbing my forehead. 'Me too.'

There was a long pause.

'I'm not imagining things, am I?' she whispered. 'You *are* different, aren't you?'

I flinched. It was my turn now, my moment to step forward, to close the gap. But how? There was no way I could tell her I was a gargoyle. It was too bizarre, and I only half-believed it myself. I had to say something. The way she was looking at me was melting all my resolve. But I had to know something first.

'Why didn't you tell Quentin the whole truth about tonight?'

Josephine folded her hands in her lap and examined them. 'I should have. I mean, it's his job to protect us. But if I told him about those things on the road, then I would've had to tell him about you.' She shook her head, sending a rush of hair over her shoulders. 'I couldn't do that, Sebastian, because . . . I want you to trust me.'

Another step.

'Well, about leveling with each other,' I began. 'I know this is going to sound crazy . . . '

I went cold all over. My shoulders tensed, and a decidedly animal-like sound left my throat before I could stop it.

Josephine jerked in surprise. Quentin's voice rang out, smooth and commanding, from the opening of the tent.

'Josephine, it's been long enough.'

I dove beneath the bleachers and crouched in the shadows. Josephine stood over my hiding place. 'I'm almost done.'

'Ten more minutes,' I heard him say.

So much for revealing any secrets tonight, crazy or not.

'He's gone,' said Josephine in a whisper.

I rose cautiously. 'I need to go. I don't want you getting in trouble.'

She moved closer, and sparks lit the edges of my vision. I found myself holding my breath as those brilliant emerald eyes searched mine. 'Listen, Sebastian, whatever it is, you don't have to tell me everything tonight. I can see in your eyes that you aren't ready, and it's okay. I can wait.' She held me trapped in the depths of her gaze. 'But please, stay.'

Tiny explosions went off in my head. 'Why?'

'Because I feel . . . safe . . . around you,' she replied.

She looked so vulnerable, and her voice was so pleading. Even if I'd wanted to, there was no way I could refuse. Still, I was determined to try. For her own good. And for mine.

'Maybe it's better if I . . . '

'I know it doesn't make any sense,' she quickly cut me off.

'But Josephine . . . '

She reached out, gingerly touching my arm, almost as if she were afraid to. 'Just until I've finished my routine.'

Josephine smiled, and what little resolve I had left burned away. 'Okay.'

What else could I do?

'Thanks, Sebastian. I'll just be a few minutes.'

She returned to the stage and pressed a button on the small sound system near the steps. Music filled the tent. The sound was haunting and otherworldly, like something from a different time.

A part of me wanted to finish the conversation and tell her what I was, or what everyone *thought* I was. But how would she react? Josephine moved gracefully to the center of the stage and posed. My heart sped up at the sight of her. No, I wasn't going to say anything.

Not yet.

Her long skirt fell back from her leg, revealing several dangling anklets. Then she began to dance. Her hands wafted around her face, fingers flowing, every bangle and bracelet sparkling in the light. I stood, mesmerized, unable to take my eyes off her. Time melted into oblivion, and everything phased out of focus except her. Josephine Romany was the only thing that existed in my world.

After what seemed like an eternity, the music drifted away. Josephine's arms lowered, and her eyes found mine. A current of electricity leapt up my arms. In that moment, something passed between us.

And we both knew it.

'So, I guess I'll see you later?' she asked, breaking the connection.

The hopeful tone of her voice made my heart soar.

'Yes, Josephine,' I said softly. 'You will.'

18. Smoke and Mirrors

When I returned to the *Gypsy Ink*, it was nearly dawn, and Hugo was waiting for me. I'd forgotten about the attack until I saw him. He lounged on the counter, wearing a T-shirt and a pair of ripped jeans. The bandage on his cheek was gone, but his tattooed arms didn't obscure the claw marks I'd given him earlier.

'How are you feeling?' I asked, throat raw with guilt.

His face was wiped clean of any emotion. 'Much better.'

Vincent, James, and Kris entered from the hallway, their expressions shadowed against the pre-dawn darkness. I'd never seen any of the guys arrive at the shop so early.

'Morning,' I said, watching them warily.

Outwardly I sounded calm, but my blood was racing. These weren't the same rough-and-tumble tattoo artists I'd known before. They'd become strangers, and a whole lot more intimidating. I surveyed the array of shattered glass still littering the floor. Lying in the middle of the debris was the painting of the Gypsy caravan.

Quentin's words came back to me.

'We're not associating with that clan! They don't have any regard for our laws!'

He'd been referring to us. No, I corrected myself. Not me, them. *They* were the Gypsies. I was . . .

Something else.

I broke from my thoughts as I realized no one had responded to my greeting. Once again, I was met with that creepy wall of silence.

'Okay, what is it?' I demanded.

Hugo leaned forward. 'Where've you been?'

'Out.'

'You disobeyed my orders.'

I gawked at him. 'You have got to be kidding me, Hugo. I'm not your kid.'

'No,' he replied. 'But you're with us.'

'You know, it's funny, Hugo,' I said, fighting against my simmering emotions. I didn't want to lose control. 'But I don't ever remember making that choice.'

'Because it's not yours to make,' he said steadily. 'You belong to this clan. It's not something you can walk away from. But more importantly, you can't just go out whenever and wherever you please. You're a gargoyle, Sebastian. It's not safe.'

I ground my fingers into my temples as snippets of Augustine's conversation jarred my brain. Who was I supposed to believe? I wanted it to be Hugo, but the longer this went on, the less reassured I felt. 'I thought you said you were going to fix this?'

'I am,' he replied. 'But you aren't helping. Storming out like that tonight was foolish, Sebastian. And dangerous.'

'You were attacked, Hugo. What was I supposed to do?'

'You were supposed to listen to your brother. You don't have a clue about our world or your place in it.' His eyes narrowed, and then he sighed. Lines furrowed across his forehead. 'I'm on your side, Sebastian, I really am. But it's taking time to get the information I need, and every moment you go out with your own agenda, you're messing with the process. You're only hurting yourself, don't you see that?'

'I know,' I said, feeling suddenly desperate. 'But I can't help it. It's like I'm fighting this war inside, all the time. Everything's pulling on me at once . . . like these instincts that won't let go, and I try to stop, Hugo, but I just can't.'

For the first time since my brother told me what I was, his stoic mask cracked. I saw a struggle inside Hugo I hadn't seen before, coupled with a strange pity in his gaze. 'You have to, Sebastian, and not just for the sake of everyone around you.' He clasped my shoulder. 'You have to try harder . . . for your own sake.'

I backed away, out of his reach, holding my head. I felt wildly uncertain, too many impulses hitting me at once. The thing inside me – with all its fierce urges and instincts – was getting stronger. I could feel it banging on the back of my skull. It wanted out. And I was growing too tired to fight. I needed to be alone.

'I'm going to bed,' I said.

Then I tensed, waiting for the Gypsies to block my exit, like they'd done before. But no one moved. I backpedaled slowly to the edge of the room. Then I turned and stormed down the hall, slamming the apartment door behind me.

My cell phone woke me from a dreamless slumber. I rolled groggily in bed and answered the call.

'Hello?' My voice was thick.

A familiar, chipper voice came from the other end. 'Hey, it's Katie.'

'Hi, Katie.'

'Where've you been?' she demanded. 'You haven't returned any of my calls.'

I hadn't? I struggled to remember what day it was. My stiff muscles protested as I sat up and rubbed my eyes. 'What day is it?'

'It's Saturday,' she replied, sounding confused.

'Oh, I . . . uh . . . had a late night,' I replied. 'Been sleeping it off.'

'Must have been some night.'

'Yeah, you could say that.'

Katie paused. 'Did something happen after you took Josephine home?'

'Nope,' I replied in my calmest voice. 'Just hung out here with the guys. You know, same old same old.'

Thankfully, Katie didn't push me for details.

'So,' she continued in a tone way too perky for my nagging headache. 'A bunch of us are going to the movies, and we want you to come. I'll even swing by and get you.'

I stumbled out of bed and peeked through the blinds. It was late afternoon, by the looks of things. 'I don't know,' I said noncommittally. 'Hugo might have some stuff for me to do in the shop.' I rubbed my shoulders. 'Besides, I've been feeling kind of sick lately.'

'Sebastian Grey, you are coming to this movie,' Katie ordered. 'And then, afterwards, it's back to my house to work on our drama project, which is due Monday and which you've barely contributed to in class over the last couple of weeks, just in case you've forgotten.'

I had to appreciate her persistence. I glanced quickly at my reflection in the dresser mirror. Sick was an understatement. I looked like death had had a party all over my face. Still, a little normalcy sounded appealing – something to take my mind off of everything – even if it did involve schoolwork later.

'Okay, Katie,' I relented. 'When are you picking me up?'

Fifteen minutes later, Katie's red Mini Cooper pulled into the lot. I slipped around the side of the building, careful to avoid the open windows at the front of the shop. I opened the passenger seat, ducked my head, and climbed in before my guilty conscience stopped me. I didn't like defying Hugo, but I wasn't going to stay cooped up, either. I wasn't an animal. I leaned deeper into the seat and tugged on the hood of my jacket, feeling more self-conscious than ever about the way I looked.

Katie had her music blasting. Her tastes were far edgier than her personality suggested. But the screaming vocals of the *Putrid Melons* – along with the fluffy pink die hanging from the rearview mirror – put me at ease. This was what I knew. No Gypsies, no stone-faced strangers. Just hanging with friends.

Like normal people.

'Hey, Sebastian, I'm really glad you're coming,' Katie yelled over the music.

'Did I really have a choice?' I yelled back.

'Of course not.'

Katie pulled out onto the highway, speeding towards town. I made sure my seat belt was tightly buckled.

'Are we late to the movie?' I asked, slamming against the door as she took a sharp turn.

'Nope.'

'Ah, so it's just a death-wish, then?'

She laughed like a deranged lunatic and made no attempt to slow down. Not that I was surprised. How ironic that, after everything I'd been through the last few weeks, I was going to meet my demise at the hands of a blonde speed demon.

'So when are you going to fix that bad dye job?' she asked while plowing through an intersection. 'I mean, the hooded thing's all tortured and mysterious, and I get it, but honestly.'

'Tortured and mysterious?'

'You know what I mean.' She rolled her eyes. 'It's not my thing, but I guess some girls are into it.'

Katie Lewis was nothing if not honest. I pondered her statement about girls for a moment, but found myself thinking about Josephine. I growled softly under my breath. I wasn't going to think about her right now. Okay, maybe that wasn't possible. But I was determined to distract myself.

We screeched into the Sixes Six Cinema. Katie squealed into a spot next to Avery's Jeep. I bolted out of the car, grateful to be alive.

'Katie, let me get your ticket,' I said as we reached the window. 'It's the least I can do, since you drove.'

She winked at me. 'Always the gentlemen, aren't you?'

I passed the money under the glass. 'Well, I try.'

The scent of concessions hit me hard, and my stomach immediately complained. I couldn't remember how long it'd been since I'd eaten, and I was feeling the effects. I could smell the food with such clarity that it overwhelmed my senses. An urge to leap over the counter and bury my face in a tub of popcorn gripped me so strongly that I had to hold onto a movie display to keep from actually doing it. I sniffed the air eagerly.

Katie gave me a weird look, her eyes crinkling at the corners. 'Sebastian, you're salivating at the concessions guy.'

'I'm a little hungry,' I confessed. In no time, Katie had me loaded down with boxes of candy and a giant tub of popcorn. 'Thanks for the invite,' I said, scarfing down the fluffy kernels. 'I really needed to get out for a while.'

'Is your brother on your case again?'

'Something like that.'

'Well, I totally understand. Mom is all over me about my college applications and junk. I'm just so not ready for next year.'

'Me neither,' I replied, nodding absently. I really needed to get my head back into school. I wasn't going to let all that had happened the last few weeks derail me, no matter how whacked out things were. We entered the auditorium. A flight of stairs led to rows of stadium seating. I put my foot on the bottom step, but Katie stopped me.

'Sebastian, are you really okay?' Her blue eyes searched for mine, but I kept my head low. 'You're so checked out these days. I miss the old you.'

I didn't want to lie to Katie. She was the closest thing I had to a best friend. But what could I say that would even make sense? My new life wasn't a subject I could just spill my guts about. But I owed her something.

'Hugo's involved with some things I don't approve of, and I don't want to get mixed up in it.' I sighed. 'But sometimes, I feel like I don't really have a choice.'

Katie let out a slow breath. 'Sounds pretty serious. Is it anything you can tell me?'

She wanted to know, but she wasn't going to pry. If I hadn't had my hands so full of concessions, I would've hugged her. Instead, I shook my head. 'I can't right now, Katie. Maybe eventually. There's a whole lot I still don't understand myself.'

'Okay, Sebastian. Well, I'm here for you if you need anything, okay?'

I looked up from the shelter of my hood. 'Thanks.'

Katie started up the stairs, fumbling for the railing. 'Do they seriously have to keep it so dark in here? Avery said he'd save us some seats, but I can't see a thing.'

'He's right there,' I said, pointing to the middle of one row. Avery was sitting next to Mitchell, showing him something on his cell phone. Brandon and Emma sat in front of them, twisted like a piece of licorice, their lips glued together.

Katie's brows shot up. 'You can see him?'

'What? Oh, well yeah,' I cleared my throat. 'My eyes adjust pretty quickly, I guess.'

'You lead the way, then,' Katie said, taking my arm. 'And don't you dare let me fall on my face like some uncoordinated idiot.'

I grinned, ready to slide into my seat and let the movie take me away. Then, my crazy radar went off. I sucked in air through clenched teeth. Josephine was one row above the others, with Quentin at her side. I jerked to a halt, my hand crushing the popcorn tub. Fluffy kernels spewed, and Katie rammed into me, gasping in surprise.

'What are you doing?' she cried.

'I didn't know they were going to be here,' I whispered.

'I said a bunch of us were coming.'

The blood raced to my head. Josephine's warmth filtered through me, combined with frigid cold as I stared at Quentin. I braced myself against the stair rail.

'Oh.'

'What's wrong?' Katie asked, trying to peer into my hood.

'Nothing.'

Josephine laughed at something Quentin said and took a sip of his drink. He pulled her close. A strange sound rattled in my throat.

'Whoa there, mad dog,' Katie said, eyes wide.

'I don't like him, Katie. I don't trust him with her.'

She grabbed a fistful of my jacket, forcing me to face her. 'Sebastian, I know you like Josie, but you're going to have to play nice. You know she's got a boyfriend. Now, just get over it and enjoy the movie with us.'

My body fought my brain, and I closed my eyes. I was going to get a handle on this. I *had* to. With each breath, I willed my instincts to settle. Gradually, I felt the threatening emotions slip back into that part of me I didn't fully understand. I opened my eyes to find Katie still looking at me, her expression frozen in bewildered concern.

'Sorry,' I replied, chuckling sheepishly and pushing away from the rail. 'Temporary loss of testosterone control.' *If only it were that simple.* 'Won't happen again.'

My answer produced the laugh I was hoping for. Katie relaxed, and patted me on the arm. 'You're forgiven. Ugh. Teenaged male hormones.' She shuddered. 'Scary stuff.'

'You have no idea.'

'And let's keep it that way.'

As we reached our row, Quentin looked up. The smile that crossed his face was almost snake-like. 'Hey, guys,' he said casually.

'Hi, Quentin,' Katie bubbled. 'Hey Josie.'

Josephine glanced up quickly, nodded, and then looked away without ever making eye contact with me. The strange eagerness she'd shown the night before appeared to be gone. A splinter of emotion wedged between my ribs. But maybe it was for the best. It would be easier to break my ties with her, knowing she didn't have any with *me*.

Katie plopped next to Mitchell, nudging him playfully. I watched them exchange a round of flirting as I took my seat. Mitchell was a good guy, and Katie deserved a good guy. I

214

dumped the concessions into my lap, trying to lose myself in the smell of popcorn instead of the exotic scent behind me.

I could feel Quentin's eyes from the row above me, burning a hole in the back of my skull. I gritted my teeth, tried to concentrate on something else. Not working. I became aware of the shallowness of my own breathing, the dull ache spreading through my shoulders. My hands shifted to the armrests, and I blanched. My claws were back. I curled forward. *Calm, down. Calm down.* I repeated the mantra frantically as I curled my fingers tightly into my palms. A cell phone rang, and I heard Quentin answer.

'I'm here,' he said quietly. There was a pause. 'I'll take care of it, don't worry.' I felt him move into the aisle. 'I'll be right back, Jo.'

He sprinted down the stairs, still on his phone as he exited the auditorium. Gradually, my cramped muscles eased. My fingers relaxed, and the disgusting claws were gone. I clutched a box of chocolates and leaned back, finally able to breathe again. Sort of. There was movement, and Josephine's scent intensified. The next thing I knew, she had slipped into the empty seat next to me.

'Hey,' she said softly.

I nearly dropped my candy.

'Hey back,' I replied, trying to keep the tremor out of my voice.

'How are you?'

'Good.'

'Good.'

Josephine glanced at the auditorium doors. When she looked back, I was shaken senseless by the bright glimmer in her eyes. Everything went upside down inside me. I wracked my brain for something to say.

'How's your family?'

Her smile was one of curious surprise. 'They're okay.'

'Did they come to a decision about the Circe?' I asked, impressed with how calm I sounded.

'We're still going to open tomorrow night,' she replied. Her shoulders lifted briefly. 'Quentin met with my parents, then they called us together and told the troupe that everything was fine. The issue has been taken care of, whatever that means.'

I frowned. 'Sounds kind of strange.'

'Pretty much describes life in a Gypsy family,' she laughed quietly.

'Tell me about it.'

'Seriously, though, there's always something, some stupid disagreement or power struggle with another clan.' She shrugged and played with her earring. 'When I told you my family is important, I wasn't kidding. My dad's the *bandoleer* of our clan, but more than that, our family sort of rules over the other Outcasts . . . well, we're supposed to, anyway. It doesn't make us very popular, sometimes.'

I couldn't help leaning forward. 'Outcasts have rulers?'

Josephine nodded and glanced toward the doors again. 'Your brother never mentioned it?'

'Hugo hasn't told me much. Things have been a little too . . . hectic . . . at home for decent conversation.' I straightened in my chair. 'But he did mention your family has enemies. In fact, he's not been really happy with me lately.'

She tilted her head. 'Why?'

'Because of you,' I replied, then I rapidly redirected. 'I mean, because I've been hanging with you, you know, like at school and rehearsals and stuff.' Unbelievable. I was blabbering like an idiot again.

Josephine looked amused. 'He has a problem with me?'

'No,' I said, attempting to backtrack. 'Not you, personally. He has this thing about your clan, but from what I heard last night, your family's pretty much the same way. And Quentin doesn't like us either.'

'Quentin doesn't like anybody,' she said, still looking amused, and more beautiful than ever. 'But that's his job.'

'So,' I went on, refusing to think about Quentin. Just his name raked my nerves like a strip of sandpaper. 'The Circe's actually going to be ready to open tomorrow night?'

She made a face. 'Yeah, it will, and I've got a ridiculously long rehearsal waiting for me after the movie, which is kind of a bummer, since everyone's going out for ice cream.'

'I don't know how you do it all. Memorizing lines for the school play nearly killed me. I can't imagine doing that and a circus performance at the same time.'

'It's no big deal, really,' she replied, waving her hand dismissively. But I could detect a hint of pleasure in her tone. Josephine propped her elbow against my armrest, smiling one of my favorite smiles: the one that sat crooked on her lips. 'It's not raining in here, you know,' she said.

'What?'

She pointed to my hood. I shrank into the chair. What was it with everyone tonight? Why couldn't they just let me be freakishly gray in peace? Josephine's hand dropped to her neck, and a rippling current shot through my body as the pendant appeared. She toyed absently with the ribbon, and I clenched my hands in my lap, trying to tear my eyes away. Augustine was right about one thing: it was getting harder to resist the draw I felt towards the Gypsy girl.

But if I wanted any shot at fixing my life, I had to.

'Your boyfriend will be back soon,' I said.

Her shoulders drooped. 'I know.'

My heart hiccupped, but I immediately brushed the feeling aside. I was just reading into her reaction, I told myself. I forced a smile. 'And you're supposed to stay away from me, remember?'

She surprised me by smiling back. 'Well, I don't always do as I'm told.' Her smile widened. 'I think that's another thing we have in common, don't we?'

My head buzzed. 'I think we do.'

She studied the advertisements scrolling across the movie screen. 'I did want to ask you something, though.'

'Okay.'

'Will you come to the Circe tomorrow?' There was something in her expression I couldn't fully read, a kind of unexplained determination. 'To see the opening show, I mean. I'd feel better, if you were there.'

Protective stirrings filtered through my head, simmering, like a pot of hot coffee. 'I thought your family said everything was fine.'

'Yes, they did.'

'But you don't believe them.'

'Of course not. My dad and Quentin are good at smoothing things over with the troupe. They're in charge. People follow. It's how we work. No one questions my father. What he says goes. But I guess you could say I know him a little too well. Something's been up for a while. Something that's got them nervous.'

My chest felt tight, as though I sucked in too much air. 'Like what?'

Josephine paused, the silence like a foot hovering above a tightrope.

'I'm not sure yet,' she said. I noticed a crinkle in the corner of her eye. She was choosing her words; probably with the same care I was choosing mine. I knew my reasons. But what were hers? 'Anyway, I could use some moral support,' she continued, turning to meet my gaze. 'So will you come?'

I'd just convinced myself I needed to stay away from Josephine. Her clan, her family . . . they weren't my business. And besides, they seemed fully capable of taking care of themselves. I thought about my life before she'd arrived in town, before everything started happening to me. I wanted that back: my future, my plans. Normal hair, for crying out loud! I could walk away from this. But as my eyes continued to look into Josephine's, the conflict inside me escalated.

It was just attending a performance, right? Everyone else would be there, too. It didn't have to be more than that. Just moral support, like she said. I nodded. 'Of course I'll be there, Josephine.'

'Thanks, Sebastian,' she said, looking relieved. 'You're a good friend.'

Josephine allowed the pendant to drop from her hand, and it hung heavily against her chest, highlighted by the V-necked shape of her shirt. It glimmered like a beacon, calling to me so strongly that I couldn't resist reaching out. As I did, Josephine's eyes fixed on my wrist.

'You know, your tattoo is really beautiful,' she said, leaning closer.

My arm froze in midair, so close to her neck that I could feel the heat of her skin. Josephine's eyes widened as her gaze shifted from my tattoo to my face. That strange sensation passed through me again. I felt it keenly, but this time, I could see in Josephine's face that she felt it too.

The two dandelions were barely an inch apart.

My lungs quit working.

It was like two magnets straining to connect. My wrist ached with the force of it. Inside its glass casing, the dandelion sparked with light, and my tattoo seemed to both absorb the energy and reflect it. Was this a part of the process Augustine had talked about?

We hovered there, locked in the powerful current. Warning signals prickled my spine, but I didn't care. I just wanted to be with her, whatever that meant. I would deal with the consequences later.

'Sebastian, are you okay?'

Josephine's gaze darted over my face. I was flushed and feverish again, and it felt like everything inside me was on the verge of exploding. A cold chunk of ice settled in my stomach. I opened my mouth to say something. Anything. But I was speechless.

Then, a putrid stench filled my nostrils, jerking me from my trance. People were pointing and rising from their seats. I scanned the room, confused. And then I saw the cause of the commotion: the auditorium was filling with oily black smoke.

'What is that?' Josephine gasped, covering her mouth with the back of her hand.

Her question was answered by the screech of the fire alarm.

There was instant panic. We bolted from our seats as people poured into the aisles, pushing and shoving to get out. I sniffed the air and gagged. The smoke didn't smell like fire. Because it wasn't smoke at all.

It was mist.

We were suddenly dragged into the aisle by the wild surge of people. The crowd was in a panicked frenzy, turning quickly into a stampede. I saw Mitchell pushing Katie into the opposite aisle as Avery ploughed them a path. But our aisle was too full, and people were climbing over each other to move. I caught Josephine's arm to keep her on her feet, but it was like fighting a riptide in a churning ocean. My grip broke. She lost her balance, going down among the trampling feet. Her terrified eyes caught mine.

'Sebastian, don't leave me!'

Her fear ignited my bizarre instincts. The world sharpened; focused with crystal clarity. I pushed forward and plucked Josephine from the raging current and into an empty row. She looked at me with frantic eyes, and I began to pant against the onslaught of driving impulses. Before she could speak, I swept her into my arms.

'Hang on,' I snarled. 'I'm going to get you out.'

I braced my foot against the back of a seat and launched forward, easily clearing the row in front of me. I hit the ground and sprang again, jumping rows like hurdles until I'd cleared them all. I catapulted over the rail to the ground floor.

My feet landed like they were made of pillows. I rushed for the emergency exit beneath the screen which was nearly unoccupied. Most of the crowd had bottlenecked the auditorium doors. Wrapping my arms tighter around Josephine, I fought through stampeding horde. My only concern was getting her out. I kicked the door open and burst through.

My legs trembled with adrenaline, but the rush I felt from my new abilities was overwhelmed by my panic. What if someone had seen what I'd done? A few other patrons had followed us out, but most of the crowd had exited the front of the building. If anyone had witnessed anything, they were too wrapped up in their own hysteria to care. I shook myself off, relieved. Then I realized I was still holding Josephine in my arms. She gaped at me in astonishment.

'Oh, wow,' she breathed.

'Are you all right?' I asked, setting her down as gently – and quickly – as I could.

Josephine searched the depths of my hood. I sensed her curious uncertainty, but this time, also mingled with fear. Every emotion coming from her felt as real as my own. But I also felt the undercurrent of that connection between us; the tie I was supposed to break with her.

'Yeah, I'm fine,' she replied.

Sirens echoed in the distance, followed by the soft buzz of a phone. Josephine pressed a hand to her pocket. She knew who it was. So did I. Instead of answering the call, she blinked up at me, and I could see the whirlwind of questions in her expression. Her phone went off again. She wrapped her fingers around it, but she didn't take her eyes off me.

'You need to find him,' I said.

'I know,' she replied. Josephine looked ready to bolt and reluctant to leave, all at once. She tilted her head, scrutinizing me again. The air around me felt like a furnace. She opened her mouth, but her phone sounded again, driving a nail through whatever words were on her lips. A small line formed between her brows. 'You'll come find me tomorrow, right? You'll be at the Circe?'

'Of course,' I replied, trying to manage the adrenaline that was still wreaking havoc on my nervous system. 'I wouldn't miss it. Now hurry and find Quentin before he calls out the National Guard.'

I smiled and stepped out of the way. Josephine studied me for a moment, then turned and ran around the building. As soon as she was gone, I collapsed against the wall. I closed my eyes, groping for oxygen.

'Josephine,' I whispered.

She made me feel alive, made me feel things I'd never felt before. Her smile, her voice; everything about her made me want to shout her name from the rooftops like a crazy person. Did I really want to be free from that? I sank to the ground, my head in my hands. I didn't know the answer.

Suddenly, a hand closed around my throat. I gasped, my eyes bugging open. Something slammed me into the side of the building. Pain exploded in my skull. The edges of my vision went black. I was rocketed through the air, then my face met concrete. The snap of pain cleared my head. Two massive figures held me down, gray faces hovering over me.

'Time's up,' Anya hissed.

She rammed her hand into my neck, choking off my air. I clawed her arms frantically, but she was stronger than me. I couldn't get up, couldn't breathe. Blood pounded in my ears, and everything went blurry. Thick smoke swirled above me.

And then, all was darkness.

19. Words or Actions

I forced my eyes open and found myself staring into the high rafters of the cathedral. My head was killing me, and the dust in the room burned my parched throat. I could still see the glint of Anya's silver eyes as she strangled me.

I sat up with a start. Pain ruptured in my brain. I groaned, pressing a hand to my face. Blood was caked along my temple. The sanctuary was dark, but I had no trouble seeing. I was beginning to feel grateful for one of my strange new abilities.

I braced my hands against the stone floor and gingerly pushed myself to my feet. I was woozy and a bit weak, but otherwise fine. I took a deep breath, fighting off the pain, and called out.

'Augustine!'

My voice echoed in the sanctuary. There was no answer. Then I remembered what he'd said about the bell tower. I searched until I located a small door at the front of the room. It creaked annoyingly on its hinges. A spiral staircase – rotted and ready to collapse – wound up a narrow shaft. I placed my foot tentatively on the first step. It held. Forty steps later, I was on a small platform surrounded by dust-laden support beams. Four enormous bells hung precariously from the rafters, covered with grime and cobwebs.

224

'Augustine?'

There was a flapping sound, and I whirled just in time to duck as a swarm of bats poured from the belfry and down the shaft.

Bats in the belfry. How appropriate.

Four sets of rectangular windows opened to the outside. I eased over to the nearest one. The pale moon bathed the cathedral in an eerie light. The roof spread before me: a maze of ledges and walkways, lofty spires and ornate arches. I hoisted myself over the windowsill and stepped outside. Stationed at every corner and along the ledges were statues.

They looked ominous perched against the backdrop of night. Their granite bodies clung to the roof, their carved faces fierce and threatening. They were a silent army, protecting the cathedral from some unseen enemy. I lifted my head as the night wind jerked invisible fingers through my hair. There was something peaceful in the atmosphere. It made me feel strangely at home.

'I've been waiting for you, Sebastian.'

I dropped low behind an arch as I peered through the dark shadows. I spotted the figure of Augustine, poised between two winged statues, looking out over the town. I moved cautiously towards him.

'I was delayed due to unconsciousness.'

'My apologies,' he said. 'As I've said before, Anya tends to be impatient.'

'You told me to come back when I'd made a decision.'

Augustine turned to face me. He placed his hand on one of the stone creatures, rubbing its coarse pewter head. 'Perhaps I have grown a little impatient as well.' His eyes hardened like black marble. 'You did not follow my advice.'

'How so?'

'The Romany girl,' he replied. 'You did not stay away from her. I warned you that it would be increasingly difficult to break ties with her. There is still so much you don't understand. I am trying to help you, Sebastian Grey. You, however, are being far too stubborn.'

He stroked the back and wings of the statue, and I watched warily, half expecting the beast to come to life at any moment and crush me with its teeth and claws.

'I can't stay away from her,' I replied.

The scar along Augustine's face drew taut. 'Then you will be throwing your life away, boy. Why can you not see that? Surely you know by now that you have potential for great things, things that are above the capacity of ordinary people.'

'I don't care,' I snapped. 'Ordinary sounds just fine to me.'

Augustine propped himself against the ledge. The starlight reflected in his eyes as he glanced upward. When he spoke, his voice was carefully calm. 'Sebastian, you have a far greater destiny.'

'To be a guardian. I know that.'

Augustine's brow arched. 'Are you still so afraid to use the word, to admit what you are?' His long fingers returned to the statue, and he smiled as I watched his movements. 'Beautiful, aren't they. For centuries, gargoyles have symbolized protection. Their images are everywhere, from cathedrals to cemeteries. My ancestors helped carve many such statues, and their faces adorned our wagons and homes. It was once believed that their demonic appearance could frighten away evil spirits.'

I studied the ferocious expression on the creature's face, remembering the pictures from Hugo's book. 'But that's just superstition.'

'All superstition is rooted in truth, Sebastian.' His hand dropped from the statue. 'It was the Romany clan who first discovered how to bring gargoyles to life. The clan once consisted of skilled masons and architects, a long time ago. According to our legends, the Romanys found a way to breathe life into stone, to fashion true protectors – not just in form – but in action.' Augustine's intense gaze met mine. 'These creatures are more than just symbols.'

My chest tightened. 'So you mean these statues are . . . '

'Alive?' he said, completing my thought. 'No, not all gargoyles are like you. Most are simply architecture. But there are some that do sleep, waiting for a time when they can be awakened again.'

'How?'

'That is precisely the knowledge I hope to gain. You are intriguing, Sebastian Grey. I want to know more about you: where you came from, how you were brought to life.' He laced his fingers together. 'There was a time when I thought the Corsis might have the answers I needed. After all, they harbored a shadow creature. Unfortunately, your brother knows very little.' Augustine sighed disdainfully. 'But together, you and I can discover your past. Don't you want to know, Sebastian? Don't you ever wonder who you really are?'

'No. I don't care about my past.'

'Sentiments you carried *before* you found out you were a gargoyle. But surely, this new heritage of yours changes things.'

Bitter anger twisted up my throat. 'This isn't my heritage. And I'm not like these statues. I haven't been asleep.'

'Are you so sure about that, Sebastian?' He caressed one of the creature's long, bat-like wings. 'But it doesn't really matter what you believe. You are waking now, and once fully awakened, nothing will be able to stop the process. You will be trapped by the Gypsies, just like your brethren before you.'

227

'No,' I protested, but my voice sounded dull. My eyes fixed on the fierce statues before me. There was no way I had anything in common with these things. Then I curled my hand into a fist, and the pricks of my claws dug into my gray skin.

My *claws*.

My *gray* skin.

'So you see,' continued Augustine. 'I wouldn't make hasty decisions, if I were you. You have much to learn.' He moved towards me, his voice smooth, almost hypnotic. 'We could teach you. Train you.'

My body felt as heavy as the granite effigy around me. My head was pounding, my thoughts collapsing like fragments of a condemned building. But I had to hold it together. I had to stay focused. I steeled myself and met Augustine's gaze. 'Why would you do that?'

'So you can be free of them, once and for all,' he said urgently.

As I looked into his face, a sudden thought came to me; a question he'd never really answered. My eyes narrowed suspiciously. 'Why are you really trying to keep me from Josephine Romany?'

'That's my business,' he replied, gazing past me to the starry sky beyond. 'Not that it should matter to you. Perhaps you've been too enthralled with her to notice, but the Romany clan has its own host of protectors; *human* protectors. They have no need of you.'

'You have something against the Romanys, I take it.'

He chuckled maliciously. 'You could say that.'

'Who are you, really?'

His laughter died, and a brutal expression warped his features. 'I *was* an Outcast, and my lineage was a proud one. But that is no more. As to who I am now, I'm simply someone who wants to help you, to free you from the clutches of these ignorant clans who don't understand your potential. They don't deserve a guardian like you, Sebastian. Not the Corsis, and certainly not the Romanys.'

I regarded him carefully. Were Augustine and his little band the enemies Josephine's family had spoken of? I felt my blood growing warm with protective instincts. 'Thanks for the offer, but I'm going to stay with my brother.'

Augustine lifted his chin. 'And the Romanys?'

'That's *my* business.'

'I see,' he replied, his voice as smooth as polished glass. 'I told you to stay away from the Romany girl, and you continue to refuse. You've backed me into a corner, Sebastian Grey. I do not want to harm the girl.'

White-hot rage blazed through me. I flew forward, grabbing Augustine by the shirt, and shoved his body against the ledge. 'If you touch her . . . '

Pain seared through my side. I gasped and pulled back, catching the glint of a blade. Augustine positioned a knife threateningly in front of him.

'You're not at full strength yet, Sebastian. Don't be foolish.' He aimed the tip of the knife at my chest. The blade wasn't smooth or shiny, yet it sparkled as though it was reflecting the stars above. 'Now, I suggest you back away.'

I snarled quietly but obeyed. Blood seeped through my jacket. I struggled to remain on my feet, feeling shaky and disoriented. Augustine twirled the unusual weapon lightly in his hand as he moved past the statues.

'Despite this behavior of yours, I want you to know that my offer still stands. You can trap yourself into a life of servitude with the Gypsies, or you can come with us, and I can show you true freedom.'

I gritted my teeth. 'Some choice.'

'Yes,' Augustine replied, tucking the knife into his belt. 'But it *is* a choice. And if you don't make it, then I assure you, Sebastian Grey, we *will* make it for you. I hope you're prepared to deal with that.'

I clutched my side, feeling an awful sense of dread. What did he mean by making my choice for me? Did he already have something in mind? Before I could voice my questions, the Gypsy suddenly leapt through the tower window. I staggered forward. The sound of pounding feet on the stairs rang in my ears. By the time I reached the belfry platform, Augustine was gone. Only clouds of dust remained in his wake.

Hugo flipped the closed sign in the shop window and bolted the lock. 'You're hurt.'

'It's nothing,' I growled, pressing my hand against the wound.

Hugo stepped closer, and I leapt out of the way. I didn't want anyone near me. My emotions were wildly out of control, and I didn't trust myself. My lips quivered in a defensive snarl. I watched Hugo warily, feeling like a cornered beast. His eyes flicked to Vincent's, and the red-headed man nodded and left the room.

'You went to see *him*, didn't you,' Hugo demanded.

'Well, yeah,' I said, my voice dripping with sarcasm. 'Or I did the first time, anyway. I was sort of knocked out and dragged there this time around.'

'I told you there were enemies out there you weren't strong enough to face. You could've gotten yourself killed.'

'Ah, yeah, I got that.' I wiped my blood-covered hand against my jeans. 'How do you know this Augustine guy, anyway?'

'He's been banished from Outcast society, but he's still a Gypsy.' My brother scowled. 'And that means we're all connected, in one way or the other.'

230

My body went taut. 'I don't get it, Hugo. If you knew about Augustine, then you knew I'd end up there eventually, looking for answers.'

'That's why I ordered you to stay here,' my brother replied, his voice like a whip. 'The answers you want are going to come from us, not him. Whatever that *marime* scum said, you can't believe it. He's nothing but an exile.'

'Maybe he is,' I said. 'But right now, he's the only one talking.'

The room went instantly quiet.

Finally, Hugo took a breath, and he looked suddenly resigned. 'When a gargoyle awakens, he is given a brand using the *prah*. The Corsi clan has traditionally been the ones responsible for this. Afterwards, the clans decided who the gargoyle would protect. In some cases, it would be an individual. In others, it was a family, or even an entire clan.'

I clenched my fists. 'Like I told Augustine, I haven't been asleep. I'm just a kid without a family. I was in foster care. I lived with your parents. I came here. I'm not being awakened, Hugo.'

His eyes clouded over. 'Have you ever wondered why you can't remember things, Sebastian? Why your past is a blank page? Before my parents brought you here, you slept. I don't know where or how they got you, but when you woke up, I was ordered to give you the brand.'

The room felt like it was tipping sideways as I struggled to grasp what Hugo was saying. Augustine's words came back to me. 'How does a seal work, exactly?'

'We don't know,' Hugo snapped. 'So much knowledge has vanished from our clan's memory. There are books without pages, stories with unfilled gaps. Zindelo and Nadya spent years researching the old lore. My parents believed that branding you would be enough to seal you to the Corsi clan, and if I were the one to inject the *prah*, it would seal you to us. But they were wrong. I was wrong. Something is missing, a critical element we've overlooked.'

My gaze fell to my wrist. The stark outline of the dandelion stood out against my skin like ink on parchment. And then, it hit me like a punch in the gut. Josephine's pendant! The insane, magnetic draw between our two dandelions wasn't some chance occurrence. It was happening on purpose. Her necklace was a piece in Hugo's unfinished puzzle.

It had to be.

I wrapped my fingers around my wrist. 'So how does a seal become permanent?'

Vincent returned. My skittering stomach should have warned me that something was up, but I was too intent on getting Hugo's answer.

'You have to understand, Sebastian, you're the first gargoyle we've had in our possession in nearly a century. So much of what we knew about the shadow world has been lost. I'm going to need time to . . . .'

Fury ripped through me. I sprang forward, yanking off my hood. My brother's startled gaze met mine, and I wondered if my eyes held the same molten silver look as Anya's. Did I unnerve Hugo the way she had unnerved me?

'There's isn't any more time. Now tell me what you know,' I commanded.

My brother rose slowly. I sensed a shift in the emotional current of the room. Something was wrong. My instincts snapped awake, but I was slow, too slow. Sharp pain stabbed the back of my neck, and I jerked, arms flailing. My fist connected with something before I went down on my knees.

I heard Vincent grunt, and he staggered into my line of vision, holding his jaw. There was an object in his hand, but

I couldn't focus on it. Everything was racing around me, like a carousel spinning way too fast. I clutched my neck. My skin tingled all over. Hugo knelt in front of me as I swayed and rolled onto the floor.

'I'm sorry, Sebastian,' I heard him say as my eyes closed. 'But you should have listened to me.'

20. Everything and Nothing

Buzzing.

An annoying, whining noise.

Like an irritating mosquito, flying around my head.

But it wasn't an insect. It was something else. My eyes refused to open. The sound was slow, methodical.

Painful.

I couldn't distinguish between noise and pain. The buzzing was above me, but the hurt came from somewhere else, somewhere along my arm. The pain was sharp, biting; the kind that made me want to scream. But my mouth – like my eyelids – seemed glued shut. The buzzing noise morphed into voices.

'How long has he been out?' The voice was gruff, vaguely familiar.

'Since last night.'

The second voice belonged to Hugo. Air brushed my face, as if someone was leaning over me. I couldn't break free of the dark void. I felt pressure above my eyelid, followed by a harsh, searing light. I tried to move – to protest – but nothing worked. Then the pressure was gone, and I was in darkness again.

'You should have been more careful,' said the first voice.

'What was I supposed to do, lock him up?' Hugo sighed heavily. 'Sebastian's my brother. Orders or not, I can't do that to him.'

'I see you had no problem knocking him out,' replied the voice.

'Yeah, well I can't risk him hurting himself or our clan either.'

My arm was lifted, and I felt a sharp sting.

'You see, Karl,' said Hugo. 'Nothing's worked.'

The name and the gruff voice matched up. Karl was the Romanys' personal trainer; the old man who'd tended to me the night of Josephine's party.

'Have you tried burning the flesh?'

My brain screamed. *Burning? No!* What was going on? I struggled in vain to move. There was more shuffling, and then, a clicking sound.

'Watch,' replied Hugo.

Heat radiated up my arm, quickly becoming a jabbing ache, and then a scorching fire. My insides writhed in torture, everything pleading for him to stop.

Please, Hugo! Please!

The sharp agony dulled, leaving a lingering hurt.

'Interesting,' said Karl, his tone curious, almost apologetic.

'I don't understand it,' replied Hugo.

There was a pause. 'What are you going to do with the boy?'

Another pause was followed by more movement. I listened, frustrated, still unable to move. I felt something cool on my wrist, then more pressure. I realized my arm was being bandaged.

'I don't know yet,' Hugo answered. 'I can't fail my parents. I received word from them a few weeks ago, from a cousin of ours in Chattanooga. The letter is the first communication I've had with Zindelo and Nadya in almost a year.' I heard the crumpling of paper: the envelope Hugo had kept in his jacket pocket. 'Their orders are clear. I have to keep him here until they return. See?' The paper passed hands. 'He can't be allowed to go to the Romanys.'

'This sound serious, Hugo. But, even so, they left you in charge.'

'Of the clan, yes. But not this.' Hugo's large form paced the room, his steel-toed boots hard against the floor. 'My parents risked their lives to bring him to us, this creature. He's a gargoyle, not a Gypsy. He's supposed to serve our people, Karl. He's not supposed to look and talk and act like a kid. I didn't think it would happen like this. I never expected . . . I never meant . . . '

'To get so attached,' Karl finished softly.

Hugo was silent.

My chest felt like a sledgehammer had been dropped on it, smashing my emotions into tiny bits. I focused on my eyelids, pouring every bit of my strength into them. They twitched, and I was able to slit them open, but I could see only shadows and silhouettes. The shadow nearest me passed over my arm.

'Well, physically he's fine, Hugo. The wrist will heal, and the knife wound doesn't seem to have affected him, which is fortunate, considering. You know how dangerous diamond-coated weapons are to shadow creatures. Of course, these injuries are the least of his problems, if what you've told me is true.'

A *diamond* knife?

'Thanks for the help, Karl. I'll have to figure out where we're going from here.'

'I'm going to head back, Hugo,' he said. 'You know I can't be gone too long, especially when I'm needed at the Fairgrounds.'

'Of course.'

'I'm sorry,' said Karl. 'I know this is a difficult situation for you.'

'Come on,' replied my brother. 'I'll walk you out.'

The two forms disappeared, and I was left with nothing but shadows and silence.

I wasn't sure how long I lay there. But slowly, my vision cleared. I was on Hugo's tattoo bench, and the only light came from his small work lamp. I coaxed my stiff, heavy body into a seated position and prodded my neck with my fingers. A tender lump bulged beneath the skin. I winced. What had Vincent given me?

The clock on the wall read five o'clock. But was it morning or evening? I scrunched my brows, thinking hard. Hugo said I'd been out since last night.

Which meant it was Sunday.

I staggered to my feet, fending off the dizziness, and yanked up my shirt. Augustine's knife had left a razor-thin line just below my ribs. To my surprise it wasn't bleeding or even scabbed over. Karl had said the weapon was diamond-coated. I didn't know what that meant, but apparently, I'd been lucky. I let go of my shirt and examined my wrist.

It was wound tightly in gauze. I grabbed a pair of scissors off Hugo's cart and went to work. Several snips later, the bandage fell to the floor. The tattoo was perfectly intact, but the surrounding skin looked like it had been torched.

They'd tried to burn the brand off of me.

I clung to my wrist as I ducked into the hall. There were voices coming from the waiting room. I got a sense of déjà vu as I eased closer to listen in.

Kris' voice came first. 'We've tried everything, Hugo.'

There was a heavy pause.

237

'Not everything,' said Vincent.

'Well, then we need to decide now,' answered Kris.

'I agree,' said James. 'We can't stay out of this any longer.'

Another pause.

Then, Vincent. 'So what next, Hugo?'

'We'll take him to Ezzie's.'

I didn't know what that meant either, but I knew one thing: I was done with the Corsi clan making decisions for me. If this was my life now, then I was going to have the final say in it.

'You're not taking me anywhere.'

The effect of my appearance was almost comical. They whirled and gawked. Only Hugo remained composed. He studied me, his eyes roaming from my face to my wrist and back again. It was the same emotionless expression I'd grown used to, but now – maybe because of what I'd heard between him and Karl – I could see the hint of pained conflict in the lines between his brows.

The heaviness in my chest returned. I'd spent the last three years living a lie the Corsis had created for me. Pretending I was normal, with a family and a future that had never existed in the first place. I should've been furious. I should've been hurt beyond repair. But instead, I felt nothing, not even towards Hugo.

'I'm going to the Circe,' I said walking past the group.

'No you aren't,' Hugo said. He snatched my arm, dragging me back. 'You don't belong to the Romanys, Sebastian.'

'I don't belong to anyone, Hugo.'

'We're your clan, and we're the only ones who can help you through this transition. You're changing, Sebastian, and it won't stop until you're fully awakened.'

I wrenched free from his grasp. 'I know.'

'Then you know I'm telling you the truth.'

I stared at Hugo incredulously. 'How can you say that? It's been nothing but lies and deception from the start.'

Hugo ran his hands through his dark hair. 'You're right, Sebastian. But I had my reasons, and I'm not going to apologize for anything I've done.'

'I'm not asking for your apology. I just want you to trust *me* for once, okay? Everyone wants me to break this tie with Josephine Romany, but I can't, Hugo.'

'Sebastian, I know you feel a pull . . . '

'I *can't*.'

Hugo frowned. 'And why not?'

My heart flew wildly up my throat, like it was trying to tear itself loose. My body shook with a new emotion, one that I couldn't force back, no matter how hard I tried.

'Because I love her.'

Oh, God. I'd said it out loud. But as soon as the words left my mouth, I knew they were true. Everything fell into place. I loved her like I'd loved nothing else in my life. That's why I had to protect her. Not because of seals or duty or destiny.

Because of something far more powerful.

'I love her.' I said again.

Maybe everyone around me was right. Maybe I *was* compelled to act because I was her guardian. But what I felt went far deeper than the ink on my wrist. That truth was all that mattered.

Hugo's voice shattered my clarity.

'You're incapable of love, Sebastian.'

I stared at him. 'What?'

Hugo moved closer, his face set. 'You may think you love her, but you don't. And your feelings may even be intense, but it isn't love.'

239

I staggered back as though I'd been slapped. 'I don't believe you.'

'It doesn't matter if you do or not. Sebastian, you were designed and crafted to protect us. That's the driving force that gives you life. You may think it's love, but what you really feel is the duty and obligation of your kind.'

'My kind,' I repeated slowly. Despair crept over me, filling me like water in a sinking boat. Images of Josephine flashed though my head. 'No . . . '

'Anyone could tell you that love clouds judgment. In a guardian, it would be a weakness. Our ancestors knew that when they created the shadow creatures.'

The waters rose higher until I was drowning in them. 'I don't believe you,' I said again, but it wasn't Hugo I was trying to convince.

'Look, Sebastian,' said Vincent. 'Accept your place here with our clan and let us figure out how to deal with this. It's the only way you'll find any peace.'

James nodded. 'Make the choice while you still can.'

More choices that weren't really choices. I backed away. I needed space, needed air. Clarity was turning into confusion, and I couldn't be sucked back into that void again. 'Why am I so important?'

'In case you haven't noticed,' Vincent replied, 'there aren't too many gargoyles running around here. Just those three Augustine's managed to force under his control. But our history tells us that when gargoyles make an appearance, it means some kind of trouble's on the horizon. So yeah, Sebastian, I'd say you're kind of important to us.'

'Then why don't you break the ties yourself?' My blood boiled, making it easier to deal with the ache of their words. 'If you own me, then just make the choice for me!'

Hugo sprang up. 'We don't know how!' A heavy silence fell over the room. I blinked back at him, my body quivering with emotion. His cold demeanor was gone, and I could see the frustration in his face. 'This never should have happened,' he continued with forced calm. 'Gargoyles are sealed at the clan's discretion. It shouldn't be your decision to make in the first place.'

The dark emotions suddenly left me. 'Why do I have to be sealed at all?' I pressed. 'Why can't I just be a gargoyle free agent or something? If I'm supposed to protect Gypsies, I'll do it. I don't need some seal for that.'

'It doesn't work that way,' Hugo said. 'Once you've been branded, the process is irreversible. You must be sealed to a charge or be branded for another one.'

I looked at my wrist. 'You tried that.'

'Yeah, and it didn't work,' admitted Hugo. 'There's something different about you. When my parents brought you to us, they said they'd never encountered a shadow creature like you before.'

I slid down the wall putting my head in my hands. I'd only just found out I was a gargoyle, and now I was discovering I wasn't even a normal one, at that.

'Then what *do* you know?' I asked wearily.

'A seal is a permanent bond, and according to everything I've read, it can only be broken when the gargoyle or the charge dies. But since you aren't sealed yet, I'm not sure if that applies.'

My heart skidded to a halt.

'Do all Gypsies know that?'

Hugo frowned. 'Know what?'

'The dead part.'

His face flashed with understanding. 'Yes.'

'Oh God,' I breathed. 'Josephine.'

I leapt up, clearing the room in two bounds, heading for the door. Vincent and Kris moved almost as fast, meeting me at the entrance. They wedged their bodies between me and escape. I whirled around, frantic.

'Hugo, I have to go,' I pleaded, 'Augustine told me if I didn't make the choice, he'd make it for me. I have to get to Josephine!'

Hugo moved closer. I sensed the looming presence of the others at my back, barring the exit. I smelled their sweat and heard their ragged breathing. I hunched over, feeling the blood racing through my veins, the panic rising in my chest.

My brother nodded stiffly. 'All right.'

For a split second, I thought I'd heard wrong. Then James rushed to his side.

'Hugo, what are you doing?' he demanded. 'What about Zindelo . . . '

'Step away from the door,' Hugo ordered.

The guys glared at him with shocked faces, but they complied without another word.

Hugo fixed his gaze on me. 'Now go, before I change my mind.'

I backpedaled to the door, unsure of what was happening. But I didn't have time to think it through. I'd already wasted so much time. 'I'll come back,' I said as I grabbed the handle. 'I promise.'

I burst through the door and jumped into my van, fumbling for my keys. What if Augustine was already there? What if he'd done something to her? I raced out of the parking lot towards the Fairgrounds. She was fine, I told myself. She had to be fine. If I were connected to her, then surely I would know if . . .

242

I refused to complete the thought.

I turned onto Fairground Drive, crossed the Sutallee Bridge. And then, I hit traffic.

Opening night of the Circe de Romany.

The one-lane road was bumper to bumper all the way. Adrenaline pumped through me, and with it came fear: panicked, blinding fear. I no longer cared what was senseless and what was sane. I was going to reach Josephine, and I was going to save her. My entire being was consumed by that driving force.

I jerked the wheel, careening off the road and down the bank. It was useless driving. The trees were too thick. I parked the van in the ditch and jumped out, running for the Fairgrounds as fast as I could. I saw the front gates, ornamented with lamps that sparked against the evening sky. Just beyond, the Circe de Romany was alive with lights, sounds, and smells. Hope rose, then sank in my chest. The line at the entrance was enormous.

I raced along the perimeter, looking for an unoccupied space of fence. The Circe was swamped with people, and I shuddered, feeling trapped before I was even inside. The only thing propelling me forward was the thought of protecting Josephine Romany.

What I was *meant* to do.

I stopped running, finally finding what I needed: a sturdy tree growing near the fence. In a matter of seconds, I was up and over, landing quietly behind a carnival booth. I pulled my hood low over my face, and stepped into the crowd. The mass of humanity was suffocating. I pressed as close to the edges of the pavilions as I could. I had to hurry. Suddenly, I heard my name.

'Hey, look who it is,' Avery yelled, jogging up. 'I thought you'd gone totally AWOL, man!'

Katie and Mitchell were right behind him. Mitchell was stuffing cotton candy into his mouth. Katie looked at me, clearly disgusted.

'Thanks for calling me back, Sebastian,' she said, her voice biting with sarcasm. 'I must've left twenty messages on your phone.'

I faltered, torn between guilt and the need to find Josephine. 'I'm so sorry, Katie. I didn't mean to just disappear. The fire thing at the movies, and then I got sick again. I've been in bed all day.'

'Seriously?' she asked accusingly.

'Uh, yeah,' I replied. My excuses were lame, but I didn't know what else to do. I glanced anxiously at the Big Tent. 'I . . . ah . . . caught the flu or something.'

Avery slapped me on the shoulder, and it took everything in me not to snarl at him. 'Well, you're good now, right?' he asked. He wasn't the least bit bothered by Katie's foul mood. 'I think the show's starting soon.'

Mitchell spoke around a mouthful of pink fluff. 'Yeah, we promised Josephine we'd be there to watch.'

Josephine.

'I have to go,' I said, backing up. 'Why don't you save me a seat, okay?'

Katie looked at me as if I'd gone insane. 'Yeah, okay. Whatever, Sebastian.'

I hesitated, feeling awful. 'I'm sorry.'

Katie maneuvered out of the way. 'We'll see you inside,' she said in a tone like battery acid.

As I watched my friends walk away – taking my old life with them – the rift between my two worlds gaped opened. I'd convinced myself that I could somehow piece the two together. That I could deal with my own changes and this

244

strange Gypsy society I found myself involved with, and then just keep going on as I was.

But I'd been lying to myself the whole time. I knew that whatever happened tonight, things would never be the same again. Not with my friends. Not with me. But I couldn't stand there and dwell on it now. I turned away, letting the crowd consume me.

A series of long gates blocked the back section of the Circe from the public. I wove through pieces of equipment and large crates until I reached them. I made sure no one was around then I readied myself for what should've been an impossibly high jump. Adrenaline fueled me, and I leapt easily over the gate and landed in a soft crouch on the other side. The Holding Tent was only a few yards ahead. I prepared to sprint for it.

But I was nearly flung backwards by ice daggers through my gut, piercing to the marrow of my bones. A group of men rounded the tent from the opposite side, marching in a tightly knit group. I ducked behind a large crate. They were dressed head-to-toe in black. Bows and arrows were strapped to their backs and knives hung from belts at their waists. I wondered what their part was in the show. Then I caught sight of the man in the lead.

Quentin Marks.

I shoved myself against the wood, suppressing a growl. Quentin was in the middle of giving instructions as he passed, his smooth voice firm and commanding.

'Phillipe and Stephan,' he said, waving his hand, 'I want you to keep the back areas secure. The rest of you, patrol the perimeter. I'm not taking any chances tonight.'

The men marched past the crate, and I eased around the other side until they were out of sight. The frigid cold released me. If Quentin was out making rounds, then Josephine had to be okay. But that knowledge didn't alleviate my anxiety or lessen my resolve. I scrambled for the open doorway.

Partitions of colored drapes were arranged inside, creating numerous dressing rooms. The lighting was dim, and I moved stealthily, keeping to the shadows. I slid along the outskirts, avoiding the crowded areas, but I didn't have to search for Josephine. My freaky gargoyle radar had activated.

I knew exactly where she was.

21. *Heaven and Hell*

I followed my extrasensory homing beacon towards Josephine Romany. My senses were going haywire, everything inside me tuning in to her frequency. I paused outside a draped-off door. The fabric was parted just enough to catch a glimpse of her silhouette against the bright white bulbs of a large make-up mirror.

Suddenly her body stiffened, and I knew she felt my presence. I gathered my courage and passed through the curtain. Josephine was sitting at a dresser, surrounded by the soft glow of lights. She was in full costume and looked every bit like the Gypsy from my image; dazzling and otherworldly.

'Josephine.'

A profound calm rippled over me as I said her name. I hovered in the shadowy corner, captivated by Josephine's reflection in the glass. My heart convulsed like a caged bird. She kept her gaze averted, however, looking at a large bouquet of roses sitting nearby.

'You came,' she said softly.

There was a strange quality to her voice – something I hadn't heard before – and I wavered, almost afraid to answer. Her face was difficult to read within the mirror. She

247

touched one of the red petals, and I saw the card nestled in the bouquet. They were from Quentin. Josephine's hands shifted to her hair, smoothing it carefully into place.

'I know the show is starting soon,' I said, my voice cracking despite my best efforts. 'I didn't mean to interrupt you.'

I started to back out, but Josephine whirled in her chair, her emerald eyes stopping me in my tracks. Her hand went to her throat, and I straightened quickly, alarmed at the look on her face. 'What's wrong?'

She fiddled with the gold bangles on her arms, and her expression clouded over. 'Quentin's been secretive all day, like he's expecting something, but he won't talk to me. I know I shouldn't be worried. The Marksmen have always protected us.'

'You mean the bow and arrow guys.'

She nodded. 'They always patrol, especially during performances, but this time, it just feels different. Something we haven't dealt with before.'

My protective urges flickered to life. I clenched my teeth against the rising tension in my body, the instincts begging to take control. 'Then I need to keep you safe.'

'What do you mean?'

'Josephine,' I began slowly. It was time to lay all my cards down on the table, such as they were. 'You asked if there was something different about me.' I braced myself. 'Well, there is.'

She came around her chair slowly and looked into the shadowy corner where I was hiding. 'Step into the light.'

My head jerked up in surprise. But I couldn't refuse her request. That thing inside me – that pull – just wouldn't let me. I reached up, discarding my hood. Then I moved from the shadows. Josephine gasped softly.

'Sebastian . . . '

She searched my face, lingering on my eyes. I waited in rigid anticipation, prepared for her to turn me out. Instead, she crossed the room until she was right in front of me. Her hand was at her neck again, absently playing with the pendant. I felt the current instantly.

'You're . . . *supposed* to protect me, aren't you?' she asked, her voice soft with wonder.

My breathing doubled erratically. All I'd heard since this whole thing had started was how I was misplaced, how I wasn't supposed to be linked to Josephine Romany. But as I looked into her eyes, I knew everyone was wrong. 'Yes.'

Josephine's brows furrowed. 'But I don't understand. Quentin is our protector. The Marksmen look after our clan. It's their job. You aren't even a Gypsy, Sebastian. What reason do you have to protect me?'

Here was my moment to tell Josephine how much I loved her; how I loved every single thing about her. She was so close that I was getting dizzy, and her intoxicating scent threatened to send me to my knees.

And I couldn't tell her. Not like this. Her face was so radiant in the soft light, and every bangle, every piece of costume glittered like jewels. She was a Gypsy angel. And what was I? *A gargoyle*? If what Augustine said was true, I was nothing she'd ever consider.

Especially not now.

'I have to keep you safe,' I whispered.

'How, Sebastian? What can you offer that Quentin and the other Marksmen can't?'

My chest ached with tension. 'Have you ever heard of guardians?'

She stared hard at me, scrutinizing every detail of my face, her expression a mixture of conflicting emotions. But when she spoke, her voice was steady. 'Like from the old Roma legends.'

For some reason, I hadn't expected her to know. 'Well, that's what I am,' I said quickly, before I could change my mind. 'And that's why I need to make sure you're safe.'

Josephine leaned nearer until our breaths mingled together, both shallow and uncertain. 'How?' she asked again, her voice desperate.

My gaze fell to her pendant, and suddenly, she knew. I couldn't explain it, but she knew, just like I knew. It was some overwhelming, instinctive knowledge between us. I didn't know if that was normal or not, but I didn't care. And it didn't matter if I believed Hugo or Augustine or anybody else, or what was true or make-believe.

This moment was real.

Josephine inhaled once, slow and deliberate, and her fingers clasped the pendant. The same magnetic pull I'd felt in the movie theater took hold of me. She turned the pendant over in her fingers, and my tattoo shot sparks across my skin. The air around us seemed to carry the weight of some harbored secret.

'What will happen if they touch?' she whispered.

A sharp, biting fear snapped at my insides. For the first time, the enormity of what I was about to do hit me. What was going to happen to me, to Josephine?

How much more would I *change*?

My arm rose, and my actions were no longer my own. The inked dandelion stretched along the inside of my wrist, vulnerably exposed. Josephine held the pendant higher. The distance closed between us. I closed my eyes, helpless and terrified.

A loud voice split the silence.

'Josephine! Warning cue to the backstage!'

I recoiled into the shadows – disappointed and relieved at the same time – until Josephine followed me. A startled gasp escaped me as she ran her fingers curiously through my gray hair. I went weak at the knees, blinking hard to stay focused and upright.

But I couldn't breathe.

'Warning cue!' yelled the voice again.

Josephine's fingers froze. 'I have to perform,' she said, sounding dazed. Her fingers slipped from my hair. 'My act is next.'

She pushed aside the drape and looked out. I tried to balance my teetering emotions. I'd been so certain about everything just minutes ago. Now, I was wrenched with conflict. Josephine turned around.

'Come with me,' she said.

My brows shot up. 'What?'

'You heard me.'

Josephine smiled, though her eyes were still uncertain. I wrestled the urge to hide again as I stared into the cavern of my own feelings. I knew I loved her. My heart didn't lie. So then, what was I going to do about it? How much was I willing to risk? As those emerald eyes met mine, I realized I had my answer.

Josephine Romany was worth any sacrifice.

'All right.'

Her smile softened into something more genuine, and she dipped through the draped opening. I followed close behind. Performers darted around and stagehands in black herded them to their places. Josephine ducked into another dressing area, beckoning me inside.

'This is Andre's space,' she explained, moving to a hanger of clothes. 'You can wear his costume.'

'I can do *what*?'

'He's my partner,' she said, searching the rack. 'He's sick tonight so we're going on without him, but if you're wearing a costume, you'll blend in better backstage.'

'You want me backstage?'

She looked over the clothes and smiled. 'You said you wanted to keep me safe, right? I figured you'd want to be nearby.'

I actually found myself grinning. 'Okay.'

Josephine returned to the costumes, sorting through them with her fingers. She called back over her shoulder. 'Hurry, take off your shirt.'

My smile vacated, and I swallowed nervously. But this was no time to be self-conscious. If I wanted to keep her safe, I had to be near her. And to be near her, I had to be able to get backstage. I quickly unzipped my jacket and shrugged off my shirt, tossing them aside. Josephine yanked a hanger from the rack and spun around to face me. Her eyes widened.

'Oh . . . '

Her voice trailed off, and I looked away, my face growing hot. I caught my reflection in the dressing mirror, and I couldn't blame Josephine for her reaction. My entire body was unmistakably gray – not pale, not sallow – but gray. Every contour in my face and neck, every bulge of muscle and bone in my chest was outlined in charcoaled shadows. My eyebrows, the hollows under my eyes, and even my lips were a darker shade of the same color. I couldn't help noticing that my arms seemed more defined; my shoulders a little broader. Avery would've been impressed. But the rest of my physical alterations weren't so positive.

Josephine approached tentatively, her eyes still roaming my body. I was warm with embarrassment, but my skin was tingling. Music and applause filtered through the walls of the tent, snapping us both back to reality.

'Here,' she said, indicating the hanger of clothes. 'Get dressed and meet me backstage. I have to go before they come looking for me.'

She pressed the costume into my hand, her fingers briefly grazing mine, and then she was gone. She was sending me into a tailspin, and I felt recklessly out of control. *Focus, Sebastian, focus.* I knew there wasn't much time. Taking pains to avoid the mirror, I pulled a dark blue tunic off the hanger and slipped it over my head. There was a long cloak as well. I swung it over my shoulders and huddled gratefully into the deep hood.

I scurried through the Holding Tent – avoiding the frantic performers – and made my way outside. Josephine had been right about the costume. I spotted several others in similar attire. No one would look twice at me. I could stay nearby and keep an eye on her. If Augustine or his minions tried anything, I'd be there to stop them.

Of course, I hadn't figured out how yet.

Inside the backstage area of the Big Tent, all was muffled darkness. Monstrous curtains divided the stage from the inner workings of the Circe de Romany. Music wafted through the air, and I could feel the excitement of the audience on the other side. I scanned the area with my night vision eyes. A large platform – complete with rope ladders and a massive fly system – loomed overhead. Around it, crewmembers adjusted ropes and pulleys.

My familiar sixth-sense alerting me to Josephine's presence buzzed through me, and I turned to see her – along with a group of similarly costumed people – passing through a small opening in the curtain. Her head dipped in my direction, and she smiled briefly. Then she disappeared.

It suddenly occurred to me that I hadn't thought this whole thing through. If Josephine was performing on stage and I was stuck backstage, how was I going to look after her? For someone supposedly meant to guard Gypsies, I was really sucking it up so far. I eyed the curtain, pondering my next move, until a hand on my shoulder made me jump. I twisted around to find a pudgy man with a headset glaring at me.

'You're late, Andre,' he said, pointing his flashlight at me. 'Get out there before you miss your cue.'

Obviously not everyone knew about Andre's sickness. The last of the performers were exiting through the curtain. Before I could logic myself out of it, I rushed forward and fell into step behind the last one.

The stage was dark in preparation for the act. The audience hushed in anticipation as the performers took their places, freezing in elaborate positions. I looked for cover. There was a large speaker, just past the curtain wall. I peeled off from the group and concealed myself behind it.

I was just in time.

The lights came up, the music swelled, and the scene began. Josephine and the others – all dressed in elaborate Gypsy attire – were arranged around a brightly colored wagon. It was as though the painting in my brother's shop had come to life before my eyes. The music changed tempo, and the women began to dance.

I was mesmerized.

Skirts whirled and jewelry flashed as the performers glided over the stage like ethereal beings, and Josephine's swaying body set the blood pounding in my ears. I could have watched her forever. At that moment – unfortunately – ice clogged my veins. The tent ceiling was pitch black, but I could clearly see two figures slithering down the metal supports of the floating platform. My skin crawled as I caught the glint of silver eyes within the shadows.

They were here.

254

22. *Faith or Futility*

I crouched low as the gargoyles moved effortlessly along the ceiling. They wove through the shadows, blending with the darkness of the tent. The sensation that warned me of their presence obviously worked both ways. They were too high for me to see their faces, but I could tell by the dip of their heads that they were searching for me. I took a whiff of air, and immediately placed the scent. It belonged to Matthias and Thaddeus: Augustine's lackeys.

A Circe troupe member was stationed on the platform, busily unwinding long strips of red fabric. As he released them, they cascaded over the sides like streams of blood. The men on stage pulled the ribbons taut. The women danced towards them and took hold of the fabric as they continued to whirl in their routine. I'd seen an act like this before; I knew exactly what was about to happen.

My gaze shifted to the ceiling. The two figures landed on the platform, jostling the scaffold. The Circe performer hustled to his feet in surprise. The closest figure seized him by the neck. The man's body jerked unnaturally, and then he dropped lifeless to the platform floor.

The Gypsy women hoisted themselves into the air. The

men rotated the ribbons, and the women began to twirl. Josephine was in the middle of the lot, her body suspended high above the stage. On the platform, Matthias ripped off his thick hood and crouched at the railing. A dagger glimmered in his hand. His gray face split in a sharp-toothed grin.

Matthias positioned the blade flat against Josephine's silk ribbon. Meanwhile, the performers continued, oblivious of the danger above. The lights dimmed, and I took advantage of the change. I leapt onto a swinging rope ladder and scrambled for the platform.

Josephine was well above the stage, her body nearly upside down as she hung by one leg. Matthias's clawed fingers tightened around the ribbon. He slashed with his dagger, making the first cut. I flung myself over the rail, only to find Thaddeus in my way. His eyes sparked like metal on flint, his animalistic face malicious.

'So nice to see you again, Sebastian,' he hissed.

'Stop this. Josephine hasn't done anything to you.'

Matthias looked up from the rail. 'Oh, but she has. She's kept you from joining us.'

I held out my hands, speaking over the music. 'Look, I'll break the ties with her, okay? I'll do whatever needs to be done. Just leave her out of this.'

'Oh, it's too late for that,' Matthias answered. 'There's only one way to end this before you're sealed. The girl must die.'

He lowered his dagger to the fabric, and I rushed forward. Thaddeus gripped me by the arm, his claws sinking painfully into my flesh.

'Please,' I begged, my mind racing for a solution. 'I won't go near her again.'

Thaddeus snarled. 'You think it's so easy?'

'You're no good to us sealed,' said Matthias in a frigid tone. 'And Augustine needs you.'

'Yeah, for what?'

He smirked. 'To rid the world of *them*.'

The dagger flashed, and I lunged, wrenching free of Thaddeus. I hit Matthias hard, knocking us both to the floor of the platform. His fingers clamped over my wrists. Before I knew it, I was hurtling through the air.

Instinct alone kept me alive. I grabbed the railing as my body flew past. I slammed against the side of the platform. The music swirled to a crescendo. I hung precariously from the rail, feet dangling. Josephine was only a dozen feet below me, her back arched in a graceful pose. Another flash of movement – this one above me – and Matthias jumped into view. I stared at his gargoyle face, twisted in sadistic satisfaction. My fingers slipped against the railing.

'If you'd listened to us, Sebastian,' he hissed down at me. 'Things would have been much easier.'

The dagger reappeared, and it sliced the flesh of my hand, but the pain didn't register at first. I was too enthralled with the blade. Like Augustine's knife, it glowed with a crystalline fire, as though coated with hundreds of diamonds. Blood poured down my arm, soaking the cuff of my tunic. I yanked my hand from the rail and hung by one arm.

The performers continued their act before the captivated crowd. I wondered what they would think when the body of a dead teenager hit the stage floor. Sweat and fear drenched my skin. If I died, who would save Josephine? I was afraid of death, but I was more terrified of losing her.

Another gray face hovered over the rail. 'What are you doing?' snarled Thaddeus, his silver eyes fixed on his companion. 'Augustine wants him alive.'

'You know the fall won't kill him.' Matthias's gray lips pulled back, revealing rows of sharp, jagged teeth. He smiled wickedly down at me. 'But it'll hurt. A lot.'

In my mind, I saw myself tumbling from the Ferris wheel again. That fall hadn't killed me. But it *had* incapacitated me. 'I thought you needed me,' I said, trying to stall, though I wasn't sure of my next move. 'Is this how you treat all your potential members?'

'I never said I liked you,' Matthias replied. 'I'm just following orders.'

'From a Gypsy?' I shot back. 'Funny how you're doing the very thing you said you hated. Maybe I'm not the one who's the Gypsy pet. Maybe it's you.'

Matthias's face went dark with fury. He flashed his hideous teeth, and gripped my throat. I choked and gagged as my air supply was shut off. I clawed desperately at his hand as my body was suspended over the stage. The edges of my vision swirled black. I wasn't going to be able to save Josephine. They were going to kill her. And it was my fault. Images of her face consumed what was left of my consciousness.

'You're not playing very nice,' said a voice from the other side of the platform.

I squinted through my oxygen-deprived blur. Esmeralda Lucian was standing there, her hands on the ropes.

My attacker jerked in astonishment, letting me go. Somehow, I managed to throw an arm over the rail before I plunged to the ground. I flipped myself over the metal beam and dropped to my knees on the platform, sputtering for air.

Matthias snarled at Ms Lucian. 'How dare you!'

'This is none of your business!' growled Thaddeus.

Ms Lucian made a clucking sound in the back of her throat. 'Picking on a defenseless fledgling gargoyle? And one under the care of the Corsi clan, at that. I think that makes it my business.'

As I stared in shock at my drama teacher, I caught something flash in her hazel eyes; a silvery glimmer. 'Ms Lucian?' I rasped, my throat on fire. 'How did . . . '

'Go, Sebastian,' she said firmly. There was a thin smile on her lips, but her voice was tense with urgency. 'Go to Josephine. I'll take care of these two.'

Instantly, the platform was engulfed with mist. It surrounded Ms Lucian, concealing her from view. The gray figures flung themselves into its oily depths. Inhuman shrieks filled the air, barely obscured by the blaring music below. I watched in horrified fascination as the mist poured through the rails of the platform.

And disappeared.

I gaped at the empty space. Ms Lucian and the gargoyles were gone. I coughed and rolled over, knowing instantly what I had to do. Attached to the platform, just a few feet from my grasp, was Josephine's red ribbon, still intact. I ducked under the rail and clutched it in my hands. The audience sat enthralled with the Circe performers entwined within their ribbons. Josephine was the only one without a partner. She wound the ribbon around her waist, readying for another stunt.

Taking a deep breath, I pushed off the platform. The fabric burned into my open wound as I slid down. Josephine felt the ribbon go taut under my added weight. To her credit, only her eyes betrayed her surprise. I clasped the fabric tightly as I neared. The other performers were setting up for their own stunts, oblivious of the addition to their act.

'Sebastian,' she whispered frantically while looping her leg around the ribbon and extending her arm. '*What are you doing?*'

Despite her shock, she didn't miss a beat. She kept perfect time with the others, curling her body around mine as if I was her partner in the routine.

'Keeping you safe,' I whispered back.

Her lips moved close to my ear. 'And how's that, exactly?' She hooked her arm around my neck. 'By screwing up my entire show?'

Her warm breath against my skin made it difficult to concentrate. For a moment, I forgot I was hanging in the air in front of hundreds of people. All I could think about was Josephine Romany and the peace settling over my soul. Whatever happened, I was where I was supposed to be. I was with Josephine, and I'd keep her safe.

Safe.

I snapped back. I didn't know how Ms Lucian intended to stop Augustine's gargoyles, or if she was even capable of doing it. The tone of her voice had been less than reassuring. I had to get Josephine out of here. I wasn't going to let anyone hurt her, especially not when I was the reason her life was in jeopardy in the first place.

'You're in danger,' I said urgently. 'We need to go.'

'We can't stop the performance.'

I stared at her in alarm. 'What?'

She tipped her head, striking a pose. Then she pressed her body close to mine. I gripped the ribbon harder. Josephine smiled at me, unfazed by my announcement or my reaction.

'I trust you to keep me safe,' she said quietly. 'Now you have to trust me. The routine's almost over. Just stay with me.' She touched her cheek to mine. 'Can you do that?'

My resolve melted away. 'Yes.'

'Then just follow my lead.'

And I did. Josephine whispered instructions in my ear as she led the aerial dance. I didn't know how I managed, but somehow, our bodies entwined within the ribbon as if we'd been rehearsing for weeks. I felt in tune to her every move-ment, almost anticipating them. The red satin slid over her body. Heat rushed over mine.

'Lower me down,' she whispered finally.

The performers descended gracefully around us, like bright spiders on scarlet webs. I loosened my grip on the ribbon, grimacing as the dagger wound protested, but I did as she asked. The stage floor drew gradually closer as Josephine twirled into my chest, and her arm looped once more around my neck.

'You're not trying to steal Andre's spot, are you?' she said as our feet touched the ground.

She twirled out of my arms, and joined the other women in a bow. Applause erupted in the tent. The men stepped into line beside their partners. The audience clapped louder. Josephine reached out and pulled me next to her. I clutched her hand frantically.

'We have to go,' I hissed.

'Bow,' she whispered.

I did, while hastily searching the tent. The other gargoyles had to be nearby because my stomach was a block of ice. I couldn't see them, but I caught a glimpse of Katie and the rest of the gang, several rows back. With my hooded costume, I knew they weren't aware that I was one of the performers they were applauding. As soon as the lights went to black, I pressed my lips against Josephine's ear.

'Okay, now we *really* have to go.'

She nodded into my shoulder. The curtain parted for us, and the performers filed off the stage. Now that the act was over, I could feel Josephine growing nervous. Her hand trembled in mine as we reached the backstage area.

'So what do we do?' she asked.

I eased us out of the line of people, moving quickly to the exit. I didn't want to attract attention. For all I knew, Matthias or Thaddeus could be lurking in the shadows. As soon as we were in the open, I answered.

'We run.'

I took off, holding Josephine's hand tightly in my own. My claws touched her skin, and I felt her flinch. But I didn't let go. We dodged the fences, crates, and rigging, but as soon as we turned the corner around the Big Tent, our progress abruptly halted. The carnival was in full swing. People were crowded into every free space. I snarled in frustration and retreated behind the tent. Josephine came beside me, peering into my hood.

'Where are we going, Sebastian?'

'I don't know,' I snapped. I was feeling all kinds of weird instincts, some protective, some animal-like. They bombarded me from every direction, and I couldn't sort them out. It made it difficult to process anything clearly. 'I just need to get you away from here.'

I changed direction and pushed through the booths, growing more frustrated by the second. Where could we go? I could take her to Hugo's, though I doubted it would be any safer than the Circe. I needed a moment to regroup and think. Suddenly Josephine grabbed my tunic, stopping me short.

'Go to the woods, Sebastian.'

'What?'

'Quentin's patrolling the property,' she answered. 'He always does during performances. 'We'll find him. He can help us.'

My skin prickled. 'I don't trust him.'

She looked away, and I regretted speaking my mind. But I couldn't ignore the truth of it. There was something about him I didn't care for, and it went far beyond the simple fact that he was Josephine's boyfriend.

She turned back. 'Do you have a better idea?'

I ground my teeth so hard my jaw hurt. I didn't have a better idea. At least Quentin seemed as intent on protecting Josephine as I was. And I didn't know if I could stand up to Augustine and his minions alone. As much as I hated to admit it, Quentin was probably my best ally at the moment. If it meant keeping Josephine safe, I could deal with it.

'Where?'

'Near the bridge,' she replied. 'They have a camp there.'

'Let's go.'

This wasn't going according to the plan I didn't have.

We wove through the carnival, picking up speed as we reached the gates. As soon as we were outside the confines of the Fairgrounds, I broke into another run, pulling Josephine along with me. The wind picked up overhead – rushing through the autumn trees – and the temperature dropped, matching the ice in my veins. The night and the woods closed in around us.

I continued through trees and underbrush, letting my instincts guide me. Josephine's breaths grew labored, but we couldn't stop. We reached the gravel road, and I paused just long enough to get my bearings. It was one moment too long. An unearthly hiss rose from the wind, and I looked back at Josephine.

'Run!'

We were being chased, pursued on both sides. I couldn't see them, but I felt their presence beyond the trees, moving at the same speed. Josephine stumbled. I wrapped my arm around her waist. I wondered if I'd be able to fight them off if they overtook us. I'd die trying, I knew that much.

I heard the rush of river water. We were almost at the bridge. Suddenly an object whizzed past my face. I jerked upright as a black arrow sunk into a tree, just inches from my head. There was another. Then another. Arrows thudded into trees all around us. I shied and doubled back, pushing Josephine behind me.

'What is he *doing*?' cried Josephine. 'Quen . . . '

I clamped a clawed hand over her mouth, shaking my head. Mist was curling from the high branches. Snarls echoed around us. I shoved Josephine into the underbrush as another arrow made a pass at my face. I didn't know who was attacking who. From the sounds of things, Quentin and his men had found Augustine's minions, and I'd dragged Josephine right into the middle of the fray.

'We have to take cover,' I said. 'I think I know a place where we can hide.'

She nodded steadily. 'Okay.'

It was now or never. Josephine squeezed my hand, and we sprang from the undergrowth. I heard men shouting not far behind, and I was afraid Josephine would stop. But she continued to run – looking breathless and terrified – beside me. The river came into view. Then, fifty yards upstream, the bridge. I changed course and aimed for the old wooden over-pass. Then I saw what I searching for: an opening between the supports of the bridge on our side of the river.

'Come on,' I hissed.

Behind us, the wind whipped through half-naked trees, scattering dead leaves in its wake. Cold dread snatched at me. My chest burned from the run. Josephine was gasping.

Only a few more yards to go. I glanced over my shoulder but didn't see anyone.

I careered down the riverbank, Josephine at my heels. The bridge towered over us, and the sound of rushing water roared like cavernous falls. Just under the place where the bridge met the bank was an opening. My feet were soaked up to the ankles as I led Josephine over the rocks, sloshing towards the hole. When she saw where I was heading, she stopped, planting her feet firmly in the mud.

'We're not going in there.'

'It's okay,' I said. 'It's an abandoned mine shaft. It doesn't go far back.'

'How do you know?'

'Camping trip with the guys last summer.'

I peered through the entrance. The place was strewn with trash, but it was empty, and it would be safe. Once I had Josephine safely hidden, I could climb back out and lead our pursuers away.

'All right,' Josephine relented.

Wind howled overhead. I sheltered Josephine behind me and backed us through the opening. It was clammy and damp inside the mine entrance. The sounds of the wind and the river faded away as we retreated further in. The low ceiling allowed us just enough clearance to stand. The ground and walls reeked pungently of dirt.

'Stay here,' I said.

I returned to the opening and crouched there. I sniffed the air, testing for any foul odors, but I wasn't able to discern anything past the earthy scents of soil and stone. My stomach felt permanently frozen, giving me no helpful indication of what might be skulking nearby. All my new senses and abilities seemed frustratingly useless, right when I needed them most.

'Sebastian?'

I glanced over my shoulder. I could tell she was having a difficult time seeing me in the darkness. But I could see Josephine just fine with my night vision, her features sculpted in vivid, detailed grayscale.

'Yes?' I said with some hesitation.

I was afraid she was going to demand we leave, to go back and find Quentin. But instead, she felt her way over to me and brushed her fingertips across my jaw. My skin warmed immediately under her touch.

'You're one of them, aren't you?'

I looked outside to avoid her searching gaze. 'I told you, I'm a guardian.' I replied. 'Or, at least, I'm trying to be. I'm kind of new to this.'

'No, I mean you're like . . . like *them*.'

There was no mistaking her meaning, and once again, I was taken aback by what she knew. But she was an Outcast Gypsy, I reminded myself. This was a part of her world; a world I hadn't even realized existed just a few short weeks ago.

'I'm not like them,' I said firmly.

'You know what I mean.'

The air shifted, and Josephine was suddenly kneeling beside me in the soggy dirt. She removed the costume hood from my head and took a strand of my gray hair between her fingers. Then she slid her other hand along my arm until she found my wrist. She pressed her palm delicately to my skin. I could feel my pulse through the tattoo.

'You're a gargoyle,' she said quietly.

'Yes.'

I said the word quickly, like ripping off a bandage. Then I waited for her reaction. I couldn't read her thoughts in the quiet. She tilted her head.

'You're not what I would've expected.' Her fingers prodded my skin, tracing over the smooth surface of the dandelion. Instant heat radiated from the ink, and she gasped softly. A familiar charge buzzed in the air. 'I've heard so many stories,' she continued. 'All the folk tales from my family and my clan . . . all the Gypsy lore. I grew up listening to the fairy tales, but I never thought they were real.'

I felt precariously off-balance. 'You've known about me the whole time?'

'No,' Josephine replied quickly, holding my wrist. 'I mean, I knew you were different, somehow, even that first day I talked to you, at the call-board. It wasn't until you took me home that I realized it was something serious. The Ferris wheel, the way you acted in the woods . . . it wasn't normal. But when Quentin ordered me to stay away from you, I had to find out the real reason why.' Her eyes searched for mine in the darkness. 'I don't like unanswered questions, remember?'

I wanted to smile and gulp, all at once. 'And what did you find out?'

'There are things in our world that the *gadje* don't know exist.' Her fingers tightened across my skin. 'Dark things that have lurked in the shadows of our history, things we don't talk about from our past. It's why we have the Marksmen. Protecting us has been their family's calling for generations. Quentin's father was head of the Marksmen before him, and his grandfather before that. No one's ever questioned their role.' Josephine frowned in thought. 'But there were always tales about others, guardians that were around long before the Marksmen. Ancient creatures that were created to protect the Roma.'

Light illuminated Josephine's face as the dandelion pendant began to shine with a life of its own. She lifted my arm, and the strange ink Hugo had injected me with reflected the amber glow.

'Do you believe the stories?' I asked, my voice unsteady.

'I didn't.' She blinked up at me. 'Until now.'

She was so close that I could feel the warmth of her body. Electricity surged up my arm.

'Josephine . . .'

She licked her lips nervously. 'Yes?'

'Let me protect you.'

Her eyes flicked to my tattoo. 'Because you have to.'

'Because I love you.'

Josephine stared at me. Her mouth parted, but she didn't say anything. Emotion, as thick and heavy as the ceiling above us, weighed me down. She pulled herself to her knees, her face so close to mine that, for a moment, I dared to hope. Then her expression twisted and she dropped her gaze.

'Sebastian, I . . .'

'I know, Josephine . . . and it doesn't matter.'

She didn't return my feelings, and I didn't need her to say it out loud. Things were painful enough. But nothing was going to change my mind. I would protect Josephine Romany all the way to my last breath, if she'd let me.

My soul felt painfully bare, as though I'd torn it out and was holding it before her. It hurt worse than anything I'd ever felt. I took a shaky breath. She was worth the pain. She always would be.

Even if she didn't love me back.

Josephine looked up at me, her gaze conflicted. Finally, she nodded.

'I want you to protect me,' she whispered.

She released my wrist and took her pendant in both hands. Electricity crackled in the air as the pull between the dandelions grew unbearable. This time, I knew there would be no going back. I was on the edge of a cliff, about to jump, with no idea where or how I'd land. The dandelions flared as they drew close.

And then, they touched.

Every nerve in my body exploded in icy fire. Somewhere in the chaos, I heard Josephine's cry. Then another sound – harsh and strange – filled my ears. I gasped for air, but took in none. My body turned inside out with excruciating pain.

Everything around me turned to shadowy mist.

23. *Demons or Angels*

I was sure I was dead.

But there was no white light, no sense of peace or finality. Instead, mist wrapped around me like a shroud. And within this suffocating void of nothing, all was still. Had I been here for hours? Days? Years? Nothing registered inside my foggy coffin. I felt encased in stone.

Forever.

Then something knocked against my brain – an urgent voice – screaming out one name over and over again.

Josephine. Josephine. Josephine.

The name rang like a hammer against stone, and I felt myself cracking under the blows. I had to get out. I struggled against the petrification, willing myself to move, to escape the frosty grave. Then suddenly I burst through the surface, and the mist shattered like ice on a frozen pond.

I was lying in the mine shaft, eyes turned to the ceiling. My body felt oddly disconnected, and when I breathed in, everything inside me felt different, strange. I pushed myself up, gasping at the sharp pain in my back. It felt as though someone was ramming giant needles into my shoulder blades.

'Sebastian?'

The voice was soft and scared.

I winced against the pain and stood up. Josephine was on the opposite side of the shaft – clutching a wooden beam for support – looking pretty shaken up. The pendant still hung from her neck, but the glow was gone.

'Are you all right?' I asked.

She wrapped her arms around herself. 'Are you?'

'I think so.' I glanced at my wrist. The outline of the dandelion burned gently, like the last embers of a dying fire. Then, it stopped. My tattoo and the surrounding skin were normal again. The stabbing pricks in my back eased, and I rubbed my shoulders gingerly. I felt weird – really weird – but there wasn't time to dwell on it now. 'What happened?'

Josephine peered at me with unfocused eyes. Without the glow of her pendant, the mine shaft was dark again. 'I don't know. There was a flash of light and something threw me back. I couldn't see anything, but I heard you fall . . . and scream . . .'

'I'm fine,' I said quickly. 'Just as long as you're okay.'

I could see her nod. 'So what do we do now?'

'Wait here.'

The only sound I heard was the river rushing over the jagged rocks. I ventured closer to the opening to investigate. The wind had fallen still, and there were no whizzing arrows or hissing voices. There wasn't anyone – or anything – in sight. Perhaps Quentin had taken care of the other gargoyles.

Or they had taken care of him.

Whatever the case, I had to figure out if things were safe before I led Josephine away from the shaft. I took a deep breath. I didn't feel quite right. And yet, ironically enough, I felt very right. I stepped out onto the riverbank.

Something brushed against my legs, and I looked down to find not water, but swirling mist. I threw myself protectively in front of the entrance. Adrenaline and instincts kicked in as I searched for the source of the dark smoke.

'Sebastian, what are you doing here?' said a female voice.

A growl rumbled in my chest. 'You won't get past me.'

'I have no desire to get past you,' said the voice. 'I'm here to warn you.'

I bristled. 'Warn me about what, Anya?'

'I'm not Anya.'

The mist withdrew behind a bridge support, and I tensed, lip curled back, ready to spring. There was a flash of black and red hair, framing a face that caused my jaw to drop.

'Ms Lucian!'

'Esmeralda, please.' She waved her hand dismissively.

'But . . . '

'I've already helped you more than I should. But I can't stop the other gargoyles.' She glanced up, and I could have sworn she sniffed the air. 'They're close, and I wouldn't recommend you pinning yourself up in the cave. They'll corner you like prey.'

'This was just temporary,' I protested, still trying to get over my shock. 'I was going to leave Josephine here, so she'd be safe.'

Ms Lucian shot me a stern look. 'You'd leave your charge?'

I took a sharp breath. 'How did you . . . '

'You've sealed yourself to her, haven't you?' she snapped. Her gaze traveled pointedly to my wrist. 'I tried to keep you from this. I warned Hugo of what might happen if he gave you free rein, but he allowed his brotherly sentiment to over-rule logic. Hugo thought the brand was powerful enough, but he neglected the *sclav*.'

I frowned at the unfamiliar word. 'What's that?'

She sighed impatiently. 'A *sclav* is needed to complete the process. It can be any physical object, but it must belong to

272

the Gypsy whom the gargoyle is meant to protect.' She saw the look on my face and silenced me with her hand. 'Yes, I'm aware that the Corsis are without that bit of information, and it is not without intention. A guardian-charge bond is not to be taken lightly or tossed about on a whim. Once the gargoyle is sealed, he belongs to that Gypsy or clan, and it becomes his duty to protect them, no matter the risk.'

'How do you know this?'

Ms Lucian's eyes blazed. 'Because I know. It is not something that the Gypsies will ever fully understand.'

I glanced towards the mine shaft. I felt charged all over, as if I'd walked through a live current. 'So when our dandelions touched . . . '

'The seal became permanent.'

I rubbed my wrist, my thoughts returning to the gray figures. 'I screwed up, didn't I? I'm supposed to be with the Corsis, but I refused to listen because I felt . . . I thought . . . ' My words were pinched off by a frustrated, painful sigh.

'It wasn't your action alone,' she said, jutting her chin in the direction of the cave. 'You both shared in it.'

I could still feel Josephine's tender touch, her fingertips on my wrist. 'Can the seal be broken?' Cold terror poured through me. 'You heard Matthias's threat at the Circe. Now Josephine's in danger because of me, and . . . '

'No,' said Ms Lucian, stopping me. 'She would be in more danger without you. Augustine may have used the girl to draw you out, but this isn't just about you. Josephine Romany is special. A gargoyle doesn't awaken without a purpose, Sebastian. You may have initiated the contact, but the Gypsy must complete the bond.' Her hazel eyes sparked silver as her gaze lingered on the entrance to the cave. 'There's a reason Josephine accepted that choice, a greater and more important one than she realizes now, but a reason, nonetheless.'

My eyes narrowed. 'You know something.'

'There's no more time for talk,' Ms Lucian said quickly. 'What's done is done. This is what's important now. You're sealed to the girl, which means you're about to fully awaken. But the others aren't aware of what you've done yet. Use that to your advantage.'

'How?'

'When the moment arrives, your instincts will urge you to act. Don't fight them, Sebastian. Listen to them. They'll tell you exactly what to do.'

'I don't understand.'

'Don't worry,' she replied. 'You will.'

A breeze wafted between us. Ms Lucian surveyed the sky. This time, I was certain she smelled the air. Her expression hardened. 'You need to hurry.'

'But where do I go?'

'Out in the open, Sebastian, somewhere you can defend yourself and the girl. Let your instincts give you the answers. I can't help you any more than that.' She pointed to the cave. 'But if I were you, I'd start by getting the girl out of this death trap.'

Ms Lucian stepped into the mist, and suddenly, she was gone. I stared, unblinking, at the place where she'd been. But before I could grasp what had just happened, fiery ice exploded in my gut, the sensation stronger than it had ever been before.

'Josephine,' I called, clutching my stomach. She appeared in the opening. I grabbed her hand, ignoring the shudder that ran up her arm as I did so. 'They're coming. We have to get out of here.'

I clawed my way up the bank, pulling Josephine with me. We reached the road, and I looked for signs of the gray figures. The bridge stretched over the rushing water.

'Come on,' I urged.

With the Circe underway, the traffic was gone, leaving the bridge and the road deserted. I prayed that my van was still on the other side, parked in the ditch where I'd left it. I'd drive Josephine back to town. Surely a trio of supernatural gray figures wouldn't attack us in the middle of Main Street.

We were more than halfway over the bridge when a sharp wind ripped through the trees. The wind materialized into black mist and hovered across our path. I jerked to a halt, pulling Josephine behind me. Matthias and Thaddeus stood between us and freedom.

Josephine clung to my arm. Her fear ignited my blood. I hunched defensively, shoulders rolled back, positioning my body squarely in front of her, my lips thrust wide in a snarl. Matthias regarded me with his molten eyes.

'Hello again, Sebastian.'

Something dark moved within the mist behind them, generating a fierce windstorm. Dead leaves skittered over the bridge, and I shielded my head from the gust. Thaddeus curled forward, mirroring my stance.

'We've come to finish what we started,' he growled.

My insides felt as if they were exploding. I panted heavily between clenched teeth, trying to fight the instincts that were taking over. Josephine's face was pale, and I could feel her hand trembling on my arm.

'Go find Quentin,' I hissed softly. My instincts screamed in protest, but I beat them back. 'He'll keep you safe.'

She stared at me. 'What?'

I studied the gargoyles, calculating my odds. They weren't too good. But Josephine's safety was all that mattered, and if she could make it back to Quentin, she'd be all right.

'You heard me,' I whispered. 'I think I can hold them off, give you time to reach him. He can't be too far away.'

'I'm not leaving you.'

'Yes, you are,' I replied, ignoring my heart.

Matthias and Thaddeus sauntered forward. Their slow movements only heightened the terrible reality of what was about to happen. I could feel Josephine's hesitation and fear. I wanted her with me, but I was not going to be stupid about this. I took a deep breath and whirled on her.

'Go!'

She flinched at my command, then she turned and fled in the direction we'd come. I ripped the hooded cloak from my shoulders and flung it aside. Then I faced my pursuers, ready for the attack. I offered a silent prayer that I'd at least be able to buy Josephine enough time.

Suddenly, another gust of wind shot along the bridge. A cloud of mist formed at the bridge's entrance, cutting off Josephine's escape. Anya materialized through the smoke. Her bright silver eyes fastened on the Gypsy girl.

'Time to die.'

There was no getting passed now. The gargoyles had us hemmed in on both sides. Anya's lips pulled back, revealing her sharp teeth. Josephine jolted backward, then tripped and fell hard against the bridge. She scrambled for something to defend herself with, but there was nothing. Her terrified eyes met mine.

'Sebastian!' she screamed.

My instincts kicked in.

And this time, I listened.

I dashed forward, sweeping Josephine into my arms. Matthias and Thaddeus sprang, closing the distance with remarkable speed. I curled my upper body around Josephine. A fierce snarl erupted from my chest as the thing inside me I'd fought so long finally awakened.

It poured through my veins like lava, shutting down my logical thought. But I didn't try to fight it. Instead, I let it rush through me, engulfing me with fire. Sweat poured down my back, my shoulders jerked, and my body coiled. I heard Josephine gasp.

'Close your eyes,' I growled.

She obeyed, burying her head against my chest. I bolted for Matthias and Thaddeus, running as fast as I could go. Wind whipped my hair and stung my eyes as my feet pounded over the wooden slats. I clenched my teeth, gathered my strength, and leapt into the air.

The force of my spring was unbelievable. I sailed upward like a high vault jumper with Josephine tucked in my arms. The gray figures hissed in surprise as we passed over their heads. For a split second, I felt a twinge of hope that we might actually escape.

Then, without warning, pain – a pain like I'd never experienced before – ripped my back, tearing it apart. I screamed in agony as I felt muscles rupture. My shirt tore from my body as spears of pain thrust through my shoulder blades. I heard bones crack, skin split, and my lungs heaved for air that wouldn't come.

My body convulsed. I plummeted towards the bridge with Josephine's muffled screams hot in my ears. I lost my grip as we hit. Josephine was thrown free with the force of the impact, but I was helpless to stop her. I collapsed to my knees – screaming again – as the pain overwhelmed me.

My claws elongated and ruptured through my fingertips, sinking deep into the wooden planks of the bridge. The remains of my shredded tunic fell away as I writhed and jerked, consumed with the torturous pain in my back. Tears poured down my cheeks, my eyes burned in their sockets. I felt my teeth slice into my lip. I tasted my own blood.

I prayed to die.

And then, suddenly, the pain stopped.

My body arched as my lungs expanded with precious oxygen. A strange energy buzzed along my skin. My senses returned, and with them, the intense protection instincts. I lurched to my feet but staggered forward, my center of gravity off. I tried to compensate as I searched frantically for Josephine.

She was pressed against the railing of the bridge, staring at me, terrified. Her eyes darted from my face to my bare chest, and then over my shoulder, fixating on something just behind me. I looked back.

At first, my brain couldn't comprehend what I saw. Two massive objects hovered over my shoulders, flapping gently in the breeze. Folds of grayish-black leathery membranes spread over long, bony appendages that seemed to be attached . . . to me. My throat constricted as my mind finally produced the word it had been searching for.

Wings.

I doubled over in horror, but the movement threw me off again. I widened my stance, trying to keep my balance. The massive objects shuddered violently in response.

No . . .

I stared at my hands. The gray skin was stretched thick over muscles; the claws were far more hideous than before. I clenched them into fists. Oh, God, what had I done?

Josephine was still frozen; the color drained from her face, her wide eyes fixed on me.

'Josephine,' I whispered.

She pulled herself up, clinging to the railing, her body trembling. But before I could say anything else, warning prickles went down my arms.

I turned, moving unsteadily on my feet. Anya and the others stood motionless in the center of the bridge, their silver eyes blazing with fury. Why hadn't they attacked while I was down? Anya lifted her chin and sniffed the air. Suddenly, the three figures vanished into the mist.

A group of men burst onto the road, their cloaks billowing in the breeze. Arrows sliced the air, embedding in the bridge around me. Josephine screamed. I spotted Quentin at the head of the group. He notched an arrow to his bow.

'Get away from her, gargoyle!' he yelled.

Something sliced through my arm, just above the shoulder, and I snarled as Quentin's arrow sunk into a wooden beam behind me. Blood wet my skin where the arrow had grazed my flesh. I fell back, lava heating in my veins, and everything clarified before me. There were ten men with Quentin, all armed with bows and arrows, their faces twisted with hatred. I snarled again, taking in the sharp, glittering arrowheads aimed straight at my heart.

'Quentin, don't hurt him!' Josephine cried.

The tall Gypsy notched another arrow, his face dark. 'Get away from him, Josephine,' he ordered. His silken voice was laced with malice. 'He's one of *them*.'

She stared at me as though I was a stranger, her emerald eyes full of fear. And if the gray figures were any indication of my present condition, I could hardly blame her. She turned to Quentin.

'No, he was trying to protect me.'

'Don't let him fool you, Josephine. He'll kill you if he gets the chance. He's been deceiving you all along.'

'That's not true,' I shot back.

My voice sounded strange: thick and tinged with a growl.

I struggled forward, but two men lunged in front of me – blocking my path – and two arrows were suddenly at my throat. Their sharp tips pricked my skin. I gnashed my teeth, feeling an uncontrollable desire to attack. But my actions disturbed Josephine. Her hand flew to her mouth, and she backed away, straight to Quentin. The Gypsy lowered his bow and placed his arm around her trembling shoulders.

'I tried to warn you, Josephine. But now you see him for what he *really* is.'

'He's a guardian,' she protested.

Quentin scowled. 'Those are just fairy tales, you know that. Do you honestly think he's some kind of guardian angel? No, Josephine. Look at him. He's a demon.'

Her gaze returned to me, and the uncertain look in her eyes hurt me far worse than any arrow ever could. 'Josephine,' I pleaded, 'don't believe him.'

Quentin shouldered his bow and approached. He studied the fluttering things at my sides. When he looked at me again, his face was a mixture of amusement and disgust.

'I don't know how the Corsis did it,' he said. 'Keeping you hidden away, looking so human. If I'd known they were harboring an abomination like you, I'd have stuck an arrow in your gut the second we arrived in Sixes. Your kind doesn't deserve to live.'

'Let me go.'

'I'm afraid I can't do that,' he replied. 'I have to protect Josephine from you.'

I couldn't hide the wounded look I knew passed over my face. Quentin seemed pleased that his words struck such a chord.

'I would never harm her,' I said softly. 'I only want to keep her safe.'

'I'm the only protector she needs.' His voice was as biting as liquid poison. 'You're just like the rest of them, an animal that needs exterminating. You're the enemy, gargoyle,' he sneered, pressing his face close to mine. 'And before this is over, Josephine will thank me for killing you.'

I let out a roar and grabbed for his throat, but I found myself flat on the ground as the two men hit me hard. I flailed, but a knee pressed into my neck, holding me down. Quentin leaned over me, a wicked smile on his face.

Suddenly, my new wings came to life, stirring up dirt and rocks in a violent whirlwind. Quentin leapt out of the way. I kicked hard, and my wings snapped out at the same time. The force of the blow sent the men hurtling backwards. I rolled into a crouch. My new sense of strength was exhilarating. Quentin hesitated, and for the first time, I saw uncertainty – even fear – in his eyes.

I braced myself, concentrating on the long extensions jutting out of my back, letting my instincts guide me. I rolled my shoulders; the wings moved in tandem. I flexed my back, and the wings collapsed and folded against me. The weight of my body immediately shifted, and I could move freely again. My lip quivered with a threatening growl.

Quentin's bow was up in a flash, an arrow gleaming. 'That's enough, gargoyle.'

There was a horrible screech, and two figures dropped from the trees, landing between us: Matthias and Thaddeus. They were without their cover of mist, and I saw the massive wings sprouting from their backs.

Wings just like mine.

I was temporarily forgotten as all arrows were trained on the other two gargoyles. The men spread out, taking aim and preparing to strike. Matthias laughed, his teeth glinting his defiance in the dim light. Quentin ordered Josephine behind him. Then I realized that one gargoyle was missing.

Anya.

A blast of wind knocked Josephine off her feet. But she landed and rolled, cushioning her impact with the skilled movements of a performer, and threw her hands protectively in front of her face. Smoke billowed, and Anya's form appeared. With movements so fast I could barely register them, she wrenched Quentin's bow from his hands and sent him sprawling through the air.

Arrows flew and gargoyles leapt into the group of Marksmen. Anya had one hand around Josephine's throat, dragging her across the bridge, taunting me. Josephine kicked and fought in her grasp. My entire world went blood red. I broke free of the battle around me and ran after them.

Josephine lashed out, striking the gargoyle across the face. Anya hissed between her sharp teeth and squeezed tighter. Josephine gagged and clutched at the iron fingers around her neck. Anya leapt onto the railing, dragging Josephine with her. And then, they both slipped over the edge.

'Josephine!'

I retreated to the other side of the bridge, hardly believing what I was about to do. My feet dug into the planks, and I pushed off, picking up speed as I sprinted for the rail. My back jolted as my wings suddenly unfurled to their full span and caught the air with one heavy flap.

I was airborne.

My body knew instinctively what to do, but I couldn't make everything cooperate. For a panicked moment, I careered wildly out of control, losing altitude and plummeting towards the river. Desperately I tried to right myself as my wings folded back on themselves like an umbrella in a windstorm. Somewhere up ahead, Josephine was in danger, and that one thought pumped fresh adrenaline into my veins. A roar ripped from my chest, and I pushed upward with everything I had.

Air caught the leathery folds as my wings expanded once more, and I concentrated on beating them rapidly. My muscles ached with the exertion, but the action worked. My downward spiral stopped as the world turned right again. I soared upward into the night sky.

Smoke curled through the forest, making Anya's wake easy to follow. I pressed forward, leaving the bridge and the river behind. But as soon as I hit the tree line, I realized my mistake. Anya had led me here on purpose. My mammoth wings were too large for my new and uncoordinated muscles to maneuver.

Branches littered my path, and I did my best to dodge them, but it was no use. I didn't have enough control to reduce my speed. The branches slung me around like a rag doll as I ploughed through them. Then, mercifully, I was through the trees and into the open. I spread my wings wide, my shoulder blades cramping. I hissed in frustration. What good were wings if I could barely stay aloft?

A mass of gold and red loomed before me: The Circe tent. Below, people were everywhere, filing out of pavilions and lining up for rides and concessions. A new panic overtook me. What if Anya had taken Josephine inside the circus? How was I supposed to go after her?

I sniffed the air, searching frantically for her foul scent. She had to be close. The trail of mist had expanded, billowing high above my head. I worked my new wings harder, ascending rapidly to meet it. But Josephine and her gray kidnapper were nowhere to be found.

Something bowled into me, and I pitched forward, tumbling through the air. Two masses were on me at once. I lashed out with my claws but grasped nothing but smoke. Matthias materialized with a loud hiss, wings convulsing violently. An arrow had sliced cleanly through his shoulder. Its tip gleamed like diamonds. Cloaked men burst through the trees as Quentin notched another arrow and took aim.

Matthias gripped my arm. 'Stop trying to protect these Gypsies. They're our enemies!'

I shoved his hand away, wrestling to stay airborne. 'Where's Josephine?'

Another arrow flew into the expanse of mist around me. Anya's body fluttered into view. She roared in fury, and ripped the arrow from her leg. A scream pierced the air; one I knew too well. Josephine shot out of the plume of smoke, and Anya's grasp, plunging towards the ground.

'Josephine!'

I pinned my wings against my back and dropped out of the sky like a hawk diving for prey. But, oh God, I wasn't going to be fast enough! She stared helplessly up at me as she fell. I stretched my arms. Josephine's screams rang in my ears. And then, I caught her. I pulled her into my chest as I rocketed to the ground.

I couldn't stop. Nothing obeyed, and my wings were useless. I roared in agony. Josephine wasn't going to die this way. Not this way! In a last ditch effort, I rolled my body over, trying to spread my wings. They fluttered like a failed parachute. Then we collided with the ground.

The impact knocked the breath from my lungs. I stared at the sky, trying to focus, trying to move. Everything was coated in a haze of red. But I could hear Josephine's heartbeat against my chest, and I nearly cried in relief.

She was alive.

24. Alive or Dead

Josephine rolled frantically off my chest and cringed in the dirt like a frightened animal, eyes wild, and choking back a sob, her hand pressed to her mouth. I blinked hard to keep her in focus.

'Are you all right?' I asked, hearing the slur of my own words.

Josephine's hand dropped, and she looked at me, dazed. I wondered if she was in shock. She nodded stiffly.

'Hunt them down!' I heard Quentin shout. 'The demons are heading south!'

A group of Marksmen stormed past us towards the woods, arrows aimed at the sky. I could hear the screeching laughter of the creatures in the distance, along with the shouts of Quentin's men in pursuit. Then, oddly enough, the sound of motorcycle engines approaching.

Several Marksmen ran towards me as well, their weapons drawn. I'd saved Josephine from the fall, but I wasn't going to be able to save myself from the Gypsies. I shut my eyes, bracing myself for an arrow to the chest, when someone yelled above the commotion.

'Call them off!'

There was Hugo, straddled on his motorcycle, the other guys just behind him. He launched off his bike and marched

286

across the clearing, his gaze fixed on Quentin. I'd never seen my brother look so furious. He jabbed his finger at the approaching men.

'I said call them off!'

Quentin held up his hand. The Marksmen immediately halted, but their bows remained taut. I could hear the hum of the strings in my ears. I squinted painfully. My head pounded, and I lay back, suddenly too exhausted to move.

A shadow fell across my face.

'Sebastian . . . oh, man . . . ' Vincent knelt over me, his expression wary. He seemed hesitant to touch me.

'How is he?' asked Hugo.

I groaned and growled, all at once. 'I'm okay.'

Vincent jerked back, as though he was surprised to hear me speak. My brother appeared over his shoulder. His brows knotted harshly over his eyes. 'We've got to get him out of here,' he said. 'The Circe's letting out. Someone might see him.'

Quentin came into my line of vision. 'I don't think so, Corsi,' he said darkly. 'The gargoyle is ours to kill. He endangered a member of my clan.'

Hugo looked from me to Quentin. 'You've got bigger problems than this gargoyle fledgling.'

The Marksmen leader strolled with measured calm to Josephine, who was still cringing nearby. He helped her to her feet, and Josephine wrapped an arm shakily around his waist for support. Her normally bright eyes were glazed and dull. My protective instincts strained against my exhaustion, and I could feel muscles tightening under my skin, urging me to move.

'My men will take them down,' said Quentin. 'It's only a matter of time.'

'Are you sure of that, Marks?' asked Hugo in a tone like a knife's edge. 'When I arrived, it looked like your men had their hands full. If I were you, I'd get the girl home and go check on your boys. You wouldn't want your inadequacies getting back to the Romany family, now would you?'

Quentin's lips went white with anger, but he kept his expression carefully controlled. 'Watch yourself, Corsi.'

'And I thought Augustine was your responsibility. Obviously you aren't doing such a great job with that, either.'

'We'll deal with that banished traitor soon enough,' Quentin snapped. 'After we've killed off his pets.'

'Yeah, you'd better,' said Hugo, returning to his motorcycle. 'Or I'm going to take this up with people who can. The Romanys may be using Sixes as a Haven, but you aren't in charge here. This is our town.'

'Keep out of our business, Corsi.'

'And you keep out of ours,' Hugo replied. 'Now, we're taking what's ours and leaving.'

I bolted upright in blind panic. Vincent ducked as my wings nearly took him out. 'I'm not going anywhere,' I hissed.

My brother's eyes flicked to Vincent, and my brain screamed a warning. I'd seen that look before. I clambered to my feet, but before I could get my balance, I felt a sharp prick against my neck. I gasped as a cold burn flooded my veins. Vincent pulled back, the now all too familiar syringe in his hand.

'Why . . . '

My tongue was too thick for words, and I stumbled as my vision blurred. I tried to move, but it was like running underwater. I felt myself falling, but I couldn't stop the motion, and I hit the ground with a thud, my wings collapsing around me. Hugo was speaking, but it was garbled in my ears. My body felt like stone.

There were arms under me, lifting me up, carrying me. I was laid on a hard, grooved surface. I could smell gasoline and metal. Something was spread over me. A blanket? An engine roared to life, and I realized I was in the back of a truck. It jarred forward and bounced down the gravel road.

I was frozen in some drug-induced paralysis. Images flashed through my head: The mine shaft, the dandelions touching, the gargoyles on the bridge. And then – the most vivid of all – the look in Josephine's eyes when she saw me . . .

Changed.

I'd never forget that look.

But like Esmeralda Lucian said, what was done was done. I was Josephine's guardian now – whether by choice or by fate – and there was no turning back. Even though I knew she'd never see me as anything but this *thing* I'd now become.

My heart ached inside my frozen chest, but beat with new determination. No matter how painful this new life was, I would find a way to protect Josephine Romany.

Why?

Because it was my duty.

Swirling gray mist . . .

Night winds piercing . . .

Shrieks in the dark . . .

The woman runs frantically, trying to escape, eyes wide with fear. She flees into a meadow filled with Gypsy wagons. As she passes, they burst into flames.

A terrifying shriek fills the air.

The woman trips, falls to the ground. She rolls, gasping, searching the trees. A growl rumbles in the night. Something steps from the shadows.

Horns spiral from its forehead. Eyes brim with molten silver. Dark lips curl back from threatening teeth as leathery wings beat the air. Clawed hands reach out as the darkness retreats. A face comes into view; gray and terrifying.

It's my face.

The Gypsy girl screams.

I jerked up, gasping for air. I couldn't see. Everything was dark. I thrashed wildly. Heavy hands shoved me down. I tried to speak, but no words came. Snarls rang in my ears. The hands held me down. Pain pricked my neck. I went cold. I fought, but the hands were too strong. Or I was too weak. My head swirled. I was tired.

So tired.

I wanted to sleep. That's all that mattered.

Just sleep.

My body went limp. A thick haze closed over me, and everything faded into nothing.

'What are we supposed to do with him, Hugo?'

The harsh whisper cut through my slumber. I tried to stir, but my body was still unresponsive. Other voices whispered around me, blending together.

'It's been two days.'

'How long are we going to keep him like this?'

'What does the book say?'

'The book is useless,' snapped a voice closer to me than the others. I recognized it as Hugo's. 'We'll have to find another way.'

'And what if there isn't one?'

'Maybe Zindelo was wrong.'

'No!' Hugo yelled. The other voices went silent. 'I refuse to believe that. Nothing's changed, do you hear me? We'll figure this out.'

'And the Romanys?'

'We'll break the seal before it comes to that,' said Hugo, his tone low and final.

My chest heaved in panic. I didn't care what they did to me, but I wouldn't let them break this seal. It was my promise to Josephine. I couldn't lose it, not after everything I'd already lost.

I wrestled my drug-heavy body for control. Muscles bulged along my back, followed by a loud flapping.

'Strap them down!' commanded Hugo. 'Or he'll tear up the room!'

I was forced onto my stomach. My shoulder blades popped. I couldn't find my voice, couldn't scream. My muscles cramped and strained.

Please, stop!

My neck stung, and all went cold and dark.

A light.

There was a light somewhere. My eyelids fluttered open. Everything was blurry at first, and then – for the first time in what felt like an eternity – my vision cleared.

I was in my room, the blinds and curtains tightly closed. My desk lamp cast dull images against the walls. It was the only light in the room, but even that small glow hurt. I blinked my still sensitive eyes. My body felt like stone, heavy and cold. But I could move, at least, a little. I wiggled my fingers tentatively. My throat was dry. My tongue tasted like gravel. Everything was sore.

'You need to eat.'

A strong arm looped around my shoulders, hoisting me up. The aroma of food wafted across my nostrils. I squinted at the figure hovering over me. It was Hugo. He held a plate in his other hand, and my mouth watered as I saw the heaping pile of chicken and mashed potatoes. I coughed and attempted to form words, but Hugo set the plate on my lap.

'Don't try to talk, Sebastian. Just eat.'

My stomach cramped violently with hunger. I greedily scooped up a handful of potatoes and shoved them into my mouth, but when I chewed, something felt wrong. It wasn't until I ripped into the chicken like a starving dog that I realized it was my teeth. They sank with unnerving ease into the meat, slicing through it like knives. But I was so hungry I didn't care. As soon as my plate was empty, Hugo removed it and lowered me back down. I groaned at the pain in my shoulders. Every muscle ached. I blinked up at my brother. He seemed a little fuzzy. I was suddenly exhausted.

'Get some sleep,' he said.

Hugo clasped my shoulder then turned his face away from me. He stood and walked across the room. I followed him with my eyes. The effort made me lightheaded. His large form was completely out of focus. Dimly, I wondered if they'd drugged the food. I worked my jaw, determined to communicate.

'Why . . . are you . . . doing this . . . to me?'

He studied me a moment, his hand on the door. 'To keep you from doing anything stupid, Sebastian,' he replied. I thought I saw something like regret pass over his face, but everything was blurry. 'Now, sleep,' he ordered softly.

And I did.

*

I was propped upright against the pillows when I woke again. I was still a bit stiff, but I felt better than I had the last time I'd been conscious. The haziness was gone. But my back was killing me. I shifted, trying to alleviate the cramped muscles.

I was strapped to the headboard. Metal cords ran under my arms, crisscrossing my chest and digging into my ribcage. They were locked into place at each bedpost. There was enough slack to sit up, but there was no way I could reach the locks.

The blinds were open and the curtains pulled back. Outside it was twilight, and the sky was faded violet. My body was tucked under the covers from the waist down. I shifted my legs, testing my muscles. Everything seemed to be working again. The blankets were hot, and I kicked them off.

There was a knock at the door. Hugo stood in the frame with Vincent behind him.

'Stay away from me,' I snarled. It was difficult to talk around my new mouthful of sharp teeth. A tear escaped the corner of my eye and trickled down my cheek. I didn't bother to wipe it away.

'How are you feeling?' Hugo asked.

I almost laughed. He was actually asking me that after keeping me drugged in my room for who knows how long? I glanced sideways at him, checking for more syringes or plates of tainted food.

'I'm perfect, thank you,' I muttered. 'Now leave me alone.'

'Very well,' he replied.

The way he looked at me sent a surge of anger up my spine. I clenched my hands into fists, feeling claws cut into flesh. A fresh tear forged a trail along the edge of my nose.

'So you've always known about me. You've always known I was a freak.'

Hugo shook his head. 'You're not a freak, Sebastian. You're a gargoyle.'

'Same thing.'

'No,' he answered evenly. 'It's not.'

'Where's Josephine?'

'You know where she is, Sebastian.'

'I need to be with her, Hugo. Why can't you see that?'

My brother opened his mouth as if to answer, then shook his head. A quick nod at Vincent, and the door pulled closed again.

No one came to visit me after that.

I drifted in and out of sleep. When I was awake, I thought about Josephine. I replayed every conversation we'd had so I could hear her voice. I traced the curves of her face in my mind. I imagined myself kissing her lips and daydreamed about how they would be against mine. I could smell her hair; I could feel it against my cheek as she leaned into my chest.

I imagined her voice calling to me; the voice from the callboard that had changed the course of my life. In my dream, she wanted me to come to her.

To be hers. To love her.

Forever.

'Sebastian, wake up.'

The voice was so soft that I thought I was still dreaming.

'Mmmm,' I murmured groggily.

'It's Esmeralda,' said the voice.

My body jolted awake. Ms Lucian was sitting on the edge of my desk, her hands folded in her lap. I tried in vain to push myself up.

'I wouldn't do that if I were you,' Ms Lucian admonished. 'They've got your wings pretty well strapped. There's no sense in hurting yourself.'

My wings.

I pressed a hand to my forehead as nightmares and horrible images taunted my mind. But this wasn't a dream. This was real. I was lying restrained in my bed with a monstrous set of leathery wings pinned to my back

'What are you doing here?'

'Homework,' she replied simply. She patted a pile of books sitting next to her on the desk.

'Homework,' I repeated, dumbfounded.

'Of course, Sebastian. After all, you've been out of school for several days now, not to mention you have some unexcused absences from last week. Since you won't be returning to your classes, I thought it best to come up with some story before Social Services decided to investigate.'

I frowned, confused. 'A story?'

'Yes,' Ms Lucian replied. 'You were in an accident after the Circe de Romany performance and totaled your van. It's a wonder you survived.' She picked up a book, glancing at it casually. 'Your recovery will be a long one, so the school has appointed me your homebound studies teacher for the remainder of the school year.'

'Nice.'

'Well, I *am* the drama teacher, you know.'

My back muscles were cramping. I rolled my shoulders, but I refused to touch the hideous things behind me. It was easier to pretend they weren't actually there, so I ignored the pain and rubbed my wrist. Touching the dandelion made me feel better. And worse.

'She's safe, Sebastian.'

My hand jerked. 'Are you sure?'

'I've been keeping an eye on her.'

I took a deep breath. 'You're a gargoyle.'

It was still hard to say the word. Give me a league of costumed superheroes or a coven of blood-sucking vampires, those, I could deal with. But this was just too much.

A hint of a smile played along the corner of her mouth, and her fingers traced the cover of the top book. 'You need to keep up with your studies,' she went on. 'You're far too close to graduating to let a few complications get in the way.'

Complications?

'You can't be serious.'

'Totally serious,' she replied, smiling coolly. 'So you can't attend school, and you may not be able to walk with your class for graduation, but there's no reason you can't complete all your credits and get your diploma anyway.'

I scowled. 'Yeah, like school really matters now.'

Ms Lucian's smile faded. Her gaze moved to my back. After a moment's hesitation, I looked over my shoulder. The massive abominations were strapped down with the same cords that confined me to my bed. They ran across my bare chest, back under my arms, and were tied off someplace I couldn't see. No wonder I'd hardly been able to move.

'I did have another reason for visiting,' Ms Lucian continued softly. She leaned forward. 'I came to warn you.'

'If it's about staying away from Josephine . . . '

'No,' Ms Lucian said. 'You're sealed to Josephine Romany, and it's natural for a guardian to want to be by his charge's side.'

'Then, what's the warning?'

Her eyes narrowed. 'You're in love with her.'

There was no use denying it. 'Yes.'

'Sebastian, I realize you don't understand the depth of your sealed fate. But you have a duty to Josephine Romany now, and it's something you can't break.'

'I understand that.'

'No, I'm afraid you don't.'

'What do you mean?' I asked suspiciously.

Ms Lucian slid from the desk and moved to the window. 'Gargoyles were created to protect Gypsies. The Roma designed us with that innate compulsion. When we are asleep, we dream about our charges. When we are awake, we are compelled to be near them. Being guardians has been both our calling and our curse for centuries.' She glanced back at me, and she seemed suddenly ancient. 'But we weren't created with the capacity to love, Sebastian. It's against our nature.'

I didn't care how many people told me that. It wouldn't change how I felt. 'So what about you?' I asked, pointedly ignoring Ms Lucian's comment. 'If you're a gargoyle, why don't you look like . . . ' I didn't need to finish the sentence. My appearance was statement enough.

'It's a long story,' she said. I could hear the strain in her voice. 'And it's not important right now.'

'How can you say that?' I demanded. 'If there's some way that I can reverse this, a way to be normal . . . '

'There's not.' Ms Lucian looked suddenly commanding, more than she ever had as my teacher. 'Sebastian, there are reasons I'm like this, reasons I can't get into now. But believe me when I say that you can't change what's happened to you.' Her eyes hardened. 'But you need to listen to my warning. Love between a guardian and a charge is dangerous and forbidden.'

'But you said that guardians weren't capable of love.'

'Yes.' She looked out the window again. 'The Roma were very careful to ensure that it would never happen.'

'Then why would it have to be forbidden?'

For a moment, Ms Lucian was silent, her posture rigid. When she finally turned to me, she looked pained. 'Because of me,' she answered. 'His name was Markus. And I . . . I failed.'

Ms Lucian swept aside her red-tinted hair. On the side of her neck was a tattoo so faded I couldn't make out the design. She'd been branded.

'What happened?' I asked, stunned by her confession.

Ms Lucian allowed her hair fall back into place. 'No more questions. This isn't about me. I'm only saying this much because I don't want you to make the same mistake I did.' I caught a glint of silver in her eyes as she spoke. 'You've got to control your feelings, Sebastian. You must protect Josephine, yes. But you can't love her.'

'It doesn't matter if I do or not,' I replied. 'Josephine doesn't love me in return.'

'It does matter, fledgling,' Ms Lucian snapped. 'Your love will keep you from doing your duty.'

'I can't accept that.'

Esmeralda Lucian sighed. 'I can't force you not to love her, Sebastian. But let me ask you this. If Josephine Romany doesn't return your love, then why do you torture yourself this way?'

'Because my heart will never belong to anyone else.'

I looked down, feeling so raw that I ached. Then, suddenly, Ms Lucian was at my side. She placed her finger under my chin and lifted my head. I met her gaze, and in that moment, I saw my pain reflected in her eyes. And I knew it was something we both understood.

'Then I wish you well, Sebastian Grey,' Ms Lucian said softly. 'If she never returns your love, I pray you find peace in that. And if one day, God forbid, she does . . . then I pity you both.'

Her fingers left my chin. She walked silently out of the room, closing the door behind her.

25. Reluctance and Surrender

'Sebastian.'

I pulled my gaze from the window, where I'd been observing a mass of fat clouds drifting across the evening sky. James was standing in the doorway, holding the customary plate of food in his hand. I scowled and looked away. They'd had me at their mercy for days. I didn't want their drugged food, but I couldn't go without the nourishment either.

It was a sucky conundrum.

'Dinner,' he said.

'I'm not hungry,' I replied.

'Since when are you *not* hungry, Sebastian?'

'Since the neighbor's dog started looking tasty.'

My gaze flicked back to James. He was studying me as if he wasn't sure whether I was joking. And the truth was, I wasn't sure either.

After a moment of careful consideration, James entered and set the plate on the nightstand. The scent of cubed steak was pure torture, but I clenched my jaw, trying to resist as long as possible. While the lethargy brought on by the food was preferable to stone-cold paralysis, I still wasn't anxious to experience it again. Soon enough, though, the horrible ache in the pit of my stomach would win.

I expected James to leave me to my meal, as he'd been doing the last several times, but instead, the burly Gypsy remained where he was. I wiped my mouth and glared suspiciously at him from the corner of my eye.

'What?'

James produced a small key and inserted it into the padlock that was hanging from the bedposts. I heard a small click, and the metal cords loosened. My wings were still bound, but I was no longer attached to the bed. I shifted my surprised gaze back to James as he pocketed the key.

'Go ahead and eat, Sebastian. There's nothing in the food today.'

'Did you run out?' I asked, sarcastically, trying to ignore the hunger nausea. 'Or is this some reward for my good behavior?'

'Neither,' James replied, smiling grimly.

My hand reached for the plate against my will. The scent was irresistible. My stomach lurched, a mixture of starvation and disgust at how easily I gave in. I snatched a piece of meat with my clawed hands, unconcerned with the fork.

'Then what's the reason?' I asked.

I took a huge bite and whimpered. It was amazing. I chewed greedily and swallowed, juices running down my chin. James watched me take several more mouthfuls before answering.

'It'll be easier to walk if you're not so groggy.'

I paused in mid-bite. 'You're letting me out?'

He shrugged. 'If you don't go trying to escape.'

I could see James taking in my new, monstrous appearance, and I huffed. 'Doubtful.'

300

Of course, escaping was *exactly* what I intended to do. A plan began forming in my head, even as I polished off the steak and moved on to the heaping pile of rice. Regardless of the feelings I had – or was told I didn't have – towards Josephine Romany, I *was* supposed to protect her. And I was going to find a way back to her, even if it killed me.

I pushed the empty plate away and wiped my chin clean. James was right. The food wasn't drugged. I grabbed an old water bottle from the nightstand and downed what was left of the contents while I did a mental inventory of my physical condition. I felt okay, but unfortunately, I was still too weak to leap off the bed or bolt for the door. I'd need a little time before I could make good on my plan.

'Ready?' asked James, watching me carefully.

'Where are we going?'

'Just to the living room,' he replied. 'There are some people who want to see you.'

'Well, I don't want to see them.'

'Look, Sebastian,' James said calmly. 'I know this hasn't been the best situation, but you have to understand. We had to keep you hidden until things got under control.'

Anger boiled inside me, but I ordered it back. 'So I'm just suddenly free now, is that it?'

James crossed his arms. 'Well, you're not chained to the bed anymore, are you?'

'No more needles in the neck?'

'Nope.'

'How thoughtful of you,' I muttered.

James blinked. 'You were unstable, Sebastian.'

Something about his reply shot fire through my veins, igniting the anger again. I narrowed my eyes, lips pulling back from my teeth. And I allowed myself to snarl. James seemed a little unnerved by my reaction, and he backed up to the door, eyeing me warily. I took a deep breath and forced my lips down. I'd never get anywhere if they thought I was still . . .

Unstable.

My anger dissipated as quickly as it had come.

'Okay,' I said resolutely.

I pushed the covers away and gingerly swung my legs over the side of the bed. Surprisingly, my body wasn't stiff. But it wasn't easy to move. Everything felt weighted down, like I was carrying a load of sandbags. The things on my back were wrapped so tightly I could barely see them, but I could feel all the new nerves tingling. It was a weird, uncomfortable sensation.

I grabbed the bedpost and stood up. I wobbled on my feet, but I didn't fall. I worked on putting one foot in front of the other until I had successfully crossed the room. I leaned on the dresser for support while I caught my breath. A flash of something in the mirror caught my eye, and I went numb to the fingers as I found myself staring at my own reflection.

I knew my transformation had been extreme, but I'd been too worried about Josephine, too busy fighting and being drugged to take it all in. I'd pretended it away, ignored the obvious. But not anymore. As I stood gaping at myself in the mirror, the enormity of what had happened to me finally struck home.

The shape of my body was different; not larger, but thicker and more streamlined, almost as if I'd grown into it overnight. I ran my clawed hand across my stomach. My skin still felt like skin, but it looked like gray stone. It stretched over my chest and abs, defining muscles I didn't know I'd had before.

I let my eyes roam over my new appearance, but this wasn't some Peter Parker moment; he'd *enjoyed* his radioactive spider infused physique. But take away the red and blue costume and Spiderman was still a normal-looking guy.

The creature staring back at me wasn't.

I barely recognized the gray face in the mirror. My features were shadowed, more sunken and angular than before. Two rows of sharp teeth glinted behind my darkened lips, and elongated, harshly tipped ears peeked through my pewter hair. The irises of my eyes were no longer gray but silver, and they glimmered eerily back at me.

This was the face Josephine had seen.

I was suddenly filled with so much disgust that I could taste it, like acid on my tongue. An inhuman sound erupted from my throat, and I swung my hand. Glass splintered into a giant spider web across the mirror. I pursed my lips against a sob and turned away. James didn't say anything, but I could feel his gaze.

'What are you looking at?' I growled.

'You, obviously,' he answered calmly.

I fixed my silver gaze threateningly in his direction. 'Well, don't.'

I sensed his wariness, but he crossed his arms and leaned casually against the doorframe, meeting my gaze steadily. 'You gotta admit, you're pretty impressive, Sebastian. I mean, I wouldn't want to meet up with you in a dark alley.'

I stared down at my shirtless chest, completely uncomfortable in this new body. 'Is that supposed to make me feel better?'

'No, I guess not,' he replied, glancing at the broken mirror. 'Come on, they're waiting for you.'

I followed him with reluctant obedience. Each step was an effort, and my footfalls echoed heavily as I made my way to the living room. My mouth felt like a wad of cotton. I didn't want to face Hugo or any of the others, but what choice did I have?

At the moment, I was nothing more than their pet.

Just like Augustine had said.

The room was full of Gypsies. All the guys were there, along with James's wife, Genella and Vincent's girlfriend, Dali. Hugo sat in the corner. Beside him stood a gray-headed man: Karl from the Circe. Whatever had been going on prior to my entrance stopped immediately. Every eye fixed on me.

I hunched defensively, and pressed against the wall, feeling all cornered animal again. My instincts screamed at me to bolt, but I curled my claws into my palms and forced myself to meet every stare.

It was Karl who broke the silence.

'Good evening, Sebastian.' He started to approach, and I tensed. Seeing my reaction, he remained where he was, offering a disarming smile instead. 'I came by to see how you were doing.'

I was immediately suspicious. 'Why?'

He smiled again, and the smile was genuine. 'Well, to begin with, Hugo asked me to come and make sure you were all right. You see, I wasn't always a trainer at the Circe, Sebastian. I used to be a doctor, specializing in your kind.'

My kind.

I shifted nervously. Did this mean more drugs and restraints? I felt like the victim in some sci-fi novel.

Karl held out his hands, which were empty. 'I'm not going to do anything to you,' he said gently. 'I just want to see how your transition is coming along.' He gestured to the sofa. 'Will you come and sit?'

My gaze shifted to Hugo. He was leaning forward, elbows propped on knees. His eyes were bagged with dark circles, and his expression was strained, as though it was an effort to stay upright. He nodded at me, a slow movement that I took to be encouraging. I looked back at Karl uncertainly. So he was some kind of gargoyle expert?

'Sit down, Sebastian,' Karl said, his tone gently coaxing rather than demanding. 'One quick examination, and then we'll talk about everything over dinner, all right?'

There was something calming about the old man's presence. I could see how he might have once been a doctor. His bedside manner was pretty effective.

'All right,' I said quietly.

Everyone continued to watch me as I lumbered to the couch. I sat and focused my attention on the floor. Hugo really did need to get his carpets cleaned. I felt the cushion deflate beside me as the circus trainer joined me. Karl's hands moved to the lumps at my back, testing the crisscrossed section of cords.

'You really shouldn't keep these strapped down like this all the time,' he said.

'You didn't see what he did to the walls,' said Kris from the other side of the room.

'It takes time to develop control,' the circus trainer replied with an agreeing nod. 'But harnessing them will greatly affect his future potential.'

'Why don't you just cut them off?' I muttered.

Karl leaned forward, searching my face. 'Why would you want to do that, Sebastian?'

'Oh, I don't know,' I snapped. 'Maybe because they're *wings*? Maybe because I look like a *freak*?'

'You're a majestic creature,' he countered.

I almost laughed. 'You obviously don't know me.'

'No,' Karl said. 'But I know what you're capable of.'

I lifted my head and studied him warily, feeling my lip curling back. But Karl didn't seem bothered by me, not in the way the others were.

'Impressive teeth, Sebastian,' he said, clinically. 'And in good condition.'

I raised an eyebrow at his casual response, but the circus trainer didn't seem to notice. I ran my tongue hesitantly along my new teeth, feeling their jagged points. Karl's gaze shifted to my shoulders, questioningly.

'May I?'

He produced a pocketknife and cut the cords that were wrapped around my back and torso. Instantly, my wings expanded like a leathery accordion. They fell limply to each side, taking up the entire length of the couch. Karl began to examine them, probing with skilled hands. Despite my disgust for the hideous things, I found myself interested in his inspection.

'The muscles and bones appear strong,' Karl said as he worked. 'And the wing talons are well proportioned.'

Wing talons?

I couldn't help glancing back. I'd never really looked at them before, but now that I was looking, I could see that Karl was right. The tip of each section of wing ended in a curved, bony claw.

'The wings are a bit dull, though,' Karl said. He looked past me to Hugo. 'What dosage have you been giving him?'

'I hadn't really been measuring,' Hugo replied. 'Enough to keep him out of it. We couldn't afford to have him escape.'

I glared at my brother and growled. Karl immediately patted my shoulder like he was trying to calm a bristling dog. Hugo met my gaze with a hard look in his eye.

'You'll be shot on sight if they see you at the Fairgrounds,' my brother said with cold certainty. 'Marks knows what you are now, and you can bet his men are on high alert, keeping their precious clan safe. You, Sebastian, are their primary enemy right now.'

My already low spirits plummeted – not because I cared about Quentin or his band of less-than-merry men – but because my plan to get to Josephine instantly went from slim to nearly impossible.

'The Marksmen have orders to kill you, Sebastian,' Karl explained. 'Your brother's just been trying to keep you safe.'

'He has a funny way of showing his concern,' I said, scowling at him.

'I had to get you away from the Circe and out of sight before the place was crawling with *gadje*,' Hugo replied. 'Drugging you was the quickest way. You were wild and disoriented, and I couldn't fight both you and Marks at the same time.'

'But you didn't have to keep . . . '

'Yeah, I did. If I hadn't, you'd have bolted for the Fairgrounds the first chance you got.' The furrows in Hugo's face deepened, and his voice dropped low, like a confessional, just between us. 'I'm right, aren't I?'

The anger cooled. I propped my head in my hands and nodded reluctantly. 'Yes.'

Hugo's face hardened, but my answer seemed to hit him with the same force as if I'd struck him with my claws. I remembered the hushed conversation he and Karl had exchanged over my lifeless body, and I grimaced. I didn't know what else to say, if there was anything to say at all.

Karl returned to studying my wings. 'I know you're concerned about Josephine, but there's no need to worry, Sebastian. I assure you, she's perfectly safe.'

'I've heard that before,' I replied. 'But I can't believe it.'

'Well, you're going to have to,' Hugo said firmly.

Karl jumped in before I could reply.

'All that being said about the dosage, you really should be more careful, Hugo. Too much Vitamin D, and you'll have poor Sebastian turning into a statue. He'll be no good to anyone, then.'

I went rigid all over. 'A what?'

Karl kept examining my wings, folding them in and out. 'Gargoyles have unusually high levels of melatonin in their systems. We've found that injecting the creatures with Vitamin D disrupts the levels, making the gargoyle lethargic. But too much of it can be dangerous.'

'Vitamin D,' I repeated, confused.

'Yes,' he replied, prodding the muscles around my spine. 'I'm sure you've noticed that the sun bothers you. It will grow increasingly difficult for you to be in broad daylight as time goes on. It's one of your unique traits.' He finished his examination. 'Your wings should have a more shimmering look at this stage, but I'm sure the dullness is due to the high dosage you've been receiving. You'll be feeling more like yourself soon.'

'A statue?' I asked, again. I hadn't considered that possibility before. Everything had happened so fast.

The old man scratched his beard. 'Well, yes. After all . . . '

Hugo stood abruptly. 'That's enough, Karl. Sebastian doesn't need things to be any more complicated than they are now. He's got enough to deal with as it is.'

I stared at Hugo in surprise.

'Yes, of course,' Karl replied, apologetically.

'Let's eat,' Hugo said, moving into the kitchen.

For the first time, everyone turned their attention from me to my brother. It was an odd shift, to be sure. One moment, Karl was sitting on the couch examining the two leather kites sticking out of my back, and the next, Hugo was calling everyone into dinner as if we were some ordinary family in the suburbs.

I was still amazed at how readily the others obeyed him. Hugo had always been the one in charge, but I'd never realized just how much authority he had, then again, that was back before I knew he was the head of a Gypsy clan.

Genella and Dali headed up the distribution of bowls piled high with seasoned noodles, the good salty packaged kind. Sodas were passed around, and soon everyone had taken up residence in either the kitchen or the living room. I sat motionless on the couch, watching the scene.

I'd heard people refer to an unspoken tension as the 'elephant in the room'. Now, I realized, I *was* that elephant. The others moved around me, talking in scattered conversations as they ate. No one paid much attention to me, yet my presence was overwhelmingly obvious in the room. I sat alone, my hideous new additions taking up the entire piece of furniture. The whole thing was enough to send me over the edge of the emotional cliff I'd been teetering on for days. I ran a shaking hand through my hair, trying to remain calm.

I had to think.

'Here, Sebastian.'

I glanced up. James was holding out a bowl of noodles, along with a plate of leftover chicken and biscuits.

'Thanks.'

I ate in silence, head bowed over my food, attempting to ignore my gray hands. But the wicked-looking claws and the dandelion tattoo on my wrist made that impossible. The sharp points of my teeth got in the way as I chewed, drawing pricks of blood from my bottom lip. The food tasted like ash and settled heavily on my stomach. My throat tightened with a sob, but I forced the food down rapidly so I wouldn't break down. I couldn't lose it, not here, in front of everyone. I was an outsider now, an object. A possession.

A pet.

Karl returned to the couch. 'Does the food help?' he asked.

I tapped a claw against my empty bowl. 'I suppose so.'

'That's good. I know your kind requires a large amount of sustenance.'

My hands tightened around the plastic. 'Could you please refrain from using that term? You make me sound like an alien.'

'I'm sorry,' he replied, sympathetically, 'but acceptance will come as your transition completes itself, Sebastian. Just give it time.'

'I know you're trying to help,' I said. 'But you'll forgive me for saying it provides little comfort.'

Karl regarded me for a moment, as if debating something. Then, suddenly, he shifted closer. He reached out, as though he was examining my wing again, but he leaned into my ear.

'Listen, Sebastian,' he said in a voice meant for only me to hear. 'I want you to promise Hugo that you won't go to the Fairgrounds.' A growl rumbled in my chest. I could feel Karl tense, but he continued. 'It's the only way you'll get them off your back. And we need you to stay safe.'

My growl died in my throat. 'What do you mean?' I whispered back. So far, no one was paying any attention to us. 'Who is "we"?'

'There are still some of us who hold true to the tradition of the guardian. You were meant to be sealed to Josephine, despite the claims of the Corsi clan. Deep down, I believe Hugo knows it as well.'

My eyes flicked in the direction of the kitchen. 'If he does, then why is he forcing me to stay? I haven't seen Hugo's parents in over two years. What kind of hold can they have over him that would make him treat his own family this way?'

Karl's old face wrinkled even more. 'Zindelo holds more power than you know, Sebastian, and defying a *bandoleer* is unacceptable. Punishable. Your brother is honor-bound to keep his father's wishes.'

'So why couldn't he just tell me that?'

'There's a delicate balance of power within the structure of the Outcast nation. The Corsis are one of the oldest and most respected clans in our society, but Hugo must be careful not to appear weak. Leaders can't allow personal feelings to interfere with decisions made for the good of the clan.'

'Okay, I get why he wants me here.' I wiped my hand across my mouth, hating the way speaking around my new teeth both sounded and felt. 'But how does my staying help Josephine?'

Karl glanced over his shoulder and I knew our time was drawing short. 'The manner of your awakening has overridden all traditional protocols, so I believe there's an unusual importance to Josephine that could very well put her at risk, should you go to her and be exposed as her guardian before the clan. Until the true purpose is revealed, you need to keep yourself safe . . . for her sake.'

My ears burned with the heat of his words, which so eerily mirrored Ms Lucian's, this mysterious, unanswered reason Josephine had been singled out as my charge. But before I could say anything in return, Hugo entered from the kitchen. I pulled away quickly. Karl moved as well, taking one of my wings and folding it to my spine with an easy flair.

'We'll strap these down for now, Sebastian,' the trainer said, loud enough to be heard throughout the room. 'But remember to stretch them as often as you can, to allow for proper development.'

Then he was busy pinning my wings. He used nylon straps instead of wire and fastened them with Velcro. It was still uncomfortable, but not unbearably so. The deformities disappeared behind my back.

Hugo planted himself on the arm of the couch. As if sensing that something was about to happen, the rest of the group gathered around, finding spots to sit either on the sparse furniture or along the floor. Karl fastened one last strap on my back and then sat forward. Hugo crossed his arms over his chest.

'Well, let's hear it,' said Hugo.

Karl stroked his beard. 'Nicolas is being stubborn. He insists the Circe continue on with the run at the Fairgrounds. Our contract is through spring, and he wants the twins to be able to finish up schooling here. But, after everything that has happened, Quentin Marks is pushing for a much earlier departure.'

My heart jerked in my chest. 'Departure?'

Karl shot me a look. 'Yes, from Sixes.'

'Do you know why, exactly?' Vincent asked from across the room. 'Does it have anything to do with Augustine?'

I bristled at the name.

'I don't think so,' Karl answered. 'He's disappeared, along with his creatures. The Marksmen have been over the whole town and the surrounding area. Quentin's furious that they managed to escape. We're keeping on alert, but Quentin's convinced Augustine's moved on.' The old circus trainer frowned. 'We've received news that there's been some unrest among a few Outcast clans up north. The council decided it was best to head that way and connect with some of the Romany family there.'

Hugo huffed. 'Well, the sooner they're gone, the better.'

I wanted to lunge across the room and sink my new teeth into my brother right then. The involuntary sensation scared me, and I shook it off as quickly as I could.

'The Romanys are not as bad as you make them out to be, Hugo,' said Karl. 'I've lived with them long enough to know that much.'

Vincent scowled. 'Yeah, but trouble follows them like the plague. And when one clan's affected, so are the others. We've seen it before.'

'They don't want you involved in their troubles.'

James dipped his head in my direction. 'But we are involved.'

'No, you're not,' said Karl sternly. 'If Sebastian is separated from the Romany girl, then there *is* no involvement. And with the Romanys gone, Sebastian will be yours.'

My breaths were dangerously shallow, and I gripped the edge of the couch with my claws. My head was thumping so hard that the room bounced in my vision. I hated being talked about as if I wasn't in the room. Only Karl's whispered conversation with me moments before kept me in my seat. Instinctively, I believed him. So I remained silent.

Hugo put his head in his palm, tattooed fingers rubbing his forehead, looking weary but determined. 'Then I have no choice but to keep him sedated.'

Karl frowned. 'I don't think that's necessary, Hugo. He knows that the Marksmen are ordered to shoot him on sight. I believe Sebastian can be trusted to stay away from the Romany girl until the Circe leaves town.'

Hugo finally lifted his head and addressed me. 'I need to hear it from you.'

Suddenly, it was my turn. I knew I had to play my cards right. Even if Karl wasn't telling the truth, it didn't matter.

If I was going to see Josephine again, I had to make them believe I wasn't going to do anything rash. I ground my jagged teeth together, beating back every roaring instinct in my body.

'I'll stay here,' I said.

Lines creased around my brother's brown eyes, and I could feel him searching for something in my voice or my face. I remained as stoic as I could manage. My wings quivered against my back, and I was thankful they were strapped down tight.

'You've said that before' Hugo replied. 'What's changed your mind?'

'After what happened on the bridge,' I began, hearing the tremble in my voice, but determined to put this to rest. 'After Josephine saw me change . . . I knew she didn't want anything to do with me.' I couldn't look at anyone, especially my brother. If I did, I knew I would crack.

There was a heavy silence in the room.

'Okay,' said Hugo, breaking it. 'Everything's settled, then.'

26. Mended and Torn

'Katie's on the phone.'

I continued to stare at the television.

'Take a message.'

'He'll call you back.' Hugo clicked the button on the phone and set it down on the counter. Then he crossed his arms. 'You know, you haven't talked to any of your friends since this happened.'

'Yeah, and what am I supposed to say?' I huffed back. "Hey, sorry I haven't been at school all week but I can't fit my wings through the front door'?'

The look on Hugo's face made the hair on the back of my neck rise, and a low, reactive growl rumbled in my chest. I hadn't totally forgiven him for keeping me drugged in my room, but I didn't blame him either. I'd seen enough of my reflection in the apartment mirrors, that is, before I'd smashed them all into tiny bits. I was an unstable danger, and Hugo was scared of me, whether he admitted it or not. Even my slight growl seemed to set him on edge.

I found some enjoyment in that, at least.

Hugo plopped in the armchair. I watched him from my position on the floor. Sitting in chairs was difficult with wings.

I'd played the good gargoyle freak and stayed confined, but it didn't mean I'd been happy about it.

'Esmeralda says you're refusing to do any make-up work,' he said evenly. 'There's no reason why you can't finish school with the homebound program she's offering.'

'Why does it matter?' I said acidly. 'Is there some secret gargoyle college I don't know about?'

'School stuff gives you something to do,' he replied with casual calm. 'I know being cooped inside sucks, but you can't sit in front of the TV twenty-four-seven.'

'Yeah? Watch me.'

My attitude was vile, but I was going crazy under house arrest, especially when I knew that Josephine was out there without me.

It had done very little for my mood.

But as vicious as I was on the outside, on the inside, it felt as if I was dying. Little by little, pieces of my heart atrophied, and I could do nothing to stop it. Karl's occasional reports on Josephine's well-being – whispered to me when the others weren't around – didn't ease the torture. Twice I'd nearly thrown caution to the wind and left, but Karl's words haunted me like Hamlet's ghost.

We need you to stay safe . . . for Josephine's sake.

It was that admonition alone that kept me rooted. If there was anything I could do to ensure her safety, I would do it, even if it meant going against every screaming fiber of my being.

I sprawled onto my stomach and propped my chin in my hands. My wings fanned out on either side of my body, unhindered by the straps I wore the majority of the time. Though I preferred keeping the deformities bound, I had to admit – deep down – that it felt really good to stretch them out. Hugo was still looking at me.

I sighed. 'What is it?'

'We're no closer to finding out how to break the seal.'

I stayed carefully controlled, though his words chilled me to the bone. I would have rather died than have my seal to Josephine Romany broken. But I had to make Hugo think I no longer cared. 'Maybe if I didn't have a charge, I could be normal again.' I gestured to the large flap of leather beside me.

'You *are* normal, Sebastian. This is who you were created to be. I want this seal broken because you don't belong to the Romanys. They've balked at these traditions for years. They have under their employ a man whose entire clan has devoted their lives to destroying the guardians. They believe you're a plague on the Roma.'

'Quentin Marks.'

'He's just one of many,' my brother replied. 'Just because you're a guardian doesn't mean you don't need protecting yourself. You'll be safer with us, Sebastian. And I don't want you throwing your life away for a clan that doesn't deserve it. I care about you too much to watch that happen.'

He looked quickly away, but his mask had slipped and underneath was complete sincerity. For the first time, I felt my anger and resentment fade away. I saw the massive burden on my brother's shoulders, the demands on him that I wasn't privy to. Hugo Corsi was the head of a clan, after all. He was looking out for them.

And me.

'Thanks,' I said, not knowing how else to respond.

'You're not going to change your mind about her, are you?'

His question caught me by surprise. He'd never mentioned Josephine directly. The quiver that shot through my spine extended out into my wings. 'No, I'm not,' I replied. 'Though it makes little difference anymore, I can't help the way I feel.'

A small part of me crumpled, replaced quickly with resolve. 'I'll never rest until I know she's completely safe.'

'I didn't do this to you, Sebastian,' he said, gesturing to my gray body. 'It's who you are. You can't take the gargoyle out of your blood any more than I can take the Gypsy out of mine. The sooner you learn to accept that, the better.'

'Accept it.' I rolled into a seated position and hugged my knees to my chest. 'That's a good piece of advice from someone who can still go out in public for Chinese food or bowling on a Friday night.'

My brother's gaze drifted from my face to my wings and back again. 'Well, there's always Halloween.'

I shot him a look and then – oddly enough – I actually laughed. 'Yeah, or the next sci-fi convention.'

I didn't totally understand my foster brother, and I certainly didn't get all his actions. Trust was a tender thing at that moment and not something I was comfortable with, not yet. But something *had* changed between us, and for the first time since all this began, I realized he actually cared about me.

And that was something.

'Sebastian.' Hugo knelt beside me, careful to avoid my wing. 'I'm sorry this happened to you, more sorry than I've allowed you to believe.' His eyes searched mine, and as I studied his face, I realized his emotional blinds were gone. 'I guess I hadn't even realized how much I was hoping my parents were wrong, that maybe you *were* just a boy, that your biggest problem would be who to ask to the Prom. And the longer you were with us, living under my roof, the more I convinced myself that you were simply my little brother.'

I swallowed past the lump rising hard in my throat. 'I still am, Hugo.'

*

A small smile tugged at the corner of Hugo's mouth, and he put his hand atop my gray head, ruffling my hair like he used to do. And for a moment, it felt as though nothing had changed between us, that the clock had turned back and we'd returned to our old lives. Then he stood and moved back across the room.

'You won't be able to keep me here forever, Hugo,' I said as he reached the kitchen.

He looked steadily back at me. 'I'm hoping I won't have to.' Hugo picked up the phone and tossed it at me. 'Now call your friends and get them off our backs.' Hugo Corsi was all business once again. 'The last thing we need is a bunch of people snooping around here.'

With that, my brother left the apartment.

The minutes passed by, but I was scarcely aware of anything except the phone in my hand and the pressing anxiety in my soul. How could I call Katie? After a week of no communication whatsoever, what could I possibly say to her? Would she even talk to me? She'd probably never forgive me, and it wasn't like I could tell her the truth anyway. But, if she really was my friend, then she at least needed to hear from me.

She picked up on the first ring.

'Hey, Katie.'

There was a bitter silence on the other end. I could feel the anger straight through the phone when she finally replied. 'Hey.'

'Katie, I'm sorry,' I said, hating the pattern I'd fallen into, the lies that continued to form on my lips. 'I know I haven't called. I've just been . . . '

'I know, I know.' Her voice softened. 'We heard about the accident. I've wanted to come by, but I was told you're in bad shape and can't be seen. God, I've been worried sick, Sebastian.'

'I'm okay. My brother tends to exaggerate.'

There was another pause on the other end of the line.

'It wasn't Hugo who told me. It was Josephine.'

My breath went ragged at the sound of her name. 'Josephine?' I managed to choke out. 'What did she say?'

'Exactly what I just told you,' Katie replied, the edge returning to her voice. 'Josie's hardly spoken to me all week, and when she's not at school, she's with Quentin. I don't know, I think she's got something going on with her family.'

I tried to sound calm. 'I see.'

Neither of us spoke. Each beat of silence was like poison, infecting the already festering wound of our friendship. Then I heard Katie's intake of breath.

'So when are you coming back, Sebastian? We all miss you.'

My wings fluttered behind me, and I jumped at the still unfamiliar sensation. 'I'm not sure.' This was tough. Avoidance had been easier. But I couldn't leave things the way they were. 'I'm going through some stuff,' I said quietly as I stared at my clawed hand. 'I can't say any more than that right now . . . and I know I don't deserve your friendship, but Katie, I want you to know you've been the best friend anyone could ever ask for.'

'Sebastian,' Katie said, worry and suspicion creeping into her voice. 'What's wrong?'

'Nothing,' I said, gulping down my emotions. The earthquake that was my life refused to cease. Aftershocks rocked me to the core, and I felt each tremor down to my bones, in the deep recesses of hurt I hadn't even had a chance to explore. I cleared my throat painfully. 'Listen, Katie, I may be going away for a while, and if I do, I don't know when I'll be back. And . . . and I just wanted you to know that, okay?'

The pause that followed was heavy, and I could hear the blood beating monotonously in my ears. Every thump was a funeral dirge, keeping time with the harsh melody of reality.

No more late night movies, sprawled out on someone's living room floor.

No more breakneck drives through town or camping trips near the river.

No more school, no more talk of futures and plans.

No more Avery or Mitchell, or even Brandon and Emma.

No more . . .

Katie.

The drumming sound of each bitter void and stinging loss filled the quiet; a silence that was more profound than I could express to Katie Lewis, no matter how desperately I wanted to. I closed my eyes and dropped my head. Every realization crashed down on me like a boulder, flattening my chest, burying me alive. The weight was so excruciating that I could barely hold the phone to my ear.

'Okay,' Katie finally replied.

'Okay,' I echoed, a pointless word, filled with nothing and everything.

'Sebastian?'

'Yes?'

'You're a great friend, too.'

I smiled gratefully, even though she couldn't see it. 'Thanks.'

'Hey, look,' she said suddenly. 'When you're feeling better, we're all going to go out and do something fun, okay?'

'Sure thing,' I said, barely holding it together now. I had to get off the phone before I broke down completely. I couldn't let Katie know they extent of my feelings. If I did, she'd be beating down my door in a matter of minutes. And I couldn't let that happen. She couldn't see me.

Not like this.

'I'll talk to you later, Katie.'

She sighed; a disappointed, resigned sound. 'Okay, Sebastian. Bye.'

The click hit me like a death knell. The phone slipped from my fingers and landed with a dull thud beside me. My composure crumpled, and I went weak all over. I was thankful I was already on the floor. Knowing I was separated from Katie – and from every part of my old life that she represented – sliced a fresh notch straight through my chest cavity. My life was gone. She was gone. I curled up and pressed my face into the carpet, trying uselessly to smother my grief.

My hollowed, gnawing insides finally got the better of me. I sat up and wiped my face with the back of my hand. The apartment was silent and empty. My emotions had hardened to a painful rock, just behind my sternum. Every time I took a breath, my chest ached.

I plodded into the kitchen to appease my grumbling stomach, and to distract myself. But before I could find anything to eat, the door to the apartment opened. I turned, expecting to find Hugo, but instead, Karl stood in the doorway.

'What is it?' I said, moving quickly to him as dread gripped my insides. 'Is Josephine okay?'

Karl glanced down the hall then ducked inside the apartment and shut the door. 'She's fine. But that's not why I'm here.'

'Then what is it?'

The old man looked at me. 'We're leaving, Sebastian.'

'The . . . the Circe?'

'Yeah,' Karl said reluctantly. 'You're not supposed to know. Hugo thought you'd try and do something . . . unwise. They weren't going to tell you until after the Romanys were well out of town.'

The room swirled, and I put a hand out to steady myself. 'Leaving?'

'Quentin won,' Karl went on. 'He convinced Nicolas that we needed to leave now. We've cancelled the shows, been packing since yesterday. The caravan pulls out in an hour.' My wings shuddered violently. Karl put his hands on my shoulders. 'Easy, son. Don't forget what I said before. We need to keep you safe in order to keep Josephine safe. There's a reason you're here, Sebastian. We just don't know what it is yet.' His wrinkled face softened. 'She'll be fine with us. The Marksmen will make sure of that.'

I shrugged out of his grasp, growling. 'Why did you come tell me, then? What's the point, if I'm supposed to just stay here?'

'I thought you might want to say goodbye.'

The word pierced me like a knife.

'I'm on the Marksmen's most wanted list, remember?' I curled my claws into my palms, struggling with yet another round of fierce emotions. 'I doubt they'd let me waltz through their front gate.'

'Most of Quentin's men left a few hours ago. They like to go ahead and scope out our next destination. Only a few are patrolling the Fairgrounds and half the troupe's already on the road.'

I raised my eyes hopefully. 'But Josephine's still here?'

'Not for long. Like I said, the remainder of the caravan leaves within the hour. It's your last chance to see her.' Karl stepped back and opened the door. 'But if you decide to come, just be careful. There's still a Marksman or two around. Now, I've got to get back before I'm missed.' He smiled gently. 'I'll see you around, Sebastian.'

Karl hurried out. My heart drummed against my chest. I had to get to the Fairgrounds! Screw Hugo and all these plans. I wasn't staying here any longer. I was going with Josephine Romany.

And no one was going to stop me.

27. Flesh and Stone

I hadn't learned the fine art of strapping wings. I draped the nylon binding over my chest and tried fastening the closures, but I couldn't get it to work. I pitched the straps across the room with a frustrated snarl. I scowled at my half-naked body then rushed to the closet. I snagged one of Hugo's long jackets. I pressed my wings to my back and shrugged it on, but when I attempted the buttons, my claws got in the way. I gave up and yanked open the back door, then I fled into the night.

The last week of October had come and gone while I'd been in confinement. My mind strayed briefly to Halloween, and I wondered what parties I'd missed, but then, just as quickly, I remembered why I'd missed them. I'd never have to dress up as a monster again.

Because now, I *was* one.

It was colder, and the November air smacked me hard in the face as I ran. But instead of chilling me, it revived me. I was breathing heavily by the time I reached the Sutallee Bridge, and I felt better than I had in days. I was done with people telling me what I could and couldn't do with my life. The old Sebastian was gone. Hugo was right about one thing: It was time I accepted who I'd become.

I slowed, sniffing the air cautiously. My gargoyle senses were on heightened alert as I made my way across the bridge to the iron gates of the Fairgrounds. Just beyond, I could see the ruins of the Circe de Romany.

The tents were gone, and the rides had been rooted up and loaded into the line of tractor-trailers parked just inside the fence. Everything looked dead, like some carnival cemetery. A few discarded booths remained, boarded up and empty, their pennants flapping sluggishly in the breeze.

There were several people milling about, and a handful of Marksmen, but I didn't see any of the Romanys. I sprinted around the outside of the fence, keeping to the shadows. I couldn't see the family's trailer anywhere. I reached the back lot and stopped, grabbing hold of the iron bars. I was going to have to scale the fence again.

A shock of ice blasted my stomach, and I melted into the safety of a nearby oak. Quentin Marks strolled near the front of the caravan, surveying the empty lot. I snarled under my breath. I wanted to blame him for crushing my dreams, but it would've been a lie. I'd had little chance with Josephine to begin with, even before I'd become a hideous freak.

I pushed those thoughts from my mind. My feelings didn't matter, I told myself for the thousandth time. I was here to protect Josephine, and I was going to make sure she was safe. That was my purpose. I surveyed the caravan. I could stow away in one of the trailers easily enough.

I'd figure out the rest later.

Without warning, a familiar scent rushed across my nose. I snapped to attention, eyes wide. Then I ground my feet into the gravel and slowly turned around.

'What are you doing here, Hugo?'

He leaned against a pine tree, his dark T-shirt and jeans fading into the darkness around him. 'You know why,' he replied, his gaze roaming past me to the gate. 'I caught Karl on his way out of the shop.'

I dropped my head, choosing to look at the ground. 'Hugo, I know I said I'd stay with the Corsis, but you don't understand . . . '

'Yes, I do, Sebastian. And I'm not going to stop you. Not anymore.'

My head shot up. 'What? But your parents . . . '

'Doesn't matter,' he said, picking at the bark of the tree, jaw working as he chose his words. 'I'll deal with the consequences when they come. Zindelo and Nadya have their responsibilities, and they have to do what's best for the clan. But I have a brother.' Hugo's eyes met mine, 'and I have to do what's best for him.'

As we stood there, I felt the rift between us finally close. 'Hugo,' I began.

He raised his hand. 'You want to hang around here shooting the breeze? Stop wasting my time and go do what you need to do.' He squinted at the Gypsies on the other side of the fence. 'Of course, from the looks of things, you'll need a distraction.' He smirked. 'Good thing I showed up.'

He clasped my shoulder – that comforting, familiar gesture I knew so well – and then he disappeared into the trees in the direction of the front gate. I didn't get the chance to ponder Hugo's decision. Suddenly, the overwhelming feeling of Josephine's presence consumed me. I let it filter through me, greedy for that small sense of peace that I'd been denied while in captivity. And then I saw her. She came around the front of Quentin's black SUV and threw herself into his arms.

She looked so happy. And that was as it should be. I hoped to God that Quentin knew how precious the girl in his arms really was. A Marksman jogged up. He motioned towards the front gate, and I knew he was informing them of my brother's arrival. I huddled against the tree trunk, waiting for them to leave so I could leap over the fence. But as Josephine pulled away from Quentin, something passed over her face. It was only a slight change, but I could see it clearly.

She knew I was here.

Josephine put a hand on Quentin's arm. I couldn't hear what she said, but he caressed her shoulder and nodded. He and the Marksman headed for gate, and were soon obscured from view by several trailers.

But Josephine didn't follow. She moved casually along the line of vehicles, speaking to the occasional person standing outside a trailer or bus. At the last moment, she passed through the caravan and out of sight. Without thinking, I slipped through the shadows on my side of the fence, heading in the same direction. And then, there she was, near the gate. Alone. She was scanning the trees, looking – I knew – for me.

As I paused behind a tree, I slipped my hands into the pockets of Hugo's jacket. My claws brushed against something. An envelope. My breath caught, and I slowly drew out the letter. *The letter*. Of all Hugo's coats, I had to grab this one. With shaky fingers, I held the envelope up to my face. It was addressed to Hugo in a flowing hand that I vaguely recognized – like from a distant memory – as that of Zindelo Corsi.

I looked to the front gate. I couldn't see my brother, but I knew he was there, keeping Quentin away, distracting the Romanys; all the while knowing that I was going to be gone when he returned. He was defying his parents for me, but what was he getting in exchange?

'Sebastian?'

Josephine's voice shattered my thoughts, and everything I'd ever felt for the Gypsy girl crashed over my soul like a tidal wave. The breeze caught strands of her hair and they fluttered across her face as her gaze swept over my hiding place. She clasped her hands tightly in front of her.

'Sebastian?'

She didn't move, but her head tilted towards me. The distance between us was painful, but the silence was worse. She looked ready to bolt at any moment, and she glanced nervously towards the caravan.

'I'm here, Josephine,' I said.

'How are you?' The words sounded awkward, forced, even. 'I know I haven't called.'

I shrugged, but my wings were so heavy under Hugo's jacket that my body barely registered the action. I was glad Josephine couldn't see me in the shadows. 'I'm all right. And believe me, I understand.'

She made a little sound and looked at the ground. 'Thank you.'

'I'm sorry for what happened that night,' I went on. 'I never should've put you in that kind of danger. I didn't know what I was doing. This is all still so new to me.'

She took a deep breath. 'Let me see you.'

There was no one on this side of the caravan, but I didn't want to leave the safety of the shadows. Leaving them made me vulnerable. Still, her request was something I couldn't refuse. I shoved the envelope back in the pocket and let Hugo's jacket drop from my shoulders, leaving my upper body bare. It was pointless to pretend she didn't know what I looked like now. I sucked in a breath and stepped forward.

The shadows seemed just as hesitant to relinquish me as I was to leave them.

As I passed into the dim light, Josephine tensed. I waited patiently as she took me in; my gargoyle body, the enormous dark wings pressed against my back, and then, finally, lingering on my face.

'You saved my life that night, Sebastian,' she said softly. 'Please don't apologize for that. And for what it's worth, I don't believe you're one of the bad guys, no matter what the others say. I believe my father's old stories. I believe you were meant to protect . . . Gypsies.' She shook her head slightly. 'You're just a different kind of guardian angel.'

I flinched. 'A hideous one.'

Josephine was at the fence; her hands took hold of the bars as she looked at me.

'No, you're not, Sebastian.' Her voice was sincere. 'There is something noble about you. Like a statue, come to life.'

I stared at her, scared to hope. 'Then you're not . . . afraid of me . . . like this?'

She bit her lip, then released it. 'I'm not afraid, exactly. Maybe just a little . . . uncomfortable.'

'Yeah, that makes two of us,' I replied, smiling softly.

'Oh, Sebastian,' she breathed. There were tears in her eyes. 'I'm so sorry that you had to go through this for me. I didn't know this would happen, otherwise I never would've agreed to it. Please, believe me.'

'It was my choice, Josephine.'

Her fingers moved to her neck, tracing the pendant. 'Not totally.'

'No, it was,' I said. 'Hugo tried to stop me, but I wouldn't listen. It was supposed to happen this way. I've never felt so sure of anything before, and if time was reversed, and I had another

330

chance, I'd do it again.' I couldn't look away from those eyes; those eyes that brought me peace, even in turmoil. 'In a heartbeat.'

The moonlight reflected off her hair as she leaned against the fence. She broke eye contact. 'I can't do this, Sebastian,' she whispered. Her hand closed around the glass dandelion. Her face was suddenly pale. 'I feel something when I'm with you, something powerful that I can't explain. But everything is all wrong.' Her fingers trembled around her pendant. 'I can't love you back, Sebastian.'

'Josephine, I'm not asking you to.'

Her eyes returned to mine. She reached through the bars as though to touch me. Then she pulled back. No matter what she'd said, I could still see the lingering fear and wariness in her expression. She was scared of me, too.

Then she reached out once more, her fingers extending. She looked meaningfully at my hand. I fought back a panic-filled sob. Slowly, I lifted my gray hand towards hers. She clasped hold of it with resolve. And this time, she didn't flinch.

Instead, she pulled my hand gently to her face and pressed my palm against her cheek. She leaned into my touch, as she had done when we rehearsed for the play, ages ago and in another world. A current of electricity ran through my body, and the air grew thick around us. Josephine's breathing was shaky.

So was mine.

We stood there, unmoving, wrapped in winter's arms, surrounded by autumn's decay. It was the most powerful moment of my life. I didn't want it to end. She slowly removed my hand and squeezed it gently as a tear ran down her cheek.

'Why did you come, Sebastian?'

I closed my eyes and breathed in, slow and deep. I wanted desperately to go with her, to be with her, this Gypsy girl, the daughter of a *bandoleer*, surrounded by protectors, accustomed to being in the limelight. There was still so much I didn't know about this world, so much I couldn't provide. Was my presence really the safest thing for her?

'I came . . . '

Suddenly, I felt the weight of all I'd done to reach this moment, of what Hugo had risked in helping me. And now, the weight of what I was asking Josephine to sacrifice by allowing me to come with her. As I stood there, shivering in the cold night air, I finally understood. My need to be with Josephine had clouded my vision. But now, things were clear. In that one moment, everything changed, and I realized the truth.

You didn't always protect something you loved by holding it close.

Sometimes, you had to let it go.

'I came to say goodbye.'

The conflict etched in her expression seared my soul. 'You don't . . . '

'All I've ever wanted was to keep you safe, and right now, this is the best way to do that.' I released her hand and stepped from the fence. 'You'd better get back to Quentin,' I said. My voice sounded strangely deep and calm. 'He'll be worrying about you.'

'Sebastian . . . '

There was a pleading in her voice, but it wasn't the same as mine. The sound of it strengthened my resolve.

'Go on,' I whispered, encouragingly.

She looked at me for a long moment. I saw the conflict ease behind her eyes even as another tear slid along her cheek. She unclasped her pendant and reached through the fence, pressing the necklace into my palm and closing my clawed fingers around it. The pendant burned into my skin and my tattoo burned along with it. The bars between us created a distance that went far deeper than mere space.

My only ray of sunlight was about to walk away. And I wasn't going to stop her.

'Goodbye, Sebastian.'

I held the pendant to my chest as my heart ripped underneath it. She turned around to leave. I rushed to the fence, clutching the bars. 'I'll always be here, Josephine,' I breathed desperately. 'If you ever need me.'

She turned. Her eyes met mine. Her gaze held an electric intensity. The current shifted between us. A soft smile appeared across her lips.

'I'm counting on it,' she whispered.

And then she walked away.

As suddenly as she had appeared in my life, she was gone. The sunlight in my clouded world faded away, leaving me with nothing but empty gray shadows.

I stepped back and let them embrace me.

They were coldly comforting.

But they were all that I had.

I perched on the railing of the Sutallee Bridge, staring out over the churning river. The moon cast a silvery sheen on the water, capping the rapids in halos of white. A soft breeze whispered through the trees and swirled across the bridge. It caressed my face and chest. It fluttered my wings. I'd left the jacket at the Fairgrounds. But I didn't care. I closed my eyes and listened to the night.

A motorcycle rumbled in the distance. It grew louder as it approached. In a few moments, I heard the engine cut off. A kickstand clicked. Gravel crunched. Then the boards of the bridge creaked behind me. I leaned back in my crouch and sniffed the air.

'How did you know I was here?'

Hugo stepped to the rail and propped his arms on the wood. 'Call it brotherly intuition. Or maybe the fact that I saw you sprinting across the road when I left the Fairgrounds.'

A half-smile tugged at my lips. 'I'm still working on the stealthy thing.'

We were silent for several minutes. I touched the pocket of my jeans. I could feel the warmth of the pendant through the thick denim. I sighed and hugged my bare abdomen, feeling hollow inside.

'Why didn't you go with the Romanys, Sebastian?'

I stared at the moon-drenched rocks. 'I changed my mind.'

'It's all you've wanted since you met her,' he replied. 'You said you loved her.'

An owl hooted mournfully from the treetops. There was a flapping of wings as it pushed from the branch and took flight. Its dark form rose into the sky, surrounded by the blanket of stars. I followed its path until it disappeared from view.

'I know . . . and I do. And maybe that's the problem.' I felt my wings shudder against my back. 'Esmeralda was right. My feelings would've gotten in the way. Josephine deserves to be protected and happy. And she can have both with Quentin Marks. I'm not the kind of guardian she needs.' The confession enabled me to swallow down the last of my emotions. 'She's safer without me.'

'You really believe that?' he asked.

'Yeah,' I said, setting my shoulders. 'I do. Besides, I've got a family here that needs looking after. I couldn't just abandon them.' I cast a sideways look at Hugo. 'Especially after what they've done for me.'

Hugo sighed and shook his head. 'Sebastian, I wish I'd . . . '

'Of course, you're going to have to up my food allowance,' I said, cutting him off. I smiled and patted my stomach with my clawed hand. 'You do know that, right?'

'Hmm,' said Hugo, and I saw the corner of his lip twitch. 'Guess I'd better find some more clients. It's going to take a lot of tattoos to cover the grocery bill.'

I shrugged. 'I'm a growing gargoyle, Hugo.'

'Yeah,' he said. 'But you're still my little brother.' I smiled again, but this time, it was easier. I tilted my chin and let the wind ruffle my hair. Hugo studied me a moment. 'Of course, maybe we should start with finding you a shirt.'

I glanced at my gray body. 'Good idea.'

Hugo's hand fell on my shoulder. The gesture was warm and genuine. 'We'll figure all this out together. Okay?'

For the first time since I'd become a gargoyle, I felt things were right between us again. I wasn't in this alone. I folded my wings and leapt off the railing. Hugo and I walked side by side across the bridge. He straddled his bike.

'Want a ride back to the shop?' he asked, strapping on his helmet.

'Actually, I think I'll walk,' I replied, taking a deep breath of air. 'It's nice out.'

'Suit yourself.' He started the engine.

'Hey, Hugo,' I said suddenly. He looked up at me. 'So no more secrets, right?'

The moonlight illuminated my brother's unreadable face.

'We're Outcast Gypsies, Sebastian,' he said with a grin. 'We always have secrets.'

The motorcycle lurched ahead, and my brother vanished into the night.

Acknowledgements

Above anything else . . . Thank you God, for your many blessings and for the gift of your Son Jesus. Thank you for never giving up on me, and for loving me too much to leave me as I am. Jeremiah 29:11, Proverbs 16:3, Psalm 34:1.

There are so many people in my life I want to thank, and I'm terrified I'll forget someone. If I do, please forgive me. I'll send you chocolate.

Thanks . . .

To my amazing critique group. This never would've happened without your advice, your encouragement, and, most of all, your friendship. Thank you Shannon, Tosha, Colleen, Shanda, Kim, Aaron, Vaughan, and Bonnie. You talented people are the absolute best. Go Trail Mix!

To the Society of Children's Book Writers and Illustrators (SCBWI) for giving me hope and motivation.

To my earliest readers and loyal fans from the beginning: Kasey, Chad, Emily, Allie, Erica, and others who graciously read scattered pages, roughly-written chapters, or listened to me ramble on the phone about plot frustrations and character woes. You mean the world to me. To Christina Lewis, for being an awesome writing partner and helper. And Patti, for never doubting and for giving me dandelion-themed gifts to remind me.

To all my students from days gone by: my inspiration, always.

To my sweet friends, who always have my back and are spectacular. And like coffee. And tea. And chatting for hours. And are sometimes as socially awkward as I am.

To my rock star agent Jill Corcoran and the Jill Corcoran Literary Agency. Thanks for bringing me into the fold, having faith in my work, and being splendid in all ways.

Thank you to everyone at HarperCollins who has been involved in this process, and particularly to the lovely ladies at Harper *Voyager* UK: Natasha Bardon and Eleanor Ashfield. Many thanks to my brilliant copyeditor Janette Currie for catching everything with style, and to the talented Cherie Chapman for such a stunning cover. And a very special thank you to my dazzling editor, Rachel Winterbottom. You have been nothing short of gracious and wonderful, and you have made my experience as a debut author one of the best things ever.

To my family. There aren't words to properly express how much I love and appreciate you. From my parents to my in-laws, and to everyone in between, I am truly blessed. Thank you for always supporting your weird, geeky, artsy girl. I love you all.

Saving the best for last . . . To my sons, Liam and Justin. My hobbit, you are my joy and have been since the beginning. Man-cub, you are a gift to our family. You boys have my heart.

And finally, to my husband Doug—my very own hero and protector. You are my soul mate, my best friend, and you have always been my biggest fan. I thank God every day that I get to experience life at your side. I love you forever.